The Scarlet Cord

The Scarlet Cord

A Novel By

Deborah Elder Champagne
&
Mary Ellen Keith

Thomas Nelson Publishers
Nashville • Camden • New York

Published in Nashville, Tennessee, by Thomas Nelson,
Inc. and distributed in Canada by Lawson Falle, Ltd.,
Cambridge, Ontario.

Printed in the United States of America.

Some Scripture quotations are from the King James
Version of the Bible.

Scripture quotations noted NEB are from The New English
Bible. © The Delegates of the Oxford University Press
and the Syndics of the Cambridge University Press 1961,
1970. Reprinted by permission.

Scripture quotations noted NIV are from The Holy Bible:
New International Version. Copyright © 1978 by the
New York International Bible Society. Used by permission
of Zondervan Bible Publishers.

Scripture quotations noted NASB are from the New Ameri-
can Standard Bible, © The Lockman Foundation 1960,
1962, 1963, 1968, 1971, 1972, 1973, 1975, 1977, and are
used by permission.

Scripture quotations noted RSV are from the Revised
Standard Version of the Bible, copyrighted 1946, 1952, ©
1971, 1973 by the Division of Christian Education of the
National Council of Churches of Christ in the U.S.A.
and used by permission.

Library of Congress Cataloging-in-Publication Data

Champagne, Deborah Elder.
  The scarlet cord.

  1. Rahab (Biblical character)—Fiction. I. Keith,
Mary Ellen. II. Title.
PS3553.H2645S3   1985   813'.54   85-21512
ISBN 0-8407-5994-0

The cultural settings of this novel are based on extensive research and are both historically accurate and true to the spirit of the times.

This novel is dedicated with grateful appreciation to the many friends, too numerous to name, who loved, encouraged, supported and put up with us during its creation.

Special thanks go to our mothers, Nettie Davenport and Ollie Elder Graves; to our church family at Believers Bible Fellowship; to Lance Homeniuk, for his dauntless scouting in the shelves of the Dallas Theological Seminary library; to Sharon Masingale Bell and Maxine Savells, whose spirits shirred up our courage; to Wiley College, where it all started; to Evangel College and to Dr. James Edwards for truth *and* education; to Dr. Rosa Bludworth and San Angelo College; to Morton Kelsey and Franky Schaeffer V, who inspired us with their visions; to Robert Flowers, whose sage philosophical insights incited us; and especially to Mary Ellen's husband Don, who listened and laughed, and brought us coffee.

PART ONE

MAID OF BAAL

These events happened as symbols,
To warn us not to set our desires on evil things as they did.
Do not be idolaters like some of them....

1 Corinthians 10:6-7 NEB

1

He had walked long days behind the stinking camels.

His nights, pillowed against the hard rocks of the Jericho escarpment, had been longer still. The camel master's coarse woolen robe bore the stains of many days' travel. Both robe and man were weighted with the clinging dust of the road. He had not bathed since he left the oasis at Jezreel, three weeks before, and his sweat mingled with the earthy odors of the Jericho streets: the pungent smells of goats and camels, and the human smells of perfume and garlic, paprika and perspiration.

The summer drought was at its height. The gods had ignored the earth, forgetting to send summer rains—rains desperately needed if a harvest were to be made. For hundreds of centuries, the gods had welcomed pilgrims, such as the camel master, as they traveled with the caravans from Byblos on the Great Sea to Memphis on the Nile. Their gifts to the gods would invoke the rains, and the rains would come. They always did.

The camel master smiled. If his participation in the ancient temple rituals would please the gods, then so much the better! But the urgency of his mission had little to do with the needs of the drought-stricken land. His body cried out for release, even as the dry earth cried out for the caress of the summer rains.

Beneath his feet, the solid earth turned to powder, and the city's dust swirled up behind him with each step, creating dancing patterns against the scorched plaster walls of Jericho. He traveled quickly through the narrow streets, surefootedly avoiding crowds and hawkers who would have delayed his progress toward Temple Baal-Jericho.

Entering the courtyard of Temple Baal-Jericho at last, he paused, allowing his eyes to adjust from the harsh sunlight of the streets. The beauty of the courtyard startled him as it always did. Even in the midst of this summer day, the tinkling fountains and the lush greens of the temple garden created an impression of cool breezes and relaxed twilight.

He breathed deeply, enjoying the scent of jasmine and the fragrance of temple incense. He was ready, had been ready since he entered the city, to do his duty—to serve the gods. Looking from the lush courtyard to the porticoes

9

where the temple courtesans relaxed, he quickly fingered the coins in his money purse. Rejecting the fat gold coins, he discovered, near the bottom of the purse, six coppers. The goddess Astarte did not require a minimum payment. He would give the gods their due from his physical essence. His finances were another matter.

Only one decision remained: with which of the maidens to serve the gods.

A teenage boy, his face not yet hinting a beard, separated himself from a small group of equally young men lounging near the fountain. As the child approached, the camel master noticed that his lips and cheeks were brightly rouged, a symbol of the Komer—the beautiful boys—consecrated to the goddess.

"The girls are tired, dusty one," the boy said, smiling. "Your caravan arrives late this season."

"We were detained by bandits," the camel master answered, "but being strong men, we overpowered them."

"The goddess honors great strength in battle, dusty one. You should be rewarded this day by more than a tired girl." The boy smiled suggestively.

"Surely not all the maidens are exhausted," the camel master said, casting an appraising glance around the courtyard. Because he enjoyed this repartee with the lad, he prolonged it. "What of those maidens over there?" He gestured to his left to a small group of women of all ages—virgin maiden to wrinkled hag. These women looked eager and restless. They chattered excitedly, and occasional suggestive giggles could be heard from amongst them.

The komer laughed derisively as he looked in the direction of the camel master's attention.

"You are right, my friend. Those maidens are not tired—nor, if you will endure my opinion—are they worth your trouble. They are unskilled."

"They are visitors, then?" the camel master asked, already knowing the answer.

"Yes," the komer said. "Like yourself, they come to pay their respects to the goddess. Some come once a year. Some come only once in a lifetime. They are eager enough to be chosen, but that is their only merit!" He paused to frown disdainfully at the women. "They are here today and gone tomorrow. They do not stay with the goddess long enough to learn her skills!"

The camel master stroked his beard as if pondering this comment, but in reality awaiting the next ploy from the komer. The lad laughed softly. His next words were almost a whisper: "You would do much better to choose me," he said.

"This is the busiest week of the caravan season. How is it that you are not exhausted, too, pretty one?" Although the camel master continued to tease the boy, in his mind he had already made a selection from among the maidens.

The boy replied, "I have had an easy day, drover. Last night I served at an

10

important banquet given by the high priest. And so," he shrugged, "I was allowed to sleep quite late; I am not too weary at all!"

"Ah, but you are too bold, boy!" the camel master said. "Boys I see every day on the caravan. Today, I think I will serve the goddess with a girl!"

The camel master laughed and walked away from the komer, who merely shrugged and rejoined his friends. Approaching the giggling women to his left, the camel master smiled down at a small-boned girl who seemed barely old enough to realize why she was in the temple. He dropped five of his six copper coins in front of her feet and held out his hand to her.

"I summon you in the name of the goddess Astarte." He said the ritual words.

Smiling innocently, the girl scooped up the coins, stood, took his hand, and followed him toward the dark curtains of the goddess' chamber.

A short time later, the camel master strode from behind the curtains and crossed the temple courtyard toward the marketplace. As he passed the seated komer, he dropped the sixth copper coin into the boy's lap.

"I'll be here again tomorrow," the camel master said without slowing his stride.

The boy laughed. "And so will I!"

Leading from the courtyard into the inner recesses of the temple were two deep green doors, studded with brass rosettes and golden bulls' heads. Behind these doors the casual visitor was not permitted, for it was here that the mysteries of the goddess were explained to the Kedeshoth and to the Komer, and it was here that the sacred rituals were enacted.

On this summer's afternoon, the high priest, Shanarbaal, was seeking the counsel of one of the city's leaders, Onuk the Fat. They lounged within an inner courtyard. The priest was slender; gray edged his beard, which was trimmed and anointed with fragrant oils. He was constantly in motion—pacing, pounding the table, and stabbing the air to make his points. Onuk, on the other hand, rested on a low couch, leaning into a pile of colorful, embroidered pillows, moving seldom and slowly—only to speak or to squint or to raise a cup of wine to his lips. His head was bald and his brown beard scraggly, anointed only with glistening droplets of sweat.

"If I am any judge of these matters, Shanarbaal—and I believe that I am!—your banquet last night was a tremendous success." The fat man sipped his wine, smiling knowingly at the high priest.

"I am pleased if that is your opinion, Onuk," the priest replied cautiously. "You know that I value your opinion. But tell me, what did you think of the king's reaction to my plan? He said little."

The fat man grinned, his eyes crinkling into slits. "I believe he liked it, Shanar. I really do. He was noncommittal last night, to be sure. But there were many people present; it must seem to be his idea, his inspiration." He shrugged, lifting his hands to expose his palms. "I think you will be hearing from him—and soon!"

"I hope you are correct," the priest said shortly. "I am not a patient man—even in my dealings with kings!"

The politician sipped thoughtfully from his round-bottomed cup.

"Think, my friend," he said at last, "think with whom you are dealing! The king is not just a man—"

The priest's eyes flashed at the politician.

"I know that the king is sacred, Onuk," the priest interrupted. "I know that the king is god, Onuk. I know that the prosperity and fertility of this community Jericho depend upon our king, Onuk."

Then his voice grew very soft, picking up speed and intensity. "But, Onuk, by the blood of the gods themselves, I know that the Jericho walls need repair! I know that the Habiru are coming! I know that they are strong!"

He banged his fist upon the low, three-legged table that held the wine pitcher.

"I tell you, Onuk," he all but shouted, "we must be ready!"

The politician was calm, unruffled by this display.

"You are right, my friend," he said soothingly. "But that does not matter. You must understand the king—what his thinking is—and then," he paused for effect, "and then, you must use that knowledge to win what you want from the king."

The priest paced from one side of the small courtyard to the other. He turned, looking at the fat politician eye to eye.

"I am right, then!" he said. "You concede it! I am right! We do need to make preparations now—to repair the walls—to prepare for siege!"

"I believe that we must, Shanar. But we must commit the king to the project. It must be to his glory. It must be his idea!"

The priest snorted. "Bah! It doesn't matter whose idea it is to me. That the job must be done—that is all!"

"To be a master of politics," Onuk explained, softly and pleasantly, "it is necessary to understand that real power comes not from the king, or from the gods—but from those who influence the king and those who influence the gods." The fat man smiled serenely. "As the high priest, Shanar, my friend, you are in the position to influence both—if you choose to do so. You read the entrails of the sacrifices to foretell the future of the king. And you speak to the gods."

The priest bowed, mockingly making obeisance to the politician.

"I honor your wisdom, Onuk-a-Baal, as always."

"There are many ways of winning a king—or a queen, for that matter," the politician said.

The priest shook his head. "Queen Asheratti is not likely to be swayed by my handsome figure, Onuk. She has a mind too keen for such simple intrigue."

"Perhaps not, my friend. Do not underestimate yourself. I have noticed how she watches you, and she does appreciate you."

Shanarbaal shrugged, and the politician continued, "Her husband, I believe, is swayed by the delightful figures of your temple servants."

"Yes," answered the priest, "that is as it should be, Onuk, since we choose the Kedeshoth carefully for their beauty—and we train them well in the mysteries of pleasure."

Both men sipped from the cups as the priest considered the temple maidens.

"No," he said finally, "they are just children. They are ignorant in affairs of state, though skilled in the calling of their service. I do not see any way that I can use our pretty doves to influence the king."

The politician settled back into the pile of pillows. Again, he smiled. "You will find a way, my friend. You will find a way."

2

The three-mile walk from the tent in the foothills to Jericho was a major undertaking for Bazarnan. Stress was evident in his face even as he set out, before the numbness of his legs became unbearable. He always walked with a shepherd's staff now—to fend off bandits, he told Kora, his wife.

He stumbled sometimes as he worked in the fields. Kora noticed, he was sure. But she never spoke of it to him. It was, rather, a mutual fear, lying unspoken between the man and his wife, but alive, nonetheless.

Now, walking carefully and determinedly toward Jericho to barter his daughter to the goddess Astarte, Bazarnan found it hard to ignore the gnawing agony of spirit that had eroded his life for the last two seasons. He was forty, ten years older than his wife, and he did not expect to live another decade.

His thoughts turned to his five children, and in particular, to his daughter Rahab. At fourteen, she was the oldest, and while she was not the most beautiful, she was his favorite. Always, Bazarnan had been close to Rahab. She was more likely to be helping him with the animals in the early morning than cooking the barley cakes with her mother. The other girls were always gathered around Kora—chattering and teasing. But Rahab! Bazarnan smiled as he walked toward Jericho, enjoying his memories of Rahab as a small child.

"Father," she had once asked, very seriously, "why does the goat get fat in the teats? She looks like a cow!"

"She will have need of her teats soon enough, little one," he had replied. "She will have a baby goat very soon, and the gods prepare her well to feed it."

"Oh, yes, the gods love us, don't they, Father! The lamb told me so this morning!" Bazarnan had laughed at this strange child. She spoke as if she meant what she said about the lamb. But to Bazarnan, the sheep revealed nothing of the gods; he had seen too many of life's cruelties to view the gods as kind or loving. His thoughts returned to the purpose of this journey, and his expression hardened. *Rahab will learn soon enough about the kindnesses of the gods*, he thought. But what he was about to do must be done.

Bazarnan was sure his health was failing, much in the same way his grandfather's health had fled. He had never known his grandfather, for the patriarch had died young. The family talked of it sometimes: the grandfather had begun to lose the use of his legs and then his arms, and then—Bazarnan shuddered—he had gone blind. After years as an invalid, carried about, a constant burden to Bazarnan's grandmother and her children, mercifully, he had died.

Bazarnan remembered the stories, and he feared that he shared the same malady. He forced himself to walk faster. If he became bedridden, the family would starve! His children would be sold into slavery. He would rather die! But if he died, poverty, hunger, and slavery would still be their lot, for he had no brothers to care for them.

The best hope for his own security, Bazarnan knew, as well as that of the family, was to get Rahab established with a wealthy and generous husband. The surest way—perhaps the only way!—to accomplish that end was to convince the priest to name Rahab a kedeshoth for a year's service. For that service the maidens earned handsome dowries and learned the skills of physical love. Rahab would then be able to serve a rich husband well.

Bazarnan smiled to himself. He had always been able to turn any dunghill into a garden of flowers. He could make the high priest Shanarbaal see beyond Rahab's dark, quiet beauty into the blossoming soul of her womanhood. Bazarnan could see the good in every situation by absolutely refusing to think about the evil, and now, having recognized his fears for the future, he dealt with them by doing what he could do and ignoring what he could not change.

Suddenly, he stumbled and almost fell. There was no feeling whatever in his left leg. It simply refused to support his weight. He was tired. He had traveled almost a mile, walking quickly. Balancing with his shepherd's staff, he sat down carefully on a rock and looked at the leg for a moment. It was as if it were dead. He turned his attention elsewhere: he would rest and make plans.

In the distance, he could see the walls of Jericho, gleaming whitely. Heat waves in the distance created the shimmer of a mirage, making the city appear to weave and swirl above the sand.

The city itself was a symbol of security to Bazarnan. It had been there for thousands of years; it would always be there. In his youth, he had traveled often to the Temple Baal-Jericho. The three-mile walk had seemed like nothing then. He had given his seed to the gods, and they had respected his devotion by sending the rains to the land.

But now, looking back, he realized that whether the rains came had little to do with the ardor of his devotion. The gods would do what the gods would do! The gods would take whom the gods would take! Bazarnan the farmer was just a man, and neither Baal nor Astarte nor any other god cared in the least what he did.

Nor did he believe that the gods cared whether Rahab became a kedeshoth, but Bazarnan cared, and he knew that Kora cared. Bazarnan the farmer would do what he could do!

Rested now, Bazarnan stood, found his balance, and resumed his journey. The ancient walls of Jericho shimmered in the summer sunlight, waiting.

3

"But I have not seen the maiden!" The High Priest Shanarbaal gazed incredulously at the man before him. "What is wrong with her that you would have me vow her acceptance before I have examined her? Is she malformed? Crippled? Fat?"

"No, no! Of course not, your lordship. Rahab is a strong beauty." The right words flowed naturally to Bazarnan's lips as they always did. "Some girls," he said, "are like little flowers, delicate and fragile in the sun, fading quickly, before the noonday's passion."

The priest raised his eyebrows. This farmer had a way with words. Perhaps it would be worth listening to him.

"There is much to be said for delicacy," he replied smoothly, "and as for passion, is it not true that the bee is drawn to the nectar of the delicate flower?"

"Yes, my lord, the bee does seek sweet nectar, but a man—" Bazarnan spread his hands expressively —"a man seeks the fullness of the vine. A man appreciates the rich wine made from dark grapes."

He had captured the priest's attention, and he continued: "My daughter is like the dark grapes sought by the man of taste and culture, the dark grapes that glisten on midnight leaves beneath the secret moon."

"You are a magician of words, I think, instead of a farmer, my friend, but perhaps your daughter has a magic of her own. Tell me more."

"She is no delicate lily, my lord. She is strong, with the eyes of an eagle and the brows of a hawk. Like the hawk, she is constantly seeking, my lord the high priest. She will be an apt pupil of the goddess."

"You speak well of her." The high priest looked skeptical. "But how does she look? The best flower cannot serve the goddess in a broken vase."

"As you will see, my lord, my daughter is still growing. She is becoming, as she fulfills her womanhood, a beautiful and strong vase, useful and admirable, a worthy receptacle of the strongest of men—worthy, I think, of a man such as yourself, Shanarbaal. You will like what you see in her."

The high priest laughed, pleasantly. "You are a persuasive man, Bazarnan. I confess that I am a man who knows and appreciates worthiness and beauty."

"Is it a contract then? Will you accept Rahab into the temple service?"

The priest laughed again, shaking his head in wonder at the audacity of this hill farmer. "You have aroused my curiosity with the magic of your words, Bazarnan. Bring your daughter to the temple tomorrow. We will see if she has a magic of her own!"

The sound came slowly, softly, insistently. The heartbeat of the drums. A command: an invitation to come! She stood before dark green doors, huge doors studded with golden ornaments. Behind them? She didn't want to know—she wanted to turn, to flee, to run. But the beat of the drums called her forward. She would have pulled back, but she could not. The doors began to open, slowly, without a sound, and behind them—darkness, blackness. There was no sound except the beating of the drums. Louder now. Terror rose within her, but the call was too strong. She could not resist. The doors were open, gaping now. Within, a dark stairway beckoned her downward, into blackness. The black below was not void. She felt a coldness there, a tangible thing, waiting.

The terror was too much. She screamed and awakened to discover her mother, shaking her.

16

"Rahab! Wake up! What's the matter? Are you all right?"

The scream still on her lips, Rahab gasped for breath. Her eyes focused on the comforting face of her mother. Her mother was here; she was safe!

"Mother!" she cried, clinging to her mother's arms. Kora's touch reassured her. "I was so scared," she sobbed. "I had a bad dream."

"It's all right, little one. You're safe." Her mother's arms held her. "What was it?"

Rahab searched for the memory, but it was gone, leaving only the cold, trembling fear and the terror. "I don't know," she whispered. "I can't remember."

"It's all right," her mother said. "Come on. Get up now—it's almost morning anyway. There's no time to waste. We must prepare the barley cakes for the goddess." Kora's voice was suddenly very cheery. "Today will be a great day for you!"

Rahab sighed. Her mother's arms were solid and reassuring, and she was not eager to break away from them.

"Mother," she said, not moving, "you served a night in the temple. What was it like?"

Her mother was silent.

The girl repeated her question. "What was it like, Mother?"

"Oh, it was before you were even born, Rahab. But I know that I served the goddess well. I did my duty, and she was pleased."

She gave Rahab a quick hug.

"Don't worry. You will please her too!"

The child looked a little beetle-browed, the high priest thought. She stood quietly, her eyes appropriately downcast.

His examination was quick but thorough: she was a study in earth tones and gentle curves. Her skin was a sun-browned olive, and her off-white robe crossed over her breasts. A brown, knotted-rope girdle accented her waist, and he could trace the curves of her thighs and legs from the sunlight shining through the thin fabric of the robe. Her breasts would grow. All in all, she seemed sturdy, yet feminine, a girl accustomed to physical work—from her coloring, outside work.

Her head was bowed in deference to him, so that the shadows hid her face.

"What is your magic, little dove?" he asked suddenly, deliberately without warning.

Her head jerked up and her deep brown eyes met his—direct and clear. The directness of her gaze surprised him; he waited for a reply.

"My lord, I know no magic, but I could tell you of sheeps and goats and quails."

The voice was soft—childlike, yet controlled, he noted. It was the boldness of her eyes that impressed the priest. He laughed.

"And is there no magic in sheep and goats and quail?" he asked, half-mocking, correcting her grammar.

Her smile was quick, relieved. He decided she did not understand the rebuke.

"Oh, yes, my lord," she answered, still meeting his eyes. Then she giggled—nervously? he wondered—as she added, "but I thought you meant magic of another kind, like the magic of the gods."

"Your father has magic with words," he said. "What is your magic, Rahab?"

"Oh—my magic is with the animals," she answered. "I can get a nanny goat to suckle the lambs."

The priest laughed, amused by the candor and the innocence of her response. The boldness of her eyes, combined with her demure demeanor, was unusual in one so young. And she was not afraid to speak!

Bazarnan, who had been standing quietly a few steps behind Rahab, feared that the child had said too much, had too much exposed her lack of sophistication. He feared the priest was laughing at the girl.

"My lord," he interjected apologetically. "Rahab is intelligent. She knows the ways of the farm, but she can quickly learn the ways of the temple."

Shanarbaal turned his eyes to the father. Clearly the man was tense, anxious, and this was puzzling to the priest. Was something wrong with the girl? Shanar considered himself a connoisseur of all things beautiful, particularly maidens.

This young woman was not ugly. Her brows were too thick and straight, her lips a little thin—but the artistry of the priestess could remedy those defects.

What was wrong with the girl? Was she disobedient? Had she gotten herself with child?

Shanar raised himself to his full height and glared down at the girl, speaking with all the authority and power of the high priest of Jericho-Baal: "You are aware that all maidens in the service of light must be virgins," he intoned. "You are comely, but are you a virgin?"

Rahab cast her gaze toward the floor. She was awed by the splendor of this man, his striking good looks and his astonishing elegance. She understood what he was asking, and she blushed, but she answered in a clear, strong voice. "I am a virgin, my lord."

Bazarnan answered quickly also, too quickly. "The child has never been alone with a man, my lord."

Shanar's eyes flashed at the father. "But you said that she is intelligent. I assume she can learn." Before the father could respond, the priest turned his attention back to the girl, who had recovered from her discomfiture and was again looking directly at him.

"Why do you wish to serve the goddess, girl?" he asked.

"Always I have worshipped. Now I am of an age to serve," she began. Then she flashed the priest a bright smile of perfect innocence. "I am told, my lord, that after I have served the goddess, I will have a dowry—and the skills to please a husband!"

Shanar was delighted with this answer. So that was it! They needed the money!

"Your candor and modesty are charming, Rahab of Bazarnan," the priest said. "But they are not the qualities you will need for the service of light. I think that your magic with animals will serve you better here."

He addressed her father then. "The god accepts your gift, farmer. For one year, Rahab will belong to the goddess."

4

City girls, she thought.

And for the first time in her life, Rahab felt terribly inadequate. Five other girls waited in the temple room that Rahab had just entered. Each was beautifully dressed, and to Rahab, each seemed an embodiment of elegance and sophistication.

I am completely unlike them, she thought. *Why was I even chosen?*

Rahab stood just inside the door of the temple room, waiting awkwardly, unsure of what she should do or say. She did not wait long, for one of the girls approached her immediately and stood, arms crossed, disdainfully examining Rahab's dusty sandals, plain cotton robe, unadorned throat, and simple headdress.

The girl's nose crinkled, as if she smelled something unpleasant, and her derisive question was spoken loudly for the entertainment of the group: "Where did *you* come from?"

Rahab was unprepared for this sudden attack, and she stammered as she attempted to answer appropriately. "My name is Rahab," she said, "and I have just come to Jericho."

The girl sneered, "Well, *that* is obvious!"

Several of the girls laughed knowingly. Asabaal had apparently decided to give this odd country girl a difficult time.

"The high priest has chosen me for the temple," Rahab answered. "I have come to honor the goddess in the service of light."

The other girl grinned wickedly. "The service of light, you say! How quaint you are! Such service as you'll see is best done in the darkness." She laughed at her own joke, looking toward the other girls for approval. "Of course, it is pleasant in the light, too," she said. "I myself am looking forward to my time of service." Her emphasis was on the last word.

Rahab did not know what to say. She did not even understand what the other girl had said.

"Stop teasing her, Asabaal!" The girl who came to Rahab's defense was especially beautiful. Her gentle face was framed by wispy curls, and her long hair glowed like well-polished ebony. "She has come here for the same reason we all have. Come join us," she invited Rahab, ignoring Asabaal's frown.

Rahab smiled gratefully and moved past Asabaal, whose lip curled, pouting, at having her sport thus ended.

"How long are they going to keep us waiting?" Asabaal complained. "There's nothing to do!"

"We were told to wait," the beautiful girl responded. "They'll come for us soon enough."

"Well, it's soon enough for me now!" Asabaal responded. "I can have more fun than this at home."

"Well, you won't be home for quite a while," one of the other girls answered her. This girl, the shortest of the group, was gently rounded everywhere. Her full, pouting lips were painted red, and there were smudges of charcoal above her eyes. "You might as well get used to it. Myself, I'm just as glad to be away from home. At least here I won't have to take care of my screaming baby brothers. You can't imagine how tired I get of them!"

She continued, "I tell you, if you had to do as much housework as I do, you'd be pleased to wait here to serve the goddess. I never get to do anything at home except work. Even this morning, when I should have been painting my face, my mother made me stop to feed Enoch. He never shuts up—"

"We know where he learned that, don't we, Enath?" Asabaal interrupted loudly. "It must run in the family," she laughed.

Enath was quiet, but only for a moment. Rahab was astonished; she had never heard such rude talk. Insults fell like pigeon droppings!

"At least in my family, we know who our father is, Asabaal," Enath retorted, finding an appropriate insult.

Rahab was shocked. From Asabaal's sharp glance, she expected a slap to be the immediate response. Instead, Asabaal laughed. "Small comfort that must be," she said, "knowing *your* father!"

The beautiful girl addressed Rahab again. "I am Bishna," she said. "You have just watched the beauties of Jericho performing, though not at their best."

"Performing?" Rahab asked. "What do you mean?"

"Oh, they are merely throwing insults," Bishna replied. "They are quite talented at it, especially Asabaal and Enath."

"You should know, Bishna," Asabaal responded.

Rahab sighed. This was going to be very different from the country!

Bishna smiled warmly. "Don't worry, Rahab. We'll teach you!"

Rahab wondered, wryly, if she wanted to learn.

The repartee was broken as a servant ushered a number of other girls into the room. Including herself, Rahab counted thirteen.

There were greetings. Everyone seemed to know everyone else, except Rahab. The other girls had been waiting all day and chattered incessantly. Rahab had only just arrived, but already she wished she were at home.

The girls were startled into silence by the clanging of a gong. The sound was repeated twice. At the end of the room, curtains parted, and a beautifully muscled young boy stepped through the opening. His hair was as carefully arranged as that of the girls, and he spoke through lips painted red.

"Silence, the goddess calls!" the tones of his soprano rang out. "Silence, the goddess cometh in the aspect of her handmaiden, high priestess of Temple Baal-Jericho!" He paused, relishing the drama of his pronouncement.

"The lady Amaranthe-Astarte. Prostrate thee once; prostrate thee twice; and do her honor!"

He stepped back with a flourish, and every girl in the room dropped to her knees in a gesture of obeisance. Rahab hastily followed suit.

The tall, red-haired woman who entered the room was no stranger to most of the girls gathered there. Her presence was recognized throughout the city. She was, indeed, impossible to miss in any gathering: her hair, like tongues of red flame, flowed down her back in brilliant contrast to the pallor of her complexion. But there was nothing pale about the black eyes that examined each of the maidens, making them feel suddenly very shy, young, vulnerable, embarrassed.

Rahab, because she was a country girl, had never seen the high priestess before. She was startled by the woman's vivacity. She had never dreamed that hair could be so vividly colored, so like fire. Even the clothing of the high priestess impressed Rahab with the strangeness that her new life in the temple would bring.

Asabaal, who was kneeling nearest Rahab, could not resist the urge to whisper: "I'll wager you that the camel drovers never get a chance at that one!"

21

Rahab tried to look as if she understood. She had no idea what the girl was talking about. She hoped Asabaal would keep quiet so the high priestess would not think them irreverent.

The priestess spoke: "I am Amaranthe-Astarte," she said, her eyes never moving. Her voice was low, and, Rahab thought, almost musical. "I am high priestess of Temple Baal-Jericho, and I will be your teacher in the weeks to come. You have much to learn and much to enjoy in your time of service to the goddess. You are privileged maidens—virgins, like the goddess herself—virgins to be initiated into the mysteries of life."

Beside her, Rahab heard Asabaal chuckle. She wished the girl would be quiet. She, herself, had heard nothing amusing, and she did not want to be distracted. She ignored Asabaal and returned her full attention to the high priestess.

"As the high priestess of Astarte, I am to be respected as the aspect of the goddess in the temple. You will obey me as you would obey the goddess herself, for I speak her will as it is revealed to me. This is never to be questioned. I am never to be questioned."

The maidens exchanged glances. Asabaal smiled derisively, but Bishna's eyes, as Rahab met them, were filled with awe.

The priestess tossed her flaming hair, lifting her chin and almost smiling: "I have many secrets to share with you. Now, you are barely more than children. Your bodies only begin to flower forth, but already each of you thinks of a husband, babies, and a home." She paused and gazed at each of the girls in turn. "Yet you are here for one year. In this time, you must serve the goddess with all your intensity."

Her voice hardened. "Give your hopes for the future to the goddess. Vow to her your total dedication, and I assure you, little girls, little doves, you will leave here women—masters of secrets that will make all men long for you as the earth cries out for the rains, as Baal longs for and finds satisfaction in Astarte. I am a woman and the high priestess. These things I know."

Her voice was hypnotic, rising almost to a chant, gathering speed. "What the goddess has revealed to me, I will share with you. Obey me, and you will discover pleasures undreamed of. Disobey me, and the goddess will not hesitate in her justice. You are the consecrated ones—the Kedeshoth. Astarte's will is your law."

The high priestess turned and was gone so quickly that the girls were not sure they had seen her depart, but her words echoed in the temple chamber: "Astarte's will is your law!"

5

In the days that followed, the girls learned that everything in the temple had a symbolic meaning.

Even the attire of the high priestess displayed the traditions of the cult. Her ceremonial headdress, worn only on ritual occasions, thrust upward boldly with golden, crescent-shaped horns. And always Amaranthe wore the symbol of the bull as a golden ring on her left hand, her stronger hand, symbolizing her own marriage to the god. She never removed it. Around her neck was a heavy golden chain that held a golden amulet warding off the enemies of the god and calling forth good fortune. A golden girdle encircled her waist in the shape of a sword belt to signify Astarte in her warrior aspect. From the girdle hung a dagger encrusted with rubies; it was symbolic of the god's virility and power.

Wearing full ceremonial attire, Amaranthe taught the girls the symbolic mysteries of the temple. She began this lesson in the open worshipper's courtyard. The courtyard was centered by a square, tiled fountain. Using a long, pointed wand, Amaranthe explained each scene on the fountain. With the zeal of belief, she recounted the stories portrayed in the shining mosaics: Autumn, with its torrential rains and the rebirth of the god Baal; winter, with the marriage of Baal and the goddess Astarte; spring, with the death of Baal, gored by the sacrificial bull; and finally summer, with its killing drought and Astarte—in her warrior aspect—breaking the gates of the underworld to rescue the god and return the life-giving rains to the earth.

Despite the enthusiasm of the high priestess, Rahab's attention wandered. She was fascinated by the massive green doors, leading from the courtyard into—what? The girls had been shown all of the famous temple, except what lay behind those doors. She wondered vaguely why they had not been explained—were they, perhaps, the gates to the underworld?

She shuddered, suddenly reliving the nightmare of the week before. Dark green doors stood before her, opening slowly, on silent hinges, a wordless invitation bidding her to enter, the approaching darkness, the waiting corridor, the dark stone stairs, leading—

"Rahab!" Bishna hissed. "Come on!"

Startled from the memory and stunned by its impact, Rahab looked about wildly and hurried to catch up with the group already filing out of the courtyard behind the high priestess.

Much of Rahab's time in the next few days was spent in lessons. Always she had worshipped the gods, but never before had she learned so much about them.

As the stories of the gods told by the high priestess fascinated Rahab, even more did the charisma of the priestess herself. Rahab had never seen a woman like Amaranthe-Astarte. Amaranthe was unpredictable, and intense. She conveyed the feeling that she, the high priestess, was inhabited by the goddess.

Amaranthe's moods might change on the instant. She was grace and tenderness at one moment, biting anger and sarcasm the next, but always she was with the girls, teaching, encouraging, berating, chiding, complaining. Always she was there with a story or an example of what temple service must be. Always she was in control.

"Life!" she said one day. "You must master it or it will master you! Power to master life comes from the gods. They know our destinies and can give us the ability to rule them. If you would master life, you must know life."

"And I'll bet you do," Asabaal muttered.

Amaranthe heard, but ignored the comment and continued, "Your dedication to the gods must be total. Your wills, like your bodies, must be given completely to the service of the gods."

Asabaal chuckled. Amaranthe's lecture went on. "Only from the gods comes the power to rule your own destiny."

Asabaal snorted. Amaranthe turned and fixed the girl with a cold stare. "The goddess will not endure irreverence." Her voice was like ice. "Two kinds of banquets the goddess hates," she continued. "Three kinds of banquets the lady of battles despises: a banquet of baseness, a banquet of murmurings, a banquet of handmaidens' lewdness."

Asabaal snickered, unimpressed by Amaranthe's rhetoric. The high priestess glared at her. "Hold your tongue, Asabaal, or you will endure the consequences!"

Amaranthe resumed her lecture impatiently. "Astarte fulfills herself in your union with the temple worshippers. Your physical union with the celebrants represents, and is, in mystic fact, the union of the god with the goddess. You must never underestimate the importance of temple service to the spiritual world. One does not function without the other."

Asabaal yawned and sighed, rolling her eyes disdainfully in an exaggerated expression of boredom.

Amaranthe whirled on Asabaal. Rahab glimpsed only a flash of gold in the air before she hears Asabaal's gasp.

Asabaal for once did not look disdainful. She strugled for breath, but breath did not come. Instead, her eyes widened, as, tasting blood, she saw the red stain spread across her own bosom. Collapsing, she realized that she was, already, dead.

Amaranthe stood, the blade of her dagger dripping with Asabaal's blood. Rahab's eyes were drawn to the hand holding the dagger. The bull's head ring seemed to glow, almost with its own fire. Amaranthe glared at the girls, but her voice was flat, emotionless. "You have seen the consequences of disobedience to the goddess."

Rahab was reminded of snakes she had seen striking mice on the desert: death without warning. The girls stood motionless before the wrath of the high priestess, stunned by the violence of the goddess herself.

Amaranthe whirled and was gone.

6

In only a matter of minutes the news spread throughout the temple. The goddess had been angered; her vengeance had been swift.

The komer who informed Shanarbaal of Asabaal's death did so with great hesitancy. He had served Shanarbaal for many years and had known his master to deal harshly with the bearers of bad tidings. Shanarbaal, to his credit, dealt with the komer hardly at all. He was learning, as he approached middle age, to deal harshly where harshness was most justly deserved.

Shanarbaal's only response to the news was a thin-lipped command in an extremely tight voice: "Tell the high priestess I wish to see her immediately." The komer was only too glad to bow and quickly leave his master's presence.

Alone in his chamber, Shanarbaal gave vent to his true emotions. "By the gods!" he swore loudly, bringing his fist down hard on the wooden table in front of him. "She has done it again! The woman will never learn. Again and again I have told her—not during the first week! She will not listen!"

Exhaling heavily, his nostrils flaring with the wrath of each breath, the high priest paced his antechamber. In a remarkably short time, he was not alone. The high priestess stood framed by the doorway, awaiting his command to enter.

Seeing her, Shanarbaal responded to her presence with a snakelike hiss. "S-s-s-certainly, you must enter, Lady, Bright One of Astarte!" His sarcasm stung, but she had encountered it before. She was not afraid of him.

"Thank you, my gracious lord," she responded with only a hint of irony.

Her soft response touched off his fury. He glared at her. "How dare you break my command again?" he demanded.

"How dare I?" she asked, laughing, but the laughter was as cold as marble. "Do you suggest that my lord's wishes have preeminence over the lady's?"

"I suggest nothing." He spat the words at her. "I know simply that I gave you a definite command which you have broken less than an hour ago in this temple!"

"It was the will of the goddess."

"The will of the goddess? By all the wills of the Baalim combined, woman, it was no one's will but your own!"

"The goddess will not endure irreverence. She punishes as it pleases her!"

"Don't quote ritual at me, and don't try to cloud the issue. Astarte will not endure irreverence. Indeed, more truthful to say, Amaranthe will not endure impudence!"

Amaranthe shrugged her shoulders. "It is the same thing," she said.

Shanar shook both his fists in the air. "By the light of the goddess, woman, it is not the same thing. It is no joking matter to say, 'My will is the will of the gods.' "

"You are right, as usual, my lord Shanarbaal." Amaranthe was herself no amateur at sarcasm. "It is no joking matter, and I was not joking. The goddess wanted Asabaal punished. Her aspect within me urged the action I took. I did not act alone."

"You acted irresponsibly. Did I not, only last spring, insist that you take no sacrificial victims from among the Kedeshoth? The gods know enough of the Kedeshoth die in temple service anyway."

"Yet, Shanarbaal," Amaranthe replied, her voice growing subtle and conciliatory, "it was not my intention that she be a sacrifice. The truth is that her death is to be an example to the others. This is a stubborn group of novitiates. Have no doubts, my lord, that without a stern example set before them, they would give us weeks, perhaps months, of trouble. Now they will know enough to fear the gods, and—" she paused to punctuate her point—"to be obedient!"

"You would teach them obedience?" His laugh was short and curt. "You know it so well yourself!"

"I have given you my reasons, my lord. If you will accept them, accept them. If not, I await judgment."

Shanarbaal was not easily mollified, but what Amaranthe said about examples made sense. "Do you really perceive this group as more difficult than usual?" he barked at her. "Why?"

Amaranthe chose her words carefully. "It is not what they say which convinces me of their rebellious attitudes, but rather the way they watch me as I give them instructions. I have trained many kedeshoth, Shanar, and never have I seen so many angry eyes in one group of novitiates, so many rebellious spirits."

"Are you so unskilled at your craft that your only control over the maidens is fear?" Shanar asked coldly.

"Of course not. I have other means, but surely you, too, have seen the time when expediency ruled subtlety? It was expedient that these girls be disciplined from early in their training. Subtle discipline is best, but one does not always have time for subtlety, my lord. Asabaal was an arrogant little fool, and from her talk, she was no virgin. I am glad to be rid of her. But I am gladder still to have put the fear of Astarte into Rahab, with her eagle brows, and Bishna, with her wise tongue, not to mention Enath, who takes nothing seriously. One example is worth a year and a day of instruction."

Shanarbaal glowered at her. He was not appeased, but at least he was answered. He was continually surprised by the logic that backed even Amaranthe's most impulsive actions. She was no fool, and as a high priestess she served the gods well. Although he was angry with her, he had no desire to lose her—yet. He did not have a replacement trained; nor did he like to admit, even to himself, that in a test of power, he was not completely confident of his mastery over her. It was better that they remain cautious equals: he, as aspect of the possessor god; she, as aspect of the earth, the mother goddess.

He shook his head and lifted one hand upward, signifying that the audience was over. "I do not approve of your actions, but what is done, is done. Remember, however, that this is not to happen again. If it does, the god himself may 'punish whom he pleases.' "

Amaranthe-Astarte smiled as she left the high priest's chambers. Once again the goddess had blessed her. She hummed a bit of an Astarte chant, singing the words softly to herself, "Grant me my wish, my want, my will, and I shall be me-er-ry."

She felt invincibly wrapped in the power of the goddess.

7

The teachings of Amaranthe-Astarte began to take root in the girls. Each day the maidens grew more sure-footed in their dance, more graceful in their movements, more artistic in their facial designs. As Amaranthe could not help noticing, each day, too, saw the maidens grow more double-tongued, speaking with ever-increasing awe and slyness of the mysteries, the rituals, and the rites of the goddess. The conversation of these virgins changed from the open and innocent babble of children to the soft and sultry calls of courtesans. Even their humor took on different dimensions as they learned to laugh from deep within their bosoms, their breasts trembling delicately with the vibrations.

Sitting before her brightly polished brazen mirror, Amaranthe thought with pleasure of how effectively she had squelched the rebellious spirit of these kedeshoth. The killing of Asabaal was exactly what the others had needed, she thought, combing her long red hair and smiling at her image in the mirror. Despite Shanarbaal's objections, she had done the right thing. She knew that the goddess had approved. Shanarbaal, after all, was hardly to be expected to see anything with spiritual eyes these days.

Amaranthe thought with a cold distaste that Shanarbaal was each day becoming less involved with the truly spiritual levels of their religion. Each day saw him more involved in secret manipulations of the political world, and each night saw him more embroiled in the acts of physical pleasure. He could be—and was in public—a ceremonial magician of breathtaking technique, but in private he was becoming more and more a man of physical hungers only.

This subtle change in Shanarbaal was, to Amaranthe's mind, very dangerous. As his spiritual appetites declined, his physical hungers grew. And worse, as Shanarbaal grew older, the objects of his desire grew younger.

It was not that Amaranthe objected to Shanarbaal's enjoyment of the maidens. That was his right and privilege as the embodiment of the god. But with every measure of her dedication to the goddess, she resented Shanarbaal's preference for the maidens. Shanarbaal's lust for youth was a threat to Amaranthe. As he turned more and more often to the temple's children and less and less often to her, he robbed her of the power gained from union with the god. The temple service required the union of the gods! The temple needed—and Amaranthe needed—the power of their physical union. Shanarbaal's neglect of this priestly duty was too much for Amaranthe's pride to endure. The goddess must not be ignored; the high priestess must not be slighted.

Amaranthe knew that the high priestess should be the consummate ruler of the temple. The consort god certainly had his role to fulfill, but to proclaim him the equal of the great mother, as Shanarbaal had done in their last encounter, was, in her mind, no less than blasphemy! Amaranthe sensed with all of Astarte within her that to make the god the master of the goddess was a sacrilege, an inversion of the natural order.

Amaranthe had only one consolation. Even as she watched Shanar's spiritual power weaken, she felt a growing supremacy, the power of the goddess within herself. And she knew that she must maintain that supremacy by her own control of the high priest. It could be done, and she knew how to do it!

As the time approached, Amaranthe prepared the Kedeshoth carefully for the temple dedication.

"You must be aware," she warned them, "that the ways of the goddess are secret and holy. The goddess does not need to explain her ways to mortals, nor does she. What she is, she is, and you must count yourself blessed that she condescends to allow her aspect to fulfill itself in you."

That the girls did not understand half of what she said did not disturb the high priestess. As she told Shanarbaal in the privacy of his bed chamber, "It is better that they be confused and perhaps a little terrified. It enhances the mystery, creating a purer dedication of their bodies to the goddess. After all, the secrets of the gods are not to be revealed to everyone."

Amaranthe spoke lazily as she lifted herself from Shanarbaal's embrace. She had come to his chambers without an invitation, but she had known how to make herself welcome. Now, as he rested comfortably beside her, she chose her words carefully, desiring that he recognize the supremacy of the high priestess over the simple temple maidens who had lately taken his fancy.

"Only to the few are given the secrets of the inner circle, the all-consuming fire," she said, running her fingers through her red hair as if to point out her oneness with Astarte.

Shanarbaal watched Amaranthe through half-closed eyelids. He sometimes wondered if the high priestess had not made her long hair red for purposes other than the fire vow she had proclaimed so loudly in the temple. He was well aware of the woman's wiles. He faintly remembered the whisper of silver that had begun to make itself heard around Amaranthe's temples and brow shortly before she made the special pledge to the goddess that caused her to henna her hair so religiously. The gods could certainly ordain things conveniently.

Shanar regarded this affectation of Amaranthe with amusement. Certainly her spirit belonged to the goddess despite her secret gray locks, and her body served the deity with the intensity of a she-goat. Amaranthe's hair might be

29

old, but her spirit was not. She had proved that to him many times in the past, and her surprising performance today had shown no signs of aging. Despite his private musing over her advancing age—her years were forty if they were a day—he realized that she was still a very skilled high priestess. She could undoubtedly initiate a score of young priests in the sacred grove. Her energies were unflagging.

Thinking of the sacred grove brought to Shanar's mind the temple dedication service to be performed that evening. Raising himself on one elbow, he regarded Amaranthe with more than his usual, tolerant amusement.

"Are your maidens ready to receive the goddess tonight?" he asked.

Amaranthe was startled by his question. He knew she had been preparing the maidens for days! The man could certainly be irritating.

"Of course they are ready!" she responded indignantly. "I always do my duty to the goddess, and you know it! You would do the goddess better service to ask your Komer if they have cleansed all the sacrificial implements. I do not want my maidens poisoned by filthy implantations."

Shanarbaal laughed. He was well accustomed to Amaranthe's temper. She flared as quickly as a Baalfire beneath the sacred powders. This time he chose to appease her, speaking in the rhetoric of their religion.

"Come, come, Sacred Lady. You know that no maidens have died from the planting time in many seasons. I nourish them as I nourish you, my life, my own."

He reached for her, and she did not pull away. "Ah, that's better," he murmured, drawing her to him.

"Remember," he whispered, "all acts of love and pleasure are her rituals!"

8

That night, as Rahab prepared herself for the dedication ceremony, she wondered what the high priestess had meant by the phrase "receiving the goddess within." *It sounds very awesome and holy,* she thought as she lowered herself into a deep basin and recited the purification ritual she had learned earlier that afternoon. Incense hung heavily in the air around her. Censers burned all over the temple tonight. Their fragrance, rising up of the gods, seemed sweeter and stronger than on less-holy occasions.

Rahab had been told that the high priest, Shanarbaal, had prepared all the incense and the ritual instruments to be used tonight. She was a bit confused concerning the purpose of the ritual instruments, but she was impressed that the high priest himself should prepare the emblems to be used in her dedication to the goddess. Into her bathwater she dropped the precious crystals given her by the high priestess. With a deep breath, she blew out the flame of the solitary oil lamp that had lighted her cell. In the darkness that followed, she repeated the simple chant:

> "I shall eat twice of the barley cake;
> I shall drink thrice of the sacred wine.
> I shall carry the secret goddess;
> The possessor bridegroom shall be mine."

Allowing the water to cover her body, she relaxed in the caressing ripples and enjoyed the new sensation of bathing in total darkness.

At moonrise, the girls gathered in the outer court of the temple with the high priestess. The fountains sang softly. On this night, the main gates were closed, for it was the last week before the midsummer solstice. Like the other girls, Rahab had dressed carefully in a flowing red robe. The color, they had been taught by Amaranthe, was symbolic of their womanhood, the monthly cycle of the goddess. Embroidered around the neckline were golden swirls: a clear red stone centered each one. Each girl's hair was carefully pulled back and twisted into a knot, which was surrounded by a golden circlet holding a short, ruby-red veil covering their faces. Only the girls' eyes were revealed, and each girl had applied the green and golden paint of the goddess to her eyelids as the high priestess had instructed. Rahab was exhilarated, caught up in the mystery and the magic of the dedication. She felt excited, important, and humble at the same time.

"The goddess calls you, my children!" Amaranthe-Astarte spoke, intoning each word carefully and separately. "Come with me into the inner courts, into the bosom of Astarte."

A soft, slightly discordant music came from the inner court—the tinkling sounds of bells and harps, punctuated by the heavy, hollow heartbeat of the drums.

Following their instruction of the previous week, the girls formed a line and followed the priestess, walking slowly, taking one step with each beat of the drum. As they passed slowly across the tiled courtyard, Rahab tensed, feeling the hairs prickle on the back of her neck. The huge double doors opened to greet them, opened soundlessly on jeweled movements. Heavy incense flowed into the cool night air of the courtyard from the passageway within, and Rahab felt a sudden nausea tinged with fear. A narrow stairway led downward. She recognized this place!

She suppressed a desire to scream, to turn and run. This was the place of her nightmare! The green door opened. The procession continued inexorably, down into the earth, into the bowels of the temple of the goddess. Walking with the handmaidens of Baal to the dedication ceremony, Rahab wondered why she was so frightened, so foolish. The gods would not harm her.

Fat, round columns of limestone lined the passageway, disappearing into the darkness above. Torchlight flickered from sconces on the walls, lighting the friezes of the goddess Astarte and the bulls: dancing, feasting, copulating, pouring out their libations, making sacrifice. The flickering light seemed to give them life.

As the girls entered an antechamber at the bottom of the stairs, they were startled by the sudden presence of the high priest before them. He faced them, resplendent in black robes that glimmered in the torchlight, their embroidery shining and seeming, like the friezes on the walls, to dance. Snakes, bulls, and flames of fire shimmered across his vestment, motivated, it seemed, by wills of their own. Surely it was a trick of the light and the fabric, thought Rahab, but it was startling just the same.

The high priest greeted each maiden by name, surprising them. He looked at each one as if she were his special lover. His eyes, wise in the secrets of men and gods, embraced the virgins boldly.

"Greetings, maidens of Astarte. Tonight I greet you as one who holds the honor of introducing you to the gods. I am come to awaken the goddess within you, to give you her token, to authorize your actions, embodied by her love. Follow me!"

As the small group led by Shanarbaal approached a wide space in the hall, which opened into an altar room, Amaranthe-Astarte gathered them into a circle around a brass brazier. The girls were awed by her appearance in the flickering torchlight. Across her brow, she wore the golden headdress ornamented with its glittering horns. The goddess, protectoress of all the herds, was thus figured before them. Her red hair gleamed, too, in the torchlight, but dully, against the golden luster of the crown. Her robe was white, embroidered over with tiny shoots of green to create a delicately fluid pattern of forest ferns honoring the goddess as the mother of all life.

Rahab had never seen Amaranthe-Astarte look so beautiful nor so young. In her arms the high priestess held a woven basket covered with an embroidered cloth that matched her robe. When she spoke to the girls, her voice was at once seductive and frightening, as it echoed against the stone walls of the anteroom.

"Barley cakes, barley cakes, my doves.
The queen of heaven calls you.
Receive her as you receive me:
Destiny waits in my arms!"

Having said this, Amaranthe held the basket out to the first girl, Enath, who, realizing her role, reached inside and drew out a small cake formed in the traditional curves and hollows of the shape of the goddess. Dotting the center of the cake was a red crescent moon.

Amaranthe-Astarte smiled at the girl. "It is well that you so choose," she said encouragingly. "Tonight you share your first communion with the gods."

With a smile that seemed meant to assure the girls of the delights to come, Amaranthe passed the basket to each maiden. The third girl to reach into the basket, Bishna, was surprised to discover that the crescent-shaped dot decorating her cake was not red as the others had been, but instead was a bright, shining green.

"Ah!" Amaranthe's smile seemed to blaze with the torchlight. "You are twice blessed tonight. In this evening you shall meet the double love of both the god and the goddess, and their union shall bring new life to the earth. Oh, my doves!" she said, soothing the confusion she read clearly on each face. "Don't be afraid. All that the goddess does, she does well. This means deeply and means for good. You will see!"

She continued to pass the basket of cakes among the girls. Rahab was the eleventh girl to draw out a cake. Three girls thus far had chosen cakes with green crescents. Rahab scarcely knew what to hope for. The green crescents seemed to imply a special blessedness, but the green door of her nightmare had always brought forth fear. Frightened by the color, she held her breath and reached into the basket.

A red crescent! She had chosen a red crescent, but what did it mean?

Amaranthe smiled. Rahab noticed the beauty of her flaming red hair against the embroidered robe. "Tonight each of you will become one with the goddess," the priestess said. "Tonight each of you will become ritual wife to the possessor god. So that you may understand, my doves, that the mysteries of the god are varied, the ways of the goddess are myriad and vast, some of you shall receive the goddess by symbol, and some of you shall receive her by rite."

The girls looked at each other questioningly. Not one of them comprehended what it meant to become the bride of both the god and the goddess.

Amaranthe took the girls who had drawn green into another passageway, and Shanarbaal took Rahab and her companions into the altar room, deep within the temple. The altar room was centered with a huge rock, and behind it was the goddess herself. Larger than life, Astarte in her warrior aspect dominated the room. She held a spear in one hand and a snake in the other. Her face was a grimace of ferocity; Rahab was reminded of Amaranthe when she struck Asabaal. The goddess was fearful indeed!

Although Rahab had sung many of the Astarte chants before, they took on new meaning as she lifted her voice and her hands before the stone altar. The words seemed to lilt from her. The cadence and the rhythm of the singing seemed under a control other than her own. She noted a change in the pitch of the voices, as with each repetition the voices grew higher and the words seemed to take on a new intensity and a new speed. And always, she heard the underlying beat of the drums, incessant and compelling.

Nine people had entered the altar room, the eight girls and the high priest. There they had been met by four eunuch priests, the komer who were to join them in their circle. Each of these komer carried a cage. Within each cage were two white doves.

"These doves," said Shanarbaal, after symbolically closing the circle of the group, "are the sacrifices, as you, my doves, are the sacrifices. Their purity is your purity; their blood spilled is your blood spilled in dedication to the goddess."

With the assistance of the komer, Shanarbaal sacrificed the eight doves, their lifeblood spilling on the altar, a tiny trickle from each precious body. This done, he lifted from the altar a golden cup filled with a rich, red wine.

"Tonight their maidenhood is forfeit, O goddess!" he exclaimed, lifting the cup high. "Drink deeply, the cup of the goddess, daughters. Twice, three times, you are her aspects!" He appeared to drink deeply from the cup and passed it to the first maiden, Migdallah.

"Thou art goddess," he said to her.

Taking the cup from his hand, she repeated the ritual words to him. "Thou art the god."

Drinking deeply, she passed the cup to the next girl, stating softly, "Thou art goddess."

In this way the cup came round the circle to Rahab, who, taking a deep drink, was surprised by the potency of the wine. She looked up at the komer to whom she must pass the cup. The gravity of the situation escaped her, and she almost giggled—but not quite—as she tried to remember how to address a eunuch. Hoping that she guessed right, she passed him the cup whispering, "Thou art goddess."

She had chosen well and was rewarded by his smile as he responded and drank from the cup.

With similar ceremony, Shanarbaal introduced the cakes. Each girl ate her bitter cake reverently, and each thought curiously for a moment of the four others in a different part of the temple that night.

The rest of the evening swam before Rahab's eyes. She later attributed her fuzziness to excitement and fatigue, but in this she was naive, for Shanarbaal was not a man to leave things to chance Both the wine and the cakes had been specially prepared to make the evening's activities flow smoothly.

The symbols of the goddess were of two forms for the dedication ceremonies. The first was a long wooden stick known as the *ashera,* a symbol as old as the religion itself. The second symbol of the goddess had been Shanarbaal's gift to the temple. This symbol, a small golden spiral, had made the Jericho temple one of the most popular in Canaan. Shanarbaal had discovered its use during his travels in Egypt as a young man. There, in the temples of Isis, he had questioned why the joy-maidens did not become heavy with child. A variety of coins in a variety of palms had brought him the answer: "The goddess within."

By implanting this tiny golden spiral, as a symbol of the goddess, deep within the maidens of his own temple, Shanarbaal solved the problem of temple women's bearing children. By carrying the goddess of fertility within their wombs, they became barren. Shanarbaal smiled. The temple coffers filled when the maidens of Astarte were unhindered by motherhood. His discovery of the goddess within had provided him control over the number of births in the Jericho temple. It had also helped to make him a very rich and very powerful man.

Naturally, he guarded his secret wisely, and only after the maidens were heavily sedated, did he and the komer greet them with the ashera, the instrument of the ritual deflowering, and then implant within them the goddess herself. Only Amaranthe and the komer who assisted Shanarbaal knew the secret of the goddess within, and they were sworn to secrecy.

Usually, after the spiral was implanted within each maiden, she was covered with a blanket and carried back to her cell by one of the komer. On this evening, however, the high priest himself chose to carry one of the maidens back to her cell. Shanarbaal waited until each of the eunuchs had left the temple room with a maiden. Then he picked up Rahab, and, taking a small detour, carried her into his own bedchamber.

Never before had Shanarbaal broken the ceremonial law of the dedication ceremony; never before had he taken the personal liberty of consummating the marriage rite of the god with one of the maidens on the dedication eve itself. Ritual law did not allow it. But a high priest is higher than the law, he reasoned, choosing to discover for himself whether or not Rahab's magic held the potential he desired.

As Rahab awakened, she was surprised by the quiet. The room was dark, but she sensed that it was already morning. She raised herself on one elbow and looked about. She was back in her own cell.

She did not remember returning there. Rubbing her eyes, she became aware of the throbbing pain in her forehead. Strange half-memories struggled across her consciousness.

What had happened? She could not be sure. Perhaps she had merely dreamed.

Confused, she remembered the circle, the cup, the high priest, and the other maidens. Groaning—remembering the ashera—Rahab whispered, "Maidens, no more."

So that had been the symbol, she thought wryly. "May the gods preserve me from the rite!"

Her sarcastic mood stood her well in the next few moments as she recalled scenes from the night before. Blood from the doves had seemed to splatter all over the altar room. She had hated to see Shanarbaal destroy the tiny little things so easily. Shanarbaal's words came back to her: "This blood spilled is your own blood spilled in dedication to the goddess."

How, she wondered, noticing her own blanket, had she managed to get *herself* so bloody? It was not her time of the moon. Perhaps she had touched the doves? Their blood—her blood. It was too complex.

Rising from her mat, she felt a sharp pain deep inside her—*the goddess,* she thought, and then wondered at the strangeness of the idea. Why should she equate this pain with Astarte?

It doesn't really matter, she thought, grimacing at the twinge within her. *There will be no spiral dancing for the girls today.* The word *spiral* sounded again in her mind. She sought the association, but it eluded her: spiral dance, spiral gods, spiral goddess—"the goddess within." Dimly, she remembered Shanarbaal's face looking down at her. "The goddess within," he had said. But that was as much as the memory told her. In her dreams, Shanarbaal's voice had whispered other things: mysteries, temptations—or had they been promises? Rahab could not be sure, and she shook her head harshly, hurting herself in the process, as if to dispel both the dreams and the nightmares of the evening that had passed.

9

Shanarbaal's villa awaited them, visible long before they reached it, shimmering atop one of the high hills northeast of Jericho. Looking toward it, Rahab realized that life in the country need not always be simple. The trip from Jericho to Shanarbaal's villa carried them very close to her father's land.

As they passed familiar landmarks, Rahab longed to leave the small temple caravan behind and hurry toward her father's tents. Homesickness engulfed her. She longed to see her parents, to feel their embrace, to touch and enjoy once more her favorite animals, the lambs.

Around her now the other kedeshoth chattered and looked nervously about. The were out of place, Rahab realized. These city girls were uncomfortable, and yes, even afraid out here in the open territory. She laughed softly. *At least I have something above them here,* she thought. *Here, I am comfortable!*

They are probably afraid of bandits, she mused. She could have reassured them that the chances of bandits' attacking here were very small since this was not a regular caravan route. She did not reassure them, however. *Let them worry,* she thought. They had caused her enough worries in the last few weeks.

She was glad they would soon reach their destination, for the temple sandals she wore were too ornate to be comfortable for walking; several of the city girls were already limping. *Blisters,* Rahab thought.

"Careful, fool, would you jolt me to the ground?" Amaranthe's sharp voice startled Rahab. The high priestess spoke angrily to one of the komer who carried her jeweled litter.

"Your pardon, lady," Alcion, the komer, responded with grace. "Such clumsiness is inexcusable. Our burden is much too precious to be treated lightly."

Rahab, overhearing this comment, giggled. Was the komer playing with the word *lightly* in regard to Amaranthe's weight? *Surely not,* she thought. *He wouldn't dare!* Still, she felt certain she glimpsed a twinkle in the komer's eye as he received Amaranthe's sharp reply: "Very well, but be more careful."

Men, even eunuchs, are eminently useless, the high priestess thought. *Were it not for siring children and carrying litters, women would have no use for them at all!*

High on her list of eminently useless men on this afternoon was Shanarbaal himself. He would be waiting for them when they reached the villa, for he had traveled there yesterday with Mari, Mishana, and Alshebeth. Amaranthe's fury at Shanarbaal centered on the fact that he had taken those three maidens of the second circle with him instead of the high priestess herself. Each time Amaranthe thought she was gaining control over Shanarbaal, he demonstrated to her how truly uncontrollable he was. This time he had ordered, commanded, by the authority of the Baalim, that she accompany the first-level kedeshoth on the day after his journey to the villa. Amaranthe could easily imagine the scene that must have taken place at the villa the night before. The high priestess spat angrily into the dust below her.

"He is a goat!" she muttered, "but worse, he is a goat with no taste!" Again he had preferred youngsters, second-level novitiates, to the high priestess!

Amaranthe soothed herself with the knowledge that she still had a few tricks Shanarbaal had not seen. The veil dance she planned for the evening of the Kedeshoth initiation would surprise even the high priest. Amaranthe had designed her costume on the previous evening as her anger at Shanarbaal had given rise to amazing creativity. The veil dance would be far superior to any that had ever been performed in the sacred grove. She smiled in anticipation of the attention she would receive. All the Kedeshoth combined, all of them in all of their virginal innocence, she thought with contempt, could do nothing to compare to the glory of a high priestess performing the sacred dance. She would be breathtaking: They would worship her!

Her mood greatly improved, Amaranthe greeted the gatekeeper of Shanarbaal's villa.

At his villa that morning, awaiting the arrival of the Kedeshoth and the high priestess, Shanarbaal prepared the barley cakes for the rituals of the next day.

The midday ritual would be significant, for then he would give the maidens their portions of the sacred cakes. Contrary to Amaranthe's imaginings, Shanar had not come to the villa early for the purpose of enjoying a night of pleasure with the maidens. Although some dalliance had, indeed, taken place, it had been inconsequential compared to the value of the time that Shanar had used to prepare the mushrooms. Mushrooms, gathered every spring on the hill of the secret longings, were carefully preserved in the cool, dry cellars of the villa. These special mushrooms, ground and mixed into the barley flour, would add magical touches to the eve of the summer solstice.

Shanar knew how important it was that the maidens believe in the gods. Temple duties were strenuous and often difficult at best. At worst—well, the worst had already happened to the girl Asabaal. The use of the herbs to enhance the maidens' spiritual vision would be a vital element in their dedication to the goddess.

How well Shanarbaal remembered his first encounter with the god and the goddess. He, too, had been young and influenced by special barley cakes, although he had been unaware of it at the time. Before his eyes, the aged crone who had been his high priestess had become a young and vibrant aspect of the goddess; beside her, her old husband, the high priest, had straightened and become young, a handsome and virile god. With them, Shanarbaal had performed his sacred duties, and his essence had belonged to the gods from that time forth.

Now, he was older, wiser; the innocent mantle of youth had long ago fallen from his shoulders to be replaced by the secretive cloak of the ceremonial magician. But still he remembered the first time he had seen the cedars dance and the first time he floated with the spirits in the emerald pool.

He shook himself. This was, indeed, a magical place, a place of the gods. Their old spell was enchanting him again. Even as he mixed the herbs that would bring their magic to life for the Kedeshoth, he felt their calling. Surely, if the gods existed, they had foreordained the mushrooms here on the sacred hill.

Shanarbaal laughed at himself as he prepared the cakes. *I do not know myself anymore*, he thought cynically. *The gods or the drugs, or perhaps both, have had their way with me. But it is as it should be; I shall have my way with the Kedeshoth.*

This place is a fortress, Rahab thought as she watched the high priestess greet the guard. The villa's walls rose dramatically against the higher hills to the east. They seemed to Rahab a tiny replica of the Jericho ramparts. Bandits who found this place would certainly be discouraged by these high, guarded walls.

At Amaranthe's word, the small caravan entered the courtyard. Rahab had been plagued all morning by a persistent and sharp pain low in her stomach. Now she could almost forget the discomfort in her eagerness to learn the mysteries of the villa. Here, on the following evening, she would meet the god Baal himself in the rite of mystic union—the celebration of the celestial dance. Amaranthe had been training the Kedeshoth for days in the proper movements, the intricate steps of the dance ceremony. The high priestess had insisted upon perfection and the dance had become a part of their beings, as natural to them as breathing.

The fragrance of the courtyard dispelled her daydreams, drawing her instead to the spell woven by Shanarbaal's garden, by the fruit trees, palm trees, herbs, and floral vines.

Once inside the villa, Amaranthe immediately took charge of everything. Alighting royally from her litter, she instructed the komer on the proper placement and storage of the caravan equipment. Then she turned to the Kedeshoth, saying simply, "Follow me." She exited through the courtyard so quickly that the surprised girls had to hurry to catch up with her.

"You will find your chambers here are very similar to those at the temple," Amaranthe told the girls as she directed each into a private cell, devoid of furniture.

"Arrange your sleeping mats and wait here. You will be brought food. After that, you must rest until I call you."

Amaranthe then turned to inspect her own chambers. Central in the north wall was the apartment of the high priestess. This apartment consisted of two rooms, well-lighted because of the large windows that opened out onto the villa's second courtyard. The rooms were spacious, and with the furnishings Amaranthe had brought from the temple, they would be very comfortable.

The high priestess, however, was not pleased. This apartment, like everything else lately, served only to increase Amaranthe's irritation with Shanarbaal. Amaranthe remembered only too well that in times past these chambers had been shared by the high priest and the high priestess. When she was younger, Amaranthe had shared many ritual nights with Shanarbaal in these rooms. In recent years, however, Shanarbaal had chosen to reside across the courtyard—in chambers adjoining the king's royal suite.

This separation of herself from both the high priest and the king offended

Amaranthe's pride in a way that neither luxurious furnishings nor spacious chambers could amend. Looking out the large windows and across the courtyard toward Shanarbaal's chambers, Amaranthe snorted. Perhaps Shanarbaal felt himself omnipotent with the god and the king beside him, but the goddess would soon reveal her own power.

And let all mortal men tremble, Amaranthe thought, *especially Shanarbaal!*

Several hours had elapsed when Rahab was awakened by a knock at her door. The komer Alcion smiled at her goodnaturedly.

"Get up, dreaming one," he said, laughing at her sleepy state. "You have slept the afternoon away. The high priestess bids you come to her chambers."

Rahab smiled and stretched. The nap had restored her energies. She followed Alcion into the corridor where they were joined by Bishna, who smiled wearily and said she had not been able to sleep at all. "Too much excitement, I guess," she surmised simply.

Rahab nodded. She found Bishna fascinating—beautiful to the point of excess, but innocent and unusually gentle in comparison to the other city girls. This city girl was at home with the ruder, harsher girls, yet she was neither snide nor cruel to Rahab, as many of the others were. Rahab loved Bishna's gentleness and was flattered by her friendship, for Bishna obviously preferred Rahab to the city girls of the Kedeshoth.

As the two girls entered the main room of the priestess's chambers, Rahab's breath caught in her throat. She looked around in wonder. The walls were covered with sensuous tapestries depicting the glories of the goddess. A rich carpet cushioned Rahab's steps. Large and beautifully embroidered pillows filled the floor space, and the curtains draping the windows were richly colored in blues, reds, and purples, and heavily ornamented with gold. Rahab had never entered the chambers of the high priestess before, and she was awed by the splendor. *This is enough to attract any bandit,* she thought. Instantly, she realized that these things were not permanent furnishings of the villa but had, instead, arrived with the high priestess in the temple caravan. Rahab had noticed the unusual number of young boys carrying parcels. Now she understood why. The high priestess would live in luxury everywhere!

Amaranthe, standing at the front of the room, cleared her throat and scowled at the two girls, who simply stood in the doorway, wide-eyed.

"Come in, late ones," she said mockingly. Rahab and Bishna quickly joined the Kedeshoth who were already in the room, seated on pillows scattered across the floor.

Amaranthe glanced confidently at the girls around her. They were so young and so simple-minded. *Easy to manipulate,* she thought, *easy to shape.* Amaranthe's desire now was to weave the magic of the goddess so intricately around the girls' hearts that there could be no extricating them. *They will serve the goddess from hearts of fire, as I do,* Amaranthe thought. Smiling, she began the lesson.

"Two powers exist in the universe," she said, "the female and the male." Her voice caressed the Kedeshoth. "You, yourselves, are tiny shades of the goddess, the perfect female. As you obey her, you become more like her. She is the perfect one of power.

"The male deities are numberless, yet all gods are manifestations of the perfect male. He is El, our high god and distant ruler."

Amaranthe's voice rose and fell gently and quietly to cast a spell around the maidens at her feet. She continued, "The goddess, too, has many aspects. She is the mother earth who first gave birth to men; for this reason, her power over men is invincible and incomparable. She is Anat, the goddess of blood and war, perfect in vengeance. She is Astarte, she it is who is eternally fertile, yet eternally pure. She it is who satisfies all men's longings: the eternal mother, eternal virgin, and eternal harlot." Here Amaranthe laughed deeply, consumed by the mythology of her religion.

"Astarte is our city's goddess," she continued. "She is patron goddess of Jericho, and her consort is the great rider of the clouds, Baal. It is he who controls our crops and our harvest, and it is to him that we bring our sacrifices in the sacred grove. He is the god of the storm, and he must be appeased."

She smiled, her eyes lighting with the pleasure she felt in worshipping her gods. "Today I shall tell you secret things. Today you shall see the wonders of the gods. In their sacred grove, you shall learn their mysteries." She laughed again and clapped her hands, startling the girls out of their mesmerism. Amaranthe's red hair blazed against the light of the doorway as she barked the command: "Follow me!"

Following the high priestess was no simple matter, for she led the girls across the courtyard, through the villa's north gate, and into the woods beyond. Amaranthe's step was as quick and fleet as a mountain goat's. These were her hills, her trees; this was her sacred grove. She knew every inch of the area as she knew the curves of her own body. Many of the Kedeshoth stumbled over vines or rocks in their haste to keep up with the high priestess, but Amaranthe was oblivious to the clumsiness of the girls behind her. She was at one with her goddess, at home in her grove.

She led the girls along the Baalpath, an ancient way that descended into a limestone gorge near the villa and followed the banks of a small stream that flowed noisily down from the high places to meet the Jordan.

Huge cypress trees lined the meanderings of the stream, creating the sacred grove. Rahab was unprepared for the power of these enormous trees. The small streams that fed her father's lands nearby were bordered only with larger, greener versions of the desert trees and bushes. Rahab had never seen such tall trees, trees of such strength. The sacred trees, Amaranthe had called them. Their deeply lined trunks reached for the sky; their huge girth suggested the ancient strength of the spirits who inhabited them. The roots of these huge cypresses curved and curled like beds of snakes, wrapping themselves around the limestone ledges along the river to drink deeply of their life source, the water itself. Graceful arching branches bent low to the water, carrying delicate wings of leaves that reminded Rahab of feathers. These leaves were always green. Never dying, like the goddess. Rahab easily believed these trees to be sacred, special to the gods. She was awed by their power.

The Baalpath left the water and wound its way for a short distance to a clearing formed by a circle of boulders. Each rock was as big as a house, twice as tall as a man. The girls were dwarfed by their mass. Rahab wondered how these stones had been so perfectly arranged. Even many slaves, using rollers and pulleys, could not have done it.

"The gods themselves arranged these stones," Amaranthe said suddenly, almost as if she had seen into Rahab's questioning mind. "They threw them down from the high places in a great battle when the earth was young. It is here that on the morrow the gods will receive you. Come," she said, turning and proceeding up the Baalpath, "let us be prepared!"

The girls followed her up the path, which ascended steeply to the hillside behind the tall cliffs, away from the river. Gravel and rocks defined its ancient curves and twists as it climbed toward the high places. Limestone steps were laid—or had they, too, been carved by the gods? Rahab suddenly visualized the gods El and Baal out on the cliffs sweating with giant hammers and chisels. She giggled.

"Quiet, foolish girls! This is sacred ground!" Amaranthe snapped without looking back. Rahab's vision evaporated.

As the party approached the crest of the cliff overlooking the sacred grove, the goddess spoke within Amaranthe's spirit. Her imagination carried her backward, to a time when there had been no temple, no city of Jericho. There had been only the sacred grove and the gods. It was here that her ancestors had first worshipped the sacred ones, here that they had prayed to the ancient aspects of the god and the goddess, the rocks and the trees. Amaranthe breathed deeply and sighed in her pleasure; she had led the girls up into the hills, and now she stopped before an altar. Next to the altar were a huge stone and a high wooden pole.

Amaranthe spoke. Her voice now was loud and resounding: "This is the high place of your gods, O mortal Kedeshoth. This is the center of wisdom of the earth. In front of you are the symbols of the gods, erected by the Old Ones: this high pole, the ashera, the symbol of the goddess, sacred beyond words, filled with her power; this huge rock, the god's *masheba*, created by his hands, representing his power. This masheba, a portrait of the god in his aspect as the bull, was given to the Old Ones by the god himself. It arose out of the depths of the sacred pool when Baal's power shook the earth. It is a symbol of his love for the goddess and his protection of the fields of men. Bow down before him, maidens. Bow down before her, maidens. Behold your gods!"

As she spoke, Amaranthe gestured broadly to the ashera. Behind it, the red ball of the setting sun appeared to be impaled upon the jutting pole.

"Thus the goddess takes the god in his chariot," Amaranthe said.

Rahab shivered uncomfortably. The Kedeshoth, stunned by the intensity of Amaranthe's enthusiasm, dropped to their knees before the ashera and the masheba, the wooden pole and the giant rock, their gods.

"Worship here," Amaranthe commanded them, "and when you have done so, return to your rooms."

Amaranthe turned, leaving the girls to worship a rock and a pole and to find their own way back to the villa. She would worship alone near the sacred pond, as befitted the high priestess of Baal-Jericho.

10

Captured by the magic of Amaranthe's spell and the setting sun, the maidens were silent for a time. This hilltop, with its ancient symbols of the gods, was their first glimpse of the mystery and power promised by Amaranthe. Rahab was captured by the awesome beauty of the place; it was so like her home, yet so different.

Standing now on the high cliff, the girls could look past the ashera and the masheba, out over the sacred grove. The stream below was hidden by the cypress trees, but they could hear its music; the arpeggio of its rapids and waterfalls was the only sound in the magic twilight. The golden lights of Shanarbaal's villa gleamed below them, and behind them, an almost full moon began its ascent into a cloudless sky.

Rahab was so entranced that she did not notice the other girls had left until Bishna's gentle touch startled her from her reverie.

"Rahab!" Bishna said softly. "Don't you think we should leave now? It will soon be quite dark!"

"It is so beautiful," Rahab said, almost to herself. "I am in no hurry to leave this place."

"The sun is gone, Rahab. It will be dark soon—and it's a long way back down the Baalpath. Let's go!"

Rahab looked around. "The others have gone on ahead, haven't they?"

"Yes. Come on, Rahab—we need to be going, too," Bishna insisted, adding under her breath, "I don't want to be caught out here alone at night!"

Rahab laughed. "Bishna, really! You're afraid!"

The city girl frowned. "There may be bandits! Snakes! Evil spirits! We could get lost—anything!"

"Oh, no! We are surely quite safe here. This is the sacred place! The gods will keep us safe!"

"But it's getting dark!" Bishna's voice rose.

"All right, Bishna, we can go. But look, the moon god is rising. He will light our way! Have no fear."

"It will take a long time to get back. Let's hurry."

"Then let's go directly," Rahab answered, turning down a small pathway that angled away from the meandering Baalpath to descend the edge of the cliff itself.

"I don't know. We might get lost," Bishna answered, hesitantly.

"No, Bishna," Rahab answered confidently, going on ahead. "I grew up in country like this. See, the moon gives us direction, and as long as we are going down from here, we have to cross the Baalpath since it follows the river. We won't get lost. Come on!"

The city girl still hesitated. "I'm afraid!" she said.

"Trust me, Bishna. I know what I'm saying. If we cut directly down here, we'll shorten our journey by half. I am sure of it!"

"I hope you're right," Bishna answered as she followed reluctantly.

The going was rough, but not impossible. The girls went single file, for the path was narrow, and they held hands, for the way was steep. By the time they had descended the cliff path, the last fading light of day was gone and they were left in the grayed brilliance of the moon, which cast deceptive shadows on the rocks and bushes along the trail. The summer night air had a softness that reminded Rahab of childhood evenings, delighting and reassuring her. But Bishna was tense and quiet.

A small, wild creature scuttled away through the underbrush as the girls approached. Bishna hesitated; Rahab seemed not to notice. As the pathway entered the sacred grove, the towering trees cut out much of the moonlight, and near the stream the air was still and humid, in sharp contrast to the drier atmosphere of the cliffs.

"I don't like this, Rahab. It's too dark!"

"We are safe," Rahab answered confidently. "Nothing will harm the maidens of Astarte in Astarte's sacred grove."

Rahab was sure of herself. She had learned the ways of the desert as a child. Her father had taught her well, for the desert child who got lost might easily lose his life.

In the darkness, the girls almost missed another path that crossed at right angles, heading directly toward the villa to the south.

"Look!" Rahab said suddenly. "Others have taken this shortcut, too!"

"Well, at least if it's a path, it must lead somewhere," Bishna replied cautiously.

"I think it must go in the same direction as the Baalpath, so it should go directly to the villa," Rahab reasoned.

"All right, Rahab, if you say so, but one direction seems exactly like another to me."

"Oh!" Rahab's exclamation was one of pain.

"What is it?" Bishna's concern for her friend was intensified by her fear of their surroundings. She had never desired adventure, and her life in the city had been sheltered and safe.

Rahab stood very still, catching her breath, leaning against one of the giant cypress trees.

"I'm sorry, Bishna. I didn't intend to upset you," she said. "It was a sharp pain in my stomach. I've been having it for several days now."

"Oh, dear," Bishna's voice was tender. "Could it be serious? Are you all right now?"

"I think so....It stabs me, and then, as quickly as it comes, it's gone."

The girls resumed their walk. Now that they were in the grove, the going was easier and faster. To their left, they could hear the stream singing to the moon.

A sudden bright circle of moonlight surprised them. The path widened, and they were in a small clearing, bathed in the moonlight. They could see clearly the gnarled and twisted roots of cypress trees, the eerie swirls of hanging mosses, and an outcropping of limestone on the far side of the clearing. The moonlight filled the open space and reflected whitely on the smooth stones to reveal—

"Is it an altar?" Bishna asked in a hushed voice.

"I don't know, but let's see if it makes a resting place," Rahab suggested, feeling weak and trembly from the exertion of the climb and the intensity of the pain. She went directly to the stone and sat down.

"This is strange, Bishna. I'm normally very healthy. I'm not accustomed to pain."

"When did it start, Rahab?"

"I don't know—well, let me think—the first one I remember was the morning after the dedication ceremony, but I was quite sick that morning anyway, so it could just have been part of my illness."

"What was wrong? Have you been sick at your stomach lately, Rahab?"

45

"No, not at all. Well, yes—the morning after the dedication, I was sick, but I think that was from the wine. I haven't been sick since—except that I keep having this stabbing pain in my stomach. It comes and goes without any reason that I can tell."

"Oh, well, the reason I asked is that I've been nauseated a lot the last two days. I thought we might have the same problem."

"Have you had any sharp pains?"

"No, only the nausea. Are you feeling better now? It's getting late—the moon is high." Bishna was impatient.

As the girls stood, the limestone bench made a hollow grating sound.

"Rahab!" Bishna shrieked. "What was that?"

"It's just the bench," Rahab said, pushing it back into place. The stone was heavy, but she was strong enough to move it. "It's a secret hiding place—or maybe it's a tomb—or maybe...maybe it's the entrance to the underworld!"

"Oooh, hush, Rahab! Let's get out of here!"

"If you insist," Rahab said with a laugh. "Follow me!"

The girls followed the path back into the darkness of the sacred grove. They had not gone far when, again, the path widened. The moonlight revealed that they stood at the edge of a quiet, dark pond. The river rushed by somewhere in the darkness to their left, leaving behind the backwaters that lay before them, serene and still under the almost-full moon. The water was dark, black and deep, except where the moon was reflected, and there, directly across from where the girls stood, it created a silver mirror, so still and so smooth that the feathery pattern of the cypress leaves was etched on its crystal surface.

"Bishna!" Rahab breathed softly, "Surely this place is sacred!"

"It gives me gooseflesh," Bishna answered impatiently. "Let's go!"

The girls followed the edge of the pond to a low limestone crossing. In times of rain, the crossing would be covered with water, but now, in the dry season, the stone separated this pond from another, smaller pond. The second pond was defined by a limestone ledge, an outcropping forming a cliff a little taller than a man, which would be a waterfall in wet weather.

Silhouetted by the moonlight on that cliff knelt Amaranthe-Astarte. She was worshipping, praying to her gods. The girls stopped instantly, looking at one another with wide eyes. They certainly did not wish to intrude upon the high priestess at her worship! Even as they stood, wondering whether to retreat or press forward, the priestess rose from her knees and stretched her arms to the sky.

"Ai-eee-eee, Astarte!" her cry carried easily across the pond, echoing eerily within the limestone gorge. Then she turned and walked regally around the edge of the cliffs, coming down to the pathway and turning toward the villa.

Carefully, quietly, Rahab and Bishna followed her back to the gardens of Shanarbaal.

11

Morning came quickly, and the girls prepared for the rituals of the day. These would be the last of their ceremonial instructions before final initiation into the Kedeshoth. The most sacred ceremonies in the religion were held at midsummer, midwinter, the vernal equinox, and the autumn equinox. On these special days, blood sacrifices were offered at the altar here, above the sacred grove. These ceremonies, secret and ancient, had been repeated for thousands of generations. Jericho itself was thousands of years old; these rituals were older still. Their roots were hidden deep in antiquity when the tribesmen of Canaan had worshipped at the Oasis of Jericho, had, in fact, worshipped the oasis itself, with its flowing springs, its beautiful palm trees, and its refuge in the sacred mountains.

Now, in the late morning sun of the midsummer day, the Kedeshoth gathered in a circle in the villa garden to drink the communion of their gods. The maidens were dressed as they had been instructed in sheer white linen robes. They sat among the flowers of the garden waiting for the arrival of the high priestess, passing the time by braiding flowers into one another's hair.

"Be still, Bishna," Enath said to the other girl good-humoredly. "If I am ever to get these daisies into place, you must sit still!"

Bishna sighed in gentle exasperation. "Oh, Enath, it doesn't matter. I don't have to have flowers in my hair. Work on someone else for a while."

"Well, I've almost got it now, Bishna. There's no sense in quitting before I'm finished. All you have to do is sit still."

"I'm sorry, Enath," Bishna replied, trying to smile. "I'm just not in the mood for a ceremony, I guess. My stomach has been giving me fits."

Rahab looked worriedly at Bishna, who was nauseated again today. *How odd*, Rahab thought. Although Rahab herself continued to feel an occasional sharp twinge within her own stomach and in her legs, she felt no queasiness. She had eaten the figs, barley cakes, and goat cheese this morning with great satisfaction. Bishna had not felt like eating, and Enath was only making matters worse by her constant, irritating chatter.

"Here, Enath," Rahab said, coming to her friend's rescue. "Work on my hair. You know how unmanageable it is. Can you make these poppies look right? I'd like them to come down and curve around my temples."

Enath touched the flowers she had been adjusting over Bishna's ear. "Yes, that's just right," she said. "All right, Rahab, let's see what we can do with

47

you. The high priestess is right, you know. You really are a challenge."

Rahab gritted her teeth and allowed her hair to be caught up in Enath's ministrations.

By midday the sun had grown quite warm, and the maidens of the Kedeshoth had waited almost longer than their patience would endure when, at last, the high priestess arrived.

Rahab gasped. She never failed to be awed by the beauty of the high priestess. Today in the bright sunlight, Amaranthe, dressed only in armor, was a highly painted and fierce beauty, a beauty that seemed as dangerous as it was provocative. The horns on her headdress glistened in the sun. She arrived on one path as the high priest—dressed totally in black including even a hood—arrived on a path from the opposite direction. Alcion and Barukna, two of the high priest's special attendants, carried golden dishes and followed their master. Behind them came the rest of the Komer, who now joined the circle.

The priestess dropped to one knee and proclaimed in a loud voice, "This ceremony is dedicated to Baal, the dying god."

The high priest knelt in response, proclaiming, "This ritual is consecrated to Anat-Astarte, the warrior goddess."

Both the priest and priestess rose and moved to face each other from separate sides of the Kedeshoth circle.

The priestess cried out the ancient ritual words, the words that carried the power of their religion, their belief in a god who was resurrected every autumn.

> "Wounded, wounded is Baal the beloved;
> Seventy-seven wounds hath the rider of the clouds;
> Yea, eighty wounds hath the beloved;
> Ninety wounds have killed the rider of the skies."

The priest responded to her lamentation. His voice was as dark as the black robe that covered him:

> "Mot hath killed Baal;
> The enemy has triumphed.
> All nature mourns Baal—the rider of the skies.
> The heavens search for him;
> The stars call his name;
> The sun seeks after him;
> Scorching the high places—
> One place, two places, he cannot be found."

The Kedeshoth had been well trained; they knew the ritual answer.

"One place, two places," they cried out, their voices wailing in the appropriate chant:

> "He is descended into darkness!
> Who can save him? Not one thousand,
> Not ten thousand! Even none!"

A ripe ear of corn appeared suddenly in the hands of the high priestess. Her voice rang out powerfully:

> "Astarte arises to avenge her beloved,
> To revenge the death of her brother,
> Her husband!
> Mot, Baal's destroyer shall destruction see!"

Amaranthe plunged her dagger into the sheaf of corn and cried out:

> "With her sword she cleans him.
> She cleaves him; she winnows him."

The priestess stripped the shucks from the corn as if in fury.

"She burns him!" said the high priest, stepping forward and causing sparks to fly from his hands. The Kedeshoth maidens gasped.

"With millstones she grinds him," Amaranthe said, dropping the ear of corn and grinding it beneath her heel.

Then, kneeling, she spread dust over the corn, as Shanarbaal said,

> "In the fields she plants him,
> So the birds do not eat his flesh."

Amaranthe stood and spoke again:

> "Let the earth rejoice!
> Mot, the destroyer, has destruction seen!
> Astarte, queen of heaven, has rescued her king.
> Baal is returned to the throne of his kingship.
> Cease your mourning, all ye thousands!
> Cease your mourning, all ye ten thousands!
> The life of the fields is returned to the land!"

Shanarbaal clapped his hands and the Komer stepped forward. In the golden dishes were the special barley cakes Shanarbaal had prepared the day before, flavored strongly by the ritual mushrooms. One barley cake with an extra portion of the mushrooms had been set aside for Rahab. The Komer stepped forward again, carrying golden cups filled with wine. Shanarbaal had added herbs to the drink to further ensure the religious fervor of the novitiates for this evening.

The Komer passed the barley cakes to each of the girls. Handing Rahab her special cake, the komer Alcion whispered quickly, "Only taste it!"

Misunderstanding his words, Rahab ate the cake quickly and smiled. *Don't waste it, indeed!* she thought, drinking her wine. *As if I would waste the communion of the gods.*

"We shall meet at sundown at the circle of stones," Shanarbaal told the assembly. "The gods await us there already. You may meet them on the pathway—or you may meet the spirits of the trees or the spirits of the river. Do not fear, but respect their power. From this moment, your initiation into the mysteries is consecrated. As the moon rises tonight, your union shall be consummated. You shall be one with the earth and with the strength of the gods. Nature, the mother, will reveal herself to you."

A gong sounded. The priest and priestess bowed deeply to one another and departed.

Hushed, the Komer and the maidens arose, and each went alone to prepare for the evening ahead.

Rahab was dizzy with excitement, eager for the evening's adventure. She would take the shortcut by the pond. As she fastened the belt of her robe, her fingers began to tingle. Her upper lip felt numb as well, but she was too caught up in her preparations to care. Tonight she would meet the gods!

Of course. She should have realized. The rhythm of the waves was the rhythm of nature, herself. Shanarbaal was right, of course. The concept became simple and clear to her as she lay at the edge of the emerald pond, feeling the gentle rhythmic waves flow over her. Without volition, she began to move her hands, pushing herself off the bank, away from the sodden leaves which clung to her hair. Her body freed itself of the pool's edge, and she felt the freedom of the deep green water at once beneath her and surrounding her.

She floated effortlessly. The tiniest flutter of her fingers guided her tranquil body across the pool. Simple, it was all so simple—nature, the mother, the goddess, caressed her with the rhythm of the waves. The waves carried her without effort, as the earth carried the trees, and so it should. She was at one with the earth, at one with the strength of Astarte. She floated, breathing deeply, feeling the earth breathe with her. Her thoughts rose and fell with her relaxed body on the quiet water.

Closing her eyes, she sensed, or perhaps she saw with inner eyes, the spirits of the water, aspects of the goddess playing among the ripples. She felt their hands tenderly touch her body, their caresses pulsing with the rhythm of the waves. Half-teasing, half-tempting, these laughing spirits caressed her and befriended her. She laughed softly, delightedly. As she floated amongst them, she sensed that they recognized her consecration, welcoming the goddess within her. Childlike in their eagerness for a companion, they required no reverence. They invited her to be their playmate.

She laughed aloud, but was startled as the pillow of water disappeared from beneath her head, suddenly replaced by rough, rocky ground. Opening her eyes at this sudden intrusion, she was surprised to see a canopy of feathery leaves and mosses where she had expected to see only cloudless azure sky. She had floated all the way across the pond, coming to rest on the limestone ledge that divided the two pools. With languid ease, she shifted her shoulders to a more comfortable position against sand instead of rock.

With the delightful drowsiness of the sun-drenched afternoon, she allowed her pleasant daylight fantasies to tantalize her imagination. Within the feathery pattern of the leaves, Baal, now the sun god, darted in and out of the hanging mosses, creating dappled patterns of shadow that, like the water, touched her, kissed her, caressed her body.

With quiet surprise, she realized that the persistent pain in her stomach was gone; it simply was not there. In her mind, but not by her own volition, words formed and a voice spoke to her: "Baal has taken your pain; great are Baal's gifts to his beloved kedeshoth!"

The god Baal, a ray of unexpected sunlight, escaped the curtain of mosses and assaulted her eyes. Squinting, she turned her face away from the brightness of his sunlit dagger, into the dirt on which she lay.

The unpleasant grating of sand and pebbles beneath her cheek was quickly forgotten as she opened her eyes to see before them a rock—or was it a precious stone? Without hesitation, she reached for it, sensing rather than hearing a quiet, masculine laugh and then words: "I give you this masheba in the sacred shape and from my own hands. I, Baal, greet you, Rahab!"

Rahab blinked, discovering that her eyes were suddenly filled with tears. This was awesome. The god himself had acknowledged her! She drew the masheba to her breast, studying its lines: she saw the face of the bull, its horns, the folds of skin that formed his neck, the beautiful play of greens and ambers across the face of the stone. With humility and reverence, she lifted the gift to her lips and kissed it. She closed her eyes and blessed the gods, thanking the great and powerful Baal.

She had no idea how much time had passed when next she opened her eyes. The sun was low as she slowly raised herself out of the water, her limbs heavy. Before her, the surface of the second pool, the ruby pool, danced to the crimson music of the setting sun. Red and gemlike, the ripples reflected a thousand ruby lights from the glowing sky. *So the vision continues,* Rahab thought, realizing she still clutched the precious masheba to her breast.

These are the mysteries Shanarbaal said I would learn: to see with the eyes of the goddess within, to share Astarte's rapture in the possessor god. The scarlet pond, brilliant with the red light of the evening sun, appeared to her a confirmation of all that she had experienced.

Her immediate desire was to hide the masheba so she would not have to share her special secret with the others—not with the girls, not with Shanarbaal, not even with Amaranthe. It was her gift from the god; she would relish it alone. She must find a place to hide it!

Almost at once she knew the hiding place, and she turned toward the clearing where she had rested with Bishna. Surrounded by the cypress trees, the limestone bench seemed as old as the earth itself. Carefully, quietly, as if in a dream, she pushed the stone. It was heavier than she remembered, but Baal gave her the strength. A cavity was exposed within the bench, an empty hollow into which she placed her masheba, the gift of the god. Slowly, reverently, she replaced the stone seat on the bench. The image of the god, made by him for her, was safe.

As she rested then, renewing her strength, her thoughts turned back to her childhood, and she sought a memory, another time when the person she had been was touched by the gods. Her mind struggled to find the memory, but she was brought back from her reverie as the komer Barukna stood before her. He held a basin with water and a linen cloth, and he carried a fresh white linen robe, her ritual costume.

"Rahab-Kedeshoth, consecrated to Baal," the komer said, "this night you serve the god. Baal-Jericho calls you to be his bride!"

Bathing in the water that he brought, she fastened the linen robe around her shoulders and tied its girdle at her waist.

"I am ready, my lord," she said.

12

In the approaching darkness, Rahab followed the messenger up the Baalpath through the grove. In the distance, she heard the lowing of the sacrificial bull.

He was frightened, lonely, calling to the herd of temple cows with whom he had shared the pastoral pleasures of the god until this evening, when the bull dancers had ensnared him with ropes and led him to this small, demeaning enclosure. He cried out to the herd, screaming his confusion, his frustration, his fear.

The komer who walked before Rahab did not observe her subtle movement away from the Baalpath and into the brush. Accustomed as he was to Kedeshoth obedience, he assumed her to be following meekly behind him. Instead, her quick and quiet steps had veered away from the path and toward the animal pens.

The bull's cry called to Rahab. The brush was thick, but not impassable. Her hands easily pushed aside the veils of moss beshrouding the cypress trees. Traveling quickly among their ancient trunks, she soon stopped before the pen that held the bellowing bull. The enclosure was made of strong cypress wood, heavy and solid. Rahab understood that the bull, if sufficiently angered, could easily knock down even these stout posts and pillars.

The bull's crying was to his friends, the cows, but it was Rahab who answered. Now she stood just outside the enclosure in the rapidly failing daylight. Her filmy white robe blew in the evening wind, catching the eye of the bull. She felt, rather than saw, his looming mass, for his darkness melted into the darkening night. He had been pacing the edges of the pen, wondering where his herd had gone, crying out to his mates, when suddenly this strange and filmy form distracted him with its white billowing. He was totally terrified by the white apparition. He snorted and readied for combat, lowering his head and pawing the earth.

Staring into the dark eyes of the beast, Rahab felt his earthy strength and power. The bull, the symbol of the god in all his animal virility, returned her stare, captivated. His bellowing stopped. The god drew Rahab forward. Slowly, her human awareness, her identity, and her free will disappeared into the compelling gaze of the terrified animal. His eyes, black pools of infinite depth, drew her. Suddenly, she laughed loudly, but as the laugh left her body, so did she.

She felt her being surge forward to meld itself into the massive creature in front of her. Joining the bull, she knew its awesome simplicity, its desire, its fear. The god himself was with her for only a moment before his presence was obliterated by the animal's raw power and sensuality. The strength of many men surged through this body. The heartbeat was so strong, so thunderous, that it seemed to shake her with its pounding. She was all emotion. Fury and fear fought within her: rage at the posts and bars before her and terror of the strange, white, trembling body of the human being outside the fence. With a bizarre awareness, Rahab realized that the person was herself. Her confusion was too great! She screamed out her rage. But the sound of that rage was a roaring bellow which could be heard throughout the grove, starting low and ending on a high shriek, like the trumpeting call of the sentry to battle.

Shanarbaal, standing in the clearing at some distance, heard the bellow and listened carefully. Something strange was happening to the sacrificial animal. Clapping his hands, he commanded two komer to check the bull pen. They left without hesitation—they knew better than to hesitate—although to them the bull sounded little different from before.

53

With the release of the bellow, the web which had spun itself across Rahab's consciousness was torn. The spell was broken, and she found herself outside the fence, in her own body, her heart racing and her breath coming fast and short. Before her, the maddened bull began to paw the ground and pace the fence line, preparing to attack both the fence and the girl. Aware of the pressing danger but unable to move, Rahab stood, a trembling statue, before the bull.

As Shanarbaal's two servants entered the clearing, the komer Alcion perceived the situation and responded immediately by jumping the fence into the bull pen. This unexpected movement drew the bull's attention away from Rahab. Taking charge of herself, she fled from the clearing. She ran blindly through the sacred grove, becoming entangled in the waving arms of the mosses and vines; she had no choice but to stop, to slowly and deliberately free herself from their dancing, strangling swirls. She thought gratefully of the komer in the bull pen behind her. How had he been there at exactly the right moment? How had he dared to jump into the pen? Surely the god himself must have sent the komer to protect her.

She turned and walked deeper into the grove. Finding the Baalpath again, she searched for the clearing and the high priest.

Ahead of her through the trees she could see the flickering of the Baal fire. Already she could hear the ceremonial drums. Shanarbaal intended to waste not one moment of the precious darkness. The initiation would begin, as did all grove ceremonies, immediately after the sun had set.

With this in mind, early in the day, Shanarbaal had sent all of the Kedeshoth to gather firewood. All of the Kedeshoth, that is, except one: for Shanarbaal, with his usual perception, had recognized the intensity of Rahab's response to the Baal cakes, and he had left her where he had seen her, floating in the pond. Rahab would be the high priest's favorite in the circle that night, and he had prepared her well. Not only had she been given the special cake, but also Rahab's Baaldrink had contained twice the potency of any other cup lifted at the midday ceremony. That afternoon, when Shanar had ascertained that Rahab's awareness was clouding, he had spent a few special moments gazing into her eyes. Invested as he was with the ancient wisdom, Shanarbaal understood the secrets of mesmerism. The irresistible gaze was but one of the many techniques he used to strengthen the dedication of the Kedeshoth. He could not know exactly what Rahab had experienced, but his years as a priest assured him that she would come to the Baalfire this night as one ready to receive the god. The smile flickering around Shanar's lips reflected his assurance that, in his own person, the god would not disappoint Rahab.

As Rahab approached the clearing, her eyes were drawn to the figure of the high priest. Standing behind the Baalfire, Shanar was illuminated by the dancing light of the flames. Even his eyes reflected the red and gold of the god in the fire. Rahab watched his smile grow as he became aware of her presence.

The smile lit his eyes as he raised his right arm and, with a dramatic wave, invited her near.

"You have taken your time in joining us tonight, Rahab." Shanar's eyes appreciated her body as he spoke. "Your hair is still wet from your encounter with the pond spirits—you met them, did you not?"

"I have met more gods than I dreamed possible," Rahab answered, her voice still weak and breathless. "At first the spirits were so gentle, and the pond was beautiful against the red sky, but a moment ago, at the bull pen—my lord, I fear I may have caused the death of one of the Komer."

"Death? Is one of my servants dead then? Tell me what happened!" His voice was a cold command.

"I do not really know if he is dead," Rahab answered. "But one of the Komer—the one called Alcion—jumped into the bull pen to save me!" She trembled, dropping her eyes. "I am ashamed, my lord, that I did not stay to help him."

To Rahab's great surprise, Shanarbaal laughed.

"Oh, Rahab, what a foolish little creature you are! Alcion dead, indeed! That boy was born in the bull pen. He is a bull dancer, my dear, and of great reputation. Were he not dedicated to the goddess, he would bring a fine price at the market, for he has many skills. Slaves of his ability are highly sought. He is alive and no doubt laughing at the bull even now." Shanarbaal watched the light return to Rahab's eyes.

"Oh, I'm so glad, my lord," she said. "Such a worthy servant should not die for me."

The priest laughed again. "So you met the spirit of the bull. Did you also meet the pond spirits?" he asked.

"Yes, they met me with great joy, my lord," Rahab answered, surprising herself. Warmed by the light in Shanar's eyes, she could almost forget the terror of the bull pen.

She was tempted to tell him all, but she did not. Shanar was not Baal, even if he was his representative. Her memory was safe. Shanar would not know of her masheba. No one would know of her masheba. Her secret was still hers.

"I have known the water spirits myself on many occasions," Shanarbaal continued. "But for me the fire always carries the stronger aspect of the god. Do you sense him here, Rahab? Look into the flames."

Rahab responded immediately by turning to stare into the leaping flames. She answered, "I have known him here in the grove today, my lord." She stared into the altering colors within the flames. Shanar passed his hands before the fire, causing the flames to leap up in an ecstasy of color and motion. The music rose to a hypnotic chant punctuated with the heartbeat of drums.

Rahab smiled up at Shanar. "He is with us now, isn't he?" she asked.

"Indeed," he answered. "This grove has been a ritual site since the ancient times. The wisdom of the earth is strong here. I, myself, have served the

Baalim here since my boyhood, for I knew very early that the goddess called me to the divine service as she is calling you. Tonight, Rahab, you shall be received into the mysteries of the gods."

Rahab smiled. "But that has already begun, master. You have not forgotten my dedication in the temple?" Her understanding had never seemed so deep, so acutely perceptive.

Shanarbaal laughed. She was so simple, and she still had so much to learn! What pleasure there would be in the teaching.

"Of course," he said, "the temple dedication was a symbol of your union with the god. Tonight you will know the reality of that union."

Shanarbaal touched her. Relishing his private memory of the ritual act he had shared with her before, his eyes captured her struggling spirit. "The god is ready for the dance," he said. The continuous pounding of the drums gained in intensity. The pipes shrieked. The Baalim would be served.

From all directions, out of the darkness of the grove, the young male dancers came forth. Their bodies gleamed with costly oils and paints. The young men, many of them newly brought to the temple, danced forward, their heads thrown back, their legs arching upward, swirling to the relentless rhythm of the drums.

The drums reached a peak of frenzy as the dancers circled the fire, spinning, kicking, leaping. Suddenly, the rhythm changed, and the drums beat slowly and softly. The dancers relaxed, then quietly dropped to the ground, their chests heaving from the exertion. Rahab felt the persistent beat of the drums—the throbbing, beating, pounding, promising beat of the drums. She was at one with the magic of the dance.

A shrill scream pierced the grove.

"Aii-eee, Astarte!"

The drums replied, echoing the rhythm of the shriek.

In the light from the fire, the goddess appeared above them, poised on one of the huge rocks. Her voice burst out again in the ritual beginning of the incantation.

"Aii-eeeee, Astart-te!"

Rahab perceived with some part of her being that this magnificent vision was Amaranthe, but the priestess was so clothed in the radiance of the goddess that her individuality had ceased to exist. For all the purposes of the sacred grove, she was the goddess.

Her red hair shimmered beneath her golden-horned crown. Her fluid body glistened, seeming at one moment to be completely shrouded in floating veils, yet at the same time to be stunning in its bare simplicity. Rahab could not understand how the priestess could appear both fully clothed and naked at the same time. As the high priestess began to dance, her flowing body swirled in a mystical veil of colors. The irregular dance of the firelight across her face made her appear at one moment to be the essence of desire and seduction and

56

at the next moment to be the embodiment of evil and death. Thus the dual nature of the goddess danced on the face of the high priestess before the astonished eyes of the worshippers in the sacred grove.

Even Shanarbaal was surprised by the vision. Amaranthe could keep a secret! He had not known that she planned a veil dance. With his eyes he applauded her. She was very much the high priestess still!

Rahab was bewitched. So this was what it was to be the high priestess, to be wrapped in the radiance of the goddess herself. It was an honor and a glory much to be desired.

The grove came to life then as the music rose and the young male dancers joined Amaranthe's movements. Linking arms, the dancers began the spiral movement that would create the magic circle. The night would be filled with awe and ecstasy, with the blood of the bull and the love gift of the virgins. The ancient cypress trees themselves, gray-bearded with heavy mosses, joined in the spiral dance; their shadows and the firelight swirled together before Rahab's blurring vision.

Far above them, the clouds trembled. Thunder in the distance echoed the rumble of the drums as the light of the full moon was suddenly gone from the grove. Lightning called forth by the intense heat of the solstice day danced behind and through the cloud banks. The firelight danced as well, illuminating Shanarbaal who, like the high priestess, wore a horned crown, the symbol of the god. Its fiercely pointed horns arched skyward, calling to the goddess in the moon, who remained hidden within the embrace of the clouds. The gold of his crown, flashing in the firelight, brought to Rahab's mind the golden symbols on the green door of her nightmare. She trembled.

For an instant, the images stopped their dance. Reality? Rahab groped for it. *This could not be reality!* The bellow of the frightened bull, closer now, being led to the circle, cut through the rhythm of the drums, and, for an instant, animal terror gripped Rahab. The sacrifice would come! The grove swirled around her once more as she struggled to free herself from the surreal mood of the dance, but she could not escape.

Shanarbaal's voice drew her toward the arching fire. "Come, maidens of Astarte," his voice caressed, seduced, commanded. "The Baalim call you. Answer the calling of the gods; enter into the celestial dance."

The beat of the drums swirled with the high piercing call of the pipes. The fire gained intensity, throwing its spiraling shadows across the faces, into the depths of the grove. The moon remained hidden by darkening clouds so that the grove was lighted only by the dance of the multicolored flames—green, red, blue and gold—flaring against the shadows of the rocks and of the cypresses. The light blazing upward created soaring, shrieking patterns on the feathery trees and mosses above.

Rahab's spirit soared, too, lifting with the light and the shadows. Feeling the fascination of the fire, she shivered in anticipation of the dreadful, awesome acts that were about to begin. With a secret smile, remembering her hidden masheba, she loosened her gown. As it dropped to her feet, she laughed and stepped forward to join the circle in the spiral dance.

In the sacred grove, time had stopped.

INTERLUDE

"Come," they say, "let us get wine and let us drink heavily of strong drink;
And tomorrow will be like today, only more so."
Are you not children of rebellion,
Offspring of deceit,
Who inflame yourselves among the oaks,
Under every luxuriant tree,
Who slaughter the children in the ravines,
Under the clefts of the crags?
Among the smooth stones of the stream is your portion, they are your lot;
Even to them you have poured out libation,
You have made a grain offering...
Upon a high and lofty mountain
You have made your bed...."

Isaiah 56:12; 57:4-7 NASB

13

Consciousness returned in a haze of pain and light. For a few moments, Rahab was aware only of the hot, searing pain in her stomach and the heavy ache behind her eyes. Lying very still, she fought nausea. Light flooded into her cell through the open door from the courtyard—bright, harsh, painful. She was uncovered, cold, and utterly miserable. As the nausea gradually subsided, memories of the night before returned: Shanarbaal illuminated by the firelight, the celestial dance, the insistent beating of the drums, the dagger of the god himself. He had accepted her. She closed her eyes, and through the pain, she remembered his gift to her, she remembered the dancing twilight of the ruby pond, she remembered the precious image of Baal, made by him, given to her. She must recapture that beauty, that wonder! She would return to the grove, to the ruby pond, to her masheba. A dingy, woolen cloak lay crumpled in the corner. She retched as she flung it over her shoulders. She would bathe in the ruby pond of the god; she would wash away the blood and pain of the initiation. She must make her peace with Baal. She must understand the events of the night before. She must see her own actions through the eyes of the god.

Outside, all was quiet in the brilliance of the morning. The household of the gods was asleep, though the sun had begun its journey through the day. Rahab followed the pathway through the grove. Reaching the pond, she fell to her knees and moaned aloud, for the reality of the ruby pool stunned her senses: the water was muddy, filthy with the stench of last night's blood rituals, polluted with the red life-substance of the sacrificial animals. Rahab realized that the ruby pool had not been red because of the sunset; instead the pool had been colored by the blood of the sacrifices.

And it was into this blood bath that only yesterday she had plunged so happily. She retched again and added her own vomit to the filthy waste.

She staggered to the limestone bench, but she had neither the courage nor the strength to move the stone to seek the reassurance of the god. She sat weakly on the bench and put her aching head in her hands and wept bitterly, abandoning herself to her misery. But as the sun continued to climb, its heat penetrated her body, warming and calming her. Sitting very still, she concentrated upon the peace of the morning and the caress of the sun.

14

"I'm exhausted," Rahab told Bishna on the fifth day after they had returned to the temple. Bishna laughed softly, amused at her friend's intensity. Rahab was intense about everything, Bishna thought, even about exhaustion.

"It's no wonder you're tired, my friend," Bishna said kindly. "Here, let me rub your shoulders."

Rahab accepted gratefully and relaxed on her stomach across a mat.

"I've noticed how many of the temple's visitors have chosen you this week," Bishna said. Bishna was using all the skill Amaranthe had taught her to relax Rahab's tight back muscles.

"Oh, Bishna, that feels good, but it hurts. Be a little gentler," Rahab responded to Bishna's trained massage. "I can't believe I'm so stiff, Bishna. I've never been this stiff in my life."

"Never before in your life have you spent a week such as this one, Rahab."

Rahab laughed shortly. "Yes," she answered, "that is certainly the truth—too much the truth, I'm afraid." Rahab paused, considering how to ask her friend the question that was on her mind. "Bishna, have you noticed that some of the men who come to the temple want very strange service?"

"Yes, I have noticed," her friend replied quietly, "but I think, perhaps, you know more of that than I do because you have served the goddess so much this week."

Bishna began a very gentle circling motion traveling up Rahab's spine. "Is this helping?"

"Very much," Rahab chuckled. "You are so much kinder than the camel drovers!"

Bishna laughed loudly at this comment. "I should hope so! Amaranthe's training would be wasted indeed if I were no gentler than a drover! I only wish that massage were the most difficult part of serving the goddess."

Rahab said nothing. The service of light had darkened greatly in her eyes.

Bishna stood hesitantly in the doorway of her chamber. She was not enthusiastic about the project Rahab was proposing.

"Oh, come on," Rahab said in quiet exasperation. "Would I suggest that you come with me if I thought this might get you into trouble? We'll be perfectly safe. You know Alcion told me that both the high priest and the priestess are visiting the king this afternoon. They're planning the third-level initiation rite for Mari and the other older girls. That could take all afternoon and half the night. Besides, if we don't go now, we won't have another chance!"

"I wouldn't care if we never had a chance, Rahab. I don't understand why you are so fascinated by those green doors. They only frighten me!"

"They frighten me, too, and that's the whole point. I keep dreaming about them. If we see the doors and the secret rooms behind them in the light of day, it will put our fears to rest."

"All right, I'll come, but I'm scared. I don't know why I let you talk me into these things."

"Because you know I'm right, that's why. With Shanarbaal and Amaranthe out of the temple, no one is going to be guarding those rooms. Alcion said himself that the Komer were going to be casting the die in their private court-yard. You know that if there is gambling going on, none of them will want to miss it."

Bishna laughed in agreement, but she was still nervous.

Along the corridor leading to the main courtyard and to the green doors were the chambers of the high priestess. As the two Kedeshoth maidens passed along the hallway, they were surprised to see that the door to Amaran-the's chamber was open. *Probably left that way by some careless servant,* Bishna thought.

Rahab stopped at the door and peered in. Once more she was awed by the beauty of Amaranthe's furnishings. The same rich tapestries, carpeting, and curtains that had enticed the girls at the villa greeted them here in Amaran-the's temple chamber. Apparently Amaranthe carried almost all her furnish-ings back and forth whenever she made the journey to the villa.

Rahab entered the room, looking about in delight.

"Rahab," Bishna hissed from the doorway. "Are you crazy? Come out of there. Amaranthe would kill you if she knew you were there!"

"Bishna, it's all so beautiful," Rahab said, ignoring her friend's warning and reaching out to fondle the luxurious material of Amaranthe's draperies. "The high priestess lives in constant beauty. It must be wonderful. Come in and look." As Rahab said this, she wandered farther into the chamber, behind the door where Bishna could no longer see her.

"I will not come in," Bishna responded.

"Oh!" Rahab's gasp startled Bishna.

"What is it, Rahab? Is something wrong?"

"Come here quickly, Bishna!" Rahab's voice was urgent. Forgetting her re-luctance, Bishna hurried into the chamber.

Rahab still stood in the position behind the door that had hidden her from Bishna's view. "Look," she said simply.

In the corner of the room, filling it, in fact, stood a huge brass mirror. In its golden glow stood two wide-eyed maidens who stared at themselves and at each other in amazement.

"It is wonderful," Bishna said.

"Truly it is. I've never seen anything like it," Rahab responded. "It's a thousand times clearer than the hand mirrors in our chambers."

"It is wonderful, Rahab," Bishna repeated to herself in her astonishment. "Do I really look like that?"

Rahab stared carefully at the reflection of her friend. "You really do, Bishna. How beautiful you are!"

"And look at you, Rahab. It is exactly like you as well."

"Oh, dear," Rahab responded.

Her reflection glowed with the warmth of the brass, but even the warm golden tones of the mirror could not distract Rahab from what she harshly perceived as faults in her appearance. Bishna's long legs made hers look too short in comparison. The other girl was fuller in the breast and more slim-waisted. Rahab wished she were prettier.

"How nice it would be to be pretty—as you are, Bishna," Rahab said with a sigh.

"You have a beauty all your own, Rahab. You are unique."

Rahab sighed again.

"By the Baalim, woman, this cannot continue!" Shanarbaal's voice sounded loudly and angrily from the rear of the apartments. The girls heard the door of the rear entrance slam shut. "You will not embarrass me again in front of the king!"

"Rahab, they're back," Bishna said, frozen in her place.

"Come on! Let's go!" Rahab grabbed Bishna's arm and jerked her into motion. Leaving the room, Rahab and Bishna heard Amaranthe's angry retort, "Fools! You're both fools!"

Forgetting the green doors, the girls hurriedly returned to the sanctuary of their chambers.

Lying on her mat, waiting for sleep to come, Rahab remembered her brief glimpse into the beauty and luxury of the high priestess' private chambers. *Someday,* she promised herself, *I will live in such luxury.* Remembering her image in the brazen mirror, she thought, *Someday I, too, will own such a mirror.*

Rahab had never before seen a mirror of such size. In it she had been able to see herself from head to foot. Her mind lingered on her image. *If I had not been standing beside Bishna,* she thought, *I would have liked myself better. Yet after the camel drovers choose me, they tell me that I am beautiful. When they choose me, I am standing in the courtyard with all the Kedeshoth, and they are all beautiful. Why then do the drovers choose me more than the others? I am not as pretty and they have never talked to me. When I entered the temple service, Shanarbaal told me I had a magic of my own. Was it this that he meant? Do I have a magic that attracts these men?*

Rahab smiled in the darkness. *Whatever it is, Enath certainly doesn't like it,*

Rahab thought. *I saw the looks she threw at me yesterday. She's jealous, really jealous. It's true. Already I have brought more money into the temple treasury than any of the other girls.*

On this comforting thought Rahab rolled over, sighed, and went to sleep.

15

In the months that followed, Rahab deepened her understanding of her own special magic.

Alone in her chamber, she smiled at the reflection in her hand mirror. Summer had passed quickly, and as the months of summer departed, so had her insecurities. She did not need to see herself again in Amaranthe's mirror to be aware that her child's body was becoming that of a woman, and the face that smiled back at her from the tiny hand mirror pleased her as it so often pleased the temple visitors. From Amaranthe, she had learned the secrets of facial design, becoming skilled in making her lips as inviting as a crimson flower and her eyes as alluring as the midnight pond.

As she brushed her thick, black hair, Rahab thought about her life in the temple. She had learned that men liked her—and, more importantly, that she liked them. Perhaps it was because they reassured her of her beauty, but it was also because she enjoyed pleasing them, and she learned more and more exactly how to please. She was no longer surprised when men chose her. She discovered that, for the most part, their desires were easy to satisfy—a pleasure, even. But there were a few men with whom temple service was not a pleasure; sometimes it was a definite danger. From Mari and the other girls of the third circle, Rahab learned to watch the signals. She had learned how to treat dangerous men and how, in many subtle ways, to protect herself. Some of the city's politicians, particularly Onuk the Fat, enjoyed baiting and teasing the girls; such men could be cruel. Even these men Rahab could charm into play-fulness. Life in the temple, she thought, was not without its satisfactions.

In his own chambers, Shanarbaal thought with satisfaction of the previous evening. He had spent the night quietly enjoying the simple pleasures with the maiden Rahab. To Shanarbaal, Rahab was no longer a child. She had ful-filled the promise of which her father had spoken, becoming a beautiful and strong vessel, a worthy receptacle with the magic to please a man. Often, after the feasts, Shanarbaal took Rahab to his private chambers for the night. There he proved her worth again and again. Of all the maidens, only two—Rahab and Mari—were repeatedly invited to share his chambers.

The high priest's affection for the maidens continued to offend the priest-ess, however. Amaranthe knew only too well of the special favors Shanarbaal provided to Mari and Rahab. Mari continued to be one of her own favorites, but Rahab received no such distinction. Amaranthe's pride was less injured by Shanarbaal's attention to Mari, who was by now a maiden of the third circle, than by his attention to Rahab. A *child,* Amaranthe thought, *a half-developed child!*

Although Amaranthe ignored Rahab much of the time, the high priestess was well aware that Rahab was a favorite among the drovers, merchants, and farmers. Rahab's daily contributions to the temple treasury impressed even Amaranthe, and Mari, the distant one, made small overtures of friendship to Rahab. Only with Bishna, however, did Rahab share a real closeness, a loving rapport that increased as the summer passed.

As the season passed, too, Bishna had become aware of the changes within her own body. She and the other girls who had drawn the green crescents on the dedication eve had been set aside by the gods for a very special service of light: each carried a child for the gods.

The days became shorter as autumn brought the rains. More and more, the maidens sought the shelter of their rooms when they were not actually per-forming their duties. On one particularly cold and gusty afternoon, laughter from Bishna's chamber drew Rahab to join the group of Kedeshoth sitting on the bedding mat on Bishna's floor.

"I'm so tired, I'm not even looking forward to going to Shanarbaal's villa to-morrow!" one girl complained.

"Oh, come on," scoffed Enath. "You know we'll have fun. Everyone will be there—the king, the city's chief politicians—everyone!"

"We'll dance for them, and there'll be plenty of wine. I hear there's to be a grand banquet. Besides, we've never been to the villa in the winter."

"Yes, and it will probably be cold and drafty," said another.

"Oh, don't worry!" Enath laughed. "You'll have someone to keep you warm!" The girls giggled.

"Yes," she responded. "I just hope it's not that fat man, Onuk!"

"Well, at least he's rich, and he has no wife."

"Either he divorced or killed them!" Rahab retorted. "No one could live with that man for long!"

"Yes," responded Mari, "you wouldn't think of him as a husband if you knew him. Money can't solve everything!"

"How right you are," Rahab answered, laughing. "Money can't make a fat man thin, or a mean man kind."

"And it can't give seed to a man like Habbak—I think I hate him even more than I hate Onuk," said Bishna.

"He may be a eunuch—but he has cruel desires just the same," Mari said. Rahab frowned. She had heard that an evening with Habbak, the king's treasurer, was an evening of pain and humiliation—and nothing more. "Hmmpf," she said, "let him play with the boys he seems to prefer!"

"Thank the gods that all men are not like Onuk and Habbak," said another. "Some of the city's politicians are quite acceptable!"

"Oh, yes, quite!" spoke another, and they all laughed.

As the group began to break up, each girl retiring to her own chamber to prepare for the journey of the morning, Rahab sighed. She wanted to talk. She watched the other girls leave and settled herself down more comfortably amongst Bishna's cushions.

"Are you worried about the journey tomorrow, Bishna?" she asked at last. "Do you think it will be hard on those of you who carry the children of the gods?"

"We're in good physical condition," Bishna said confidently. "We work hard in our sessions with Amaranthe, and she instructs us on many things—secret things that I cannot share even with you, Rahab."

Rahab's eyebrows shot up. She knew that the girls who were with child had long special meetings with the priestess, and they never spoke of those meetings afterward.

"Does she tell you anything you *can* share, Bishna?" she asked.

Bishna laughed gently. "She tells us that we are safe because the goddess will protect us when we carry her children, so you must have no fear on our account! The journey tomorrow will be easy."

"For some reason, I don't look forward to the ceremony," Rahab answered. "I know that this midwinter gathering involves great celebration, but I'm not eager for it."

"Not only celebration," Bishna answered, lowering her voice confidentially. "There will be ceremonies of great mystery. Rahab, if I tell you this, do you swear yourself to secrecy? I would not want Amaranthe to know I spoke of it."

Rahab nodded solemnly.

"Shanarbaal will tell the king's fortune. He will divine the future—from the entrails of a lamb!"

Rahab shook her head and sighed. "Ah, Bishna—I am sick of blood. I am sick, sick, sick of sacrifice!"

"The gods know, Rahab. We do not—but, after all," she added lightly, "what is a lamb?"

16

During the journey to the villa, Rahab could think only of her masheba. Was it still there? Though she was sorely disillusioned, bored even, with the meaningless sacrifices, still the masheba held some of the magic she had first encountered within the temple.

Her need for its reassurance was great, and she resolved that with the dawn she would seek out her gift from the god. She would speak to Baal this morning in the sacred grove.

Rising earlier than the sun, Rahab ran through the villa gardens, aiming herself like an arrow toward the east garden gate, toward the sunrise, beyond which lay the sacred grove.

Outside the garden's pathways, the rising sun blinded Rahab. She hurried onward, not waiting for her eyes to adjust, running through the sacred grove, full into the embrace of the ancient trees, deep into their ancient secrets.

The bright darkness of the cypress swamp dazzled her. A maze of vines and hanging mosses veiled the path, impeding her progress and arousing her impatience. Pushing aside the mossy elongated fingers of the cypress trees, she cursed softly as she realized that the recent rains had turned the Baalpath into mire. She forced one sandaled foot out of the sucking mud and determined impatiently to seek her own way across higher ground. The swamp was hazy. Humidity created a mist, like the smoke of Baalfire, making it difficult to breathe and playing tricks with her vision, obscuring landmarks and confusing depth perception. The area was small, and Rahab did not fear getting lost.

So sure was she of her solitude within the swamp, that the figures which appeared at a distance before her seemed, at first, only an illusion—a trick played by the swamp upon her altered senses. She realized quickly, however, that these were no spirits floating upon the swamp mist.

Rahab stopped instantly. Seeking the protection of one of the huge cypress trees, she hid behind its massive trunk. Rahab's fingers tensed on the ancient tree. What secret rite had she stumbled upon? She was both frightened and fascinated. She had to watch! Before her, across the swamp, were Amaranthe-Astarte and Shanarbaal. Their arms were raised toward the sky. Their feet were invisible; they stood ankle deep in a red pool of blood. Perhaps five feet behind Amaranthe lay the body of a small goat.

Rahab could hear clearly the rising pitch of Amaranthe's Astarte chant so familiar, yet somehow different—discordant. Straining to catch the words, Rahab realized with horror that the two were performing an invocation of the goddess—a deep magic, awesome and fearful, drawing the goddess not only to the rite, but into the very body of the priestess!

Mesmerized, Rahab watched from her hiding place as Amaranthe seemed to grow taller and taller. The beauty and the restraint of the high priestess vanished as Amaranthe's entire demeanor changed, growing bestial in its ferocity. Rahab looked through the mists and saw clearly the essence of the high priestess: this woman was evil!

The voice of Amaranthe, full-bodied and empowered now with the spirit of the goddess, carried easily across the swamp. Rahab stood without breathing as she heard the first words of the goddess: "Where are my sacrifices, O mortal man?"

To Rahab's surprise, Shanarbaal responded smoothly, calmly, as if the words were part of a ritual: "The sacrifices have been offered, O lady of battles. Twice, six times, the eunuchs are dedicated. The god is appeased!"

The goddess's shriek of anger rang through the swamp: "Astarte requires her portions, foolish mortal! What do you offer the goddess of war?"

The voices had dropped, but Rahab heard the words, "The blood of the Komer," as the priest handed the woman a golden goblet, which she drained in one long draught, flinging the empty goblet across the swamp and into the trees.

And then, to Rahab's horror, the goddess took the priest, falling fiercely upon him, pressing him into the mud, to begin their mating in the bloody swamp.

Rahab turned and fled.

17

At sundown, Amaranthe and Shanarbaal gathered all the maidens in the villa's gardens. The girls glanced uneasily at one another. Each maiden hoped that she would not be the choice of the gods—no one was eager for this honor!

"Maidens of Astarte!" Amaranthe broke the silence, calling for their attention. "The goddess calls you now for a great honor. One of you—only one—will make the sacrifice of the lamb tomorrow at sunrise."

There was no sound from the assembly. Only silence, tense and waiting.

"Bishna, come forth! The goddess calls!" the high priestess commanded.

Moving slowly, heavy now with her pregnancy, Bishna approached the priestess, her eyes respectfully downcast. She bowed, despite her bulging belly, and awaited the pleasure of the priestess.

Amaranthe dramatically held aloft an ornately woven basket, the same one that had been used at the initiation of the goddess within. The contents were hidden by the same embroidered cloth that had covered the barley cakes then. She signalled Bishna to reach into the basket, and Bishna reached in to withdraw—a white stone!

Amaranthe smiled benignly.

"You shall sacrifice a dove, my daughter. The god has chosen." Bishna's relief was almost audible, though she merely inclined her head.

The priestess' eyes swept the circle. "Mari! The goddess calls. Come forth!"

Mari stepped quickly to the priestess. Rahab envied Mari her calm poise. Nothing ever upset Mari. She seemed to have the gift of handling easily any challenge that came her way. Mari could competently handle anything—even the most difficult of the drovers!

Mari's eyes met Amaranthe's, and she took a pebble from the basket. Without glancing at it, she handed the pebble to the priestess. It was white. Amaranthe's smile was warm. *She actually likes Mari,* thought Rahab incredulously.

"You shall sacrifice a dove, my daughter. The gods have chosen."

Mari returned her smile, bowed slightly, and returned to her place in the circle.

Shamu was next. Like Bishna and Mari, her pebble was white.

"You shall sacrifice a dove, my daughter. The gods have chosen," the priestess repeated.

The remaining girls looked at one another. Tension mounted.

"Rahab!" intoned the high priestess. "Come forth—the god calls!"

Like the others, Rahab reached into the basket. Inexplicably, she had the feeling she had done this before and had drawn—the black stone! Her heart sank.

"No!" the word escaped her lips, a gasp, involuntary, with a sharp intake of air.

Amaranthe had scarcely begun the words of the ritual. She whirled in disbelief.

"What did you say, Rahab?" she snapped, her eyes narrowing dangerously.

Speaking the truth, Rahab heard herself say the words, very softly: "I do not want to kill the lamb!"

She would never forget the look on Amaranthe's face, distorted with the spirit of the goddess—pure hatred, pure evil—as Rahab had seen her in the sacred grove that morning. But now the goddess stood before her, and Rahab could not turn to flee the power of her wrath.

The priestess stared at the trembling girl in disbelief that any of these maidens, so carefully and thoroughly trained in obedience, would dare—would even think!—to speak thus.

Her goddess' eyes flashed and locked with Rahab's. She spoke one word. It was a hiss, spat between her teeth: "What?"

Rahab lowered her eyes, and once again she heard herself speak the truth: "I do not want to kill the lamb!"

A slap stung her face as the priestess vented her contempt.

Rahab cowered, holding her hands before her face to catch the trickle of blood that ran from her smarting nose.

"What you want and what the gods want are not the same!" the priestess shrieked. "Your will is not the will of Astarte! What is your will compared to the will of the gods? What do the gods care for your will? Your will is dung!"

The words came faster, falling over themselves in their haste to strike the unfortunate girl. "The ways of the gods are eternal ways. You are nothing! You have no existence! You have no meaning! You are dung!"

The priestess paused for effect or, perhaps, to catch her breath. She spoke more slowly now, deliberately. It seemed to Rahab that each word lashed her like a whip. "Who are you, Rahab, to question the goddess? You have been chosen to kill the lamb. So be it! So it is! So it will be! You *will* kill the lamb!"

Amaranthe moved back, her right hand tensed on the jeweled dagger at her side. Rahab's concentration fixed upon Amaranthe's hand as it hovered upon the dagger. The angry energy of the goddess was unmistakable. Even the veins on the back of Amaranthe's hand stood out in fury. Red fire danced from the jeweled eyes of the bull's-head ring.

Transfixed by the ruby fire within the golden ring, Rahab could only gasp. She knew that she must answer, humbly and quickly. Her life depended upon her answer. But words would not come.

The momentum of the priestess' wrath was interrupted by the smooth, controlled voice of the priest. "You have been chosen by lot, Rahab," he said, speaking very slowly, very softly. His voice seemed to revive Rahab's spirit.

"So be it." He repeated the words of the high priestess. "So it is. So it will be." He paused now, carefully phrasing: "You do not want to kill the lamb—but you will kill the lamb! Won't you, Rahab." It was not a question.

Rahab now found words. "I will, my lord," she said. She recognized that the high priest's intervention had saved her from a death like Asabaal's.

Unbelievably, Amaranthe accepted this statement. Without moving her hand from the jeweled dagger, she repeated the incantation, and her voice was as cold as marble. "So be it. So it is. So it will be."

She turned, speaking directly now to the priest. "The gods have chosen—but the goddess will triumph!"

Rahab shuddered. She was allowed to rejoin the circle, and even though the black stone had been chosen, each girl went in turn to the basket and withdrew a stone. Rahab's mind was awhirl with pain from Amaranthe's blow and with images from her childhood: her father, the fresh grass of spring, the old ewe, the bleating of a newborn lamb, the joyful wiggling of its tail as it suckled. She loved the lamb!

Rahab shuddered from her reverie as the priest and priestess departed. Quickly, without conversation, the Kedeshoth scattered, except for Rahab, who seemed fixed to the spot, and Bishna, who stayed to comfort her.

The moon goddess had come forth as the sun had disappeared. Her cold light cast pale shadows in the garden. The tall, stately cedar trees seemed frozen in time and space. Their reflections in the garden's still pool were a pale echo of the spiral symbol of the goddess.

Wordlessly, the two girls sat for a time, Bishna's arm around Rahab, like a mother, comforting her. In the quiet peace of the moonlit garden, Rahab again gave vent to her rebellion: "Bishna, I do not want to do this!"

"But it is the gods' will. They do not choose by accident. The lots are significant. They are a sign. We must obey them. You will feel stronger for it."

Perhaps it was Bishna's tone of voice, or perhaps it was the purity of her resignation to obedience that touched off in Rahab a sudden flash of anger, causing her reply to be strident, sarcastic.

"Ha!" she snorted. "I will feel stronger for it. Yes, I will feel stronger for it—just as I felt stronger the morning after the initiation. Just as I felt stronger when I saw Shanarbaal and Amaranthe—" Rahab stopped. Bishna did not know of the scene she had encountered that morning in the swamp. It had been too ugly to discuss. Bishna stared, and Rahab quickly completed the thought, "—making a sacrifice.

"Why? That's what I want to know!" Rahab continued. "Again and again we are told that we are the representatives of the goddess on earth. Our fertility with the males in the temple is the fertility of the goddess. Yet, except for you who drew the green crescent, there is no fertility. Why cannot the goddess be fertile for herself? If she is so great, why does she not bear her own children? Where is the performance of her promise? She gives only blood and pain, blood and death."

"What you speak is sacrilege!" Bishna exclaimed. "Do not say this! Do not even think it! Here in the sacred villa, she will strike you dead!"

Rahab answered bitterly, "Aye, she will strike me dead—as she struck Asabaal dead, as she almost struck me dead not ten minutes ago! It seems that fear of Amaranthe-Astarte is wiser and more necessary than the fear of the goddess herself." Rahab paused, astonished at the perception that she now recognized as accurate.

"Bishna—don't you see!—we are playthings in the hands of mortals who are mad, mad for power, and the gods look down at us and laugh!"

"I will not listen to this. Rahab, you must not speak like this! You will be punished!" Bishna was fearful for her friend. Rahab seemed taken with her mood of bitter sarcasm, and it seemed to Bishna that her beloved friend was developing a new character, a cold and frightening character.

Rahab's thoughts turned back to the sacrifice, and she said softly, "I am not the one who will be punished. Who will die tomorrow, Bishna? Tomorrow, the lamb will die. A perfect little lamb will be punished!"

Rahab could not stop her tongue: "I will be—what? The officer of judgment —the executor of justice? No—I will be merely the murderer of a little lamb!"

"The sacrifices must be performed, Rahab. It is the gods' will," Bishna's voice pleaded. What was happening to Rahab? Bishna had never seen her like this.

Rahab herself did not know why she reacted so strongly. She actually envied the other girl her simple loyalty to the temple tradition and to the gods, but she seemed compelled to vent her feelings. Her disgust and disappointment with everything about temple life now came pouring forth from her pain. Yet she could not share the core of her horror: her reaction to the scene in the swamp.

"I am not satisfied with any of this!" she shouted. "Where is the wonder? Where is the awe? Where are the blessings of the gods?"

Rahab's voice grew bitter again: "I remember very well when Amaranthe told us that the secrets of the gods were great and that we would see with spiritual eyes the mysteries of the gods. Ha!"

"We have seen much, Rahab," her friend reminded her gently.

Still Rahab ranted, "We have seen too much, Bishna! But we have seen nothing good. I have seen nothing but the blood of sacrifice and the lusts of old men. And now, now I must kill a little lamb for the goddess Astarte, the goddess of blood and lust! Why does she love blood so much, Bishna? Tell me that! Why is she so cruel?"

"I don't know, Rahab," Bishna finally said. "It is the will of the gods. It is too much for us. It is too great for our minds. We must obey. It is our duty to obey!"

Rahab could not share Bishna's dedication. She had seen too much of temple life, and she was left with too many unanswered questions. But Bishna now touched a nerve to which Rahab could respond.

"Then will you obey Shanarbaal?" she asked. "Even though he has saved your life, he still supports the ritual! You are chosen, Rahab, as I was chosen before you—I to bear a child, you to kill the lamb. We are chosen ones who have no choice: we must obey."

Rahab sighed and sank to her knees. "I suppose I must."

Encouraged at this sign of compliance, Bishna continued, "I did not balk, Rahab, when they took me to the temple room on our dedication night. I did not turn and run when I realized what the temple service required of me. I was chosen by lot. I knew it was my destiny to serve the goddess, even if suffering was required."

Rahab knew that Bishna spoke the truth.

"For two weeks I served the goddess with many men and without rest, though those of you who drew the red crescent served her for only one short night. I did not understand then, Rahab, that the gods wanted me to bear a child, but I understand now—and I do not regret it!"

Bishna stood now, grasping her friend by the shoulders, and looking her in the eyes, imploringly. "You will do what they say, Rahab, or you will suffer the consequences as Asabaal did."

Still, Rahab was not convinced.

18

Later, alone in her chamber, Rahab thought about Bishna's gentle acceptance of whatever pain the gods might deal her.

"The gods know, Rahab. We do not," Bishna had said again and again, with perfect acceptance! Rahab would have wept, but she had no tears. She struggled to balance what she strongly felt to be wrong—killing the lamb—with what she knew was required for her own survival. Rahab felt dirtied, frustrated, pushed, angry.

But her anger had no source. She could not fix blame, and that in itself made her even more angry.

She could not sleep. She knew that when the morning sun lifted the cover of heaven, she would be attired ceremonially, her face painted, and her hair arranged. Then she would hold a golden ceremonial dagger poised over the heart of a little lamb. *No! I do not want to do this!* She wanted to run from the sunrise!

Sitting on her mattress with her head on her knees, Rahab thought of the lambs of her childhood. The flock had been small—six ewes. During the day, the ewes went out to graze with other nearby flocks, and in the evening, when the shepherds brought them back, she was there with her father to put the sheep into the pen at night.

She always counted them on her fingers, saying their names as they ran through the gates. In this way, the sheep were kept safe from the predators that roamed the hills. She had—she had forgotten what happened to it—one special lamb, a pet, a friend.

Rahab had made every effort to protect each new lamb, to shepherd, to care, to nurture—but never to kill! She had hated those occasions when her father butchered one, and she had never truly enjoyed eating lamb though her mother always prepared it daintily with cinnamon, grape leaves, and barley. Her family had laughed at her for this, yet she had remained true to her own child's heart. She loved the lambs! She did not like their deaths.

Memories flooded Rahab and she wished desperately for her lost childhood, her family, her innocence, her friends—the sheep, the oxen, the goats, the quail. Even the animals of her past had been more trustworthy than the people who ruled her now.

She thought of the first time she had known the god. It was through the lamb, she knew—but what? She struggled with the certainty that she knew—whom? How had she known? Somewhere, sometime in her lost childhood, had she known a god who was real? She could not remember how, or when, but—the lamb—what lamb? Rahab was exhausted—mentally, physically, emotionally. She was confused, scattered, miserable. If only she could remember—what?

Puzzled, she felt that Baal was not the god of her childhood. She sensed, with an awareness deeper than her feelings, that the god she had known in her childhood had been a loving god—a creator, not a destroyer. The gods she had come to know in the temple were Baal the destroyer, Astarte the avenger. They could not be the creators of the lambs or of children.

She understood, then, that her anger was not really without a source. She had only been afraid to realize with whom she was angry, for she was angry with the gods. *Baal has put a pretty mask on this life,* she thought bitterly. *This religion is whitewashed like the Jericho walls, but underneath, it is rotting rubble. Why must—*

The knock on her door frame was gentle. So deep was Rahab in her bitter thoughts that she wasn't sure she had heard it until she realized it had been repeated.

"Rahab! Awaken!" It was Alcion.

Rahab was startled.

"What is it, my friend?" she asked quietly.

"The king calls you," he answered. "He would bed the one chosen by the god to ensure a favorable fortune come the dawn."

Her heart sank.

The king! It was like a call from the god Baal himself. She was incapable of pleasing any man at this moment, but she feared greatly to displease the king.

At various times the king had called for one of the Kedeshoth, but usually at the conclusion of one of the feasts, when he and all the guests were sated with wine and food. Rahab felt on those occasions that one girl was the same as any other. She knew that the king could not have recognized her nor any of the other maidens in the light of day.

But this command was different; this would be a ritual mating. The king had called for her specifically, so she must go.

She repeated Bishna's words, almost as an incantation.

"The gods know. We do not. We obey." She sighed. "I am coming, Alcion."

She followed the eunuch out into the courtyard, across the villa toward the royal apartments. As they passed through the gardens, Rahab glanced toward the Jericho plain below, toward the Jordan River, where a thunderstorm played in the heavens.

She paused to watch in fascination, wishing she could fly away into it, like an eagle, and dance with the lightning. Then she remembered the bronze statue of Baal, the god of thunder and lightning. She shuddered and hurried on behind the komer.

Approaching the door to a large chamber well within the villa, Alcion paused and motioned Rahab within. Reclining on a bed piled high with sumptuously embroidered pillows, the king awaited her.

"You have come," he said.

"I am here, my lord," Rahab answered, wondering what she should do next. She stood at the doorway, hesitantly.

"Enter, little dove," the king directed, softening his voice as if he sensed her tension and would put her at ease. She was grateful. "This night you are called by the gods," the king continued. "This night I would wed the goddess, and you are she, chosen by lot."

75

Rahab bowed her head, and answered, as if to herself, "I am she whom the god has called this night."

This man was not the ribald, laughing, staggering king of the feasts. Rahab could almost believe that he was divine, so grave and serious was his demeanor.

"Come to me, maiden," he said, sternly now. "Kneel before me. Baal would plight his troth this night."

Rahab shivered; she was compelled to serve.

The king lifted a bronze cup, drinking deeply of its contents, then offered it to Rahab.

"Drink the wedding toast, maiden," he said, handing her the heavy vessel.

She sipped the draught. It was wine, rich and red, heavy and sweet. She thought of blood. Her mind would not stop: *like the blood of the lamb.* She shuddered and quickly handed back the bowl. The king took it from her and plunged a golden ceremonial dagger into the ruby liquid. He raised it slowly, and the red drops ran slowly down the dagger—*like blood,* she thought again, pulling back.

"Thus does the god take the goddess," he said.

He drank again. Then he put the cup on a low table, with the golden dagger beside it. A small oil lamp was the only light in the room. Its flame flickered, burnishing the bronze carvings on the bowl and the golden dagger.

"So shall Baal take the daughter of Astarte!" The king did not smile. He was frowning and very serious. It seemed to Rahab that the king was under some tremendous pressure. But she was in no mood to be used. She was still angry, and in her anger, she decided that Baal would not take her, could not control her. If she were to be the goddess, she would act the role!

She stretched herself tall, taking the posture of the goddess that Amaranthe had assumed in the sacred grove in the morning mists, and looked disdainfully at the king.

"I am Astarte. Why wouldst thou wed me this night, O mortal king?" she replied in a deep tone and slowly.

The king was astonished, suddenly half afraid that he had invoked more than he had planned. He had called for the kedeshoth; had the goddess herself responded? His wits awhirl, the king was silent.

Rahab repeated the question. "Why wouldst thou wed me this night, O mortal king of Jericho?"

Rahab's demeanor was completely powerful. Her dark eyes challenged and threatened the king. *Surely this is the goddess,* he thought. *No child of the temple would speak thus to the king. Best to respond, and quickly.* But he was so taken aback that he had no words. He fell to his knees before her.

"O great lady," he finally stammered, "have mercy upon me! I am merely a mortal!"

Rahab suppressed a smile. She could feel the effect of the sacred wine, though she had not drunk deeply. The room seemed unreal to her. Only one thing was clear: the king believed she was Astarte. He knelt before her. She would make him grovel.

She repeated her question a third time. "Why wouldst thou wed me this night, O mortal king of Jericho?"

Her voice was low, but strident and slow, like Amaranthe's. One part of her was participating in this dialogue. Another part of her brain was watching and directing. To her amazement, she was enjoying herself.

"I beseech thee, O great lady," the King implored, "accept me this night. I will give thee my essence. Then intercede for me with thy consort Baal, at dawn, when the sacrifice is made, so that he will grant me my wish, my will...so that he will grant me the future...that I...want." He almost sniveled.

Rahab was amused, enjoying the thrill of the king's groveling before her.

"If I spend the night with thee in the consummation act," she said sarcastically, "then when, O mortal king, dost thou expect me to plead thy case with Baal?"

The King was obviously confused. Rahab pressed her point.

"Tell me that, O foolish mortal man. When?" she asked sharply.

The king was miserable. He had thought that to wed the chosen one would assure a favorable sign on the morrow—but now?

He hung his head, and he made his decision, speaking very softly, but with grave dignity. "Plead my case, then."

Rahab felt the ecstasy of power. She controlled the king! She had used the aspect of Astarte, but it was she, Rahab, who controlled the king. On the edges of her awareness, a small fear raised itself: would Astarte retaliate? Rahab did not care! She had not asked to be here. She had not wanted to be the one chosen to kill the lamb. She would do what she would do!

To the king, Rahab seemed to grow taller, looking down upon him. His obvious weakness made it easier for Rahab to maintain the disdainful demeanor of the goddess.

"What is your case, O mortal king of Jericho?" she said. "Set forth your case!"

The King looked up, his eyes pleading. "At the dawn," he finally said, "when you will sacrifice the lamb—and Shanarbaal will divine the future from its entrails—he will tell us whether...whether good or ill awaits Jericho: whether the Habiru—" he shuddered "—whether those violent people who wander the plains will overrun our cities—whether we should repair the walls—whether we should enlarge the fighting force here within the city. Should we seek the aid of Egypt—" As he talked, his words picked up the intensity of his emotion, revealing the depth of his fears for the future. "And—if they attack? Will I survive? Will I live to sire sons?"

Then his voice dropped, and Rahab strained to catch each word. "But there is one thing I have told no one, O goddess. It gives me great tribulation—I constantly fear, I constantly watch—this I truly need to know, and I can ask no man, only the gods: Is the queen true to me?"

Rahab was past astonishment. She could not understand his concern—for the queen might have ritual union with any commoner in the temple.

The king continued, "Sometimes, at the feasts, I see her watching the others. She looks at Shanarbaal, not at me. She sees the rippling muscles on that bull dancer, Alcion—and I see desire in her face! It is me that she must desire! Me!"

"This is what you would have me seek out Baal to learn?" she asked, incredulous.

"You must understand, O mighty lady of battles. Sons whom the queen bears must be my sons, or my dynasty is gone! If she is not faithful to me, I will—I will have her killed!"

He hung his head and sobbed. "Asheratti is my delight. I love her!"

Rahab reached out and touched his shoulder. Her voice was softer, more gentle. "It shall be as you ask, O mortal king of Jericho. Astarte will intercede for you this night. Rest easy."

She turned and hastened away.

Alcion was waiting outside. She did not speak until they were alone.

"Alcion—did you hear?" she asked.

"Yes, I did," he answered. "I couldn't believe my ears."

"Well, komer with rippling muscles," she laughed, quoting the king and lightly touching the eunuch on one bicep, "I think we must tell the high priest what has occurred this night. Will you take me to him?"

"Follow me," Alcion replied. "I never thought any man would be jealous of a woman's attention to me," he mused. "But the king is fierce in his jealousy!"

Rahab was silent. She knew that she owed Shanarbaal the favor of her own life. She must warn him! If Shanarbaal would prophesy that the queen maintained her virtue, the king would know that the goddess had indeed interceded. He would be mollified.

Shanarbaal had worked through the night. To the casual observer, he would have appeared to be in prayer and supplication to Baal. In actuality, however, he was planning, memorizing and rehearsing his prophecy presentation for the dawn. He felt all-powerful as he polished the wording. He remembered the counsel of Onuk the Fat: True power lies with those who influence kings and gods. Only he, Shanarbaal, could do both!

A gentle knock interrupted his meditations.

"Shanarbaal! High priest of Baal!"

It was the komer Alcion. Shanar was both annoyed and curious. When the priest was in communion with the gods, mortals did not interrupt without good cause! His response was impatient. "What brings you here at this hour, komer?" he demanded harshly.

In the circle of light from his lamp, he saw Rahab standing hesitantly behind Alcion. "Come in!" he said. "What is it? Speak up!"

Rahab bowed low. She was afraid to speak, but she knew she must. "High Priest, Shanarbaal, I have just left the king. I must tell you what he said. It is known only to the gods, but you must know!"

"Leave, Alcion!" the priest directed the komer. The servant bowed and left.

Quickly, softly, Rahab explained what had just occurred with the king. She carefully repeated their conversation, exactly, word for word.

Shanarbaal did not look at her once during this recital. As in their many nights of love, his eyes tonight looked elsewhere, receiving but not sharing what she offered.

When she finished, he sat on a stool near his work table and pressed his hands against his thighs.

"Leave, Rahab," he said shortly. And he began to chuckle.

As Rahab and Alcion retreated through the corridors, they heard the chuckle grow to a laugh and then a roar that reverberated through the midnight villa.

19

The priest had called Rahab forward. She stood at the altar, her back to the rising sun, grasping in her trembling hand the golden dagger of the goddess. *This is the dagger that killed Asabaal,* Rahab thought. *The goddess loves blood—blood, blood, blood. I hate this!*

"Ba-aaah." The bleat of the sacrificial lamb reminded her of home. *How beautiful the lamb is,* she thought, watching the komer lead the small animal toward the great stone altar. *This lamb is so tiny,* she thought, *and so helpless. I cannot save him, and he cannot save himself. He doesn't even know he needs to!*

Shanarbaal rested his hand upon her shoulder. The fragrance of his perfumes reassured her. She could feel the warmth of his body behind her. She felt his strength and breathed deeply as if to inhale from his essence the power she needed to kill the lamb.

His breath was warm upon her earlobe, and he spoke as if reading her thoughts: "You do not kill the lamb, Rahab. The goddess performs the sacrifice through you."

"The goddess performs the sacrifice," Rahab repeated to herself as she raised the golden dagger and closed her eyes—she could not watch! She caught her breath and plunged the dagger into the heart of the lamb.

It is finished, she thought, stepping backward away from the altar. I have killed the lamb, and—she looked down at her white robe—I am covered with his blood. If I can rub some of this off—no, it looks like—ah, gods, it looks like Asabaal's dress when she—

Other blood memories flashed through her mind: the lifeblood of the tiny doves in the dedication; her bedcoverings stained with her own blood; the bull, slain at the initiation, his blood pouring down the stone circle in the sacred grove, flooding into the ruby pond; the unending temple sacrifices that followed; and, just yesterday morning, Amaranthe and Shanarbaal copulating in the blood of the slain goat. The memories locked her into numbness. Time stopped. She knelt frozen, totally bound by the blood that had already begun to harden on her hands. Astarte is indeed a goddess of blood, she thought.

"Astarte is the goddess of blood," the high priest said. "She wages war with Mot, the enemy of Baal, and is victorious. She brings Baal back from the underworld."

His voice was hypnotic, forcing out other thoughts and other times, bringing her back into the present.

"Baal, the mighty rider of the clouds," he shouted, "returns to the earth from the darkness below. Baal, the god who speaks with the voice of thunder, returns to us now from the regions of death!"

The high priest moved purposefully from the altar to the small fire that burned between the altar and the kneeling circle of supplicants. He swirled his cloak like black wings over the flames and quickly moved back. Beneath his flourish, the fire exploded like the thunder, the flames flashing high like the lightning.

Shanarbaal is so calm! Rahab thought. But then he should be—he's done this hundreds of times. What is he doing now? I wish I could see—no, I don't want to see. How will he know what the lamb's entrails mean anyway? This is horrible!

"People of Jericho," the priest answered himself. But now his voice was deeper, fuller—the voice of Baal, Rahab thought, shivering. Rahab looked toward the king. His round face was taut with tension. His lips were pulled thin; his forehead was furrowed in deep concentration. His future was in the hands of the priest, Rahab realized.

"People of Jericho!" the priest repeated. "Thus speaks Baal, the god of thunder. Pay heed to his words: Pile stone upon stone. Make high your ramparts. The Habiru come, bringing death and destruction. Always, says Baal, men will look to the walls of Jericho as a portrait of strength and the power of the gods. Make strong your walls; build high your defenses. Fortify your strongholds—the power of the gods will be known throughout the earth!"

Again, Rahab shuddered. The Habiru would come! Almost she could hear their footsteps, their trumpets of war.

But the trumpets were the shofars of the eunuchs within the circle. The sound signalled the end of the first prophecy.

Again the priest moved purposefully from the altar to the fire, and again he swirled his cloak, black wings fluttering against scarlet flames and quickly moving back. The fire exploded in response, the flames leaping high toward the rising sun.

"Tell us, O great god Baal—what lies in the future of the king of Jericho, lord protector of the city and the lands." Again, the priest's cloak swirled, and again thunder spoke from the flames. The priest spoke then in the voice of the god: "Pay heed, O king of Jericho! Listen well, O mortal man! An heir shall come to the king—flesh of his flesh, bone of his bone, blood of his blood."

Rahab caught her breath and looked at the king. He was grinning—the furrows between his brows were erased, and his eyes were crinkled. This was the reassurance he wanted! Rahab was astonished. How subtly Shanarbaal had accomplished it. She had given him the information, this information. Her tale told in the middle of the night had become this astonishing prophecy. She had been the author of this prophecy—not the god!

Shanarbaal picked up in his hand the red entrails of the lamb, holding the string dangling aloft like a red cord, and the prophecy continued:

> "From his birth, the gods shall claim him;
> The destiny of Jericho shall be his own!"

Again the trumpets sounded. The prophecy was finished.

Later in her room, Rahab at last washed the dry, cracking blood from her hands. She would be the ceremonial bride of the king this day, and the Kedeshoth gathered to prepare her for the event. They were her maids, and they prepared her well. The bitterness of the morning began to dissipate, as Rahab was caught up in the excitement of the day.

Bathing her with warm water, poured gently from ceramic pitchers, the maidens of the Kedeshoth chattered pleasantly. They anointed Rahab with costly oils and rubbed perfume upon her body. Her hair was a major project, requiring the best of their talents and ingenuity. Finally, it, too, received their approval. Her black tresses wound upon her head in braids adorned with pink and blue wildflowers. Never had Rahab received so much attention!

"Ah, Rahab," Mari exclaimed. "Your eyebrows would challenge a magician!" Even the maidens of the highest circle worked to adorn the ceremonial bride.

Bishna, standing nearby to lend assistance, laughed delightedly. "But, Mari, you are a magician!" she trilled. "You make an arch where there was none before!"

"Nothing is too good for our king," Mari replied laughing.

Across the courtyard, the maidens stood before a golden altar. Approaching her from beneath the trellised walkway, the king was startled by her beauty. This was, of course, the same maiden who had sacrificed the lamb at sunrise, and this was, of course, the same maiden through whom the goddess had angrily spoken to him on the previous evening. Yet now an entirely different person appeared before him—a quiet beauty, a fragile and feminine aspect of the goddess of love. The king smiled and almost imperceptibly quickened his pace. Annually he fulfilled his role in the ritual wedding of Baal and Astarte, but not every year was he so pleased with the bride of the god. This year the gods had chosen well. This year the gods had chosen a maiden who was a thousand maidens, a maiden with as many aspects as the goddess herself.

Rahab watched the king's approach through the leafy trellis. He, too, was crowned in flowers. A garland of hyacinth blossoms and myrtle leaves adorned his head. The villa courtyard sang with color. The Kedeshoth and the Komer were as decorative as the garden. Standing in small semicircles, they were dressed in the finest and most brilliantly colored of their religious robes—red, rose, purple, fuschia, deep blue—the colors of the flowers themselves. Early blooming flowers, chosen especially for this garden and for this ceremony, had been tended carefully by the Komer and were protected from the northwinds by strategically placed stone walls and benches. The result of the Komer's careful planning was a winter garden that foreshadowed the springtime. Beds of hyacinths, anemones, and wildflowers danced in harmonious color along the pathway near the bridegroom's feet.

The king approached Rahab quickly, the warm smile of eagerness upon his face answering the excitement Rahab felt within herself. Suddenly, she was transported on ritual wings of anticipation. Throughout the afternoon she had been pampered and prepared as a royal bride, and although she knew that the marriage was only another symbolic ritual, she could not contain her pleasure. The king's eyes, as they met hers, answered her that today she was truly beautiful. She did not doubt it. In that moment she knew the power of a beautiful woman over a man. Rahab smiled. *The king is a man like any man,* she thought, *and I know the arts to please him!*

The king took her hands and began the ceremonial words. Only the present existed for Rahab, the present and the pleasure of her power over the king.

The great room of Shanarbaal's villa blazed with heat and light. Gigantic shadows, like dancing spirits, rose and fell against the high plaster walls of the banqueting room. Incense wafted from burners on every wall. The heady fragrance of frankincense mingled with the sweet strong perfume of sandalwood.

Laughter, strong and masculine, filled the air, answered by murmurs of a more feminine nature and the unnatural soprano chatter of the Komer.

For hours now, the hall had been filled with music and feasting. Against a background of pipes, lutes, and tambourines, the high priest, the king, and the city's major politicians had told bawdy jokes, had watched dancing girls, and had drunk and drunk and drunk. The komer who directed the table service had, hours before, served the last of the vintage wine, but at this point in the evening, his master was concerned only that the cups be continually filled. The quality of the wine became insignificant. Master and guests alike had, hours before, lost the ability to differentiate. A baby goat, simmered in its mother's milk, had been the main course of the banquet's feast.

Now, men and maids lounged against embroidered pillows pulled close to the huge braziers at either end of the room. The warmth of the fire and the wine enhanced the fires already burning within the politicians. Gradually couples or groups of three and four—politicians, komer and kedeshoth—began to move into shadowed corners of the room. Others chose to step out of the banquet hall itself, preferring the privacy of the cubicles.

Rahab lounged beside the king, her mind glowing from the wine and from the excitement of the evening. She enjoyed the flippancies and familiarities of the king, who was, himself, relaxed and grateful for the favorable prophecy of the day.

"Last night, I spoke with the goddess," the king murmured against her ear, "but tonight I would like to know the maid."

Rahab smiled lazily, lifting her chin to enjoy more fully the king's kisses against her throat. "Are you ready for me tonight, little one?" he asked her. "I am the king and therefore the god—but I am also a man."

Rahab laughed softly, enjoying her power over his desire. "Yes, my lord, and I am a woman."

"Come," the king responded. "We will go to my chambers."

Rising to go with the king, Rahab glanced at the others. The room was greatly emptied. Only a few couples in corners remained, and to the far end of the room the politicians, Onuk and Zophar, sat with the komer Bachra, still drinking and laughing with Shanarbaal. With them were several of the Kedeshoth, including Bishna.

Rahab smiled and then tripped on a pillow. The king, laughing at her, put his arms around her waist and led her out of the hall.

20

Bishna's face was distorted with the intensity of the pain that tore her body. Droplets of sweat glistened on her brow in spite of the night's chill as she crouched, panting, in the corner of the cell. She shrieked.

The sound brought Rahab running from the adjoining chamber, to which she had returned after her visit with the king.

"Bishna!" Rahab's voice was urgent. "What is wrong? What's the matter?"

"It's just cramps—gas, perhaps," Bishna answered through clenched teeth. She seemed to relax then, as the pain eased.

"What can I do, Bishna? Can I bring you some water?" Rahab could think of no real way to help.

Bishna shook her head and retched.

"It was that beast Onuk, wasn't it, Bishna? He hurt you!"

Bishna's response was a long, drawn-out moan.

Rahab was angry. "They shouldn't have made you serve! The banquets can be too harsh!"

Bishna began to sob, but she said nothing.

"Onuk hurt you, didn't he, Bishna?" Rahab accused.

The pain had eased again. Bishna caught her breath and looked directly at Rahab. Bishna's eyes were pools of dark green—the exact color of the emerald pond at sunrise, Rahab realized with a start. Dark circles underscored those enormous eyes. The green and gold paint of the goddess had smudged, making steaks down Bishna's cheeks and accenting the hollows beneath her high cheekbones. Her face was painfully thin, Rahab thought, for as the child had grown larger, Bishna had seemed to grow thinner, to wane like the moon after it had reached its fullness.

Very tenderly Rahab repeated her statement—it really wasn't a question: "Onuk hurt you, didn't he."

"It wasn't only Onuk," Bishna whispered finally, catching her breath. "They made me do the celestial dance—and they laughed. They said I looked like the moon goddess when she is full, and they were going to throw me to her—and then they—" She could speak no more. The pain tore her body again, and she vomited what was left of the sacred wine. She lay panting then as Rahab wordlessly stroked her hair. Rahab's hands were gentle, but her lips were thin and bitter and her eagle brows met across her forehead in a fierce frown. She hated Onuk the Fat.

Bishna sighed. "Rahab, I'm sorry I'm so sick. Go back to sleep—I'm better now! You see—it was the wine."

Rahab stood, wondering, and Bishna stood and began to return to her pallet, still weak and shaken. She had taken only a few, halting steps when she stumbled against Rahab, doubling over in pain. A shriek tore from deep within her, and she clutched at Rahab, leaving bruises where her fingers caught Rahab's arms. Again she retched, and Rahab held her head.

"Here, lie down, Bishna. The wine is gone–you'll be better now." Rahab eased the girl to her pallet. Bishna knelt there for a moment, holding her bulging belly and moaning softly.

As the pain eased, Bishna spoke: "The gods will do what the gods will do, Rahab. I carry the child of the goddess. I am safe." She sighed. "If I could just get comfortable now and go to sleep."

"Yes, Bishna," Rahab answered, wondering bitterly how this girl could hold her faith when she had been so abused in its service.

The service of light, Rahab thought wryly. *Asabaal was right—this service is better done in the dark.*

When she thought of the excesses, the brutalities, of the evening, she was filled with hate for Onuk. Shanarbaal should know what had happened. He could stop this sort of thing—he would, if he knew—and she determined that she would tell him when she could.

"Ah, Rahab—forgive me for disturbing your night," and then Bishna clutched her belly again, drawing up her knees with the force of the pain. "It's coming again—oh, no!" Bishna writhed on her pallet, and sweat broke out on her forehead. Then, again, the pain subsided, and she rested.

Rahab suddenly grabbed Bishna by both arms and all but shrieked: "Bishna! The baby! When my mother has babies, the pain comes and goes. Are you having the baby?"

Bishna's eyes widened in terror. Was this birth? Was this how her mother had died? Panic joined with pain as Bishna thought of the mother she had never known.

"Rahab!" she cried. "It may be! Six moons have passed—is that enough? How long does it take?"

"Something like that," Rahab answered, unwilling to admit that in spite of four younger brothers and sisters, she had no real knowledge on the subject. But she knew that when it was her mother's time, the pains came and went and came again.

"If it is the baby, Bishna, then we must get help for you. I'll go get Shanarbaal and—"

But once again the pain struck, twisting Bishna beneath its force. Bishna's eyes were wide with terror now.

"I'll get Shanarbaal now, Bishna," Rahab repeated.

"No-o-o-o!" It was a howl, a shriek wrung from the depths of Bishna's soul.

Shanarbaal's laughter rang loudest in Bishna's memory.

"Don't leave me, Rahab! You are my only friend."

"Bishna—" Rahab began, hoping to reassure her, "Shanarbaal can get the midwives. You'll need a birthing stool."

"No-o-o-o-o!" Bishna shrieked again. "Get Amaranthe-Astarte—"

"Why do you invoke me, Bishna?" the harsh voice of the high priestess interrupted. "Why do you shriek and scream and wake the villa at this hour? Have you no consideration?"

The girls were startled into silence for a moment. The priestess demanded again, "What is going on here?"

It was Rahab who found her voice: "Oh, great lady, I think the baby is coming. I was just ready to seek your assistance."

"The time is not yet passed for the coming of the child," the priestess replied.

"Yet," Rahab answered, "I have seen my mother when the babies come—it is much the same."

"Silence, Rahab!" the priestess snapped. "I will judge for myself."

"Forgive me, great lady," Bishna implored. "I did not wish to disturb your sleep."

"Lie down, Bishna, on your back. Let me see what is happening here."

The priestess appeared to know what she was doing. She placed her hands and her ear as well on Bishna's swollen belly, and she waited. Again, the pain assaulted the girl, but this time she clenched her teeth and was silent. The priestess waited, and again the pain came. Beneath the priestess' touch, Bishna writhed from the force of the recurring pain, but she maintained her silence.

"You are not screaming now, my dove," the priestess noted dryly. "Perhaps the pain is not so bad, after all." Then she turned to Rahab: "Has there been any showing of water or any blood?"

"No, great lady. She has vomited, and for some time now, the pains have become stronger," Rahab answered.

"I think you are right, Rahab. The gods send us their baby a little early—in time for the solstice. Astarte answers my prayers with a child for the solstice!" the priestess exulted. Rahab was puzzled by Amaranthe's delight.

"Have no fear, Bishna," the priestess said. "You carry the child of the gods. You are safe."

The same words that Bishna had said earlier. *Of course!* Rahab thought. *Those words must be part of a ritual.* Perhaps this was the secret of Bishna's faith.

"Rahab," ordered Amaranthe, "stay here and keep her quiet. I will get what is necessary to expedite this birth."

When the girls were alone again, Bishna seemed calmer, more relaxed. The pains continued to come, and between them Bishna rocked gently on her heels, holding her stomach as if it might break.

They heard Amaranthe returning. She entered the cubicle, followed by a komer carrying a birthing stool.

"Still no show of water?" Amaranthe asked briskly.

"No—no water," Rahab answered.

"Well, we will make the water," Amaranthe said. Rahab now noticed that Amaranthe carried the ceremonial ashera. "Lie back," the priestess commanded Bishna, and Bishna obeyed. "Now, be still—do not move," the priestess said, motioning the komer to hold Bishna motionless as, with the ashera, she loosed the amniotic fluid that would begin labor in earnest. Bishna screamed and screamed again.

Rahab watched Bishna's face, and it seemed to her that Bishna's expression, a mixture of fear and bewilderment, was much like that of the sacrificial bull on the night of their initiation—except that the bull was powerful and strong. Bishna was just a frightened little girl.

The komer helped Bishna to the birthing stool as Amaranthe watched appraisingly.

"The girl is too tense," she said. "This will take forever." The priestess clapped her hands, and the komer brought forward a small brass bottle that had been tied to his girdle.

Amaranthe took the bottle and passed her hands over it three times, ignoring the periodic screams and moans from the birthing stool, and chanting:

> "Three things please the goddess; three things the goddess loves.
> Death; her joy in battle; and
> The birth of a child of her own.
> Ai—e—eee—ee, Astarte!"

She then handed the small bottle to Bishna, who drank from it eagerly. Rahab was astonished at the cool, detached demeanor of the priestess. She appeared completely unaffected by Bishna's distress, completely in control of the situation. She had assisted at many such births, Rahab surmised.

Bishna screamed again. Amaranthe ignored her. Walking to each corner of the room, the high priestess continued her chanting.

> "Spirits of the winds, I call you.
> Spirits of the four corners of the earth,
> I invoke you by wind and fire.
> By water and blood, I call you forth,
> To bring to fruition this birth."

Again and again Bishna screamed. Finally, Amaranthe spoke. "It is time," she said. She was right. The baby came, a tiny, feeble boy, a fragile blue baby who had fought furiously against entering the world and, having entered, refused to breathe its air.

Amaranthe turned the child upside down and shook him. Still he made no sound. He would not cry! She slapped his bottom harshly and spoke in rising anger, "Cry! You must cry!"

To Rahab the baby appeared only to turn bluer, but the high priestess became crimson in her fury.

"The gods cannot take him now," she shrieked. "They must not deny me this!"

Suddenly Rahab knew what she must do. Why had she not remembered immediately?

"Lady, my brother was born this way," she said. "I saw my father make him breathe. May I—"

"Do it!" The priestess almost flung the baby into her arms. "Quickly, or we shall lose him!"

Rahab took the tiny body and breathed her own breath into his mouth. *Please, Baal,* she prayed silently, *don't take him! Please let him live.* Desperately she breathed into his mouth again. It had worked when her father had done this for her brother, Benan. *Oh, Baal, please,* she prayed, *let him breathe!*

A tiny whimper, breath inhaled, answered her prayer. The child lived! His loud cry released springs of joy within her. She had saved him! Her breath had saved Bishna's child! Bishna!

Rahab turned quickly to see her friend lying quietly, a tiny smile on her lips. "My baby?" Bishna asked.

Amaranthe took the child roughly from Rahab's arms. "He lives, though he's had little help from you, Bishna!" the priestess snapped. "Your friend is a better mother to him than you are. Here, take him, and see if you can at least give him suck."

Bishna took her baby, oblivious to Amaranthe's harsh words. "My baby," she said, softly sighing, drawing the tiny mouth to her waiting breast.

Amaranthe turned to Rahab. "She will sleep very soon. Stay with her. Call me if anything is wrong with the baby in the night. I don't want anything untimely to happen to this child!"

The gods are good to me! Amaranthe thought as she left the room. *The child came too soon, but in the time of the gods, it is perfect!* Amaranthe's satisfaction was complete: there would be a sacrifice for the winter solstice!

The bleating of the lambs welcomed Rahab. She smiled at her father as he shepherded the small flock into the pen. He smiled at her. His voice was warm and loving. "They are hungry this morning, Rahab," he said. "We must feed them." The bleating of the lambs became more insistent, so insistent that she awakened. But still they bleated. It was not the lambs! It was Bishna's baby! Bishna's wonderful, tiny baby boy!

Rahab hurried toward Bishna's pallet, stopping in horror at the sight of her friend's blood-stained mat. Bishna's baby cried hungrily, but his mother would never suckle him again.

Rahab plucked the crying baby from Bishna's arms and ran, screaming, to Amaranthe's apartment. She pounded on the door, crying and clutching the child to her breast.

Amaranthe opened the door, scowling sleepily. "What's wrong, girl?" she demanded. "Is the child alive? Is it all right?"

"Yes, my lady—I think so—but Bishna—my lady, I fear that Bishna is dead."

"How so?" asked the priestess. "What has happened?"

"I think that—" Rahab swallowed. "I think that she has bled to death in the night. The baby woke me with his crying."

"Bah!" the priestess responded. "Then we will need buckets of water—and I have other duties for the komer this day."

The priestess clapped her hands, and a komer came from within the apartment.

"Go," Amaranthe said crisply. "The maiden Bishna is dead. Get others. You will need buckets of water. Then prepare a litter. You will need to take Bishna to the high places. The birds will clean her bones. Leave someone to clean her room."

The komer bowed.

"Hurry!" Amaranthe added. "We have much to do today!"

During this exchange, Rahab stood near the door, still holding the baby, whose cries had subsided to soft whimpers.

"But, my lady," she said, forcing herself to control her sobbing. "What of the baby?"

"You have nothing else to do today," the priestess said harshly. "Keep the child safe and bring it to me at sundown."

"He will need to be fed," Rahab said softly, almost to herself.

"Then feed him!" the priestess snapped, slamming her door. Rahab stood bewildered, holding a hungry baby.

Rahab sat on an upturned feeding trough in the villa's stable. The goat tethered beside her bleated occasionally, but stood still, and was cooperative.

"I am glad you were here," Rahab said to the goat. "See how much help you are!"

She held Bishna's tiny baby in her lap under the goat's belly, watching with satisfaction as his hungry little mouth suckled at the long brown teat of the goat. *What a beautiful baby he is,* she thought, *so tiny, yet so perfect.*

"My father said I had a magic with animals, little one. Do you think I have a magic with babies, too?

"I love you, baby," she said, "as I loved your mother." The thought of Bishna brought tears to her eyes. "I will try to be a good mother to you," she told him, "if the high priestess will let me."

The goat bleated again. "You are like my friend Nana," Rahab told the goat. "She is a goat on my father's farm. She is so good. She was willing to suckle a lamb once when the wolves killed his mother." Holding the baby in her lap

89

with one hand, she rubbed the goat's back with the other.

The baby turned his head away from the goat. "Ah, you've had enough," she said, placing the baby's head at her shoulder and patting his bottom. "You need to burp."

The baby burped, and Rahab held him in her lap. He was delightful. The blue had faded, and he looked pink and healthy. "The gods have taken Bishna, but they have given you to me, baby. Perhaps the gods are not so cruel as I have thought," she sighed. "Bishna, I will take good care of your baby."

The sundown came too quickly.

With some anxiety, Rahab carried the tiny baby toward the apartment of the high priestess. "I will ask her if I may take care of you," Rahab said to him. "Surely, by now, she will see that I am able to care for you. She must let me care for you! You are too precious for any wet nurse!"

The high priestess came quickly at Rahab's knock. "Ah, you are here. You have done well. Give me the child and go to prepare yourself quickly for the evening ceremony."

Rahab hesitated. "But, my lady," she said, "I wanted to ask—"

"Go and prepare yourself," snapped the high priestess, jerking the baby from Rahab's arms. The door shut in Rahab's face, and she stood alone in the empty hallway.

21

Purposefully, Rahab sought out the sacred grove. Never had her mind been more clear. Her steps were quick and firm as she made her way on the morning following that longest, darkest night of the year. Her whole being was concentrated in anger, a total revulsion of the horror on the hilltop at last night's ceremony.

She would confront Baal himself. Baal, he who had given her himself, in his likeness of the precious masheba, and to whom she had given herself—she hated him! Baal had betrayed her! He was cruel and horrible. He had betrayed them all!

He had killed the baby!

The pond was still and, as always, dead. The morning was too cold even for the flies, and the sun had not yet crested the tops of the ancient trees. The heavy dew had frozen into flowerets within the hanging mosses and along the Baalpath. The crunch of Rahab's sandaled feet was the only sound. It was as if the grove itself was frozen in fear, awaiting the confrontation that would follow. Rahab would confront the god! She would rip him from his hiding place in the limestone bench. She would accuse him! She would throw him to the ground. She would stomp him into nothingness. He could kill her. She cared not. He could kill her as Asabaal had been killed. He could take her as Bishna had been taken, in a sacrifice of blood. He could—but her thoughts stopped when she remembered Bishna's baby.

She hurried, driven by her wrath, furious. She would beard the god face to face in his own sacred grove. She spat in fury. What if he did kill her? She hoped he would!

The force and energy of Rahab's wrath gave her the strength to push aside quickly the heavy limestone bench where she had hidden her masheba, her gift from the god. The early rays of the sun filled the cavity of the bench to reveal the reality of the god, the physically embodied Baal.

Rahab was stunned as she stared down upon the physical likeness of the god. She caught her breath, entranced at the enormity of what was now revealed. She was unaware of time. She had so carefully, so reverently, placed the likeness within the bench, selfishly concealing it even from her fellow novitiates and most certainly from the jealous and vindictive Amaranthe. Her precious masheba! She stared at it in disbelief, tracing in her mind the outline of its magical appearance on that night of ritual. She saw again the bull's face, the curved horns, the folds of skin and muscle in the neck.

Looking down at it now in disbelief, she traced the figure in its physical reality, lying cold and frozen in the sepulchre of the limestone bench, a symbol of the god's betrayal. Still there was the outline of the bull. But now she saw it clearly.

It was a dried lump of cow dung!

Rahab understood then. It came to her with stunning clarity that Baal was dead—or had never lived! There were no gods! She understood completely at that moment that Baal and Astarte had been created by men to satisfy a lust for human power. The priests controlled the people through the rituals and the endless sacrifice. She knew as well that the lust could never be satisfied—not even with the slaughter of the innocents!

The child! His life's blood had been wasted, poured onto the ground as a libation to a god who did not exist. She closed her eyes, and her breath caught

91

in a sob. It was all a lie—a cruel joke! It wasn't Baal the Betrayer. It was Baal, the lump of dung!

Slowly and deliberately then, without thought, she pushed the heavy stone back into place, sealing forever in its limestone sepulchre her god Baal. The death of the gods! A laugh that was not a laugh tore itself from her breast. The gods were less than men. To be angry at Baal was to be angry at nothing! Baal was dead, had never lived. Astarte was nothing! Less than nothing! The ceremonies were rituals in futility, for there was no meaning in gods who did not exist.

The reality that now claimed her concentration seemed to freeze her blood, to stop the beating of her heart, and to quell even the flutterings of fear that gathered around the edges of her mind. Wrath drove out any trace of fear, any hint of hesitation. She knew what she must do. The rage that had engulfed her was now driven away by cold, fierce bitterness—that men could—would— did!—use the blood of a precious baby to manipulate other men. She would have retched, but her feelings were too deep for nausea. The idiocy! The waste! The pain! The deep, deep grief, the inexpressible sorrow for the lost child—that beautiful, trusting boy baby! He could have been her own. He *was* her own! For she had given him the breath of life at birth. They had thought the gods would take him then, for he was blue and did not draw breath or cry. *He knew,* she thought bitterly. *He knew!* Her anger was too deep for tears.

Rahab sank to her knees beside the limestone bench and buried her head in her arms on the cold slab. For a moment, her thoughts relived the night before. Bishna's baby, the child of the gods—his bright brown eyes blinking against the harsh glare of the firelight reflected off the golden horns of the high priestess—the gasp of pain as the knife met his flesh, savagely, efficiently, to consummate the sacrifice. The shrill shriek of the high priestess as she held up the bleeding, lifeless child to the black sky and spread his bright red blood upon the altar—libation poured out upon the high places. Kneeling in place with the other Kedeshoth, Rahab had watched, unable to stop the tableau of death enacted at the hilltop altar.

Earlier, as the rites had begun, she had poured out her ritual wine, promising herself that she would see clearly this night the mysteries of the goddess. *I should have known,* she thought bitterly. She could have taken the child and escaped into the countryside. But she knew, with a positive certainty, that Amaranthe would have made both their lives forfeit if she had attempted to steal the child of the gods. Her desolation was too deep for tears. Her grief hurt even the marrow of her bones, numbing all physical feeling.

The sun crested the ancient treetops and warmed Rahab's back. As it had done before in the sacred grove, it reminded her of life. She forced from her mind all thought of the night before and concentrated on feeling the warmth of the sunshine that reached even here in the sacred grove. She knew, almost as if she had heard the words, what she would do. She knew, without any doubt whatsoever, that the plan would succeed.

She had knelt a girl, a slave to the gods and a slave to her own emotion. She arose, a woman. As she returned to the villa of Shanarbaal, her step was firm. Her posture was straighter and her poise was complete. She was free from Baal! Astarte no longer held her captive! Her spirit sang within her. She was free!

From this moment forth, she was no longer a maid of Baal.

She was a woman. Her own woman!

PART TWO

WOMAN OF JERICHO

...When lust has conceived, it gives birth to sin,
And when sin is accomplished,
It brings forth death.

James 1:15

22

Shanarbaal shifted beneath the woolen coverlets. Had he been dreaming? His mind was still asleep, his senses blurred in the aftermath of the night's excesses. The girl's warm breath excited his earlobe, rousing him to the morning and to the warmth of her body. The priest questioned her audacity to enter his private bedchamber unbidden, but his body did not question the pleasure of her presence.

Rahab, for her part, plied every technique of the mysteries of love that six months in the temple of Astarte had taught her.

Later, as Rahab served him breakfast, he questioned her. He was propped up against the pillows, languid and relaxed.

"Rahab, I'm curious," he said. "Why did you seek me out this morning? You are the bride of the god this day. Do you seek his priest as well?" She laughed gently, saying nothing, and he continued his questions. "Or have you brought me more tales of midnight meetings with the king?"

"I have brought you myself, my lord," she answered. "I wish to serve you."

"All the maidens of Baal wish to serve me, my sweet," he said. "How are you different?"

"I wish to serve you differently." Her steady gaze met his eyes and held them. She had his attention. Though she controlled the interview, she presented no threat; there was no confrontation in her power. The priest noticed only that she was totally poised, totally graceful.

"And how is that, Rahab-Kedeshoth?" He was intrigued with this girl. She would be capable, he knew, of using her intellect and her energy to his advantage. She had demonstrated her perception, her loyalty, and her courage only this week when she had come to him—again unbidden—to reveal the confession of the king's fears.

"My time here is almost accomplished, my lord," Rahab said, although she had served only half of her year of service.

The priest knew that when her year of service was completed, Rahab's father had arranged a wealthy marriage for the girl, and his lip curled almost imperceptibly in contempt as he thought of that man, the proposed bridegroom. From his observation of the girl, he knew that she would not welcome the match.

He nodded assent. "The gods have been pleased with your service," he assured her gently, with a self-satisfied smile.

Rahab's answer was swift. "It is you I am thinking of, my lord—not the gods!"

Shanarbaal's eyes narrowed in surprise. Certainly this girl was the opposite of Amaranthe, who attributed her every whim to the inspiration of the goddess. Rahab's candor intrigued him.

Again her gaze met his, and she hurried to explain. "My lord, I know that the temple depends upon the contributions of its patrons for its financial security and that my service has brought more than any other maiden's, even those of the third circle. I know, as well, that there are women who serve the pleasure of paying patrons outside the temple. You, as the high priest of Jericho-Baal, have a need to be close to what is going on within the city, I think—with the king, the army, the merchants, the traveling caravans."

"Yes—what are you getting at?"

"My lord," she added persuasively, "men speak more freely when they are alone with a woman in a private house. If I used my talents in your behalf within the city, you would be assured of wide and useful knowledge, to the advantage of the temple in your dealings with the king." She laughed suggestively. "You know that the king appreciates my talents!"

The priest was silent, staring at this girl, surprised at her sophistication. Rahab had no way of knowing that he had been considering her for further temple service.

Shanarbaal asked her, "Have you considered remaining at the temple after your year of service, Rahab-Kedeshoth? Your abilities have been noted. You could rise to a position of real power." He paused significantly. "Amaranthe is growing old."

Again their eyes met.

"But she does not grow kindly toward those who would threaten her power, my lord."

He was silent, remembering the intensity of Amaranthe's flash of anger at Rahab about the sacrifice of the lamb.

"I do not believe in the gods, my lord," the girl continued quietly. "I know that Baal is dead and never lived. I know that Astarte was created by men, that she is nothing."

The priest caught his breath in astonishment. No one had ever spoken such blasphemy aloud in the temple—especially to the high priest of Baal. He smiled, for in the privacy of his chamber, in those brief and candid moments when he admitted to himself that he was more magician than priest, he had thought such thoughts. But the ideas had never been voiced!

Deliberate now, Rahab went on. The priest listened with fascination.

"But I know you, too, my lord," she said. "I have watched you. I respect your strength. I would learn from you. I would serve you. I would serve you well!"

Before the priest could respond, Rahab changed her tone completely. She dropped to her knees and grasped his hand, pleading now. She looked very young, very vulnerable.

"My lord, I have tasted the pleasures of the temple. My father has doubtless chosen a husband for me, but I know my father's thinking. He will choose a wealthy man, but one who is a clod! I cannot go to one man now!"

The priest believed her. He turned her suggestion over in his mind, approved it, and then voiced his sole objection: "Rahab, little raven. You are young. You have a magic with men, it is true—but you are too young for such a dangerous game. You do not know what you ask. You would not be safe."

Rahab thought bitterly of the safety of the temple maidens, of Asabaal, of Bishna, of the baby. But those thoughts she kept to herself. She must appeal to the priest's weakness.

"I am young, my lord," she answered him, "but I pleased you this morning. Surely I could continue to do so!"

He laughed, slapping his thigh. If this raven nested with a husband, he would miss the pleasure of her company indeed!

"I believe you can!" he said. "So be it, my sweet. I shall establish you. You will be Rahab the harlot, a woman of Jericho, a woman in her own right." He laughed.

She made her final point. "It must be now, my lord. You know I have offended Amaranthe. My life is forfeit now that the sacrifice is accomplished and the wedding done."

"So be it," he said. The ritual words made it a promise.

She went to him again, and again she pleased him.

It pleased Shanarbaal to take the girl from the goddess.

Amaranthe would call it stealing! *She will turn as red as her hair,* he thought, chuckling to himself. Fine sport, to snatch the bird from the fox's paws! *Best of all,* he thought, *the priestess dare not raise a voice of complaint! Altogether delightful!*

"The god has called. The maiden must obey!" he recited the ritual loudly with great relish, although there was no one to hear. It would be done tonight, before Amaranthe's very eyes. He laughed, remembering the advice of Onuk the Fat: real power belongs to those who influence the gods and the king. Yes, the exercise of power was altogether delightful. He gloried in it, especially when it was that proud witch Amaranthe who would bow. She could not even blame him! It would be the king, speaking as the god, who would call the maiden. Tonight's feast would be a feast indeed. Shanarbaal's smile broadened as he remembered his breakfast feast. The gods were good! He would summon Amaranthe. Best to mollify the priestess before the storm.

Amaranthe was carefully applying paint to her eyelids when the komer tapped gently at her door to summon her to the high priest's chambers.

"Tell him I'll be there shortly," she answered impatiently. *Curse the man anyway!* she thought. *He doesn't care what I am doing, or whether I am occupied with other things. He says, "Come," and I must come!* "Bah!" she said aloud, throwing down the tiny fur brush she had been using. She picked up a small linen square and rubbed the eyelid she had just painted, smudging and softening the effect. She smeared the excess on the other eyelid, tossed aside the cloth, and examined herself carefully in the brass mirror. Her reflection, made golden by the brass, was very enticing. She liked her form, lean and muscular, with tiny breasts, high and small. They had never grown heavy or sagged from the weight of milk as did the breasts of other women. *Yes,* she thought, *I am Astarte, eternally virgin, yet eternally harlot. And now,* she told herself, *I must go and play the harlot to that goat Shanarbaal.* The thought that the high priest needed—desired—her was always satisfying to Amaranthe. *Ah, well,* she thought, *it serves as a pleasant enough diversion, and it suits my purposes to keep him under control. I will compliment him on a magnificent presentation yesterday— and perhaps I will learn what he is planning for this evening!*

Across the courtyard, in the royal suite, the king was enjoying an afternoon alone with Queen Asheratti.

For the first time in months, he looked upon the queen without wondering whose arms had held her last. The king was ecstatic. The queen was his and his alone. The gods had confirmed it! He almost wanted to seek out his old friend Shanar to ask his pardon. How could he have entertained evil suspicions of the queen, his wife, and the priest, his friend, and even Alcion, a eunuch! He laughed aloud.

"What is so funny, my love?" the queen asked sleepily.

"Umm, I was just thinking of yesterday," the king replied. "The ceremonies—the fortune—a son for us!"

"Even now," the queen answered with a smile, "perhaps the future grows!" The queen had been with the king for three years, but the gods had not blessed them with a son. A princess of Megiddo, she had been taught from birth that her role in life would be to bear sons for a king. But this king planted no seed for sons. *Maybe now,* she thought, *maybe today.*

She had grown impatient, even bored, through the years, and she spent her time, except when she was with the king, in pampering herself and making herself beautiful. Her dark hair and creamy golden complexion were set off by large violet eyes. She was a beautiful woman. She knew it and enjoyed her beauty.

Shanarbaal, whom she considered the most elegant of men, had spoken strangely at the divination ceremony yesterday. It was very well and good to be promised a son—she expected no less. But his comment that the queen looked at no man other than the king—it was laughable! She enjoyed any man she

desired. Shanar knew that! Suddenly, she understood. The gods wished to reassure the king so that he would know a son was truly his! This was the only
possible explanation.

"My sweet," she teased the king suddenly, kissing him quickly behind one
ear, "you were jealous, weren't you?"

"You are so lovely," he answered earnestly. "Any man would be jealous of
your love." He returned her kisses eagerly.

The queen laughed as a mother laughs at a charming child. "Make me a
son," she said.

Asheratti had retired to her bath, and the king lay relaxed, his hands behind
his head, looking idly at the ceiling. He had been puzzled by Shanar's request
this morning, but his pudgy face lit up in a lustful grin as he thought of
Shanar's plan. *The gods are good,* he thought. He was looking forward to this
evening. He would assume the role of the god Baal. He would call for the
thunder and the rain, and he would take the kedeshoth Rahab for himself! He
would proclaim that from the time she had sacrificed the lamb, she could no
longer serve the temple worshippers. She would serve only the god and his
friend, the king—and those whom the king would choose! Baal would speak
tonight.

When Asheratti returned from her bath, the king was snoring gently, a
smile across his boyish face. She began to brush her hair.

In the Kedeshoth rooms that afternoon, Rahab stood at the door of the cubicle where she had shared secrets and laughter, birth and death, with her
friend Bishna. The blood had been washed away. The Komer had carried
Bishna to the high places of the mountain tops. The birds would cleanse her
body, and perhaps someone would go and fetch down her bones, perhaps not.

Grief welled up within Rahab and tears spilled down her face. She would
leave this place of death and horror. The group was to depart in the morning;
it would not seem strange, if anyone happened by, that Rahab was gathering
her things. Rahab was leaving! She wasn't sure how Shanar would arrange it,
but she knew that he would arrange it. She was leaving. She would not return
to this room!

Sated with wine and food, the last guest had retired. Amaranthe, however,
was wakeful, angry for hours, ever since that fool of a king had stood
drunkenly to proclaim that he, the god Baal personified, claimed for himself
the kedeshoth Rahab who had performed the sacrifice. Amaranthe had been
furious. It had been a public rebuke to Astarte! How dare he execute such
power! To make it worse, he had taken the girl away with him on the spot! It
was an unbelievable effrontery!

Remembering the king's fat face as he smiled and said, "I, Baal, take the ke-

101

deshoth Rahab for my own. I claimed her with the black stone; I take her for my own," Amaranthe ground her teeth. The more she thought of it, the angrier she became.

Lamps lighted her chambers, casting a yellow glare on her face in the mirror, which reflected a mask of wrath—Astarte in her warrior image. Never had Amaranthe been so angry!

He had done it. He had taken the girl and left, and she had said nothing, done nothing. Amaranthe was even more angry with herself because she had been taken off guard. That in itself was unforgivable. She had pretended it was all right, but it was not all right! Rahab had been dedicated to Astarte, to the service of light. Even in the yellowed reflection in the mirror, a vein in Amaranthe's neck and another in her forehead were noticeably distended, throbbing with the heartbeat of her wrath. How dare he!

With great strength and force, Amaranthe systematically picked up the pots of color before her mirror and threw them, one by one, across the room. They crashed against the opposite wall, spilling paint in all directions. The violence served only to make her angrier. How dare he! That fat little fool. That overstuffed sausage of a man—mortal man, fool! How dare he!

He is so stupid, he could not have done it himself, she thought. *That goat Shanar put him up to it.*

Wrath gave wings to her feet, and wine gave them speed. She turned and dashed to the apartments of Shanarbaal. Never had Amaranthe been so angry. Never had her fury so mastered her. Never had wrath so consumed her being!

She ran from her apartments past the king's rooms. They were empty now! He had left! The fool! And she flew like an arrow to the door of the high priest.

She flung open his door and attacked. "How dare you!" she shrieked. "You have insulted me for the last time, you viper!"

Roused from a drugged slumber, Shanarbaal thought at first that he was dreaming. Amaranthe had gone mad. It was a nightmare. She was on top of him, shrieking, slapping him, choking him. He pushed her off.

As the priest blinked his eyes against the pale, grayed moonlight silhouetting Amaranthe-Astarte's flailing arms, the woman was on him again.

"You fool! You could have stopped him!" she cried, slapping him.

He struck back. "By the gods, woman! Have you lost your senses!"

"By the goddess!" she screamed. "This time you have gone too far! You have angered the goddess." She laughed crazily. "You thought you could steal the girl."

"Woman, are you mad?"

"Ai-eeee-eeee, Astarte!" she screamed, and again they struggled. Her grip was like iron, her fingers locked around his throat, and he called upon all his strength to beat her off.

"Amaranthe! You are mad!" he said sharply. He slapped her face with his open hand.

At his stinging slap, her fury seemed to grow. She stood and came at him again—Astarte in her warrior aspect. She lunged. "Aii-eee-eee, Astarte!" she shrieked, but reaching her greatest height, with the scream still on her lips, she collapsed, as if her spirit had been called forth from her body. She fell in a heap at the side of his bed.

For a few moments, there was silence. He sat on his couch and slowly shook his head. He had not experienced a nightmare; he had survived an attack. He could still feel the iron tension of her fingers.

Slowly and carefully, Shanarbaal arose and lighted a lamp, his hand shaking. In its yellow light, he looked at the heap on his floor. She appeared to be lifeless. He hoped she was!

"The woman was mad," he muttered to himself. *Surely she has awakened the household,* he thought. But no feet came running. If the Komer had heard, he decided, they had imputed the noise to the dreams that follow feasting.

Catching his breath and letting his heart settle once again in his breast, he quickly calculated the wisest course. He would carry her to her room. Let someone else tell him of her demise!

Gathering the high priestess in his arms, he was half afraid her screams would begin again, but the arms that had moments ago shown the strength of ten men were now limp and lifeless. Quietly, cautiously, he crossed the courtyard, staying in the shadows of the porticoes, out of the moonlight, and made his way to the priestess' chambers.

Her door was open; the lamp burned brightly. He saw Amaranthe's pots of colors smashed against the wall, testimony to the ferocity of her wrath. Quietly, he carried her into the room, and quickly, he let her slide to the floor at the foot of the brass mirror.

He glanced into its shining surface. He looked a little wild-eyed, he thought.

"She was mad," he said simply to the image in the mirror.

23

The sun was at its zenith when Rahab awakened. She stretched and yawned, and joy, like the winter sunlight, flooded her heart.

"I am free!" Rahab said the words aloud. "I am free!"

Eager for the new day, the new life, she rose and bathed in a large basin that centered this simple room in the house of the king. Figs had been set out for her, and she ate with simple enjoyment. Lying in the tepid water, she remembered the teachings of Amaranthe-Astarte: "You must master life or it will master you!"

Rahab promised herself, "I will master life!"

What her future life would be, however, was a mystery to Rahab. Was she to stay here with the king? Was that what Shanar had arranged, or did the high priest perhaps have other plans for her? She did not know. But of one thing she was sure: No matter where Shanar placed her, she would be her own woman.

The servant who called Rahab to her meeting with the king ushered her through a curtained entranceway and into a private audience chamber. The king, who sat at a table with his ever-present pitcher of wine and a bowl of dried grapes, waved the servant out and greeted Rahab solemnly.

"Enter, child, I have something to tell you."

Rahab was surprised by the ominous tone in the king's voice. Yesterday at the feast he had been cheerful, even jovial. A cold shiver of foreboding passed over Rahab's body. "Is something wrong, my lord?" she asked quietly.

"Ah, Rahab, I have just heard grave tidings from the temple."

Rahab trembled at his words. Had something happened to Shanarbaal?

"It is Amaranthe-Astarte," the king continued. "She has gone to join the gods."

Rahab stood in incredulous silence. "She is dead?" she finally asked.

"She is dead," the king affirmed. "A runner has just come from the villa to tell me that she was found dead in her room this morning."

"And the high priest?" Rahab had feared for his safety on the previous evening. Livid at the king's proclamation that Rahab must leave the temple, Amaranthe had gazed at the high priest in unveiled hatred. Now she was dead, but who knew what evil she had accomplished before her death? "And

Shanarbaal?" Rahab asked again, with less decorum than was due the king's rank.

The king looked at the girl in puzzlement. "The runner said that Amaranthe is dead," he responded simply. "The high priest will, of course, see that a proper ceremony is performed."

"And after that, what will happen after that, O king?" Rahab asked the question intensely, but the strength of her emotions came from her secret heart. Amaranthe was dead, and her wonderful protector, Shanarbaal, was not.

"A new priestess will be named by the oracle," the king explained. "The gods will choose. It is all the same."

"Do you mean they are all like Amaranthe-Astarte?" Rahab was aghast.

The king laughed and reached to pull her to his lap. "Let us hope not, little raven," he said. "We have seen enough of our lady of battles. We need more of our lady of loves!"

During the week that Rahab spent in the palace, her friendship with the king grew. He was a stupid man, but often pleasant and jolly. Though he would have been an excellent baker or butcher, he was less than an excellent king. *But,* she thought kindly, *what do I know of kings?* She was beginning to wonder if Shanarbaal had forgotten her when, on the seventh day of her freedom from the temple, she was called to the king's audience chamber.

She entered the audience hall to find both the king and Shanar speaking earnestly in low tones. They seemed not to notice her presence, so she stood in the shadows at a distance.

Her heart beat wildly as she awaited their notice. She savored the sight of the priest. He knew what he was about. Here was power—security and safety. He spoke with gods and with kings, and he was her protector, her benefactor! *He is so beautiful, so strong,* she thought.

Their heads close together so that none of the suppliants or servants present could hear, the two men laughed and whispered. Their laughter was music to Rahab's ears, reassuring her that all was well in spite of Amaranthe's death. Or, she thought wickedly, *because of Amaranthe's death.* Questions about that death raced through her mind. Surely Shanar would tell her all!

After a short time, she was called to the men. The king sighed heavily.

"I shall miss this little raven, Shanar," he said with a smile. Squeezing Rahab's arm playfully, he added, "But I will see you often!"

Rahab's heart sang at those words. She would be going with Shanar!

The sun was shining brightly, and the day was clear and warm as she left the palace of the king with her protector, the high priest. They climbed into his litter and started off down the twisting streets. Rahab's questions began tumbling out immediately.

"What happened? I know Amaranthe was angry, my lord. I saw her as we left. She was furious! I was worried about you....I know her moods."

"You are correct in your assessment," he assured her formally, yet smiling with amusement. "Amaranthe was indeed angry!"

"Tell me what happened, please," Rahab insisted.

The priest lowered his voice despite the privacy of the litter. "When they found her, her paints had been thrown all over the room, as if in a fit of anger."

"And you, my lord?" Rahab asked quickly. "I see scratches, bruises." Her fingers tarried on a mark at his neckline. "Did she vent her anger on you as well?"

Instantly, his manner changed; he became cold. "No one else has noticed, Rahab, so mind your tongue. She was found alone, in her own apartments. She died from the fury of her own wrath."

Rahab nodded. "I understand. I am glad you are well." Then she embraced him, burying her face in his chest. "I am so glad you are well!"

The priest laughed. The litter jolted as the slaves lowered it to the ground. "Come, Rahab, woman of Jericho. Here is your house."

"My house?" she asked.

"It is yours now to use as you suggested—to serve me. It was my mother's house while she lived. Now it shall be yours." They alighted from the litter, and Rahab looked up three stories. The house was a part of the wall of Jericho itself!

"But there is no stair!" she said. "How do you get to the upper stories?"

He laughed. "The stair is inside, country girl. This is the only house in Jericho with an inside stairway. It is my own design. Come! I think you will like this place. It is a wonderful house. There were two houses here, and I had them made into one big house for my mother. That is why there is no stairway outside."

Taking her inside, the priest continued. "It will suit our purposes well. No one will be able to see your visitors once they have entered the outer door."

Rahab was amazed again. This man's talents knew no limits. Buoyantly, joyously, she allowed him to lead her out of the sunlight and into the darkened and shuttered house in the walls of Jericho.

"My mother has been with the gods now for several months," Shanarbaal explained as he led Rahab through the entryway. "I like this house. I could not bring myself to sell it. Come! Let us go to the roof. First you must see the view. Then I will show you the rooms."

Rahab moved hesitantly, for the floor was uneven beneath her feet, and the room was dark.

"Come along!" Shanar laughed, jerking her toward the stairs.

"It's dark!" Rahab returned his laugh and stumbled after him.

"Of course it's dark. The shutters have been closed for months. Don't be afraid. You are safe with me. I won't let you fall. Come on!"

As they reached the stairway, the hairs on the back of her neck stood on end for an instant as she felt a cold draft, a flow of air coming up from the level below. She froze on the first step, remembering the nightmares of her childhood and the stairs down into the temple.

Shanar jerked her arm painfully. "Come on, woman!" he shouted.

Rahab jumped to follow, hurrying behind him up the limestone stairs. "I'm coming! I'm coming!" she said, laughing nervously.

Shanarbaal knew his way easily up every step of the three flights of stairs to the roof. But for Rahab, each step was new and uncertain, and in the darkness of the stairwell, she felt entombed. She would have felt panic except for the comforting presence of the high priest.

At last, they scrambled out onto the rooftop level, but they were still in darkness.

"We are here, Rahab!"

"But it's dark," she answered.

"Ah, country girl!" he said. "That's because we are in a room, and the door is shut."

"A room? On the roof?"

"It was my idea," he said smugly as he lifted a wooden latch, opening a heavy door into the winter sunlight. He took her hand and led her out onto the rooftop.

Rahab squinted her eyes against the stabbing brightness of the day, and the priest laughed.

"Look around you, child! The world is at your feet—below you, within the city's walls, Jericho. To the east, beneath the tree tops, is the Jordan River, the mighty Jordan. And up there, in those hills beyond, are the nations of the Amorites."

Rahab's eyes had adjusted to the light now, and she gazed with fascination as he pointed dramatically toward the east. She caught her breath.

"Shanar! This is magnificent! I never dreamed that the view from the city walls could be so wonderful. It's like standing on the mountaintops near my father's farm."

"These walls are our protection, Rahab. Out there, in the hills across the Jordan, the Habiru prowl."

He paused, and his eyes narrowed. "They attacked us once, a long time ago—maybe thirty years. I was a boy, but already I had gone away to school at the temple in Karnack to learn the mysteries of the gods. I heard about the battle, even there."

"What happened?" Rahab asked.

"Our people routed them. They fled like farmers chased by bees!" His laugh was deep and gentle, intimate. His arm encircled Rahab's shoulders tenderly, like a friend and protector.

"Do you think they will come back—the Habiru?" she asked.

"Some day they will return. After all, we have riches here—and water. One day they will make another attempt. We must be ready."

"Are we in danger, then?"

He chuckled. "No, not really. The Habiru are simple wanderers. They have no chariots, no iron, little bronze—and certainly no skills in the arts of war. They are shepherds, but there are many of them." He patted her shoulder gently. "We are safe here. These walls protect us against their numbers."

"But do you think they will attack?" she asked again.

He turned shortly and pulled her toward the stairs.

"Fear not, little raven. Your nest here is secure. I promise it. Come, let me show you!"

They entered the small structure on the rooftop that protected the stairwell, but this time he left the door open, and daylight preceded them down the stairs. The stairway divided the space on the next level, creating a bedroom to the left and a sitting room to the right. The sitting room was in the corner of the Jericho rampart itself, and, being high, it had a large window that looked to the east, toward the Jordan River. Inside wooden panels closed the window securely against bad weather, leaving the room dark, even at midday. Shanar unlatched the panels and pulled them open to let the midwinter sun warm the wide wooden planks of the floor.

"These were my mother's rooms; they are the most pleasant in the house. I think you will want them to be your own. Below us, as you will see, there are two more rooms, which may be used for sleeping, and on the street level, below them, is a large room for entertaining, a cooking area, and a room for a servant. The storage room beneath that is carved into the bedrock itself. It is always cool there, and food does not spoil."

They reclined on the low couch which had been his mother's bed, and the sun was low before they descended the stairway again.

In the days that followed, Rahab was alone in the house. Except for the stairway, the house was perfect. She found herself too often peering into the stairwell, struggling with the feeling that its darkness evoked in her. The stairway was dark all the time. It was eerie. It was evil. And she determined that it must be changed, whitewashed perhaps, lamps added.

In her mind's eye she could see the house as she would change it. It had been left just as Shanar's mother had lived in it: her furniture, her dishes, her tapestries, and her carpets. Rahab thought of many things she could change, though it was obvious that Shanar's mother had been a woman of expensive tastes. Shanar had brought many of the furnishings to his mother from his travels. There were carvings from Egypt, jewelry from Ur, wall hangings from Babylon, bronze lamps from Byblos. Everywhere she looked, she was surrounded by beautiful and expensive things, but none of them were hers. She felt she lived in the shadow of the other woman.

For two days, she cleaned. The dust and mustiness of the closed house were vanquished. Each evening, Shanar came to check on her progress. He refilled the storeroom, and they made plans for the future.

"Your main responsibility is to be my hostess—and to please the king. When I wish you to entertain, I will always give you advance notice. Other than that, you may entertain whom you wish—and such gifts as you receive will be your own. I shall expect an accounting only of that which I provide."

"It shall be as you say, my lord."

He smiled at her fondly, but his voice was flat: "Remember this, Rahab. Always, your first loyalty must be to me. You will tell others nothing, but you will tell me all. You must have no secrets from me! Remember that. It is your bargain, and you will not regret it!"

Rahab was thrilled. This was the best of all worlds. She had freedom, she had the protection of the most elegant and powerful man in Jericho, she had a fine house, and she would be rich! Nothing from her childhood dreams compared with this! Her voice was warm and her laugh genuine as she responded to the bargain: "So be it, my lord. I will not fail you!"

24

The next morning Rahab went out into the marketplace alone, carrying with her the money that Shanarbaal had given her when he first showed her the house. Rahab remembered that first evening with great pleasure. He had pressed the gold coins into her palm as he departed.

"I am your first patron," he had said. "And your most important. Remember that, and enjoy the fruit of your labor."

This morning, Rahab thought, *I shall buy something new for my house, something beautiful. Shanar will come tonight, and he will be pleased. He will admire me above all the other women he has known.* She laughed to herself, thinking that Shanar had surely known many, many women.

He will be so proud of me!

She spent the entire morning wandering amongst the twisting streets of the marketplace near her house. The bazaar was a new experience for Rahab, and she was fascinated by the smells, the sounds, the textures of the things she discovered for sale in the many tiny shops. Men looked at her appreciatively. She wondered if they remembered her from the temple; she remembered some of them!

Everything looked wonderful to Rahab that morning. *I shall buy a lamp,* she thought. *I will hang it in the stairway, and it will never be dark again! Shanar will be pleased.*

The minute she saw the little jackal, she knew that this was the lamp she wanted. It was bright yellow ceramic, with rich purple spots. Its ears pointed straight upward, and its four straight legs were poised on a piece of rose quartz from the mountains. The jackal was designed so that his body held the oil, his tail curled over his back to make a handle, and the wick was in his mouth. The flame of the lamp would stick up like a tongue and would light up his eyes, which were holes in his head, from within. It was altogether precious, she thought.

Getting the jackal installed in the stairway was not an easy task. Rahab had no help, though Shanar had promised to send her a servant soon. She wanted to install the lamp between the second and third levels so that its light would extend to her personal rooms as well as to the public rooms below. Finding a niche in the darkened stairwell was especially difficult for Rahab because she was not tall. There was no niche within her reach at any point up and down the stairway. Finally, in desperation, she carried a stool to the landing between the second and third stories, and at last she found a niche well above her normal reach where the lamp would balance without falling. She carefully lighted the lamp and then carried the stool back to her room, enjoying the luxury of the lighted stairwell.

It was dusk when Shanar threw open the door from the street and shouted harshly: "Rahab! Where are you?"

Startled by the sharp tone of his voice, Rahab jumped from the bed where she had been awaiting his arrival and ran to the stairway.

"I am up here, my lord!" she called. "What is it?"

He took the steps fiercely, two at a time, not noticing that the stairwell was lighted, until his head crashed into the quartz base of the lamp, which protruded from the niche in the wall. The niche could not have been more strategically placed had Rahab intended to waylay the tall high priest.

Rahab had seen the impending collision, but there had been no time to warn the priest. His roar of pain and anger reverberated in the plastered stairwell.

The girl caught her breath and gasped, "Oh, no. My lord, are you all right?"

"No, I'm not all right, you fool!" he shrieked. "Are you trying to kill me?"

He wiped blood from his head and looked at his hand in the yellow light of the lamp.

Rahab had never heard such angry cursing before, nor had she ever been the object of Shanar's wrath. Certainly she had not intended to harm the priest! She fell to her knees and implored his forgiveness, but he was shouting too loudly to hear her.

"By the Baalim, woman! Is it not enough that I hear tales that you have been wandering the city alone—fair game for any jackal who would steal you and take you into slavery—but I come into my home and find that you have ambushed me with—with—" he reached up then and angrily took down the lamp from its niche. He was silent for a moment as he stared incredulously at the offending object. Rahab could not believe the expression of revulsion that crossed his face as he examined her precious yellow and purple jackal. He held the still-burning lamp at arm's length, and his lip curled derisively. His voice grew dry and flat as he finished the sentence, "...with this pile of dung!"

Bringing the lamp, which he handled as if it were a piece of carrion, to the third level, he grabbed Rahab by the shoulder with his free hand, which was still bloody, and flung her across the room and onto the bed.

"This!" He spat then, pointing at the lamp. "This is what you endangered your life—and my reputation!—for in your tramping about the city today? This?"

"But my lord, I—I meant no harm," she stammered, stunned by the intensity of his anger.

"You fool. You stupid little fool. Don't you know what might have happened? Are you so naive, even after a year in the temple, that you would go alone, unprotected, into the streets of this city?"

Rahab said nothing, but she realized, with sudden sickening, that he was right. She could easily have been carried away, murdered, raped, tortured, sold into slavery. She knew he spoke the truth.

The priest continued. "In this house, you are surrounded by the finest artworks that the world has to offer. I myself have chosen them with care and taste and have brought them from the far places of the world." He shook his head as if he could not believe what he saw in his hand: a yellow and purple ceramic jackal, its eyes glowing and its mouth gleaming with a yellow tongue of flame.

"Rahab," he said, "do you not see? This is not art! This is carrion. You have contaminated my house with carrion! This thing is trash! It is dung!"

He lifted the lamp, looked at it in disbelief one last time, and flung it, still lighted, out the open window. He turned back to the quaking girl who crouched speechless on his mother's bed.

"Did you spend money on that, Rahab? How much did you spend?"

"Oh, my lord. I was wrong, wasn't I? I only wanted to *please* you with the light. Oh. I will never...again...oh, please forgive me, Shanar."

He looked down at her and shook his head. "Ah, Rahab," he sighed. "There is so much for you to learn."

She held out her arms to him, then, imploring. "Teach me," she said.

For a time, the room was quiet. Then Shanarbaal began to chuckle. "A purple and yellow jackal," he murmured, and he shook his head again. "Rahab, how could you?" The chuckle grew into a deep-bellied laugh. "How could I ever explain it?—a purple and yellow ceramic jackal, with his eyes glowing! Even our king has better taste than that. No one would believe it! No one!" His laughter grew and grew, and he rolled off the bed and flailed his arms against the floor, roaring with mirth.

Rahab sat on the bed and watched quietly, determined in her own mind that no one, ever again, would question the quality of her taste.

25

Oparu was one of the first to seek Rahab out.

He came to her house for the first time early in the morning. His booming voice beckoned Rahab from outside her door. As soon as she saw his gigantic form, taller than her door frame, she remembered him from his many visits to the temple. She liked the giant, the captain of the king's chariots.

"Rahab! Open! I come to welcome you!" His voice would waken not only her, but the entire street, Rahab thought.

"Good morning, Captain. Good morning!" She smiled at the warrior. "Welcome to my home! You are out very early, my friend."

The captain blinked. "My friend" was an unexpectedly pleasant phrase to hear from the prostitute. Bawdy compliments about his size or sniveling servitude due his rank—to these he was accustomed. But this tiny woman—her nose reached his navel!—looked up at him with unwavering eyes and called him friend as though he were her countryman, and this in a country where the presence of the sons of Anat was barely endured. The giants, he knew, were tolerated only as a matter of military expediency.

Her open courtesy inspired him to the same, and he knelt so that his eyes met hers. "Greetings, Rahab. I, Oparu, captain of the king's chariots, greet you. I have just this night returned from the Great Sea, and to what do I return but to find my entire household taken sick with some pox. It is not a serious thing, but I do not wish to be stricken by it. This morning, at the temple, I spoke with the high priest, who has sent me to you with his highest regards. And so—I kneel before you a man without a home." Oparu spread his hands and smiled wistfully.

Rahab laughed, charmed by the huge man's boyishness.

"Come then. Enter, Oparu," she said, "and may the goddess bring you joy. My house shall be your home for as long as the need exists."

"Ah, then, home it is!" Oparu said crisply, lunging past Rahab into the public room. Majestically, his hand swept to his shoulder in the traditional warrior's gesture of salute. He turned, smiled at Rahab, and collapsed.

Rahab hurried to the warrior, discovering as his tunic fell open, the dark, crusty gash that spread across his left shoulder. He had been bleeding for some time, she realized, and she hastened for healing wine, oil, and bandages.

He was still lying on the floor—Rahab could neither rouse him nor move him alone—when Shanarbaal arrived with Alcion and a cook, a woman called Nantha.

"By the gods, woman," Shanar shouted as he saw the warrior prostrate on the floor. "What have you done? Did you hit him with a lamp, too?"

"No, my lord," Rahab answered. "He has been grievously injured. I am so glad you are here! He collapsed as soon as he arrived." As Shanar and Alcion knelt to examine the warrior, Rahab continued, "I have only just this moment finished washing the wound and applying wine, oil, and bandages."

"Let's get him to the couch, Alcion," the priest said crisply. "All I need is to have the captain of the king's chariots die in this house!"

With Alcion and the two women helping, it was still difficult to get the unconscious giant to the low couch in the alcove of the public room. He stirred as they moved him, and his eyes opened and rolled.

"He is heavier than a bull, master," Alcion commented dryly.

"Let us hope he has the strength of one. I don't want him to die here!"

The giant spoke then. "I'll not die," he mumbled.

"Thank the Baalim for that," Shanar responded. "Come on, let's get you over here to the couch, where you can rest."

As they eased the huge man onto the couch, he revived, much to Rahab's relief.

Shanar began to question the warrior impatiently, even as he unbandaged

113

the wound to examine it. "What happened to you, Oparu?" Without waiting for an answer he added, "This is a deep wound, but the girl has cleaned it well. I think you are right. You will live."

"Of course I will live," the giant snorted. "But the man who did that didn't."

"When did this happen?" the priest asked.

"Two days ago, I think," the warrior answered. "I was leaving Joppa, and I was ambushed. It was a man who had hated me for many years, a kinsman." He paused and smiled. "But he hates me no more, for he is dead. I slit his throat with his own knife!" Oparu's laughter rang through the house. "The knife is worth more than the man," he said, and he pulled the dirty blade from somewhere inside his tunic.

Rahab gasped.

"You have not seen a blade such as this one, I'll wager," Oparu said, holding it out for their inspection.

Rahab was fascinated. Never before had she seen the fruits of battle. The knife was dirty with dried blood. But even so, it gleamed strangely. Its blade was a dark blue-gray, a metal that even Shanarbaal had never seen before. Its handle was finely decorated bronze.

Shanar took the weapon from Oparu and carried it to the open door, where he could examine it in the daylight.

"Rahab," he commanded, "bring me oil and a clean cloth. This knife is filthy. Don't you clean your weapons when you use them, soldier?"

"Of course I do!" Oparu snapped. "But sometimes I have others do it for me."

Wiping the blade carefully, Shanar turned it back and forth in the sunlight. It appeared to be neither iron nor brass. He tested its edge against his thumb and studied it again.

"What metal is this?" he asked at last.

"Hmmph," Oparu snorted, "I thought you priests knew everything!"

"We know more than to get in the way of a blade we cannot identify," Shanar shot back.

"I can identify it," the warrior said defensively. "It is made by the sea people, my kinsmen, and it is stronger than iron. Few such knives exist in the world, and I have earned this one."

Shanar fingered the knife appreciatively and returned it to Oparu. "So you have," he said. "So you have."

As the giant drifted off to sleep, Shanarbaal and Rahab ascended the stairway.

That night before he left, Shanarbaal sat with Rahab on his mother's bed.

"I had no idea," he said, "when I sent you Oparu, that I was sending you an invalid. He had fallen asleep in the temple this morning and sending him here seemed like a convenient solution to the problem. But he is too much for you to care for alone."

The priest continued. "I am glad I brought you Alcion. He will be able to assist in many ways—not just with Oparu. You will find Alcion useful in matters of money, for he is trained as a scribe. He is a servant of many talents." He laughed teasingly. "He can even protect you should you venture into the marketplace again—and perhaps he will instruct you in matters of artistic taste as well. He is sophisticated."

"I am pleased that you have brought him to me," she answered.

"I hope you will have no trouble with this captain of the king's chariots," Shanar mused.

"It is all right, my lord. I don't mind caring for him."

"His visit could prove useful to us. Learn what you can from this man. I am intrigued by the blue metal of his knife blade. Besides," he said with a smile, "it will do us no harm to have earned the good graces of the captain of the king's chariots! He is a man who must be watched. Befriend him, Rahab."

The instant the horse saw his master, he whinnied and pranced in excitement.

"Oparu—he has missed you!" Rahab said.

"I have missed him, too," the giant responded. "I didn't enjoy lying up for a week when I should have been working this animal."

As they approached the pen containing Oparu's horse, the huge golden-red stallion reared and snorted, galloping from one corner of the enclosure to the other and pawing the ground in his impatience.

Oparu laughed deeply. "I like this beast," he said. "He is afraid of nothing. You should see him in battle. At the first blast of the trumpet, he snorts. He can smell the battle, and he is eager for it! He loves the smell of blood."

Rahab looked up at the snorting horse, who now came to stand quietly with his muzzle pressed into his master's palm.

"He is like you, Oparu! He is a giant!"

Oparu laughed again as the stallion nuzzled his cheek. "Indeed, I brought him with me from my home country. I cannot ride the grasshopper horses of the men of Jericho. This is a horse for a man, a horse for a son of Anat, like myself."

"He is so tall and so beautiful," Rahab replied. "I have never seen a naked horse before."

"Yes, he is beautiful. His hoofs are like the thunder, and his speed is like the lightning. Do you still think that you can fly with him, little raven? You are too small even to bridle him."

"I have a magic with animals, Oparu; he will let me fly with him. But as for bridling him, you will do that for me, will you not, Captain?"

"I will," the giant agreed with her. "Your magic is with more than the animals, little one."

"It is a steep trail to the high priest's villa, Rahab," Oparu warned as he finished bridling the horse. "You will have to hold on to me tightly if you do not want to land in the dirt. And it is a long way to the dirt from the back of Thunder."

"Oh, is that his name?" Rahab asked, rubbing the animal's huge nose. "Your nose is soft and rough at the same time, Thunder—and how good you smell! He does not smell like anything else."

"He smells like a horse," Oparu answered simply as he swung up onto the horse's back and pulled Rahab up behind him.

The horse was as fast as Oparu had promised. Rahab clung to Oparu and breathed deeply, joyously, as the horse loped farther and farther away from Jericho and toward the villa of the high priest. The wind stung her face, drying her lips and whipping her hair into tangles. Her body tingled with exhilaration and the smooth rhythm of his gallop.

"Eeee-eeee-eeeeeeeeee!" Her shriek was purest joy. "Oparu, this is wonderful." She was breathless. "I could do this forever."

His laugh blew past her and was gone on a wind that also carried his scent and the scent of the horse. She pressed closer into his back to savor his maleness—the warm, strong male fragrance of leather, sweat, and horse.

The new high priestess, Mari-Astarte, had clothed herself in the power of Amaranthe-Astarte, Shanarbaal thought as he admired his new high priestess. Mari had drawn the golden lot. Shanarbaal had seen to that. It had been almost a month since Amaranthe's body was carried to the high places, and the priest's power seemed absolute. Mari was his protégée, the queen and the king were pleased with his prophecies, the leader of the king's chariots was in his debt, and with Rahab he had established a second center of activities within the city.

The party this night was given to honor the new high priestess, but it was Rahab who was the center of attention. Rahab could sense that every man's eyes were drawn to her. She drank deeply of the admiration in their eyes and of the rich wine the komer poured so freely. She could not determine the source of her exhilaration, but she felt empowered with the excitement of the evening. The men at the party were friends from her temple days. Oparu could not keep his hands off her, but she would not stay at his side. She alighted first with one group and then with another, aware that the men's eyes followed her as she moved. She had never felt so beautiful nor so happy. Mari might be the high priestess, but Rahab was the mistress of her own life!

Returning to her wine cup at Oparu's side, Rahab heard again the details of Oparu's fight with his kinsman. This time the story was even bloodier than before. *This fight grows more fierce each time I hear the tale*, she thought.

"We struggled for hours. I began to think his strength was unconquerable, but then I tripped him and he fell. I quickly grabbed his magical knife and turned its spells against him." He laughed. "His blood squirted into the trees. I slashed his throat from ear to ear. When I had finished, I tossed his head into the ravine. He wasn't laughing then, I'll tell you!"

The men around him howled with laughter. Onuk the Fat slapped his thighs. "We are fortunate, indeed, to have you on our side, Oparu. You are a man who knows how to fight."

"It is true," one of Oparu's lieutenants agreed. "I remember once when Oparu led us on a raid against the Habiru. It was a small camp, but it was a pile of ashes when we were through."

"What sport it was!" another soldier added. "The women screamed, but we took what we wanted. Habiru women do not like giants!"

Oparu grunted. "They are grasshoppers. We did them a favor to kill them before the winter came."

Onuk laughed. "All women are grasshoppers when it comes to giants such as you."

"Canaanite women can handle giants," Rahab answered.

Onuk's eyes narrowed and he smiled evilly. "I'd enjoy seeing you handle a whole regiment, my precious."

"I am not your precious, Onuk," she said, but the politician only smiled more broadly and blinked his eyes at her.

Rahab turned and walked away, but she felt the politician's eyes upon her back.

On a low dais at the end of the banqueting room, Shanarbaal and his new high priestess shared a golden goblet of the rich, red wine.

"This is your night, Mari-Astarte," the priest said to her. But Mari's eyes narrowed as she watched Rahab leave yet another group of admiring men.

"Your little country pigeon seems to think it is her night. Since you've made her a nest in the city, she's putting on airs."

"Fear not, my lady of loves. She will be useful to us."

Mari's eyebrows arched. "Not if she takes all the patrons from the temple," the new priestess answered him. "And she looks as though she is trying to do just that."

Shanar laughed wickedly. "Are you afraid? Can you not train the maidens to attract the men to the temple?" He grinned conspiratorially. "After all, you are she who influences the goddess. It is you who brings fertility to the land. Rahab cannot make it rain."

"I can handle my responsibilities, Shanar. Never think that I cannot." Now it was her turn to laugh wickedly. "Amaranthe taught me well."

A group of men at the far end of the banquet hall began to applaud and yip. Rahab was dancing, swirling her skirts and tossing her hair seductively. Mari sipped her wine and looked disdainfully at the younger woman.

117

"It looks as if Rahab has learned her lessons, too, doesn't it?" she said dryly.

26

The horse was magnificent!

His slick, shiny coat shimmered like the walls of Jericho in the morning sunlight below, and the dappled gray circles on his flanks looked like the round river stones of the wadi when the rains came, turning the valley roadways into rivers. Oparu could not have given her a better gift! She named him Shimmerance. His eyes were brown and expressive, and every ripple of his sleek, round muscle, every twitch of his ear and toss of his long, flowing tail, every flare of his nostrils, even, echoed Rahab's rapture with the morning and the glorious excitement of her journey.

She was going home!

She was free of the temple now, had lived in her own home for six months. Her parents would expect her to return home after her temple year, but she was going to surprise them. How thrilled they would be to learn of her success in Jericho!

The beauty of the morning delighted Rahab. A soft mist arose from the morning dew, which would soon be burned away by the summer sun. The horse trotted, his feet seeming almost to dance above the wadi stones.

Overhead, two ravens circled, cawing harshly. A small rodent scurried into the tall grasses and bushes, frightened by the unaccustomed clatter of the horse's hoofs.

Rahab sat easily astride the horse, using her feet and legs to direct him as Oparu had shown her. When she had ridden donkeys as a child, she had puzzled over their stubborn natures. But this creature was a horse! He seemed to understand her every thought and to respond even before she gave the signal.

"What a wonderful creature you are, Shimmerance!" she said, reaching out to caress the sleek, arching neck and flowing mane. "You know it. You know that you are wonderful and beautiful! And you are right, of course." She laughed a laugh of pure pleasure.

Before she knew it, her father's tents came into view. He would be so proud of her! Even he would have never dreamed that she could have been this successful—so soon established in her own house, with her own eunuch and her own cook and the protection of the high priest of Jericho himself! This was far better than any marriage her father could arrange.

They would all be so pleased with her. She would be rich and powerful and beautiful. She laughed aloud. Already she rode her own horse, the beautiful Shimmerance! Life was so good. She had, indeed, mastered life!

It had been an ugly scene.

Riding back to Jericho slowly, unmindful of the horse beneath her, Rahab relived the angry words.

They had welcomed her at first with great joy. The younger children had clamored around her, covering her with shouts and hugs and squeals. Her mother had hung back a little, and her father had leaned on his shepherd's staff and smiled. Her brother, Micah, who was ten now, had bypassed Rahab and run to hold the horse. It had seemed a joyous homecoming as she played with her little sisters while her mother prepared the midday meal. Her father and brothers had hurried back to the field to finish their work so that the rest of the day could be devoted to her homecoming.

That was not how it had happened, however. The meal had started happily. The children chattered, and her parents complimented her on her appearance. But when she eagerly began to tell them of her successes, icy stares and a cold silence greeted her recital. She had only started to tell about her house and its art treasures when her father stopped eating and turned to her mother.

"Is this your daughter?" he asked.

"Oh, Bazarnan," her mother replied as tears filled her eyes and spilled down her cheeks, "I do not know."

Rahab looked from her mother to her father in astonishment. "I don't understand. What's wrong? I will be rich and powerful. What is the matter?"

Her father stood slowly and crossed his arms. "I have made arrangements for your marriage," he said solemnly.

"You have what?" Rahab was incredulous.

"I have made arrangements for your marriage, Rahab," her father repeated. "He is a rich man, a leader in the city. He has been widowed three times, it is true, but this is a good match, Rahab." He paused dramatically. "You will wed Onuk-a-Baal!"

Rahab shrieked. "Onuk! Onuk the Fat! Onuk, the fat pig of the universe!"

"It is a good match, Rahab," her mother answered softly, taken aback by Rahab's response.

Rahab paid her no attention. "You are crazy!" Rahab screamed. "I will not wed Onuk. You cannot make me marry him."

"The arrangements are made, Rahab," her father said. "You have no choice."

"I have made my choice!" Rahab shouted. "I am my own woman!"

"Then you are not my daughter," her father had said coldly. He turned and left the room, limping. Her mother's moans echoed in her ears, the sobs of a woman in mourning.

Rahab could not believe it had happened. Where had she gone wrong? Her father had disowned her—for Onuk the Fat! She thought bitterly that there was more to mastering life than she had guessed, but still, she resolved, master it she would. She would show them! She would be rich and powerful!

The horse began to gallop, jolting Rahab from her reverie.

"We will show them, Shimmerance," she said, patting his neck. "We'll show them. The world will know Rahab, woman of Jericho!"

In only a few days, Onuk sought her out. Rahab was not surprised when the fat politican appeared at her door. She greeted him coldly in the words of their religion: "May the goddess grant you joy."

"May *you* grant me joy, my little precious," he responded, entering.

"I am busy, Onuk. What is it you want?" she answered.

"I have only come to pay a friendly call. All the men in the city come to visit you. I would also enjoy your pleasures."

"I have other pressing business today, Onuk. I am not receiving guests."

The man snickered. "Your father is—or he was, when I saw him last."

She whirled to face him then. "You have seen my father?" she snapped. "When?"

"Yesterday," he answered casually. "I think that we must talk, Rahab. A bargain is a bargain."

Her answer was direct. "I have made no bargains, Onuk!"

"I think you had best hear me out, Rahab. Your father is a very angry man—and he is not well."

"What do you mean—'he is not well'?"

"You had better hear me out, Rahab," the politician repeated.

"I told you I'm busy. If you wish to talk with me, you must come to the roof, for that is where I am working."

She turned and started up the stairs, with the fat man behind her. His girth barely permitted him access up the narrow stairway, and she could hear him breathing heavily behind her from the exertion of climbing the stairs. *If he wants this talk, he will have to earn it,* she thought with pleasure. As she passed the second level, where Alcion was working on the books, she said with double meaning, "Alcion, I will be on the roof."

"I will be near," he answered, instantly assessing her situation.

"All right, Onuk," Rahab said, sitting on her knees and beginning to pound stems of the flax she had stacked on the roof. "What is it you wish to discuss? And what did you mean—my father is not well?"

"You ask too many questions at once, my precious," the fat man said, still panting from the exertion of climbing the stairs. "As you well know, your father has arranged a bargain with me."

"As you well know, I have made no bargain," she answered coldly.

"You have not heard my offer, Rahab."

"You have nothing to offer me," she answered, not looking at him.

He rose then and walked to the edge of the roof, looking toward the city and the temple. He gestured expansively across the city.

"I am the richest man in Jericho," he said. "Neither the high priest nor the king can claim the fortunes that I possess. I can give you jewels, gold, clothes, houses, horses—I can give you anything that you desire in the city."

Then he turned and gestured to include the entire Jordan Valley outside the walls. "My lands extend as far as you can see and farther. I own slaves and herds and mines. They can all be yours, Rahab."

"And how do your previous wives enjoy them?" Her answer was quick and coldly sarcastic.

The politican was not deterred. He smiled and continued: "True power comes from these riches, Rahab. The high priest thinks he controls the gods and the king." He laughed softly. "But I control *all* of them. Do you want power, Rahab? Do you want respect? My gold can buy things for you. Do not fool yourself that Shanarbaal has power. He comes to me; I am his source."

"I am my own source, Onuk," she answered. "I have experienced power over men and kings. Do I not know that a man's wife is his slave? Neither you nor any other man will enslave me, Onuk. No. No, thank you!"

"It is very well for you to say these things, my precious. You are young and healthy," he began to whine, "but I am an old man. I am your father's age— you saw me climb those stairs. My heart will not last many more years. I know weakness, and I recognize a man at death's door when I see him. If your father continues the hard physical labor of the farm to feed your army of brothers and sisters, his days are truly numbered."

"What are you trying to tell me about my father? What is wrong with him?" Rahab snapped the words.

"Your father is a desperately sick man now. He will not last long. Do you not care that he suffers and that your family lives in poverty? Your father needs the comforts that wealth can bring—and he needs them now. You cannot earn enough to save your family from slavery when he dies. I can give you that, Rahab. I can give you back your family."

"You lie!" She shouted. "Get out of here! I will not marry you! I do not sleep with swine!"

He rose slowly. His face was a mask of hatred.

121

"The time will come, little precious one, when you will regret those words. You will grovel to me, and I will spit on you!"

Rahab pounded the flax stems as if the fat man were not there. Only after he slammed the wooden door to the roof and departed from her house did she sink to the floor, bury her head in her hands, and sob. She thought of her father's shepherd's staff, his ashen color, and his faltering step. *Something is wrong with him,* she thought, *but he cannot be dying. Surely my mother would let me know if it was serious.* If Rahab had believed in the gods, she would have prayed to them. Instead, she resolved that she would achieve wealth in her own right—soon!

"I won't sleep with swine," Rahab said emphatically. "Even in the temple I managed to avoid it. Certainly here in my own house, I can choose those with whom I will share my bed. I have chosen so far; I shall continue to choose!"

Alcion and Nantha sat with her around the low table as they ate their evening meal, discussing the day's events. Alcion said, "Onuk left, true enough, but he may prove to be a problem. Shanar does look to him for advice, and the priest will not want to offend his fat friend. You will need to tell Shanar what has happened between you and Onuk, but even that will not prevent your having to endure his company again if Shanar desires it."

"I am not Shanar's slave, Alcion," Rahab responded sharply.

"No," Nantha chuckled, "but you live in his house, and you do his bidding. As the reputation of your hospitality grows, you will have to deal with many men who do not please you."

Rahab looked at Nantha as if she wanted to hit her.

"But think, Rahab," Alcion murmured. "Surely you have learned enough in the temple to be able to deal with a man who likes his wine as much as Onuk does. It takes but a moment to spice a cup. Any of us here can prepare a sleeping draught which will deal with Onuk efficiently. If he comes to sleep here, that is exactly what he will do. A confrontation is not always the answer."

Rahab laughed delightedly. "Alcion, that's perfect. That is exactly what we will do. Let Onuk come. Let him pay dearly, and let him enjoy his sleep. Shanar told me you were wise. I see now that he was right." She paused and added hopefully, "He even told me that you could instruct me in matters of artistic taste."

"I have been told that I have an artist's eye," the eunuch answered wryly. "When I was younger, I was the servant of many kings, and I have lived with the art of many lands."

"Where have you lived?" Nantha asked.

Alcion laughed with something less than humor. "Where have I not lived?" he answered. "I was born in Cnossus on the Isle of Crete, but the sea people captured me and sold me to the Egyptians. I lived in the pharaoh's palace at Karnak. Then I was sold to the king at Gaza, back on the Great Sea. Then I went to the king at Megiddo and from there to Hazor; then I stayed for a long time in Damascus. Next I was sold all the way to Babylon and after that to Ur. Shanarbaal bought me there from the high priest. Believe me, Rahab, if you can survive in Jericho, you can survive anywhere!"

Both women laughed delightedly at this last comment. Alcion smirked and bowed in an exaggerated fashion. "In all of those places, ladies, never have I had a more appreciative audience."

Nantha shook her head in amazement. "You must have been a very important man," she said.

"No," he replied, "I was just a pretty slave boy, but I watched and I learned."

The next day, Rahab again sought treasures in the marketplace. This time she took Alcion with her for protection and also to teach her his worldly wisdom and his good taste.

"Alcion," she said to him, "I am a country girl; I have learned the ways of the temple, but still I know nothing of how to choose the things that will please a city man. My lord, the high priest, respects your taste. I want to learn from you as you have learned in all the places you talked about last night. Can you teach me to choose things that will please a man of culture, a man like Shanarbaal?"

"That is quite a request, Rahab, and it may take time, but since my time is yours to command, I'll be happy to teach you."

As they visited the various shops within the marketplace, Alcion became Rahab's tutor. He found her an apt pupil. He explained to her how to choose colors and textures that would evoke the responses she wanted from her patrons. He pointed out to her the differences between finely wrought copper from Egypt and the more crudely made local work. In every shop there was something to be learned. Here he explained why one piece of linen might be expected to hold its color better than a second piece; there he explained why the lines of one design were more pleasing to the eye than the lines of another.

Finally they went into the lamp shop. There, sitting just as she remembered, was another yellow and purple jackal lamp. "Alcion," she called his attention to the lamp, "this piece is really terrible, isn't it?"

He snickered. "You are learning, Rahab. It's so unbelievably bad that to call it terrible is really gracious."

"I thought so," she said.

As the shopkeeper came toward them wearing a wide smile of recognition, she hastened Alcion into the next shop.

Rahab sat on the floor in the center of her public room. She was surrounded by her purchases of the day but all her concentration centered upon the fabric she had spread before her. She had bought lengths of the sheerest Egyptian linen in shades of red, pink, and purple. It had been very expensive. She cut the material in great circles, and she layered them to create a full flowing skirt whose colors changed as she moved. This skirt she attached to a shining brass girdle. When this costume was complete, she called Alcion to test its effect.

"Even Nefertiti, the great queen of Egypt, could have worn nothing finer," he assured her enthusiastically. He assured her further that as she danced for her patrons, the costume would be seen not only as stunning, but also as tasteful.

"Oh, Alcion," Rahab sighed, "this has been such a good day. You will surely help me to become the richest woman in Jericho."

"Oh, so that is your goal? For that you could have married Onuk."

Rahab turned up her lip. "His wives don't live to enjoy his riches."

"You have to be strong to live, Rahab."

"I intend to be," she shot back. "That's why I didn't marry Onuk. I want to become wealthy in my own right. You're good with money, Alcion. What do you suggest?"

Alcion considered her question for a moment and then answered decisively, "Yes, there are some changes you could make in the way you run your business. First, I think, you must set the price of your trade. Do not sell yourself cheaply, Rahab. The rich men of Jericho can afford to pay for their pleasures. Poor men will soon learn to stay away."

"That sounds reasonable," she said. "I often wondered why they didn't do that at the temple. Some men never give more than a copper." She laughed and added emphatically: "I will accept no more coppers."

"One thing which the temple does have, however, is many girls," Alcion said thoughtfully. "You could double or triple your income very easily that way."

"Yes, that is true, and the temple has the Komer, too. They earn money as well." As Rahab said this, Alcion's face hardened.

"Fortunately, Shanarbaal valued my talents as a scribe highly, allowing me to avoid that particular service in the Jericho temple," he responded quickly. "It is a service that has treated me cruelly in the past, and I have no wish to resume it."

This was a bold thing for a slave to say, but Rahab understood. So far, she had not sold Alcion's services to any of her customers. There was no need to start now.

"I value your abilities, too, Alcion. I think that in my house I shall have only girls."

The tense lines around Alcion's mouth relaxed. Rahab liked the eunuch very much; she did not want him to be uncomfortable in her service.

"How else can we do things differently from the temple to make money?" she asked him.

Alcion spread his hands and smiled. "Serve meals," he said. "Nantha is an excellent cook. Men would come to your house for that alone, although they would certainly stay for the dance." He grinned.

"Above all, save your money," he continued. "Buy only things that will last or that will return a profit. I have noticed your interest in the flax. Buy a field, and weave. There is always a market for linen. In fact"—his eyes brightened with his own idea—"you can learn to create art yourself. Tapestries would be a good choice. If you would weave beautiful tapestries, you would make a fine profit on each one." He laughed in excitement at his ideas. "Perhaps you *can* become the richest woman in Jericho, Rahab."

To reward the scribe for this last comment, Rahab swirled her skirts, grabbed the tambourine she had bought in the marketplace, and danced around the room.

"Aha, entertaining already, and very nicely, I see." The booming voice of the high priest stopped her in midstep. The priest looked appreciatively at Rahab's outfit.

"Do you like it?" Rahab said, holding out her skirts.

The high priest nodded, answering, "The colors are well chosen. This is much better than purple-spotted jackals."

"You are pleased then, my lord?" Rahab turned so that he might see her from all angles. "I am glad. Alcion has been instructing me in color and design today."

"I am glad to see that you are serious about your work here," the priest responded, smiling. "You will have an excellent opportunity to mingle with your potential patrons tomorrow. The entire community will be at the temple for the cornerstone ceremony."

"What is that, my lord? I have not been instructed on a cornerstone ceremony."

"It occurs only once in seven years," he answered. "It is the rededication of the temple."

"Oh, yes," Rahab answered enthusiastically, "I can see why that would be a truly important event."

"It is the most majestic ceremony of our religion. Everyone attends."

Rahab was an eager listener. The ways of city life fascinated her. No two days seemed the same.

"We have already set up the altars in the temple courtyard," Shanar told her, "and the rams will be brought in at sunrise, together with the bull. Of course, you know that we have lost two of the babies that the goddess normally provides—but, no matter, we'll get by without them. If the goddess wanted a baby for the winter solstice, who are we—mere mortals—to disagree?"

Suddenly Rahab felt a stabbing pain rip through her stomach, and she was very quiet. The priest continued: "It was a shame, however, that Migdallah's child did not survive its birthing. That one was of no use whatever to the goddess. The other two girls—you will remember Shamu and Zorah—they have carried theirs and suffered no mishaps in delivery. The goddess will be pleased with these two sacrifices."

125

The priest rose to leave.

"I will send the litter for you an hour before the sun rises. You will not want to miss my ceremonial magic. If all goes as I plan, it is quite possible that some of the citizens of Jericho will offer their own sacrifices. There are many babies in Jericho this season; the goddess will be pleased. I will see you at sunrise."

The priest left quickly, assuming Rahab's answer. After he had gone, Rahab turned, clutching her stomach, and struggled up the dark stairway, stumbling as the hems of her skirts caught beneath her sandals.

"Bishna! Bishna!" she sobbed loudly. "So that was what they wanted! They wanted him for a sacrifice all along!"

As she reached the third landing and her own rooms, all her anger and despair welled up into a wordless shriek that might have been heard even at the temple.

She jerked the brilliant red skirt off and flung it into a heap in the corner, and then she threw herself across the bed. Dry, racking sobs shook her body, and she whispered the words "my baby, my baby" again and again.

Alcion awoke. Hours had passed since his mistress had run screaming to her chambers. Now the house was silent, dark. He hoped Rahab was resting. He had not felt it proper to intrude upon her earlier distress, yet he was concerned. Without lighting a lamp, he carefully ascended to the third level. Her window was open, and the room was chilled. He could make out the form of her body across the bed—she was shaking. He watched for a moment, uncertain what to do. Then he heard her whisper, "My baby, my baby!"

He was puzzled. Rahab had borne no child. "Are you all right, my lady?" he asked softly, touching her shoulder.

Her reaction was violent. She shrieked. "I cannot go, Alcion! He must not make me go! I cannot go. It is horrible!"

He comforted her as a mother comforts a crying child.

"Yes, my lady. Many things in life are horrible—but life does go on! Calm yourself. When the litter arrives, I will send it away. I will say that you are ill."

She shuddered in his arms. "Yes," she said finally, "I am ill, Alcion. I am sick of needless death."

27

As the days following the cornerstone ceremony passed, Rahab found solace in her work. She concentrated upon organizing her profit-making ventures and could almost ignore the occasional stabs of pain in her stomach and the odd, half-remembered phrase, "the goddess within."

When she was busy, there was no time for thinking: no time for grief, no time for despair. As the second year in her house passed, Rahab made herself always busy. In the early mornings, Alcion would accompany her to the stables outside the city walls where the horse Shimmerance waited, and she would ride the horse up into the wilderness for a little way, alone, while Alcion waited below. Rahab enjoyed these times.

She enjoyed her work as well. She set a high price on herself, as Alcion had suggested, and her jar of gold and silver shekels quickly filled. Of every ten shekels that she received, she set aside one for her family. Periodically, she sent Alcion to them with the money—but never did she receive a response.

Shanarbaal had always been generous in his provisions for her household, but now she was supporting her own house. He was pleased when she suggested that she undertake additional enterprises. She entertained his guests with excellent food prepared by Nantha; Alcion had been right about the cook's talents!

Even more entertaining for the men who visited the house of Rahab, however, were the dances. Her veil dances had become famous in the community. Rahab had begun with the dances she learned in the temple, but she soon added her own rhythms and movements until the dances scarcely resembled the formal recounting of the religious myths that went along with temple ritual. Rahab's dances were exciting; it seemed that she moved with the sensuous rhythms of the earth itself. Sometimes she used the tambourine, while at other times her only accompaniment was the tinkling of her jewelry and the tiny brass zills which she attached to the thumb and middle finger of each hand.

Rahab was never too busy to entertain. And after entertaining, she worked by lamplight with the flax she had purchased with her first earnings. She pounded on the heavy stalks to free the inner threads that would be woven into fabric. As she worked, her mind centered on the rhythm of the pounding, the pounding of the bricks against the stalks of flax. She felt nothing except the pounding, the exertion, and when she was too tired to lift the brick another time and her eyes were closing in spite of her will, she would extinguish her lamp and, taking her cloak, feel her way from the roof down one level of the darkened stairs and collapse into a dreamless heap.

As the seasons passed, she transformed the sitting room on the third level into a work room. She had learned the art of spinning and weaving at her mother's side. It brought her pleasure, for it consumed her. From a heavy beam across the ceiling of the room, she hung threads of wool weighted with stones, and she wove linen through the wool, as was the Canaanite custom, to create a simple fabric of sufficient weight to hang smoothly on a wall or to serve as a sitting rug.

"In Egypt," Alcion told her once, "the women of the harem weave fine linen—so white and so thin that you can see through it, with a chevron pattern,"—which he demonstrated by drawing the interlocking V's with charcoal—"they can even make it into pleating."

"I'll not try anything so fine as that!" she assured the scribe. "Rather, I think I would prefer to work designs over the completed fabric, to make pictures—beautiful scenes that could take the place of windows."

She occupied her mind in creating those designs, and with an ivory awl, given her by a patron from the east, she created beautiful, colorful tapestries of the birds and flowers and animals of her childhood.

But Rahab's sewing never kept her from the business of entertaining her guests. Her visitors expressed their appreciation in gifts as well as payment. She began to collect jewels and golden ornaments. One elderly statesman, sensing death at his door and having no family, gave her a vineyard. With her earnings from the first year, she purchased a field. Alcion was pleased. So was Shanarbaal.

"Astarte smiles on you, little raven," he said with approval one day as he watched her count the gold spilled across her bed's new coverlet, "in spite of the fact that you shun her temple services."

"My lord, when I am with the high priest, my union with the gods is complete," she responded, laughing. "I need no gods but you."

"How old are you now, Rahab? Barely sixteen? Yet you have the power to make me feel like a god. No other woman has done that! I think your magic is with men."

"It is you who taught me magic, Shanar," she answered. "You are the greatest magician the Jericho temple has ever known!"

"And you, my lady, are the greatest in your own way. I would like for you, tomorrow evening, to entertain Oparu for me. Use your own special magic."

"Entertaining Oparu will be a pleasure, my lord. It always is!"

The priest laughed. "I think the secret of your magic is your pleasure in your work, Rahab."

"I do what I want to do, my lord. It pleases me to serve you well, and it pleases me to make a profit."

She scooped her coins up, dropped them into the jar, and resumed her seat, cross-legged on the bed. Her fingers idly fondled the wool and linen coverlet. She had woven and embroidered bright flowers and black ravens to create the design, and from the moment she covered the bed, it became, in her own mind, her bed rather than his mother's.

Shanar sipped his wine and resumed his conversation. "I have heard tidings that give me cause for concern about Oparu," Shanar said. "I need to know whether the rumors that I hear are true. You can easily get Oparu to talk."

"What is it that you have heard, my lord?" Rahab was instantly serious.

"I have heard that Oparu is saying great evil about me, trying to undermine my influence with the king," he answered. "At the same time, I know that rumors are not to be trusted—they must be tested!"

"I will test this rumor for you, my lord. It will be a pleasure," she answered with a smile.

On the next evening, as Shanarbaal leaned deeply into the pillows at his back and stretched his legs out before him, he thought with great satisfaction that moving Rahab into this house had been wiser than he had known. Little had he imagined on that first morning when he had decided to move her from the temple that she would prove to be such a brilliant student of political magic. *She is growing up,* he thought. He watched as Rahab laughingly poured more wine into the cup of the Egyptian tax collector, Jamat. Beside Jamat sat Mohan—another tax collector and an even more unscrupulous one—admiring Rahab with undisguised lechery. Rahab kept the wine flowing and the men talking. She kept them entertained but not too entertained to talk, and it was to their conversation that Shanar listened with what appeared to be casual, half-bored interest. In truth, he did not miss one word or one innuendo in the conversation.

"Our fat little king is more than a little displeased," Jamat chuckled. "With every correspondence the pharaoh demands higher tribute, and worse yet—in our king's eyes—he demands more and more of it in gold and silver. Little good it does to collect sheep's wool from the farmers when every season the pharaoh says, 'Send more gold.' "

"Soon even men like Onuk will feel the sting of this scorpion's tail," Mohan agreed. "You cannot squeeze gold out of a fat pig's tail, but oh, how you can hear him squeal. Farmers may give us goat cheese and barley seed, but it is rich men like Onuk who have the hordes of gold that pharaoh demands."

Jamut drank deeply and smiled. "But Onuk alone will not bear the brunt of this taxation; he'll see to that."

Mohan smiled, too, and directed his attention to Shanarbaal, who appeared to be drifting into sleep. "The temple will undoubtedly be called upon to support the powers of its god and its king."

Shanarbaal opened heavy eyelids and apparently tried to focus on the men who spoke so freely to him. "What do you mean?" he asked.

"You may entertain us in style now, Shanar, but before long, the pharaoh will see more of the Kedeshoth earnings than you do. The king is out to find gold wherever it may be had, and he will not be unwilling to claim his rights as king-god to do it." Jamat did not seem to be at all distressed over the information he shared. "Our little king will rob the goddess herself before he will dip into his own treasury!"

Mohan laughed in comfortable agreement. "Your new high priestess may be selling her armor if the pharaoh does not deal more gently with Jericho. Egypt wants no Canaanite slaves, she wants no flax, and she wants no barley. She wants gold, and our sniveling king proclaims himself Egypt's dog and licks her feet. He will give her anyone's gold—anyone's, that is, besides his own."

Shanarbaal frowned. The situation was worse than he had anticipated. He closed his eyes, and he felt the anger rise within him. Already the temple gave one-fourth of all its profits to the king. There were other ways for the king to acquire the needed tribute, and well the king knew it. He was simply, without question, too lazy to bother. Rich men should have their lands reassessed. The goods the king collected could be resold at a profit. The tax collectors themselves could be made to give a stricter accounting of their monies—but no, those methods would require the king to think, to plan, to organize. How much simpler it was for him to steal from the temple. Shanarbaal opened his mouth and pretended to snore. The tax collectors looked at him derisively.

"It appears that the high priest is fascinated by our conversation," Jamat said laughing.

"You would think that the high priest of Baal could handle wine better than that," Mohan added thoughtfully.

Rahab pressed herself close to the saggy publican. She giggled and spoke conspiratorially. "My lord the high priest is a man of many talents, but he is also a man who enjoys mixing in his wine the special potions which he brings from the temple." She motioned to the sleeping priest. "He does this on many nights. He falls asleep across my couch, and I, alas—" she looked at the men from beneath her lashes—"must sleep alone."

The two men howled with laughter. The thought that Rahab, woman of the most popular house in Jericho, might ever sleep alone was extremely amusing to them. A loud banging on the door interrupted their merriment. The men looked at one another as if the knock confirmed their thoughts. The house of Rahab was never empty.

Rahab hurried to the door. It was, as she had expected it to be, Oparu. She stepped quickly outside to speak with him. "Oparu, I am glad you are here. You will not believe what Shanar has done to me. He told me that he had invited you here, but then he brought—you will not believe this!—he brought Mohan and Jamat here. He knows that I hate them—sickening little leeches— yet he brought them both here. Now he has passed out on the couch leaving me to deal with them. Will you help me get rid of them?"

Oparu laughed softly. Rahab was such a sport! Something exciting always happened when he was with her. "I'll throw them out for you," he answered.

"Oh, no, Oparu, that will never do. If you throw them out, they will come back tomorrow, and they will have doubled my taxes."

"Then what should I do?" the giant asked, bewildered.

"Let's scare them away," Rahab said. "If you bellow and scream, they will think that they are in danger, and they will leave and be glad to get away." Rahab giggled. "Pretend that you are angry with me. Pretend that you think I stole your purse. You can even yell at them a bit. They'll leave, and then we'll have the evening to ourselves."

The giant nodded. This was exactly the kind of fun he liked.

"Start yelling now, before we go into the house," Rahab suggested. "Oh, and pretend you are drunk. That should really scare them!"

The giant snickered for a moment and then took a deep breath.

"Don't lie to me, you little grasshopper," he roared. Rahab stepped back at the volume of it. Oparu grabbed her shoulders and winked. "I know your kind!" He kicked the door open and threw Rahab into the room, following her in and shouting. "You thought you'd get away with it, did you?" The two men sitting on Rahab's floor looked at each other anxiously.

"No one treats the captain of the king's chariots this way," Oparu shouted, seeming to stumble over a cushion on the floor. He kicked it with all his might. "Fools!" he screamed. Jars in the corner trembled at the reverberation. "Fools who think they can deceive Oparu die! Would you steal my purse, you little mouse? You steal your funeral monies!"

On the couch, Shanar still appeared to sleep.

Rahab crawled forward from the spot where she had landed on the floor. "Oh, my lord," she begged. "It was an accident. Your purse fell from your cloak when you were here last."

"Lies!" the giant started for her, but then seemed to notice the men trembling on the floor. "And who are you?" The two men quaked before him. He was obviously too drunk to recognize them.

"Jamat," the first man whispered.

"And Mohan, your friends, my lord!"

"Friends! By the canker on my dead grandmother's bones! I know you. You are the Egyptian leeches who put this harlot up to this! You told her to steal my gold for your cursed pharaoh!"

"Oh, no, my lord, we know nothing of the matter," Jamat gasped. Mohan looked as if his heart would kill him if the giant did not.

"You put her up to this!" The giant hovered over them menacingly.

"No, my lord, truly, we only came here with the high priest!"

"The high priest! That dog! If you are his friends, then I must surely kill you."

"No, no, my lord," Mohan had paled to the color of ash. "Kill him, my lord Oparu. See, he is here!" The sniveling publican pointed to the sleeping priest.

"I will not remain in the same house with that dog!" Oparu shouted. "If you are his friends, then you had better take him with you when you go." The drunken giant seemed to have forgotten about killing them. "You are going, are you not?"

"Oh, yes, my lord, we were just leaving. We're going right now!" Jamat said. Both men leaped for the door.

"Wait!" the giant roared. The men froze.

"Take this sleeping dog with you."

Never before had Rahab seen two rabbits carry a fox. She saw it now.

Oparu fingered the fine work of the woolen coverlet, and he began to laugh again. He had, in fact, not stopped laughing since the tax collectors had left, struggling beneath the burden of Shanarbaal's inert form.

"And the priest slept through it all!" he said again in amazement.

Rahab laughed, enjoying his astonishment. "I told you, he passed out. He brings drugs from the temple and puts them in his own wine. He seems to enjoy oblivion." Then Rahab's face sobered; her eyebrows appeared to knit together in an angry line. "I cannot believe he brought those little spiders into my house, Oparu. I hate tax collectors, and he knows it."

Oparu nodded his head. "Everyone hates tax collectors, Rahab. If they only went where they were liked, they would never go anywhere."

"That would be fine with me!" the girl snapped. "Every day Shanarbaal does something else to make me hate him. His visits are worthless. He sleeps on my couch more often than he sleeps in my bed. Now he brings vermin into my house. I have my standards, Oparu," she turned to the giant, running her fingers over his arm, "and I have my favorites."

"The high priest is not so wise as he thinks he is," the giant said, accepting her compliment as a matter of course. "He wastes his evenings on wine and herbs when there are finer things in life." He pulled Rahab close against his tremendous shoulder. "So your love for the high priest fades, does it, little one?"

"Bah," Rahab responded. "The high priest gives me money as all men do. It is convenient to know rich men; it is better to know strong men." She smiled up at Oparu. As he stroked her face, she reached up to caress his huge hand. "You have such strong hands, Oparu," she said.

"To be a giant is a strange thing, Rahab. Men mock you, but they fear you as well. My fist made two of any average man's. And my hand is three, perhaps four, times the size of yours. But then, you are a tiny woman."

"But a woman, nonetheless, my lord."

"A very fine woman. The high priest does not appreciate your worth. He is a fool."

"Is he, my lord?" the question was simple, direct.

"Indeed, he is a much bigger fool than he knows. He thinks he knows all there is to know of love and of war, but he knows nothing." He stroked her face again. "He is like a child building walls in the dirt and fighting imaginary wars, but he is playing with the destiny of Jericho."

"I do not understand, Captain; such matters are beyond me."

"Perhaps, but they are not beyond me, little one. The king knows I am right; even so, he listens when Shanarbaal spouts his nonsense about building walls. Why will not priests be priests and let soldiers be soldiers? But no, your wonderful Shanarbaal—"

"He is not my 'wonderful' anything, Oparu."

The giant shrugged. "He tells the king we do not need chariots. He tells the king that only the walls of Jericho can save the city from these prowlers, the Habiru. He is wrong, of course, but if he convinces the king, the entire city may pay for his arrogance."

"Is there a better way to protect the city?" Rahab asked.

"Of course there is a better way! Shanarbaal thinks that because the walls have stood for six thousand years, they will stand six thousand more. Perhaps he thinks he can stand atop the wall and mutter incantations and send the Habiru running back to Egypt. He is a fool."

"He is said to be a wise man by the people of Jericho," Rahab said. The comment was just the thing to antagonize the warrior.

"He is a fool! He has never seen a battle. He knows nothing of the camps of war. My horse knows more of war than he does. I have seen the Habiru encampment, Rahab. Their tents stretch for miles. It is true that from these walls we could kill thousands of them, but for every thousand who fell, ten thousand would rise up to take their places. They are like a plague of locusts. They stream across the desert like roaches in the cellar when you light the lamp."

"Surely, then, we are lost."

Oparu shook his head. "No, we are not lost. We are not lost if we are not afraid, but if we stay within these walls, they will smell our fear, and it will draw them as jackals are drawn to blood. We must attack them, Rahab. They are shepherds. They have no chariots; they have no weapons of war. On the plains, our chariots would terrify their numbers. They would run before us like the hart before the lion."

"I am glad, Oparu, that we have men like you, a man with the heart of a lion." Oparu groaned at her humor and pulled the coverlet over his head.

Shanar poured another cup of wine for Rahab. "Shall I spice your wine with some of my magical sleeping herbs, my dear?" His eyes twinkled wickedly.

"Oh, no, my lord. You might need them. Otherwise you might not be allowed to sleep on my couch tonight."

Shanar laughed delightedly. Despite the bad tidings of the tax assessors, he had enjoyed the events of the previous evening. It was worth the cost of all the wine that Jamat and Mohan had guzzled to see them tremble before the wrath of the giant.

"It was magnificent, Rahab. If I hadn't known better, I would have sworn that Oparu was drunken beyond mortal limits and that at any moment he was going to kill all of us!"

"Yes, he was convincing, wasn't he, my lord, but no more so than you. Are you sure that you weren't truly asleep?"

"Asleep? I was almost dead by the time they dragged me out of here. I was holding my breath to keep from laughing aloud. I've never heard such whimpering cowards—'Oh, no, my lord, don't kill us! Kill him!' Oh, Rahab, it was too funny."

"And how I wish you could have seen them drag you out of here. Their little feet had wings, my lord. The gods themselves could not have gotten away more speedily."

"Indeed, too speedily. They almost pulled my shoulder from its socket."

Rahab smiled. "It served its purpose, though. I have never seen Oparu in a better mood. He was jovial, and he was very talkative!"

"That's good. Then you learned what I needed to know?"

"I hope so. Oparu has no regard for your plans to fortify the Jericho walls. He doesn't respect your knowledge of military matters, and he feels he must influence the king to act against your advice. He thinks that we must win our battles with the Habiru with chariots and weaponry. He will do everything in his power to influence the king to strike first, in fierce battle upon the plains. He is a very dangerous man."

"How clearly you understand the situation, Rahab. You have learned exactly what I need to know. It pleases me that you have a mind sharp enough to record such military matters accurately."

"I learn what I need to learn, my lord. If it is to your advantage that I understand war, then I will understand war. Men like Oparu are all strength, but they have no reason. Oparu is as useful as a bull, but no better."

Her eyes searched Shanarbaal's and her gaze revealed the depth of her admiration for him. "Your wisdom of the ways of the world is like the wine I drink and the food I eat. I have learned much from you, my lord, the high priest, my wonderful lord Shanarbaal."

Shimmering through her window, the brilliant light of the morning sun danced in dappled patterns across the delicately woven coverlet of her bed. She stirred and stretched.

Uhmmm, hmmmm, Ohh, morning. She stretched, reaching for him. *Oh, he is gone already, returned in the night to the temple. Oh, Shanar, I wish you were here. …How delightful, how pleasant is your magic, O priest, how satisfying is your caress.*

Pleasures abound in the world, and I, Rahab, am master of them all. Ah, if there were gods, I would thank them.

"Good morning, good morning, Sun! How brightly you shine through my window! How warmly you greet me!"

Surely when we have been so close…surely he loves me! Oh, we shall be so powerful! Together we form a union incomparable to any. The pharaoh and his sister-bride may have such power, perhaps—but no one else.

What Shanarbaal had told her was true: the men who influence the kings and the gods hold real power. And more powerful still are the women who influence those men! You have done well, Rahab. You feed your household, you satisfy your lord, and you show a profit!

The sun, which had been streaming so brightly into the room, passed behind a cloud, and for an instant the room darkened and was chilled.

I must get up, she thought. *I must be about my business.*

28

Nantha smiled proudly as she looked over her accomplishments of the morning. They looked exactly as she had hoped they would, and they would fit perfectly into the corner niches of her kitchen. In all her time in Rahab's house, only one thing had been missing to make her perfectly happy. She had needed her own household gods.

At several different times during her life, she had tried to make her own gods, but never before had she been successful. In her mind, she knew exactly how they must look, and nothing else would do. They were the same gods who had protected her mother's kitchen—or, more accurately, the kitchen of her mother's master, the kitchen where her mother had been head cook, a position of honor for a slave who had begun her service as a scrubber of pots. Nantha had grown up in that kitchen, watched after by those little gods nestling in the rafters and guarding all that took place. Their harsh faces sneered, and sharp little teeth protruded beneath their fat, puffy cheeks. She had been afraid of them when she was little. But her mother had explained to her that they were not malicious gods. Their entire purpose was to protect the hearth stones from wandering evil spirits. Gradually, she had come not only to accept those gods, but to like them.

When she was sold, she had left all that she knew and loved. The memory of those little gods had come to represent home to her. Never in all the marketplaces she had seen was she able to find images of the same beings. She had, at various times, bought other household gods, but none of them could bring her the comfort of the gods of her mother's kitchen. Now, in Rahab's kitchen—in her kitchen, for that is how she thought of it—she had made the gods of her hearth with her own hands, following the memory etched deeply into her heart, and now they lay before her—little gods shaped out of barley dough.

Only one thing remained to be done. She had purchased pots of color in the marketplace; now she must paint them. Then they would be complete, and they would leer down upon her kitchen with their strange mixture of vengeance and love.

Nantha painted the little figurines with great care. She remembered their colors from her childhood, and though she was no artist, she knew what she wanted and could achieve a fair approximation of the painted gods she had seen in the past.

"You are much more brightly colored than my mother's gods, but they were very old," she told the sneering little faces. "In time you will fade a bit, and then you will be just right."

"I am very pleased to finally get your shapes right," she said as she dabbed bright spots of yellow onto the face of one of the images. "I was a little girl when I last saw you, and now I have been a woman for many, many years, but I have always remembered you, and I have wanted you to be with me." She cleaned the yellow off her brush with olive oil, reaching for the polished pebbles that would serve as eyes for the little gods.

"I could never get your shapes right when I worked at the temple," she said, picking up the third figure. "Perhaps you did not want to live in the temple of Astarte, hmmmm? She is a great and fearful goddess. You are much happier to come to live here in the kitchen of the house of Rahab, are you not? I, too, am happier here. That must be it. You have joined me now because we have finally found a home."

When a voice answered her, Nantha jumped, almost spilling her paint.

"I am glad you like it here, Nantha, but who on earth are you talking to?"

"Oh, mistress!" Nantha responded. "I did not know you were there. I am talking to my gods. I have just made them, but they are the same ones who protected me in childhood. See?" Nantha held her creations up for Rahab's inspection.

Rahab looked at the fat little doughballs that Nantha held up so proudly. "Do they have strong magic, Nantha?" she asked.

"They have magic, mistress; they are protectors of the hearth. They will watch over the kitchen as the alcove god watches over the house."

"The alcove god?" Rahab asked in puzzlement. "What are you talking about, Nantha?"

"The little god in the alcove of the public room. You know, the one who sits between the rafters above the bed. He is surely the household god."

Rahab looked at the other woman strangely. Had she lived in her own house for two years without ever seeing this alcove god? Certainly she had noticed that there were no threshhold gods, and she had thought it strange. But she had never bothered to replace them. She had, indeed, been glad that they were not there. Alcion could protect her house better than any lump of clay fresh off a potter's wheel.

"Show me this god, Nantha," she said.

The cook looked at Rahab as if she had lost her mind, but she complied, leading Rahab into the alcove and pointing up into a dark corner where two rafters met. Rahab found herself looking straight into the eyes of a grotesque lion whose arching feathered wings met over his back. Shivers went over her body.

"He has always been there, Nantha?" she asked softly.

"As long as I have been here, mistress. I thought he was yours."

"He is not mine."

"Then he must be the god of the house, for he has been here longer than we have," the cook reasoned.

"Whatever he is, I do not like him," Rahab responded.

"Oh, don't say that, lady. You don't want to anger him."

"No, and I don't want to stay in the same room with him either. Come, Nantha, tell me what you have planned for our supper."

Later that day, Rahab called Alcion into the alcove to look at the statue in the rafters. He, too, was surprised.

"No, I had not seen it before, but then I seldom come into this room."

"And I use it only in the evening, Alcion, when I use it at all. I never looked into the rafters above the bed. Why would I?"

Alcion climbed onto the bed and reached into the rafters, carefully bringing the figure down and handing it to Rahab. "It is Ninunta," he said.

Rahab held the dusty idol and turned it in her hands. It had a bird's body and a lion's head. "Who is Ninunta?" she asked.

"He is the Assyrian god of the thunder. Someone has brought him here from a long way off."

"Probably Shanarbaal," she said.

"It would seem most likely."

The thunder god...just like Baal, she thought. *Wherever I go these gods follow*

137

me. Rahab looked at the carved stone image. It was heavy and finely wrought, expensive. "Take it to the marketplace, Alcion, and sell it." She turned and left the alcove. She would let Nantha keep her silly little kitchen gods if having them brought her pleasure, but Rahab wanted no Assyrian thunderer looking down on her. *Let the gods stay in the temple where they belong,* she thought. *The house of Rahab needs no god!*

29

Seven days had passed and the high priest had not visited the house of Rahab. It was the first time since Shanarbaal had brought her to the house that he had failed to visit her at least once during the week. When she mentioned this to Nantha, the cook frowned and said, "It's probably the vengeance of the god of the alcove. You should have left him where he was. Gods don't like to be interfered with."

"Nonsense," Rahab snapped. "That thing was no more a god than you are!" She stormed out of the room.

"Don't mind her," Nantha said to the little deities who stared down at her. "She says a lot of things she doesn't mean."

Rahab refused to let Nantha's superstitious comments annoy her. The best way, she decided, to find out why Shanarbaal did not visit her was to ask him. She determined to do just that.

Shanarbaal's reception of her visit put all her worries to rest.

"Rahab," he all but shouted as a komer ushered her into the priest's private chamber. "It's wonderful to see you. Come in." The priest turned to the komer. "Bring us wine and cheese, and bring a basket of fruit." He turned to Rahab. "I just realized that I have not eaten today. You will join me, of course?"

"Of course, my lord," she answered, surprised by the exuberance of his welcome.

"Here, sit at this table." He pulled out the long bench for her. "I want to show you what I have been working on. I am delighted with it." On the table were sheets of papyrus, another Egyptian innovation the high priest had adopted.

"Rahab, I have solved the problem that the tax assessors were so happy to announce the other evening at your house. On these sheets, I have devised a completely new way to assess the taxes of the farmers and the rich men of Jericho. I have been working on this for days, and this morning I have finally finished it.

"I have an audience with the king tomorrow, and I'm sure he will adopt my plan—especially since it requires almost no work on his part. Best of all, it will completely override the need for the king to dig into the temple treasury. The king will have his taxes, the pharaoh will have his tribute, and the temple will keep her gold!"

For the next two hours Rahab listened to Shanar explain his plan. She used every ploy she knew to remain animated, interested, and charmed; it kept her from falling asleep.

Shanarbaal put aside the last of the papyra—which he had explained thoroughly to compensate for the fact that Rahab could not read. She was finally able to ask the question that had brought her to the temple.

"My lord, has the house of Rahab offended you in any way?" she asked softly.

"Offended me? Of course not, Rahab. You have been of the utmost help to me. Why would you ask such a question?" The high priest looked startled by her question and touched her shoulder gently.

"You have not visited me in seven days, my lord."

"What? Seven days? Has it been so long? It cannot have been seven days?"

"Yes, my lord, it has been seven days."

"My dearest Rahab," he said, spreading his hands, "I am so sorry. I have been working on this plan. I've worked into the night and started again at daybreak, but as you can see, it has been worth it. The king will accept this plan." He stared vaguely at the papyra, then remembered himself. "But...but seven days," he sighed. "I must beg your forgiveness. With your permission, I will visit you tonight."

"I should be most happy to have you visit me tonight, my lord the high priest," Rahab said with a smile, but her voice was very formal.

Shanarbaal did something she had never seen him do before. He pushed out his lower lip, and he pouted. "Am I no longer your 'wonderful lord Shanarbaal'?" he asked in a sulky voice.

She went to him then. "Yes, my wonderful lord Shanarbaal, more wonderful than you know."

The komer who passed the door a few moments later closed it discreetly.

Rahab smiled as she walked quickly through the temple hallways. *Let Nan-*

tha say that the Thunderer is angry with me now, she thought happily. *No Assyrian lion with feathers can change Shanar's feelings for me.* She hugged herself in pleasure. *I really am his favorite,* she thought with satisfaction. Of course he had been consumed by his work, but this tax plan was very important. A loving woman would learn to accept the odd quirks of a man like Shanarbaal, a man of great importance. It should not surprise her that a man of such brilliance was a bit strange.

A small whimpering sound interrupted Rahab's thoughts. She stopped. It came from around the corner, from the slave quarters. Rahab followed the sound. She pushed open one of the doors to the tiny slave chambers and saw, exposed in the bright shaft of light from the doorway, a young girl, lying partially covered by a coarse woolen cloak. Bruises, obviously left by large, rough hands, marked her upper arms. Shadows—or were they bruises too?—circled her eyes and dried blood crusted her upper lip.

Rahab gasped. She knelt beside the child. *Oh, she looks like Bishna,* Rahab thought, and her stomach clenched.

"What happened to you?" Rahab demanded. "Who has done this?"

The girl's eyes slowly focused on the woman at her side. The harsh light from the corridor silhouetted Rahab's shape against the open doorway.

"It was the soldiers, lady," she answered softly, simply.

"Sons of Sheol!" Rahab cursed. "They are too rough! The temple lets them go too far!"

The girl moaned.

"What is your name, girl?" Rahab snapped, making the decision that this sparrow would escape the hunter's net.

"I am Kinah," the girl answered softly.

Rahab whirled and left the room.

In the chambers, Shanarbaal was once again lost in the study of his tax plan. As Rahab burst into the room, Shanarbaal looked up from his tablets in sudden irritation and began to speak just as Rahab did.

"What—" they both said.

"What is it?" Shanar asked impatiently.

"What is happening here with this Kinah?" Rahab shot back.

"What," he demanded, "is a Kinah?"

"She is a slave girl," Rahab answered. "Shanar, she's hurt, and she's totally unattended. She needs care. Let me take her home with me."

"Take her then!" he all but shouted. "She's little good to us here if she's injured." He turned from her, and his attention returned to his work. It was as if Rahab had never entered.

"My lord," Rahab interrupted him again, "I will need a litter."

"Send for one then," he said without looking up. "Tell them I ordered it," he added, obviously dismissing her.

Rahab was the most glamorous woman Kinah had ever seen—and the kindest.

At the temple, Kinah had known the high priestess Mari, a vain and cruel woman, as were many of the owners she had known in her short life, but never before had she known a mistress who treated her slaves as friends and cared for them with her own hands, as Rahab did.

During the first fevered days of her sickness, Kinah had awakened many time to find Rahab bending over her, washing her face or changing the herbs and bandages on her wounds. Kinah, in return for Rahab's care, worshipped the older woman.

As Kinah healed, she watched Rahab's household with interest. Alcion was a quiet wonder. He was handsome and strong—not soft like so many eunuchs—and he was the smartest man Kinah had ever talked to, though Kinah never made it a habit to speak with men—it was too dangerous.

Nantha was a funny one—not old, not young, merely there, and always doing something. She cooked, she cleaned, she entertained guests, and she complained. Consistently and constantly, she complained. Rahab ignored the complaints or laughed at them.

Rahab was perfect. She was beautiful. When Rahab danced, Kinah's eyes followed her in amazement. This was what a woman in charge of her own life could be—beautiful, rich, perfect. There was no one quite like Rahab in the whole world; Kinah was sure of it. No one else had a house so beautifully arranged; no one else could carry herself so proudly in any company. Rahab was so wise and so mature. Kinah wanted to be just like her.

Shanarbaal, the high priest, visited often, and Kinah noticed that Rahab seemed to come to life when the high priest visited. Her eyes danced, and her smile was quick and vibrant, as was her laughter. Shanarbaal seemed to be the master of the house, yet he was not. Rahab was mistress of her own house. She directed Alcion and Nantha in their duties, and she made decisions.

Rahab never seemed to tire of her work. She entertained politicians, merchants, soldiers, tax collectors, and travelers. Kinah saw the tremendous number of gold and silver shekels they left.

In addition, Kinah watched Rahab spin, weave, and sew. Kinah was fascinated with the colorful, embroidered tapestries that Rahab created by lamplight after all the guests had gone.

Often, Rahab's needle was still at work when the sun rose across the Jordan. Rahab made clothing for all her household, and she began to teach Kinah some of the same skills. The girl was quickly adept at pounding the flax stems to produce the long strings that would become, with Rahab's touch, linen tapestries for the marketplace.

Kinah never mentioned the abuse she had received at the temple; Rahab never asked. Rahab taught, and Kinah learned. Kinah thought she was fortunate indeed to have become part of a household where her masters were kind.

She would have done anything Rahab asked, and she tried to anticipate Rahab's desires. Nothing pleased her more than an expression of approval from Rahab or Alcion.

In three weeks' time, Kinah was living and working in the house of Rahab as if she had been there always. Her bruises had faded, and her resemblance to Bishna was more pronounced as she smiled and laughed in the safety of Rahab's household.

"I think you are greatly recovered, aren't you, little one?" Alcion asked her one morning as he watched her straighten the public room.

"I am almost well," Kinah agreed happily.

"Well enough to accompany me to the market this morning?" he asked.

"Oh, Alcion, may I?" Kinah's eyes sparkled delightedly. "I would love to go with you."

"Then get your veil and come along," Alcion said, smiling at her eagerness. Kinah showed the promise of becoming the most beautiful woman he had ever seen, and he had no desire to tempt ruffians in the market with her unveiled loveliness.

In the marketplace, Kinah reminded Alcion of Rahab when he had first met her. She was pleased by everything she looked at, and she looked at everything. Her delighted laugh brightened the marketplace, causing heads to turn. Alcion was glad she was veiled.

"Alcion, look," she suddenly exclaimed, tugging at his sleeve and pointing to a small booth.

Alcion turned obligingly, looking where Kinah pointed. In the middle of the stall sat a harp, of the sort made by the Egyptians. It was an L-shaped wooden instrument, brightly polished and gently carved, with its taut strings attached to bright brass nails.

"That is a harp, Kinah; it is for making music."

"Oh, yes, I know!" the child responded, surprising him. "I have seen them played," she said, hurrying toward the stall. Alcion followed her agreeably.

Kinah brushed the harp's strings with her fingers. The sound hovered, a soft magic upon the air. "Oh, it is wonderful!"

"Where did you learn of harps?" Alcion teased.

For an instant, the girl's eyes clouded. Alcion wondered if she were going to cry. She blinked and answered seriously: "I think I have always known. The only thing I remember of my mother is that she played a harp."

Alcion plucked a string of the harp. A discordant twang resulted, and he made a face. The girl laughed and touched the string to still its vibrations.

"No, no, Alcion. It's like this." She laughed and ran her fingers across the strings. Harmonies filled the shop.

Alcion shrugged. "You have a gift from the gods, I think," he said with a smile. "Perhaps you should have a gift from the house of Rahab as well."

Instantly she gasped. Alcion could almost see her smile through the veils.

"Rahab's guests would find your music a great addition to the entertain-ments of the house," Alcion remarked, the decision already made. "How much for the harp?" he asked the grinning shopkeeper.

Kinah's magic was with the harp. She found her greatest pleasure in creat-ing melodies upon its strings. Alcion had been right; Kinah's music wove shimmering threads of sound across the tapestry of Rahab's entertainment. The guests were delighted, friends met at Rahab's house to laugh, to eat, to hear the music, and to see the dance, and later, as the wine cups emptied and the lamplight softened, to disappear for a while with one of the women and to reappear pleased to the point of generosity with their evening's pleasures.

As the third year passed, the prosperity of Rahab's house grew, and so did the self-satisfaction of its mistress.

30

The knife lay between them like a thing alive.

Its burnished brass handle gleamed, reflecting the golden tones of the lamp-light, carved brass, ornate, designed in curls and swirls that reminded Rahab of the goddess Astarte. The knife was cleaned and polished now and Rahab examined it closely, remembering the first time she had seen it, when Oparu had almost died in her house. Its blade was blue-gray, cold, and darkly deadly. The knife's cold fire seemed reflected in Shanar's eyes as they flashed in anger. He spoke softly, however.

Rahab knew that the determined set of his beard, the slight narrowing of his eyes, and the soft voice meant that a serious wrath burned beneath his pol-ished manners.

But Oparu was so intent on conveying his message, so sure of his strength, that he was oblivious to the dangerous mood he was arousing in the priest.

Never soft or quiet—the giant saw quietness as weakness—he was all but shouting in his desire to get his point across.

"Don't you see!" His voice rose. "This is not ordinary iron. It has been to the underworld. The gods have given it the strength of their loins and blessed it."

"Don't tell me about the gods. I know what the gods will do—and what they will not do," Shanar answered.

"On the plains, my kinsmen have whole chariots made of this metal. They are invincible! Their spears are tipped with this magic metal. It will pierce our armor and go right through our shields. But our spears are turned aside by it."

"I can see that is is very hard indeed, and no doubt it would serve us well—but, Oparu! It is more precious than gold!" Shanar shook his head. "What you ask is incredible, impossible."

Oparu's voice grew louder still. "You can convince the king! The gods know I have tried to convince the king! These weapons are our best chance. They are essential!"

"Come, now, Oparu! Nothing is essential," Shanar spoke with only a hint of sarcasm.

"Don't you see?" the warrior asked, and the unspoken insult to Shanar's intelligence was as loud as Oparu's booming voice. How could the priest be so thickheaded! "These desert wanderers who yip at us do not have chariots, but there are numberless thousands of them. They outnumber us by the tens of thousands! Without these weapons, we shall be overrun by the Habiru hordes!"

Shanar looked at Oparu as he would have looked at an imbecile child. "I thought you called them grasshoppers! Is the great warrior afraid?"

"Even grasshoppers can destroy the farmer's field," Oparu snarled in defense.

"They will not destroy what they cannot reach, and they cannot reach us behind these walls, Oparu." The priest's lip curled. "It is easy to see that you are not a student of history. You put your trust in might and brute strength." He laughed softly, pleasantly.

Rahab watched Oparu, who stared balefully at the priest, open-mouthed, breathing heavily, not understanding. Shanar stood, posing elegantly to continue his lecture on history. The warrior looked down at the knife, silent.

"The world of reality is not so simple as you think, O mighty warrior," the priest said, speaking the title with emphasis, sarcastically. "For thousands of years, these walls have repelled such hordes, invaders who would have taken us. We have the springs—water that never runs dry—and the walls are invincible. So are we. Weapons are not of vital importance when we are protected by the walls. You and your horsemen are a sufficient force for such fighting as we shall need. Your valor, not your weaponry, is all that we need to maintain this city!"

Oparu reached, then, for the knife. He toyed with it, sliding its deadly blade between his fingers. Rahab wondered if he longed to test its strength on the priest's throat.

"O great high priest of Baal," the giant said at last. "You have heard my words of wisdom. If you do not pay heed, you will pay with your life."

The priest snorted. "Do you threaten me, Oparu?"

"I foretell your future—and the future of this rotting city!"

Oparu spat the words, turning as he spoke, and stomped out of the room and into the night. He carried with him the knife of tempered iron. The room was weighted with silence.

"More wine, my lord?" Rahab asked at last.

The priest held out his cup. "Bah!" he said. "The man is a fool." He drank deeply, sinking down into the pile of pillows near the table.

"He sounds convincing, and he has the ear of the king."

"The king listens to me, Rahab," the priest said shortly. "It is I who influence the king."

Shanar pulled Rahab onto the pile of pillows. His smile was one of enjoyment. He dismissed Oparu from his concern with a promise: "If I hear that Oparu has tried to undermine my influence with the king, my sweet, it is Oparu who will pay with his life."

Rahab laughed with him. "Yes, my lord," she answered. "It is Oparu who will pay."

31

Shanarbaal stood angrily and paced the floor. Never had Rahab seen him so coldly furious.

"You are sure he intends to do this?" he asked her, whirling and fixing her with an icy stare. His eyes were black, black and cold as onyx.

"He was quite explicit, my lord. He said that he has lost his patience with that fool of a high priest who knows nothing of war, and the time has come to buy chariots, even if it takes the entire treasury of the temple—and that the king has already agreed." She spoke quickly, accurately summarizing an evening's chatter with the giant Oparu, and she spoke without emotion.

"Curse the fool!" Shanarbaal said softly. "Go back to your sewing, Rahab. I must think."

Rahab picked up the ivory awl that she had used for almost four years now. It had worn, become finer, through the years of constant sewing, and Rahab's fingers had become more adept in its use. She had spent many nights, working late as the oil burned in her lamps, creating the designs for coverlets and wall hangings that Alcion sold in the market for her through the same merchant who had years before dealt in lamps. Now he sold rugs and wall hangings. He had, as well, become a devoted patron of her house.

The priest sat on the low bed and sipped his cup of wine without speaking as Rahab continued with her needlework. She was using green threads, stitching diagonally across the warp and woof of white wool that made the base fabric on which she now created the feathery green leaves of the trees of the sacred grove. It was a pleasant design, a special order for Mari-Astarte, for her fourth year as high priestess.

Rahab could not believe that the time had passed so quickly. She thought with satisfaction that her life with Shanarbaal had been profitable. She had earned substantial sums, and she had been given many valuable gifts. But still, she worked with unflagging energies. In sewing, she found release, for it took all her powers of concentration, and she thought of nothing else when she was creating beauty with the colored threads.

Finally, she looked up at the priest. He sat with his head in his hands, deep in meditation, perhaps.

"More wine, my lord?" she asked softly.

He looked up, his concentration gone, and he held out his cup. She put down her thread and rose to pour the wine.

"It is becoming a desperate situation, is it not?" she said.

"It seems that my alternatives become fewer and fewer, Rahab. If Oparu has indeed persuaded the king to use the temple funds to purchase chariots, then we are in grave trouble."

"We? My lord, do you mean you in the temple?"

"Not only the temple, Rahab. I mean the city as a whole. It seems that every time the king needs to find extra monies, he looks to the temple coffers."

"Surely this is nothing new," Rahab said.

"Except for one thing, Rahab. The cost of these chariots will exhaust all of the funds in the king's treasury and most of the temple funds. Should the Egyptians raise the tribute again this year, we would not be able to pay it."

"And they are sure to do so—they do it every year," Rahab said.

"Furthermore, if this mad plan of Oparu's is followed, it is doomed to failure. The chariots will not work here. They may be workable in the flat plains near the coast where Oparu's people live, but here, the terrain is much too hilly."

"You mean, even if he gets the iron chariots he wants, they will not be able to protect the city."

"Exactly, my sweet. He could never get them to the plains to fight. The Habiru will stay on the mountains until they decide to attack. And if they attack here, the walls are our best hope. Chariots are useless within the city. There's no room to maneuver."

Rahab sighed. "Oparu is such a warrior, Shanar...such a man. Why is he so thick-headed?"

"He is a stupid fool—that's why. Warriors are meant to fight and not to think. When Oparu began trying to think, he stepped outside his realm."

"You tried to persuade him. You have tried again and again. It seems the more sense you make, the more stubborn he becomes." Rahab sighed again. She liked the giant.

"He has been talking against me to the king for years now, and I begin to sense a change in the king's demeanor toward me. He no longer trusts me as he did."

"But he has never had the child that you divined," Rahab interjected. "Is that not perhaps the true reason that the king has become colder toward you? I do not think Oparu could influence the king so much."

"No, Rahab, it all goes together. Oparu derides me on every occasion. The repetition takes its toll. Oparu must be stopped."

"Do you want me to talk to him?"

"You have talked to him. I have talked to him. He does not listen. He is a dolt, a fool. Iron chariots are on his brain, and his brain is as stubborn as iron! He is determined to have iron chariots—and if he lives, he will have them."

"If he lives? He is not in ill health."

The priest sighed now. "Rahab, if this man lives, he will bring his plan to fruition, and if he does that, the city of Jericho is doomed. Sooner or later, the Habiru will attack. If we have used all our resources on a useless fool's toy that will not repel the enemy and we have permitted our one real defense—the walls—to crumble in disrepair, then the city is fallen."

"But, my lord, Oparu is strong. He is mighty in battle. He will not fall if we are attacked."

"Rahab, you are not hearing what I say. If Oparu lives, he will succeed in his plan with the king. And if that happens, this city is doomed. The temple treasury is depleted; the people are killed; your pretty nest here is gone, wiped out, fallen! Do you understand my meaning? Can I make it more clear?"

She caught her breath.

"Oparu must not live!" the priest said sharply.

Rahab trembled, biting her lip, then protested: "But he means well."

"His well-meaning will kill us all," the priest answered. "It is necessary for the city that this man die."

"Oh, no," Rahab wailed. "I never thought it would come to this."

"If the city would be saved, Rahab, it is expedient."

"Yes," she answered finally, "we must save the city."

Shanar spoke compellingly. "That is the nature of war, Rahab—that some must die to save the city."

"Yes, that one must die to save the city...but, oh, he is a good man!" she wailed again.

"He is a foolish man! And he must die. You do understand the necessity for this death, don't you, Rahab?" He paused, sipped his wine, and continued: "We do not wish that Oparu would die, but he must. Do you remember the lamb we sacrificed together, Rahab? It is the same. It must be done, and we will do it."

She looked down at her tapestry, at the feathery leaves of the trees in the sacred grove—the trees that never died. She envied the trees, and her tears fell silently to the tapestry in her lap.

"Yes, my lord Shanarbaal," she answered him at last.

Late in the night, long after Shanarbaal had left and darkness had covered the city of Jericho, one lamp burned in the sewing room of the house of Rahab. One lamp burned, and nimble fingers sewed into the night. Rahab, woman of Jericho, sewed and sewed and refused to think. Only one phrase echoed chantlike against the blank wall of her mind: "One man must die to save the city."

Onuk the Fat sat at his table poking huge hunks of roasted fowl into his mouth. As he ate, he watched his companion, a thin man who ate delicately but drank even more heavily than Onuk himself.

"Why have you invited me here?" the thin man asked. Never before had the king's eunuch been invited to eat with the city's richest politician. "What can I do for you, Onuk?'

"Oh, my friend," Onuk responded expansively, spreading his hands apart. "It is not what you can do for me, but what I can do for you that has prompted this meeting."

Across the table, the eunuch's eyes glimmered through two tiny slits. *He looks like a starving mole,* Onuk thought contemptuously.

"What can you do for me, Onuk? And what will you ask in return?"

"You are too suspicious of me, Habbak," Onuk replied. "We should be friends. We could be very useful to another."

The eunuch sipped his wine and listened as the politician continued, "I hear many things in my dealings in the city. I learn many secrets which could tickle the ear of the king."

"I have ways to learn the secrets of the city, Onuk. I have not been the chief eunuch of the king of Jericho these five years without learning something of the ways to intrigue a king."

Onuk smiled, "Yes, Habbak, I know. I know of your informers—slave boys and temple girls, children—children and servants. What you need, Habbak, is not a string of children to tell you tales they hear in the street. What you need is a cohort, a friendly conspirator, a man who frequents the tables—and the bedrooms—of the city's richest families. What you need is a friend such as myself. There is a chain of power in this city, Habbak, and I know its every link. If you wish to be the favorite of the king, you will need my help."

"You make a most promising offer, Onuk, an offer I should be most ungrateful to refuse, but in every covenant, there are two sides. What will this bargain cost me?"

The eunuch's eyes were invisible, tiny slits above his wine cup.

Onuk laughed, "Always suspicious, aren't you, Habbak, and rightly so. There is a small favor which you can do for me in return for my—what shall we call it—my patronage. I would like to read this newest defense plan which Shanarbaal has devised. The rumors say that it is a plan to defend the city and that every man in the king's guard is against it. A year ago when Shanar convinced the king to raise all nobles' taxes, it cost me dearly." He frowned, sipped his wine, and continued. "Shanar has a sharp mind, but he tends to forget who his friends are. If I see the plan now, before the king makes his decision, perhaps I can think of a way to keep this new plan from costing me so heavily. There are other rich men in the city besides me!"

Habbak laughed softly, a rough sound rather like the rustle of parchment. "So that is what you want! Yes, that can be arranged. Those papers are spread across a table in the king's anteroom. I can get you in and out of there any morning of the week, and no one will be the wiser."

"No one, except me," Onuk grinned. "And that is as it should be."

The eunuch returned his smile. This evening with the city's highest politician showed the promise of great reward, and at so small a cost to himself!

"Then it is a bargain!" Onuk slammed his fist onto the table. "You will show me the plan tomorrow?" he asked.

"It is a bargain," Habbak replied. "You must come to my quarters shortly before sunrise."

"And so I shall," Onuk answered, "but now, my friend, our business is done. Let us relax and talk of more pleasant things. Friends should enjoy each other's company. We need not always talk of taxes, kings, and wars. There are more important thing to discuss: good wine, good food, beautiful women, beautiful boys! Indeed, I have seen perhaps the most beautiful boy in Jericho just this morning."

The eunuch sat up a bit straighter and asked with unfeigned interest, "Oh, really? And who do you say is the most beautiful boy in Jericho?"

Onuk licked his lips. The mole had taken the bait; now to set the trap.

"Oh, he is undoubtedly the eunuch of the house of Rahab. He is her scribe, I believe—a considerable waste of talent, in my opinion. He is a beautiful young man: tall, strong, with waving hair, a quick smile, but a quicker wit. Surely you know him? His name is Alcion. He was scribe to Shanarbaal for some time, but apparently has fallen into the high priest's disfavor, for he has lived with Rahab for over three years. Do you not remember him?"

"Yes," the eunuch sighed, feeling the heavy pull of the wine. "I do remember him—tall, lithe—a Cretan as I recall—slender as a reed, and swift. He avoided me well at villa gatherings. I had assumed he was sold out of the city."

"He is very much in Jericho. Early every morning, I see him in the market-place," the fat man chuckled, "hours before you venture out, I'm sure. The harlot, Rahab, rarely leaves her home—hates wearing a veil, I hear—but this Alcion does all her trading for her at the market. He stands at the stalls shifting his weight from one elegant leg to the other and bartering for all he's worth. You'd swear he was posing, but he's so artlessly beautiful that he doesn't need to pose." Onuk watched the eunuch's reaction to his words and knew his plan was working.

"You say he's been with Rahab for three years now?" Habbak asked.

"A little more than that, actually. Rahab values him highly, but I dare say she'll lose him to some amorous customer one day. That boy is too fine to sit all day at books."

"I have recently lost such a companion," Habbak said in a low voice.

"Yes, and I grieve with your loss. Perhaps...but no, Rahab is too fond of Alcion. She could not be persuaded to sell him," the politician responded thoughtfully.

"A high prize is worth a high price, Onuk," Habbak responded with a familiar saying.

"True enough, but Rahab is a strange woman, Habbak. She buys and sells, but she has a pride that is not easily purchased."

"Gold is but one of the metals of persuasion, Onuk. It may be that I shall test Rahab's mettle and that of her scribe."

Onuk merely nodded. "He is a beautiful boy," he murmured again, and smiled. *The seeds I have planted tonight will bring Rahab a bitter harvest,* he thought, licking his lips at the sweet taste of his revenge.

Across the table from the politician, Habbak smiled. Tomorrow, he thought, tomorrow there would be time to visit the marketplace and to see pretty boys, but tonight there was a new alliance to bond, an alliance that could prove most useful in the future.

Onuk leaned across the table to refill the eunuch's wine cup. "So," the politician said softly, "you have learned much of the ways to intrigue a king, have you?"

The eunuch laughed coquettishly and reached across the table to touch Onuk's hand. "And of the ways to please a politician," he whispered.

Breakfast had not yet been prepared when a young voice shouted outside. "Rahab! Is this the house of Rahab?"

"Yes, yes, fool," Nantha said, hurriedly opening the door. "This is her house, but what would such as you want here?" She laughed at the ragged teenage boy who stood at the door. "You obviously cannot afford her services."

The boy drew himself up proudly and eyed the woman with disdain. "She is my sister, old woman, and I want to see her."

"Your sister! Name of the gods! What you are doing here? Well, come in, then. I'll take you to her."

Nantha hurriedly led the boy to the roof where Rahab and Kinah sat, pounding flax.

"Rahab!" Nantha said breathlessly. "It's your brother!"

"Micah!" Rahab exclaimed, jumping up to embrace the boy. "Why are you here? What's wrong?"

At her question, the boy's proud demeanor collapsed. In tears, he answered her, "Rahab, Father is really sick. Yesterday he couldn't get up. Mother says we will starve if we don't get help."

"Don't cry, Micah. It will be all right. Tell me what's wrong with Father. What did Mother say exactly? Did she send you here?"

"Yes, she's worried, Rahab. I've never seen them like this. Father can't get up, and Mother says we won't be able to get the fields plowed this year, so there won't be any food."

"Did Father fall? Has he broken something?" Rahab asked anxiously.

"No, no, it's not like that, Rahab. He's been getting sicker and sicker for a long time. Nobody knows what it is, and nothing helps. His legs just won't hold him. He can't stand up."

"He's been getting sicker and sicker, and no one has even told me!" she said angrily. She remembered Onuk's veiled threats concerning her father's health, but she couldn't have trusted Onuk. For years, she'd sent her parents money, and they had never even thanked her. Now, when her life was already too complicated—now, they needed her help. Her irritation overrode her concern.

"What does Father think of your coming here? Does he know Mother sent you?"

"I don't know, Rahab. Sometimes he talks about you, but he always sounds as if he thinks you are dead."

Rahab shook her head. She understood. She had been disowned: for her father it was the same as if she were dead. But she was not dead, and now her mother needed her.

"Very well," she sighed. "I will have Alcion take you back home."

Micah's lips pouted and tears welled up in his eyes again. Rahab laughed and hugged the young boy. "Do not worry, little brother, I will not let you starve. Your sister is the richest woman in Jericho. The family of Rahab will not starve."

Rahab released the boy and called Alcion. It had been several weeks since she had sent him up the wadi with money for her parents. He had reported nothing amiss at the time, though she had not asked. Now, she asked: "Alcion, when you went to my father's farm the last time, was anything wrong there?"

The scribe looked puzzled. "No, my lady. Everything seemed the same as always. Your parents were polite, as they always are. But I do not stop to pass the time with them. Your mother takes the money, she thanks me, and I leave."

"Did you see my father the last time?" Rahab asked.

"Yes, the family was at the midday meal. He was eating."

"Then you did not see how he was walking? Micah says he cannot walk at all now."

"That's right, Alcion," the boy interjected. "Mother says we will starve."

"Alcion," Rahab commanded, ignoring the boy's interruption, "I want you to take Micah home, and I want you to determine how serious matters are there. I do not know if Father still considers me dead, but Mother has sent Micah here for help. You must be my eyes and my advisor."

It was evening when the eunuch returned. His face was grave. Rahab was dancing for two rich merchants. The eunuch glanced at her briefly and ascended the stairs without a word.

Rahab did something she had never done before: she stopped her dance and sent her guests away. Rahab and Alcion talked late into the night, their voices too low for Kinah and Nantha to hear. Finally Alcion said, "I think that your parents cannot object." With that comment, the decision was made. Rahab's family would move to Jericho. Alcion would find a place for them to live and Rahab would support them. Her father might never admit that Rahab had been right in her decision not to marry Onuk, but he would have to admit that his oldest daughter was well able to support the family. The move would have to be accomplished quickly, or the rainy season would be upon them.

Rahab herself was too busy to attend to the move, but Alcion borrowed slaves from the temple and brought Rahab's family to a small house that she purchased within the city walls. Rahab's mother could become a merchant, and Bazarnan could sit on his couch, using his magic with words to good advantage in the marketplace. Rahab's sister, Leal, and her husband stayed at the farm, doing what they could. The others made the move: Bazarnan and Kora, their daughter Tirnah and her husband, Jaben, and Rahab's brothers, Micah and Benan.

Shanarbaal had graciously lent his slaves. The next two weeks would be a busy time for Rahab, he thought, for she would be hostess at a major banquet at Shanar's villa. He had laid his plans well; Rahab would be honored to be his choice. There were certain necessities to be handled at this particular banquet, and Shanar wanted no mistakes.

"The deed must be accomplished quickly," Shanar explained to Rahab, "for the king must never know."

Rahab frowned. "Must it be I, my lord? Why not Mari? She is always your hostess for banquets at the villa. Would I not arouse suspicion?"

Shanar laughed shortly. "The king must never know, Rahab."

"I know that, my lord. I understand," Rahab answered.

"Then understand this wisdom, Rahab. The fewer those who know, the fewer those who can tell. You know already. That is enough. I have trusted you in this. I have no need to trust Mari."

"I am honored that you trust me," Rahab answered, "but how can I be hostess?"

The priest laughed again. "Mari will become violently ill the day of the party. I assure you that she will not be well enough to travel to the villa—much less to act as my hostess."

Rahab was astonished at the intricacy of his planning. The priest was a master of his craft.

He continued. "I will call on you at the last moment, and you—" he smiled and bowed to her, "—you will graciously agree to take her place. No one will wonder. They all know you entertain for me here."

Rahab listened quietly. The priest's voice hardened. "You will make sure that Oparu gets very drunk indeed so that he will fly when he visits the gods. That is all you have to do."

"And I will do it," Rahab murmured. "We must save the city."

32

Rahab crouched at the foot of the tree. It afforded little protection from the icy, stinging rain assaulting the sacred grove. Heavy, black clouds came down from the high places and obscured the cliffs, flying before a howling wind that blew the ancient cypress trees and shrieked down the wadi between the limestone cliffs. It sounded to Rahab like voices crying, wailing in despair.

Shelter! Surely somewhere there was shelter. Her eyes searched the sacred grove. Nearby she could see the river, but its song of rushing water had been overridden, obliterated by the howl of the angry winds. The water had changed in the last few minutes. No longer were the blues, greens, and grays of the water to be seen; it was black from the darkness of the storm. Even the white foam had turned dark, reflecting the anger of the sky.

Pulling her cloak tightly about her and clinging to the basket of mushrooms she had been picking as the storm caught her, Rahab turned from the water and ran deeper into the grove.

Often, when the storms brought violent rains, the waters rose and filled the wadi. *This is not a place to be now,* she thought. *If the rains have been heavy toward the high places, the water here may rise suddenly. I could drown, be washed away to the Jordan before anyone even knew. Why did I not tell Shanarbaal I would be here? I have barely picked a dozen mushrooms—and already they are soaked. I am soaked. I must find shelter!*

She looked about wildly. The limestone cliffs towered above her to her right. To her left, the river, noticeably higher than just a few minutes ago, raged toward the Jordan. Her eyes strained through the driving rain. She had heard stories of people trapped in a wadi when the rains came. The waters from the high places would come down like a wall, washing away everything before them, roaring like the shout of Baal's anger.

Hailstones, small and icy, began to hit her. She felt them even through her heavy woolen cloak, and they stung her face. *The gods are angry,* she thought. *I must get back to the villa.* But there were no pathways up from this part of the sacred grove. She must follow the wadi.

"Aaaiiii-eeeee!" the wind shrieked, and she almost heard it add, "Astarte!" Lightning flashed near her, crackling, and instantaneously the storm gods roared. She approached the emerald pond. For a moment the rains stopped, and the pond lay still and black, like a huge onyx. Rahab stood transfixed, looking into the pond, which darkly reflected the ancient cypress trees, silhouetted shapes, black on black. She remembered the first night she had stood here, in the light of a full moon, with Bishna, poor Bishna, who had been so frightened.

"Aaaiii-eeeeeee!" The scream was torn from Rahab, from the depths of her own terror and despair. She knelt by the black water, and her tears poured into the pond. The rain began again, pelting furiously, but she did not feel it. Now she understood Bishna's fear of the sacred grove; she had never felt fear like this. She understood, too, the ancient worship of the storm god, for now she knew his wrath.

If the waters rose, they would cut off her passage across the limestone bridge between the ponds. She stood, tucking the basket with its magical mushrooms beneath her cloak, and ran. Her feet were sucked into the mud and water. Her sandals would be ruined! No matter—she would live to wear other sandals. She must. Passing the limestone bench, she remembered the masheba, her gift of dung from the god! The winds pulled at her cloak as she paused to stare at the bench, where she and Bishna had sat and rested and where she had so self-ishly hidden her great gift of nothing. She burned with sudden anger.

"Baal!" she shrieked at the screaming winds. "You are nothing! You are less than nothing! You do not frighten me! I am Rahab, woman of Jericho! Do you hear that, Nothing? You do not exist!"

The winds shrieked, and she thought she heard wild laughter from the high places. She fled across the passage between the ponds, with the water rising, pulling at her feet and skirts, trying to pull her down, into the pond. She picked up her feet and ran. She would not be pulled into the black waters!

She reached the other side, laughing and crying hysterically. Then, with her feet securely upon the earth, she turned and looked back. The winds bent the cypress branches, and the sodden, feathery mosses swirled like celestial dancers. Rahab looked across the ruby pond, its filthy waters purged by the pouring rains. The pelting torrent made thousands of tiny splashes hitting the surface of the water. Her eyes followed the lines of the limestone cliff that enclosed and created the pond, and she remembered the night when she and Bishna had first seen this place and had surprised the high priestess worshiping on those rocks. The sound of the priestess's cry rang through her memory: "Ai-eee-eee, Astarte!"

"You are nothing!" she screamed to the wind and the rain. The memory of the blood in the ruby pond assailed her senses, as she thought of the morning after the dedication when she had added her own vomit to its stinking filth. "Astarte, you are nothing! You do not exist! You and Baal deserve each other! You are not even death! You are nothing! Can you hear me? Nothing!"

Lightning flashed from the high places, striking an ancient cypress that stood near the limestone cliffs. It split with a wrenching groan and crashed to the sodden earth.

"You deserve each other!" Rahab shrieked again, turning to run deeper into the trees and away from the rising waters of the wadi. She approached the circle of monoliths, the huge boulders where she had joined the celestial dance at her dedication.

Perhaps there would be shelter here, within the rocks. They towered in their primeval circle, with nooks and niches that might protect her from the rain and hail.

Is there safety here? she asked herself as she drew instinctively into the black shadow of the rock. Its mass protected her from the force of the winds, and she breathed quietly for a moment. Her heart was beating wildly. Terror was all around her. She could not escape it. From this place of refuge in the rock, she could not see the waters of the river, but in her mind's eye they rose steadily.

She could imagine the roar of the wall of flood waters rushing down the wadi, between the limestone cliffs. She would have stayed in the shelter of the rock, but she dared not.

Rahab turned back into the fury of the storm, running against the wind, pursued by fear, pushing toward the path that led up the cliffs to Shanar's villa. *I will save myself,* she thought. *I will not stay here where the waters rise and where the torrents beat upon me. I will get back to the villa!*

She could have shouted for joy when at last she found the rock steps leading up the cliffside to the villa. She started up the stairway. Exposed now to the true fury of the storm, she felt the rain slashing at her face and the wind clawing at her cloak, trying to force her off the narrow stairway.

Even so, she paused halfway up the hillside and looked back at the sacred grove. The clouds were black and green; hanging low, they seemed to chase each other across the sky. Lightning glimmered within the clouds as they raced from one side of the high places to the other. Then it crashed down in vertical fury to the wadi. Thunder reverberated between the limestone cliffs and grew loud on its own echoes. It was magnificent! Rahab heaved a sigh of relief that she was above the danger of the rising waters in the wadi, safe now, only minutes from the villa. She could truly understand the superstition of the ancient ones. It looked as though the gods were real! But she knew better! She ran quickly up the steps and through the gardens of the villa.

Shanarbaal was taking his ease in the banqueting room when Rahab entered, soaking and dripping, with her basket of magical mushrooms. Astonished at her disheveled appearance, he jumped to his feet to assist her.

"Rahab, little raven!" he exclaimed. "You've been out in the storm! What were you doing? Don't you know that the wadi floods in storms like this?"

She laughed delightedly. She was safe! "I met the gods of the storm, my lord, and I ran away from them!"

She dropped her sodden cloak to the floor.

"I see you have a basket of—what?" he asked.

"I was picking mushrooms before the rain," Rahab answered. "I wanted to be ready for this evening's festivities."

"Aha!" he said, understanding her intent.

"Oparu will have a good journey this evening, my lord. The gods will welcome him."

Shanarbaal smiled and pulled her to him. "Let me dry your hair, little one," he said.

Gradually, the fury of the storm abated, and the lightning ceased, but the heavy clouds lingered, and all day the rains fell. The warriors and politicians began to arrive in late afternoon, disgusted with the rains, which had descended upon them at the halfway point of their journey.

"Curse the gods to make it rain today, anyway!" grumbled one merchant from Jericho. "I've been looking forward to this banquet for days—and now

I'm frozen and soaked. I'll probably die of pox!"

"Come, come, my friend," said Shanarbaal lightheartedly. "Only a month ago you were giving your essence in the temple and praying that it would bring rains to the land."

"It wasn't his essence that brought rains to the land," said another man, pulling off his streaming cloak and dumping it on the stone floor.

"I suppose it was yours, then!" the merchant snarled.

"The goddess knows!" came the answer, with a lewd laugh.

"And she'll never tell, will she!" Rahab said as she joined the men, giving each an embrace of welcome. "Come to the fire and warm yourselves."

She clapped her hands, and a komer brought steaming bowls of hot wine for the shivering guests.

Others began arriving, and the komer were busy making arrangements for litters, men, slaves, and horses. The politicians soon dried. They stood in small clusters sharing Jericho gossip and news.

Rahab moved from group to group, laughing. Kedeshoth from the temple danced and drank wine with the guests. Dinner was served in courses—fruit first, then lamb roasted in grape leaves, olives, bread with oil, and, as always, wine.

While the guests reclined at the table, a sudden blast of cold air chilled the room as the last arrival flung open the double doors and entered the room with a shout.

"Not even Baal himself could keep me from this banquet!" Oparu's loud voice was rich and jolly, silencing every other sound in the room.

"Welcome, great captain of the king's chariots," Shanar responded. "We are pleased that the storms did not keep you away."

"When my mind is set upon a goal, nothing keeps me from it!" The giant seemed to speak with double meaning. Shanar wondered if his mind were that subtle.

"Was the water high when you came through?" a merchant asked.

"It was getting fierce, but Thunder swam the torrents as if they were nothing," Oparu bragged. Shanar looked at him with thinly veiled disgust. *He always brags*, Shanar thought. *How tiresome.*

"Come near the fire—warm yourself—have some wine!" The priest played the role of the gracious host. He was pleased that the giant had arrived at the banquet, but not for the reason his guests supposed.

As the evening progressed, the room grew warmer. Rahab watched her guests, thinking of the night to come. These men from the city were not likely to go out in this weather! They would sleep on their cloaks in the banqueting room; so would the kedeshoth and the komer.

Rahab drank with unaccustomed abandon. She filled the wine cup of Oparu again and again, and her own as well. Into Oparu's wine went the extract she had prepared earlier in the day of the mushrooms and other magical herbs.

157

She refused to think of what was to come for him, but she considered the drugs a kindness. They would make him sleepy, and they would give him pleasant dreams even before he slept!

She moved from group to group, a bit unsteadily, her laugh a little louder than she realized. She focused her entire concentration on each group as she joined it. She no longer felt her hands and feet. Her guests did not notice her clumsiness, and her blurred words were drowned in their own drunken laughter.

The hour grew late. The rains continued as though they would never cease. A sodden komer ran in from outside, straight for Shanarbaal. He knelt and whispered into the priest's ear. Rahab watched as Shanar's face grew cold and sober. He got up quickly and sought out the giant, who was telling loud and bawdy stories with a group of merchants. The two men whispered together for a moment, and then Oparu lurched drunkenly to the place where Rahab sat in earnest conversation with a seller of fine rugs.

The giant pulled her outside, under the portico, where they were sheltered from the rain and their privacy was secure.

"Rahab, I have been called. I must go," he whispered urgently into her ear.

"What do you mean, Captain?" she asked, though she knew better than he who had called him.

"The king has sent word—and so I shall go out into the night to serve the king."

"Oparu! Is it safe? The waters were high when you arrived! It's late. Surely," she added with a special smile, "it can wait until the morning's light."

"Serving the king is never safe, little one, when you are a captain of the king's chariots!" He laughed. "But I am Oparu, a son of Anat. I am equal to the challenge!" He leaned down to her. "Give me a kiss, then."

Rahab tiptoed, raising her face to his, catching his own unsteady arm to balance herself, turning her face so that his kiss caught her lightly on the cheek.

"Your beard is scratchy!" she giggled, pushing him away. "Get out of here, warrior, if the king is more important than your friend! Go into the night! Go into the storm!"

"Until the sun shines, Rahab!" he shouted, lurching into the night without his cloak, oblivious to the stinging rain that beat upon his bare shoulders.

It was much later, as Rahab slept in the chambers of Shanarbaal, that the high priest joined her. She awakened groggily as he lighted a lamp and poured a cup of strong red wine.

"Wine?" the priest asked her.

"Yes, my lord," she said, sipping from his cup. "Is it done?" she asked. "Did he fight?"

"You ask too many questions at once, my sweet, as always." He sipped on the wine, deliberately making her wait for his answers. "Yes, it is done. Fight? Your mushrooms and the wine did their work well. He couldn't have connected a spear point with the side of the hill of Bashan. But he kept his knife. It goes back to the gods. I would have liked to have had that knife!"

He handed her the cup, and she sipped the heady wine.

"Then it is done?" she repeated her original question.

"Oparu, by now, is well past Jericho, and the waters of the wadi have carried him to the Jordan." He laughed softly and coldly. "Now he knows who is wise in the ways of war."

She had helped to kill a man who had been her friend for more that three years. Shanar handed her his cup. She drank again, this time deeply.

INTERLUDE

How deserted lies the city,
*   once so full of people!*
How like a widow is she,
*   who once was great among the nations!*
She who was queen among the provinces
*   has now become a slave.*

Bitterly she weeps at night,
*   tears are upon her cheeks.*
Among all her lovers
*   there is none to comfort her.*
All her friends have betrayed her;
*   they have become her enemies.*

Lamentations 1:1-2 NIV

33

Rahab watched him as he ate.

The man's eyes never wavered from the dish before him. His small, pudgy fingers worked swiftly, expertly, in concert with his knife. Conversations and laughter swirled about him, but he seemed unaware of them. His total concentration was on his food. As he ate, small droplets of oil ran down his tightly curled beard, and his right sleeve was constantly wiping them as, at the same time, he poked more food into his mouth.

It occurred to Rahab that this man—this seer of the gods—was extremely physical in his appetites for one reputed to be so spiritual. She had planned a veil dance during the meal, but she decided to postpone it. No need to dance to impress an absent audience.

"Blurrrrup!" The belch seemed to start at his toes and flower up from his belly to his toothy smile.

Rahab rose and refilled wine cups around the table. The king, Shanarbaal, and the guest had supped well on the spicy creations of Nantha. Kinah created pleasing harmonies on the harp, setting a festive mood.

"This kitchen prepares the best food in all of Jericho—but the goddess provides even greater joys here," Shanarbaal said to the guest proudly.

"Blurrrup," responded the guest, leaning back and rubbing his belly. "Better than the cursed Moabites, at least," he mumbled. His voice was deep and gravelly.

Shanarbaal and the king exchanged glances and laughed politely. The guest was the great seer of the gods, Balaam, whose reputation was known throughout the world. He had just returned from the Moabites—and, from what Shanarbaal had heard, had fared badly at the hands of the Moabite king, Balak.

It had been many years since Shanar had seen the great prophet. As a youth, Shanar had gone with his father, the high priest of Jericho, to visit Pethor in the north. At that time, Balaam's uncle was high priest of Anat, and Balaam was a young priest in the temple. Shanar remembered fondly his admiration for the wizardry of Balaam's uncle: when he made his divinations, he seemed to speak to the gods themselves, and his voice changed as he spoke the oracles, echoing from the chambers of the underworld itself. As a youngster, Shanar had been awed by the magic of the Temple of Anat.

The guest, whose reputation now far outshone that of his uncle, seemed to

161

Shanar to be a lesser man, much less, even, than Shanar himself. Even after a lifetime in the sophisticated temples of the north, his manners were no better than those of a camel driver. The fellow was coarse; he had no style; he was a buffoon! But he had seen the Habiru encampments, and Shanar was eager for information about the threat to the east.

The seer drank deeply of the wine.

"I should hope our hospitality would be finer than that of the Moabites," Shanar said agreeably. "They can hardly be expected to have been exposed to true civilization, such as we had in Pethor!"

"Humpf," said the guest, "I left Pethor six months ago. I have not seen civilization since."

This comment provided Shanar with the opening he had been seeking. "And what have you seen since you left Pethor?" he asked innocently.

The seer drank again, deeply, and held out his cup to be refilled. It was only after Rahab had filled it and he drank again that he leaned back into the pillows surrounding the table.

"Blurrrup!" he belched again, and sighed. "Indeed, what have I not seen? Shanar, my old friend, you would not believe what I have seen—for I have seen the unseen, and I have done battle with it!"

Again, the priest and the king laughed politely. Shanar sipped at his cup. "That sounds most interesting, O great seer. Tell us what you saw that was not seen?" He almost snickered, and Balaam laughed as well—drunkenly, it seemed to Rahab.

"The funny thing was—my donkey saw them all along!"

Everyone laughed, though Rahab missed the humor. She refilled the wine cups again.

"Ol' Oned—that's my donkey—she got so stubborn after we left Pethor. No matter what I did to make her go, she wouldn't budge!" The prophet leaned back into the pillows, relishing his story. "I kicked, I screamed, I tugged on the reins, and I finally beat the old fool! Every time I'd get her going, she'd stop or turn, and I'd have to beat her some more." He drank again and held out his cup to Rahab. "I tell you, Shanar, my arm finally got tired!"

Rahab wondered why: *His arm gets plenty of exercise when he drinks*, she thought. *I wish his tongue would get tired as well.*

Shanarbaal was beginning to wish he had not inquired what the seer had seen; he wasn't interested in a stubborn donkey! But Shanar could disguise his impatience well when he was after information. He hoped the wine that the prophet guzzled so freely would not silence the man's brain too soon, and he casually rubbed his left ear lobe, a signal to Rahab to water the next pitcher of wine. He realized that Balaam had returned to his story.

"...and then—here's this huge man, an angel of the Lord God Almighty—standing there before my very eyes. There's no room at all, because the walls of the vineyard are so close together that—" he hiccoughed—"that there's not

162

room enough for a fat horse, and this stupid donkey of mine was sitting down under me, refusing to go."

The men laughed and drank. Shanar wondered what an angel of the Lord God Almighty was, but he decided not to ask. He would never find out about the Habiru if the seer went off on another diversion!

"Well, it seemed," Balaam continued with exaggerated inflection, "I had angered the Lord God Almighty—his name is Yahweh—by undertaking this trip for Balak to curse the Habiru. The Lord protects these Habiru. He watches out for them, let me tell you!"

He paused only to drink again and resumed his story with increasing animation. "Well, Oned was falling down like she had seen something out of Sheol itself. We were just going through this fence row—I told you it was narrow there—when Oned started aiming for the dirt one more time. I must admit I did get upset. Well, this fool donkey was seeing something I wasn't seeing, and she was dodging it for all she was worth!"

"Oh come now, great Balaam," Shanar said. "You aren't telling us that a foolish, dumb donkey was seeing something *you* couldn't see—you said you saw—an angel?"

The guest sat straight up, and he looked Shanar in the eye—soberly. He answered softly: "That is exactly what I am telling you. And I'll tell you more than that." His voice grew loud. "The donkey wasn't dumb either. She spoke right up, and she defended herself!"

The king and Shanar guffawed loudly. What fine entertainment the great Balaam was! Never had the king heard a story so funny—especially from a priest. Shanarbaal, his own high priest, tended to be distant and aloof, always serious, always looking down on everyone—even the king!

The king controlled his laughter first. "Are you telling us, O great Balaam, seer of the gods," he finally asked between gasps of laughter, "are you telling us that your donkey talked?"

"More than that!" the seer answered. "I'll tell you what she said!" Balaam's eyes grew narrow; his smile was gone. "She rebuked me for beating her when she was only trying to save my skin!"

Shanarbaal couldn't drink for laughing. Finally, he asked, "And what about it, great one? Did you stop beating your faithful donkey?"

"Wouldn't you? With the Lord God Almighty, the God of the universe himself sending an angel down? This angel had his sword drawn, and I figured I was dead. But I did get out with my life—and my donkey. She has carried me all the way from Pethor to Kiriath-Huzoth"—he looked about, frowned, and sighed heavily—"and here!"

Shanar asked the next question quickly, before this buffoon started talking about donkeys and angels again. "We heard that you sacrificed many bulls and many rams for the Moabites. How did it go for you there?"

Balaam slammed down his wine cup so hard that it broke on the tabletop, spilling wine onto the floor. "May Balak inherit a whirlwind of a thousand fleas, ten thousand fleas, through all his insides! He treated me harshly, backed out on his agreements with me. He caused me nothing but trouble!"

"How was that?" Shanar asked.

Rahab brought the guest another cup of wine—well watered—and he continued, "I told Balak from the first that I could not utter any word unless it were given me by the Lord God Almighty. Balak took me up to the high places of Bamoth-Baal, and from there I could see part of the Habiru. They were camped by the tens of thousands, by the hundreds of thousands. We sacrificed seven bulls and seven rams on seven altars, and I spoke what the Lord God Almighty instructed me to speak: 'How can I curse whom God has not cursed? How can I denounce those whom the Lord has not denounced?' " He paused to drink again and shrugged his shoulders. "I blessed the Habiru; I had to do it."

"What?" Shanar said. This was unbelievable. "You blessed them?"

Balaam nodded and shrugged again. "How could I denounce those whom the Lord has not denounced?" he repeated.

Shanar shook his head in wonderment. Rahab's eyes met his. She shared his thoughts: the Habiru were a strong force! But the king still drank, laughing softly; he had missed the significance of what Balaam said.

"What then, O great seer?" Rahab prodded the storyteller.

"Then Balak said we should try again at another place, and so he took me to a field of Zophim on top of Pisgah. Again, we could see more of the Habiru—by the tens of thousands, by the hundreds of thousands. They were camped as far as the eye could see in every direction."

"And?" Shanar asked.

"And again, we built seven altars, and again we offered seven bulls and seven rams. The blood ran like the wadis in the rainy season. Again, I spoke the words the Lord God Almighty gave me: 'No iniquity is seen in Jacob, no misery observed in Israel. The Lord their God is with them; the shout of their King is among them. God brought them out of Egypt; they have the strength of a wild ox!' "

Again the men drank, but the laughter had stopped. The king watched solemnly. Jericho had known the Habiru were many, but this was the first eyewitness report he had heard.

"Balak still wasn't satisfied. He would try again, and this time he took me up to the top of Peor, overlooking the wasteland. Still, the Habiru camped as far as the eye could see."

"And?"

"And again we built seven altars and we sacrificed seven rams and seven bulls—seven is the perfect number, Shanar—you should remember that from your studies at our temple." He sighed. "I looked across the wasteland, into the hills and valleys of the desert." He drank again and belched again, before continuing, "I saw them through the eyes of the Lord God Almighty—and the oracle came to me, the words of the Lord himself."

"And?" Shanar asked again. "What was the oracle?"

Balaam stood now, unsteadily seeking his balance. He waved his arms and the wine cup as well, splattering wine across the table and the guests. His voice was loud and deep, and it filled Rahab's house with its foreboding:

" 'The Lord God Almighty brought them out of Egypt,' " he shouted, " 'they have the strength of a wild ox. They devour our hostile nations and break their bones in pieces; with their arrows they pierce them. Like a lion they crouch and lie down, like a lioness—who dares to rouse them?' "

He lost his balance then and sat heavily back into the pillows. He belched and continued in a hoarse whisper, so softly that only Rahab made out the words: " 'May those who bless the Habiru be blessed, and those who curse them be cursed also!' " Rahab shivered. Through his drunkenness, did he speak the truth?

But Shanar pressed for detail. "What happened then?" he asked impatiently.

The seer's eyes focused on the priest, and he answered: "Balak was furious. He refused to pay me. I was fortunate to escape with my life, and I didn't escape with any money at all." He spread his hands, holding out his almost-empty wine cup to Rahab, exaggerating the gesture of a beggar.

"I, the great Balaam, seer of the gods, known and respected all over the civilized world, am here, drinking with a small-city king and a little temple priest, in a harlot's house—and I have not even the money to pay for the evening's entertainments."

"That is of no matter, great one," Shanar quickly assured him. "Your presence honors our city, and I am pleased to see you after so many years. Your stories are wonderful. I have not laughed so much in years."

Shanar meant the comment as a compliment, but Balaam took offense. "My stories are not meant to keep you laughing. My story is true. I have seen the gods. I have seen the angels—and my donkey talked."

"Can you show me the gods?" Shanar asked. "If you can, I'll give you a hundred gold shekels, and if not—? What do you have? You can give me your donkey. I would like to have a talking donkey!" Again Shanar laughed, and the others laughed with him.

"I'll show you gods if you want to see gods," Balaam said nastily. "But if I win, I want more than a hundred gold shekels. I want the girl—that girl, the one playing the harp."

Kinah, who had been playing soft music throughout the evening, stopped instantly, her hands frozen to the harp strings.

"So may it be!" Shanar laughed again and slapped his hands together to signify that a bargain had been struck.

The seer struggled to his feet and lurched toward Kinah. He pinched her cheeks and breathed into her face. "Tomorrow, little girl, tomorrow you will be mine!" His laugh rang loudly through the room. He turned to Shanar. "Meet me at the temple before the dawn. We will see who can conjure gods and who commands the spirits."

When the guests had left, Rahab spoke angrily to Shanarbaal: "Kinah isn't yours to wager. You gave her to me. She is mine."

"You weren't mine to take either, my sweet. You belonged to Astarte. But don't worry—I can hold my own with that fat old fool."

"I hope so, Shanar," she answered. "Something about him is strange."

34

Behind the green doors of Astarte's temple, the two men met at dawn to fulfill their wager.

Shanar wore his finest, most elaborately embroidered robes. Balaam's robes were, in contrast, simple and unadorned. Above the robes, Balaam's face was severe and inscrutable; heavy jowls, shaded in gray and silver, added harshness to a face that was simultaneously dark and ashen. In this austere aspect, Balaam commanded the room. His presence seemed to reach even into its darkest corners. The man's dark eyes seemed wise and ancient, their color an indistinguishable shade, appearing first like the brown mud of the Jordan River and then like the brooding black of the midnight clouds.

Shanarbaal sat within the sorcerer's circle. Balaam had created the circle out of nothingness. Around the two men, the circumference of the circle glowed, shimmering with its own blue light. Shanar did not know how the magician had produced it, but it was impressive. Shanar was puzzled by Balaam's ceremony. The magician's style was very different from his own—less showy, less entertaining—but the man's results could not be denied. The circle glowed, but it did not burn. At a small altar within the circle, the seer performed rituals Shanarbaal had known for years, but there was a difference in the atmosphere of Balaam's circle.

Shanarbaal knew the secrets of mesmerism. He knew, therefore, that he had not been mesmerized. Only the pungent smell of Balaam's incense dulled the high priest's thinking, but in a way that was more relaxing than dangerous. Balaam's incense was strong—stronger than any used in the temple. Shanar recognized in it the heavy odor of nightshade, deadly if misused, but Balaam knew his craft. He would never mix a fatal dosage—never, unless by choice. *No, Shanar reasoned to himself, I am neither mesmerized nor drugged. What I see, I see.*

Ignoring Shanarbaal's presence, Balaam appeared to be in a trance. Continuing to chant and passing his hands above a small altar, Balaam now called upon the gods that Shanar did not know, and he quoted ritual never heard before in the Jericho temple.

"The time is now," the seer proclaimed loudly. "Return his evil unto him one hundredfold, one thousandfold."

Shanarbaal stared incredulously as, in response to Balaam's words, smoke seemed to curl out of the ritual instruments on the altar. Spiraling upward, the smoke seemed to hover in the air between the high priest and the seer.

"Go! I command it!" Balaam's voice was cold.

Light, much like swamp haze, glimmered momentarily within the smoke and then was gone. The smoke swirled upward, disappearing. Shanarbaal stared at the man before him. Gone was the drunken buffoon babbling of donkeys who talked; gone was the gluttonous country oaf whose speech annoyed even as it amused. The man who stood before Shanarbaal now presented a demeanor that could command pharaohs and that had, before Shanarbaal's eyes, commanded gods.

The high priest of the Temple Jericho-Baal was undone. He who had claimed to influence both gods and kings sat powerless, overwhelmed by the incantations of one whose spirit had communed with both the masters of darkness and the creator of light.

Shanar stood to speak to Balaam, who was even at that moment passing his hands above the perimeter of the circle and causing the glow to disappear.

"I have done you an injustice, Balaam; you have indeed won our wager. But we will talk of that later. Now, let us talk of the mysteries you have performed here. If this is the work of your Lord God Almighty, I wish to know him. I want this kind of power for myself!"

"You mistake, my friend, if you think our work this day to be that of the Lord God Almighty. He is not a god who obeys the bidding of mere mortals. I thought I had told you that. No, these are other gods whom we have served and who have served me. I am glad to say that fool of a king Balak will be sorry he ever heard the name of Balaam. I have sent a spirit to torment him, and I hope he rots in the wastelands!

167

"But the Lord God Almighty, Shanar, He is a different god. Even I cannot control the Lord God Almighty! He is a god who controls men, a god who—"

"Tell me no more of a god who controls men," Shanar said impatiently. "I will not serve him! I will have nothing to do with him. I want to know more of these gods who will do your bidding, of those you sent to torment your enemies. Tell me how I may deal with those gods!"

"All right, my friend," Balaam answered. "I can tell you anything you want to know. I have worshipped all gods, and none of their secrets are secrets to me. If you would have the masters of darkness to do your bidding, there are ways, and I can teach you."

"Then teach me!" Shanar spat. "I've had enough of trickery that masquerades as the gods. That I can do, and I do it well, but what you have done this day, that I cannot do, and I would learn it from you!"

The seer shrugged. "And so you shall, so you shall....But these are mysteries which must be learned thoroughly, for we deal with powers both dangerous and awesome. You must learn my lessons well, or you will suffer from your own stupidity."

"I will learn!" Shanar said eagerly. "Teach me now!"

The seer, having won his wager, felt inclined to placate Shanarbaal. "Come," he said. "Let us go to your most private chamber. I want a chamber that is far below the ground. Have you such?"

"We do, of course. Let us go now."

"Your eagerness is surprising, Shanar, but leave that lamp here. We will not need it. What I will teach you now is best learned in darkness and kept in the secret chambers of your soul."

It was midday when Balaam left the Temple of Jericho-Baal. He left several scrolls with Shanarbaal, and the high priest of Jericho closeted himself for study.

Balaam saddled his old donkey and rode her to the house of Rahab. He had his hundred gold shekels. Now he would claim the rest of his prize.

Rahab had been sewing with Kinah throughout the morning. The girl was tense and frightened; Rahab tried to comfort her though, secretly, she shared the girl's anxiety.

"Don't worry, Kinah—the man is a buffoon," she said.

Even Nantha, for once, expressed comfort and hope. "Our great priest, Shanarbaal, is certainly wiser than this fool," she said.

Kinah was not comforted. "I don't know, Nantha. That man pinched my cheeks hard, and he looked as though he meant it when he said that he would come to claim me."

"I know he has a great reputation as a seer," Rahab said, "but, surely, Kinah, the man's speech is as coarse as a camel driver's. He drinks too much; he has no self-control whatever. He cannot possibly be a threat."

"Trust Shanarbaal," Nantha agreed. "Look, it is almost midday. If that fool won his wager at dawn, don't you think he would be here by now?"

Then, as if planned by the gods, a pounding sounded on the door below. Balaam had come to claim his prize.

Rahab stood, her face showing no emotion. She gathered up a handful of golden coins from her cachepot. The knock sounded again. Kinah, still sitting on the floor with her sewing, began to tremble and to cry.

"Stay here," Rahab said coldly. "I think I know how to handle this man!" The coins went quickly into a small cloth sack, and Rahab descended the stairway.

She opened the door into the sunlit street and was face to face with—a donkey. The animal's soft brown eyes were eye level with Rahab—*very pleasant*, she thought, *more pleasant than the master!* Then Rahab's gaze traveled up to the leering grin of the short fat priest. She looked back at the donkey.

"Good morning, Oned!" Rahab said pleasantly, rubbing the graying muzzle of the beast. "And what news have you brought me today from the Lord God Almighty?"

But before the donkey could answer, if indeed she would have, the fat priest on her back snarled, "I have come for the girl, harlot! Bring her to me!"

Rahab laughed agreeably and continued to talk to the donkey. "I think you are more lovely than your master, Oned. You are certainly more polite!"

The priest began to shout, his voice angry and strident. "Bring me the girl. I have won her!"

At the noise, a small crowd gathered in the narrow street. Doors nearby opened, and curious neighbors looked to see what was happening. Rahab continued to talk to the donkey, speaking pleasantly but loudly enough so that the neighbors could hear her clearly. "Your master tells us that you can talk," she said, and her neighbors began to giggle. "I see that you speak more politely than your master!"

The little beast snorted gently, as if in answer, and Rahab continued to rub the donkey's muzzle.

"By the Baalim!" shouted the priest. "I said bring me the girl! She is mine! I won her from Shanarbaal!"

"Poor baby," said Rahab to the donkey. "Does your master not know that one must own something before he can wager it away? Tell your master, little donkey! Tell your master that I, Rahab, woman of Jericho, own the girl—and I have made no wager!"

The priest was livid. Rahab continued, and the crowd began to snicker loudly, mocking and laughing at the foreign priest, who looked very foolish, sitting on a fat old donkey and shouting obscenities at the richest woman in Jericho, who paid him no heed whatever.

"Do not incur my wrath, harlot!" he snarled. "I have won my wager with your priest. I will be paid!"

169

"Oh, what is that?" Rahab leaned close to the donkey, as if she were listening. "Well, I suppose we must look after you, little one, and get your fat master back to his home in civilization. Here, little donkey—here is gold in redemption for my handmaiden! Tell your master I wish him a very speedy journey!"

The priest snatched the coin purse, feeling its weightiness in his palm. It was heavy! He smiled.

"I will take your gold," he said softly. "You may keep the girl. She would, in truth, only be a burden on the journey. But I have something for you, too, harlot—something you may not want!" And then he spoke loudly, so that the crowd could listen: "Hear these words, the words of Balaam, the oracle of the gods." The laughter of the crowd ceased, and the street was instantly very still. "The words of the man who sees the mysteries of many gods: The walls of Jericho stand fortified against you, Rahab. You are an enemy of the Baalim, whom you have offended, and of your own people."

A sudden cloud covered the sun, and the street was darkened. The hairs prickled on Rahab's neck. The prophet continued. "This house is marked by the gods. After this day, this house will see me no more, but death and destruction it shall see. From this day forward, this house shall drip with unseen blood, and not all your gold nor any man's gold shall buy the redemption of your household."

He pulled at the donkey's reins and turned to leave. Looking back, he added, as if in afterthought: "May the unborn child die within your womb!"

At his words, the stabbing pain ripped through Rahab's insides. She carried no child, she was sure, yet the very core of her womanhood contracted at the prophet's curse. Balaam, the mad, the talking-donkey prophet, the fat-pig prophet, he who knew all gods and was faithful to none, had cursed a baby who did not exist. Without a word, Rahab turned and entered her house, closing the door and pressing her back against it. She had kept Kinah, but at what cost?

Nantha and Kinah had been standing in the public room, listening. Kinah was crying. "I was afraid," she said. "You cannot imagine how frightened I was!"

"Bless the gods," Nantha said. "I was frightened, too!"

Rahab smoothed the wet waves of Kinah's hair away from her eyes. "I was so afraid," the child repeated.

"You are safe now, Kinah," Rahab soothed her. "That madman prophet is gone. You have nothing to fear."

Kinah hugged Rahab tightly. "You paid him for me, didn't you? We listened. I was yours to begin with, but you have bought me back. Why did you do it? Oh, I'm so glad you did!"

Rahab laughed, relieved that the worst was over, pleased by the girl's resiliency. "Oh, yes," she teased Kinah, "you have certainly cost me enough now. The gold I gave that pig-prophet would have bought a small field or a vineyard or a pottery! Are you worth so much, little one?"

Kinah smiled, too, now, as she recognized the love in Rahab's voice. "I am not worth nearly so much, lady," she whispered.

Rahab pulled the child tightly to her breast. "You are worth much, much more, my darling. You are worth what you have cost me, Kinah. Never forget that."

"You are like a mother to me, Rahab," the girl said softly.

The prophet's curse sounded in Rahab's mind. "I am not your mother," Rahab snapped, sounding harsher than she had intended. "I am no one's mother, Kinah," she added more gently. "But I am your friend. Come, Nantha, bring us some wine. We have work to do, but I think we have earned some refreshment."

Rahab turned to ascend the dark and waiting stair.

35

The queen carried a child!

Sewing late into the night, Rahab thought with envy of the queen. Shanar had prophesied a child for the queen, but Balaam! Balaam with his dark gods! He had promised Rahab only images of death and blood. *Ha*, she thought, *I saw enough of blood at the temple. Surely blood holds no horror for me now!* But as her hands were occupied with the scarlet threads, she realized that only by keeping busy did she fend off the nightmares that would have haunted her.

This tapestry would hang in the chambers of the royal prince. It was finely woven wool; embroidered over the warp and the woof were a green tree branch and a bight red bird. The design was simple enough to please the child. *And someday*, she thought, *when he goes out into the wadi, he will hunt such a bird.*

She sighed, wishing that she could fly out her window and across the Jordan River. She wished that she could fly into the sunrise and leave behind this rotting city with its foul politics and its religion of death.

Outside, the thunder rolled. For days it had been raining, and Rahab felt the rain would never stop. The days would go on in endless repetition; the nights were never-ending troubled dreams. Better to work—busy hands, busy mind. No time for despair, no time for anguish. She concentrated instead on line, and color, and beauty! *Only in beauty lies sanity,* she thought.

Again, the thunder roared outside, echoing up from the Jordan, reverberating against the Jericho walls. The floor beneath her feet seemed to shudder.

Rahab rose, stretched, and walked slowly to the window, opening its shutters to let in the wet night air. Outside the only light that could be seen was the lightning flashing against the sky to the east. She breathed deeply and then turned, startled by the sound of a soft footfall on the stairway. It was Kinah.

"Oh, excuse me, Rahab. I didn't mean to startle you. I saw the light and came to see if there were something wrong."

"Nothing is wrong, little one," Rahab answered wearily. "It seemed a good time to work on this tapestry for our royal baby—and," she smiled, "I couldn't sleep."

"This is the third night this week that you have worked nearly all night, Rahab. You will hurt yourself if you continue this way."

"Now who is being mother to whom?" Rahab chided the girl. "I hurt myself more to lie in bed awake. This house does not run itself. There are many things that require my attention, more than I can deal with in the day."

Kinah frowned. "If you do not sleep, you will not work well—or worse, you will become ill. The plague attacks when we let ourselves grow weak."

"I won't have the plague, my dear, nor will you. The mixture Nantha puts into the wine strengthens us against it. Now, don't be troubled about me. Go back to bed."

The young girl looked at her with glowing eyes. "I worry about you because I love you. I'd be terrified here without you."

"That is a situation you will not have to face," Rahab reassured her. "I am not sick, and I will not leave you alone. Where I go, you go, and that is a promise. But for now, go to bed! When you are as old as I am, you may work all night if you please. Go!"

Rahab spoke the words firmly, but she smiled as she said them.

How very like Bishna this child was. The same gentle ways, the same loving tenderness. Much like a kitten that had been mistreated, she was always frightened, yet longing for love. That such a one should worry about her was extremely amusing.

She turned back to her work. The needle moved swiftly, requiring all her attention.

As the weeks passed, Kinah was worried by the change in her mistress. Since the visit of the prophet Balaam, Rahab seemed distracted. She did not laugh, nor did she tease and joke as the women worked during the day. Often, she worked all night. Nantha said it was because Shanarbaal had almost ceased his visits to the house.

One morning, as they worked in the sewing room, Kinah could not contain her concern. "Mistress," she said, "do you miss the high priest so much?"

Rahab looked at the younger girl in surprise, then answered her honestly. "Yes, Kinah, I do miss him. My work seems—I don't know—it seems somehow meaningless these days."

"He will return, mistress. He still comes to see you occasionally."

Rahab smiled sadly. "Yes, Kinah, but even you must have noticed the difference in him. Something has happened to him. Have you noticed how thin he has grown and how sullen? Sometimes when he is here, I am not sure it is the same man."

"Perhaps he is drinking too much, lady?" Kinah questioned.

"Yes," Rahab nodded gravely. "He is drinking, but that is not what has changed him."

"Balaam," Kinah said softly.

"Yes, Balaam!" Rahab hissed the words. "It was one thing when Shanar worshipped Baal and ran the temple of Astarte, but these dark gods that Balaam brought to Shanar—they have ruined him, Kinah. He mutters about them in the darkness, and he sleeps—Kinah, the way he sleeps, he murmurs constantly, but except for that, a woman might as well be alone. It is no wonder he seldom visits me."

"Oh, Rahab, I am so sorry," Kinah answered.

Rahab sighed. "Yes, Kinah, I too am sorry, but there is nothing we can do."

The high priestess Mari-Astarte sat before her brass mirror. The events of the past months pleased her as much as if she had planned them herself. Oparu—that thorn in the side of the high priest and in the side of the god himself—was gone, most certainly dead. Shanarbaal had not shared his plan with her, but that was of no importance—as long as it had worked. She respected his discretion. She had been ill that week. She would have been of little use to him. She would never be sure, perhaps, but she knew that Shanar had been responsible for the disappearance of the captain of the king's chariots.

She knew, too, that the giant Oparu would never trouble the priest again with his talk of iron chariots. Oparu's horse had returned to its stables alone, and after a week, a lieutenant of the charioteers had been appointed the new captain. A new captain was a weak captain, so the temple treasury was safe. Shanar had done well!

The pregnancy of Queen Asheratti was pleasing also. Mari had feared that Shanar's prophecy of a son for the king might not come true, and without that fulfillment, the king had seemed all too ready to invade the temple treasury every time the need arose. But now, with the announcement that Asheratti carried a child, and, of course, with the disappearance of Oparu, it seemed that Shanar's fortunes in the royal household had risen once again! *The arrival of a child could not be better timed,* she thought.

Most pleasing of all the recent events was the visit of the prophet Balaam. True enough, he was a crude goat, but, oh, what a change his visit wrought in Shanarbaal! Following the prophet's visit, the priest had spent weeks in deepest study. Mari smiled pleasantly at her reflection in the mirror. *He leaves the temple only rarely—which means,* she thought with feline satisfaction, *that he is not seeing Rahab!*

Mari wound her long black hair into a knot on top of her head, admired the effect, and secured it with a golden comb. She laughed. The house of Rahab had been her own source of irritation throughout her four years as priestess. Too many of the high priest's nights had been wasted at that harlot's house. Since the visit of Balaam, Shanar had shown no interest in the charms of his little city nest.

Mari grimaced—nor had he shown interest in visiting the nest of the high priestess, but that would change. Soon enough he would need respite from all his hours of closeted study. And when that time came, she would be there, waiting for him. The high priest belonged in the temple, with her.

As if in answer to her thought, the high priest appeared behind her in the mirror. She turned, startled, but pleased to see him in her chambers.

"I have need of you," Shanar said.

Mari smiled. So the time had come. "How may I serve you, my lord?"

"I require the presence of a priestess for an incantation."

"Oh." Her smile faded. "Then I am happy to assist you, of course, my lord."

"Come with me," the priest said curtly, turning to leave, but as he did, his eyes stopped upon a figure on Mari's personal altar.

"Where did you get this?" he demanded, picking up the statue almost fiercely.

Mari looked at him in surprise. Why was he so upset? "It was given to me by a temple worshipper. It is not important."

"You do not know what is important and what is not," the priest snapped at her. "This is Ninunta. He is the Assyrian god of thunder, and he is a protector of the secrets of priests. Who gave him to you?"

"As I said, Shanar, it was a temple worshipper, a man who gave his essence to the goddess and who desired her special favor."

"Where did he get it?"

"Shanar, I do not know where he got it. What difference does it make?"

Shanar looked at her as if she were insane but then, shaking his head harshly, he seemed to change his mind. "Perhaps it does not matter. Perhaps it is not important after all....Come, we have a ceremony to perform."

The high priestess stared at him but followed obediently.

174

The thunder awakened him. The room was black except for the sudden flashes of lightning. Dark shapes seemed to loom over him against the blackness of the night. The thunder roared again.

"Ninunta," Shanar whispered.

The darkness quivered in the flash of the lightning. *He is not here*, Shanar assured himself. The thunder seemed to rock the temple in answer. "Are you here then?" Shanar whispered the words into the darkness. "I did not move the statue, you know." The darkness simply waited.

"It was not my doing, I tell you," Shanar said, sitting up in his bed. "I did not know they had moved you." Shanarbaal silently hoped the god did not know that until today he had forgotten his youthful vow that the house in the city's walls would belong to Ninunta if the god would help Shanar become the high priest. The vow had been so long ago. It had seemed unimportant, but the scrolls said— The thunder sounded again.

"Ninunta, I am sorry," he pleaded. "If I have offended you, I will make amends. I will punish those who have removed your image."

The dark room was silent, but a gentle patter of rain began on the roof.

Shanar sighed and lay down again. The sound of the rain helped him sleep.

In the household of Rahab, everyone slept late. The gentle sound of the rain had formed the perfect background for sleeping well into the morning. In the kitchen, Nantha started the fire and began to prepare the breakfast. In his own room Alcion stood at the small window and looked at the rain-drenched land. He smiled and yawned. He always slept better during the rainy season.

Kinah, still lost in the last dream of the morning, sighed in the room across the stair. In her own chambers, Rahab stretched, sighed, and bounced out of bed. Rarely did she feel this well in the morning. She had slept soundly for the first night in weeks. She breathed deeply of the clean, damp air. She opened the shutters of her large window and looked out across the Jericho plain. *It is a well-washed world*, she thought.

"Where is your mistress?" The harsh shout of the high priest shattered the tranquility of the household. Nantha's answer was too quiet to be understood, but in a matter of seconds the high priest stood in Rahab's chambers.

Even as she tried to understand why Shanar was angry, Rahab was shocked by the change in his appearance. The man who stood ranting before her seemed but a skeleton of the Shanar she had loved. His color was sallow, and his eyes, sunken deeply into their sockets, glared with a feverish light. *Like the spirit of a dead one*, Rahab thought. Why was he so angry?

"Too far!" he was saying. "You have taken advantage of my kindness for the last time. I give you the house to use as your own, but is that enough? No! You must displace its gods!"

"What gods? What do you mean, Shanar?"

Shanar grabbed Rahab and propelled her roughly down the stairs and across

175

the public room, flinging aside the curtain to the alcove. "There!" he said, pointing into the empty blackness above the rafters. "What did you do with him?"

"Oh, him," she said softly, but Shanar was not amused. He received her answer as a confession. His stinging slap flung her to the bed.

"You have gone too far!" he shouted.

"My lord!" she interrupted.

"Silence!" he shrieked. "Ninunta no longer protects this house. Ninunta protects the temple now, for that is where he is. You have thrown him out!" He ground his teeth at her. "And when you threw him out, you threw me out as well!"

"But, my lord—"

"Silence!" he shrieked again. "If this is no longer Ninunta's house, it is no longer my house! I renounce all claim to it—and to you!" The high priest crouched beside the trembling woman. His snarl was unlike that of any human being. "I'll give you a prophecy, Rahab," he said, laughing suddenly, wildly. "You are an enemy of the Baalim. You are an enemy of Ninunta, whom you have offended. The protection of Jericho will not reach into this house! I leave you, now and forever, Rahab." In one movement, the priest was gone.

Rahab shuddered. Two priests had cursed her house, and in almost the same words, and one of them had been the man she loved. She ran out of the alcove and into the arms of Alcion.

The visit of Shanarbaal had its effect on everyone in the household. Nantha thought they would all be thrown out of the house into the streets, but as the days passed and no word came from the temple, she began to relax. *The high priest must be a kinder man than I realized,* she thought. *After what Rahab did to his alcove god, any punishment would have been justified!*

Alcion comforted Rahab on the morning of Shanarbaal's visit, but privately he was not comforted himself. He was concerned that Shanarbaal's vengeance on Rahab might include his own summons back to the temple. Although Alcion had not been unhappy during his time in the temple, he did not want to go back. Like Nantha, he had found a home in the house of Rahab. He would miss the warmth of her household if he were called to return to the temple of Astarte. But this summons, like Nantha's imagined message of eviction, did not come. Knowing Shanarbaal's temperament, Alcion assumed that the priest had chosen to ignore the existence of the house of Rahab. As usual, Alcion was right.

Kinah and Rahab worked harder than ever before. Rahab was supporting two households, and she did not take her responsibilities lightly. Her father's household must be fed and clothed, and recently Rahab had retained a physician, trained in Egypt, to visit her father regularly. Rahab did not mention Shanarbaal, but Kinah knew that the high priest's rejection weighed heavily upon her mistress. The long days and nights of work continued. Rahab did not demand that the members of her household work constantly, but she set an example that was hard to ignore.

Kinah worked with her mistress late into the night, but Rahab would at last send the girl to bed. Her own lamps, however, did not go out until the sunrise.

As the weeks passed without further word from the high priest, Rahab realized that he had meant what he said. He was not coming back. So she told herself that there was plenty to do without him. She was showing a greater profit than ever before, and she was beginning to re-establish a relationship with her parents.

She tried to visit her parents' household regularly. Usually she could find the time at least once a week to travel across the marketplace to the little house in the north wall where her father sold pottery and some of her tapestries. She never went alone into the city streets. She did not like to go into the city at all, but she felt it necessary to see that her father had everything he needed. Usually, Alcion walked with Rahab to her parents' house, and Micah accompanied her home. She was not afraid, but she had learned to be cautious. A woman like herself would bring a small fortune in the slave market.

36

Rahab's father was standing up when Rahab entered the main room of her parents' small house, a week later.

"Father!" Rahab exclaimed, "you are better."

Her father smiled at her, a sad but not an unkind smile. "I am better," he agreed. "The doctor you hired says my illness is one which comes and goes. Though I shall not again be well, I shall at times be better."

Rahab embraced him. "It is good news!" she said.

He smiled once more. It was, Rahab realized, the haunted smile of a man who had borne much pain. "You are a good daughter, Rahab," he said.

His simple acknowledgment warmed Rahab more than the compliments of a hundred patrons. "I am glad you are in Jericho, Father," was all that she could reply. Her mother entered the front room from the kitchen area of the house.

"Rahab, I'm glad you're here. Do you see how your father is improving? He will be well before we know it." Although Rahab's mother had been the one who had, at last, renounced family pride and called upon her disowned daughter, Kora had nevertheless failed to accept the chronic nature of her husband's disease. She always talked about what they would do when he was well again.

Rahab and her father exchanged glances. Her mother continued, "City life agrees with us, Rahab. We did well to move here." Rahab remembered how much her mother had protested at making the move to Jericho. "We will have no life in the city," she had said. "How will your father live without the fields?"

"I am grinding barley," her mother went on. "Come and join me."

Rahab obediently followed her mother into the alcove that served as kitchen. They sat on the floor. As her mother pounded the grain beneath the mill stones, Rahab smiled, remembering how often she had watched and helped with this simple chore when she was young. But she had especially enjoyed working in the fields and pastures with her father.

"Rahab, do you know that the queen will bear a child?" her mother asked.

"I have heard it," Rahab answered, immediately thinking of Shanarbaal's prophecy for the king. At last his oracle would come true. Finally Jericho would have a prince.

"Your sister, Tirnah, too, will bear another child. She needs to bear a son. Husbands love wives who give them sons."

"I am sure Tirnah will have no trouble bearing sons, Mother. She brought little Mita into the world easily. A baby boy will come easily as well."

"Yes, I hope it," her mother responded. "Mita is such a precious little girl, much like you, Rahab, when you were young. You should have a baby, Rahab. It is time. Can none of these Jericho men get you with a child?"

"I don't need a child, Mother," Rahab said with a laugh. "I am not like Tirnah. I do not have a husband who must be placated with sons."

Rahab's mother did not laugh in return. Instead she pounded the millstone harder against the barley. "You have been a woman these five and a half years since you entered the temple, yet you have borne no babies." Suddenly her mother stopped the pounding and looked at Rahab suspiciously. "I am right, am I not? You have borne no babies?" The question was almost an accusation.

"You are right, Mother," Rahab answered, seriously now. "I have borne no babies."

Her mother sighed and resumed her pounding. "You have been cursed, perhaps. The goddess is angry with you for some reason."

"I have not been cursed!" Rahab uttered the lie emphatically. "I have borne no babies because I have wanted no babies and the gods have yielded to my will—my will, Mother! Not that of the gods!"

"You talk nonsense, girl," her mother responded.

"I am going now, Mother; if you need anything, Micah can come for it. We will not talk of this again!" Rahab swept out of the room. Saying good-bye to her father, she bade Micah accompany her through the market.

37

Rahab held her veil close against her face, noting that the leers of camel drivers and of even less savory itinerants followed her in spite of—no, probably because of—her veil. She hated wearing veils, and she hated the conversation she had just ended with her mother.

She and Micah did not talk as they hurried through the crowded streets. Micah had known his sister long enough, by now, to understand that Rahab had no patience with the alliances of the market. He hurried through the streets, walking close enough to Rahab to prevent the pinches and comments that would have greeted any veiled or pretty woman. The city was a mad place.

Micah had learned much in his few months in Jericho. He had met many pretty girls, and he had found the girls of Jericho to be more than friendly. He knew that his sister's house was the most popular in the city, but he visited there only as a member of the family. Rahab treated him like a big child, and Kinah ignored him. Nantha was old enough to be his grandmother.

He had found other houses in the city, but they were so rowdy and dangerous that he had chosen to make his friends elsewhere. The few boys he knew in the city were villains, so corrupt both in manner and morality that even in Micah's most adventurous states he found them boorish. He visited the young girls who had become his friends, and he attempted to be a man and help his mother. Otherwise, he kept to himself, becoming wise in the city's ways and avoiding the city's men who were more dangerous to a young boy than lions to a sheep. Micah was glad he had grown up in the country.

One particular old merchant in the marketplace had, twice in the last month, suggested to Micah that a close alliance with him could be very profitable. Today as Micah hurried through the streets with Rahab, he took a short-cut in order to avoid the stall of that old troublemaker. Rahab did not protest. She liked shortcuts.

As the pair hurried through a sidestreet, their path was suddenly blocked by a trio of men who stepped out of a doorway and into the narrow alley. The three men had their arms about each other's waists and were obviously drunken. Two of the men were Egyptian soldiers, the man in the middle Rahab recognized with distaste. He was Habbak, the king's chief eunuch.

"What, ho!" the eunuch cried. "Who have we here? A veiled lady and a pretty boy."

"Yes, Habbak, and we're in a hurry," Rahab replied curtly.

"Oh, they're in a hurry," one of the Egyptians jeered laughingly. "To what pleasures do you hurry, lady? Do you like little boys?"

The other soldier laughed suggestively. "Yes, so it is! She likes little boys, too!"

"Don't be ridiculous," Rahab snapped. "This boy is my brother. Let us pass, Habbak."

"Her brother, Habbak! The story grows sweeter still."

"Yes," Habbak said, laughing. "He is her brother, brother of the richest harlot in Jericho. Isn't that so, Rahab? Richer than Onuk, are you? Richer than the king?"

"You are drunk, Habbak, and it is not even the middle of the day."

"Ah, my lady," Habbak said in mock dismay. "We drink only to ease our loneliness. We have no lovers."

"You can love yourself, Habbak," Rahab retorted. *No one else will love you,* she thought.

"Oh, lady, you mistake my purpose. I would not think of imposing upon the time of one so busy as yourself, but perhaps you could convince your pretty little brother to join us. There is much that a boy so young can be taught by men like ourselves. We would enjoy his company."

"Today is not the day for such revelries, Habbak. We have urgent business to be about. Let us pass!" she demanded.

One of the Egyptian soldiers reached out and tickled Micah's neck. The boy jumped as if he'd been bitten by a viper.

Rahab was incensed. "Habbak, tell your friend to leave my brother alone."

Habbak giggled unnaturally and reached out to pinch Micah's cheek. The boy roughly brushed the older man's hand away.

"There's no need to be so touchy," Habbak said, addressing Micah directly. "You're very pretty. You deserve to be admired."

Micah straightened sharply and addressed the eunuch with sudden fierceness. "I have women to admire me, eunuch! I prefer my pleasures with girls! That is, perhaps, beyond your understanding?"

"Oh, my," Habbak said surprisedly, "the little scorpion has a sting. But you mistake, boy, to think I do not know the pleasures of women. Why, ask your sister! She has on more than one occasion entertained my friends and me."

For all his city-wise manner, Micah could not contain the look of shock that passed across his face.

"But Habbak," Rahab interrupted, "the house of Rahab will not entertain you again. Your rudeness has lost you your welcome."

"Oh, but then, how shall I ever live?" the eunuch said in ironic protest. "Come, my friends," he said to the soldiers pleadingly. "You must console me in this, my deep loss."

The other men laughed and caressed Habbak in a feigned sympathy.

"Farewell, Rahab," Habbak said, in a still-mocking voice. "Today you have broken my heart."

Much to Rahab's relief, they moved on. Rahab and Micah traveled swiftly through the streets and toward her house. As they hurried, Micah asked, "Rahab, did you really entertain a eunuch?"

"He is one of the king's men, Micah. It was necessary."

"I did not think they liked women," the boy said, more innocently than he realized.

"There is nothing the men of this city do not like, and many eunuchs find ways to humiliate women and boys. You must be very careful!"

The boy was silent, aware once again of how strange life was within the walls of Jericho.

Garlands of flowers decorated the king's formal audience room, and musicians created a happy atmosphere as harps, flutes, lyres, and voices joined in a hymn of thanksgiving for the safe birth of a royal son, a prince of Jericho.

Rahab sat, holding the tapestry she had made for the royal child and feeling uncomfortable. She had not been in this room since she left the temple. She avoided such gatherings, preferring instead the heady ambiance of the intimate gatherings in her own public room. Here, she was one of the crowd, one of the admirers. Every leading citizen of Jericho was here this day, each bringing a gift to honor the royal birth.

The voices of the chanters were loud and happy:

> "A son is born in Jericho!
> Blessed be Astarte who has given us a son.
> A prince is born to Jericho, that the people may rejoice.

Happy is Queen Asheratti; happy is the king;
Happy are the people that a king-to-be is born.
The destiny of Jericho shall become his own.
Happy is the city! Her walls shout for joy!"

A great shout went up in the king's public room. The walls reverberated with the songs of the well-wishers.

Rahab wished she were at home. She could think of a hundred better ways to spend her time than waiting in the king's anteroom. She despised waiting. Still worse, she had to wait in the same room with the high priestess. Across the room from Rahab sat Mari-Astarte. In her lap, the high priestess held a golden bowl, a gift that Rahab knew was symbolic of the bountiful blessings of the goddess.

Rahab could not keep her eyes off the high priestess. *She looks older*, Rahab thought. The goddess paint no longer hid the hard lines around her eyes. She never smiled, and it was beginning to show in the set of her mouth. But her gown was lovely. She had always had good taste. Rahab's gaze traveled to Mari's hair. Was that a sprinkle of gray—or just a trick of the light? As Rahab stared, lost in her thoughts, Mari looked up, her eyes meeting Rahab's. Rahab looked down in sudden embarrassment. *This is ridiculous*, she thought. *If they do not move the people faster than this, I'll be here all day. I wish I'd brought a tapestry to work on.*

As the morning passed, slaves began to serve cool drinks. Rahab was relieved at this respite. But to her dismay, the drink was more water than wine. *The king is thrifty to the point of rudeness*, she thought. *He indulges only himself.*

At last, a servant came to bid her enter the queen's antechamber. She shot a triumphant look in the direction of the high priestess and followed the servant to the queen's anteroom. The servant left Rahab alone in the tiny room. *Good*, she thought, *this means I will be next.*

The door from the public room opened again, however, and a sniveling servant ushered the high priestess into the room. Rahab rolled her eyes. She could think of no way to avoid speaking, but Mari spoke, haughtily: "It has been a long time since I last saw you, Rahab. I thought perhaps you'd left the city. We never see you at the temple anymore."

"I don't have time for the temple, my lady," she replied respectfully. "My business keeps me occupied."

"Ah...that's nice to hear," Mari responded with exaggerated good humor. "I thought that your business might have slowed since you no longer have the patronage of the high priest."

Rahab looked surprised. "Oh, really?" she answered. "I've been too busy to notice."

Mari ignored this comment. "The high priest is quite busy these days himself," she said conversationally, "and with more important affairs. He brought

182

his gift to the king's baby yesterday in a special audience."

"Too bad the temple does not honor its babies so well," Rahab could not hold back the words.

Mari looked puzzled. "There is no greater honor than to be received by the goddess, Rahab," Mari quoted the ritual.

"The goddess protects those whom she loves," Rahab answered in ritual, adding impulsively, sarcastically, "doesn't she?"

"Well, of course she does. You know that the goddess protects her handmaidens. She protected you while you were in the temple."

"As she protected Asabaal? And Bishna?" Rahab wished that she had not spoken these words. She wished she could escape this conversation.

"Accidents happen, Rahab. The goddess did not will their deaths. Asabaal's own sharp tongue caused her death—and Bishna—well, Shanarbaal drank too much that night."

"Onuk the Fat incited them," Rahab answered sharply.

"Onuk was present, that's true, but he did not incite them. Shanar was the ringleader that night! For some reason, he wanted to see Bishna dance, and then they all got rough with her."

Rahab hoped she was misunderstanding. Shanarbaal would not have participated. "Did Shanar not try to stop them?" she asked.

"Stop them?" Mari looked at her incredulously. "I told you—he started them. He was the first—and—I think—he was the last!"

It was suddenly clear to Rahab why Bishna had not wanted her to go to Shanar for help. It was all sickeningly clear, but Mari must not know her feelings.

"What a beautiful bowl," Rahab said.

"Oh, yes," Mari said. "It was made by the sea people. It is quite expensive."

At this moment, mercifully for Rahab, a servant ushered the high priestess into the queen's chamber to present her gift. Rahab was again alone. She unrolled her tapestry and looked at its cheerful design; green branch and red bird. So she had been wrong. Four and a half years since Bishna had died, and she had been wrong all that time. She had trusted Shanarbaal, but he was no better than the rest of them. In fact, if Mari were to be believed, he was worse. He was worse even than Onuk. She had been betrayed by all of them! Shanarbaal, Amaranthe, Astarte, Baal—the very religion of Jericho had betrayed her!

Her thoughts were interrupted by the sound of a soft chuckle. She turned to see Habbak, lounging against the door frame, arms crossed, smiling at her. At her gaze, he crossed the room and joined her on the bench, sitting very close to her. Rahab shifted to acknowledge his presence, moving away from the man.

"Good day, Rahab," he said softly. "What gift have you brought to our young prince?"

She held out the tapestry. "As you can see, I have brought him this."

"You do fine work, Rahab," he said. "Yours is a house of many talents, it seems."

Rahab was puzzled by this comment. "Thank you, Habbak," she said finally.

Habbak reached inside his tunic, smiling through his teeth, and withdrew a small embroidered bag that he pressed into Rahab's hand, closing her fingers over it so that she could not withdraw. His touch was dry and cool. The bag was heavy.

"I want to buy him from you," he whispered.

"You—what?" Rahab did not understand.

"Your scribe—I want to buy him," Habbak said.

Rahab shook her head, laughed, and tried to pull away from the sallow-faced eunuch. He would not release her hand. "You what?" she asked. At first, she had thought he meant Micah.

"Alcion. I want to buy him from you," he repeated.

"You are surely joking, Habbak. Alcion is not for sale."

"I am making you an offer, Rahab," Habbak repeated sharply.

Rahab jerked her hand away, standing quickly. Habbak's bag fell to the floor. "I told you—Alcion is not for sale!"

The eunuch's eyes were cold. "It is a handsome offer, Rahab. You would do well to consider my position before you reject it. I have much influence with the king."

Rahab spoke sharply now. "Alcion is not for sale, Habbak—not to you, not to anyone!"

Habbak snatched the sack of gold from the floor and stood to leave. His eyes narrowed, and the threat rustled from clenched jaws: "Then it is you who will pay, Rahab." He turned and stalked out of the room.

38

Nantha had said long ago that Rahab's barrenness was a curse. Her comment had caused one of the worst quarrels Nantha had ever had with Rahab, and neither the curse nor the barrenness had ever been mentioned again. But Rahab was sure the older woman still remembered it.

It could not be a curse, Rahab told herself. Baal was nothing. Astarte was nothing. Two nothings could not prevent her bearing a child, yet in the almost five years that she had lived in Jericho house, no babe had been born to her.

Now, Rahab realized how deeply she desired a baby of her own. In times past, thoughts of Bishna's baby had been too painful; they had been pushed aside, buried. But the memory of the queen's baby could not be denied. So delightfully had he nestled against the beautiful Queen Asheratti's breast, that Rahab's own breast had been filled with tender longings.

She was Rahab, woman of Jericho, the woman with everything. She should have a baby. It was only right.

Rahab sat with Kinah in the sewing room. "He is a beautiful baby," Rahab said wistfully.

Kinah laughed and replied, "As you have told me three times already, Rahab!"

"Oh, so I have." Rahab laughed self-consciously at her own error. "But I am awed by how perfect he appeared. It is something to which one never grows accustomed: that each baby is so perfect and so beautiful."

"Babies are wonderful, Rahab. You are right; perhaps soon I shall be old enough to bear children. Then we will have babies in this house—Oh!" Kinah bit her lip, realizing she had said too much. Nantha had told her that Rahab's barrenness was a curse and that she must not speak of it.

Rahab looked at the younger girl intently: Kinah was already old enough to have a baby, but she matured slowly despite her work in Rahab's house. "A baby might be exactly what this house needs," she said solemnly, standing and turning away from Kinah, toward the loom.

Rahab continued to think of the queen's baby. It seemed every woman in Jericho could bear a babe except Rahab. She was the one woman in the city who had everything a woman could desire—everything, except the two things most women desired: a husband and children.

A husband she did not need. She could have children without one. *If only I could have children!* she thought. During the years that she had lived in the house in the wall there had been a few times when she had thought that perhaps, just perhaps, she carried a child. There had been months when she had hoped—almost holding her breath in her desire that nothing disturb the possibility—but always she had been disappointed. Each time her hopes had been raised, they had been destroyed as her time had come upon her cruelly, with greater pain and bleeding than was her custom.

"I did not summon you to come here," Shanarbaal said. The high priest who stared at Rahab seemed but a shade of the man she had known, had loved. Easily Rahab could have believed that the man who sat before her was Shanarbaal's father or his grandfather, but could he be the virile, powerful man she had known so well? He seemed a gray and wrinkled shell.

"I have come to make a request of you, my lord," Rahab said.

The high priest's eyes grew colder, if that were possible, more furtive than before. "What do you want?" he snapped.

Rahab hesitated. She despised herself for the hesitancy, but she could not help it. She hated with all her heart to ask anything of this man who had proved to her so completely that no one was to be loved, no one was to be trusted.

With an act of will, she pushed her pride down and faced the priest with her problem. Her voice was quiet, unusually reserved. "I have come to you because I have a problem which I cannot solve, and I hoped that you could..." she hesitated again and then forced herself to go on "...that you could forgive our differences enough to help me. I do not know what to do." She hurried on. "I have done everything that the legends of Jericho suggest and yet nothing works. I thought perhaps you would know a way—a secret, or an incantation—something that might help me."

Shanarbaal looked at the woman before him. She was babbling. What was she talking about? She must not know that he didn't understand her. Staring at her through yellowed eyes, he answered her with ritual words: "Myriad are the mysteries, the secrets of the gods, woman. What is your wish, your want, your will?"

Rahab swallowed and admitted her shame to him: "I cannot carry a child, Shanar. I want one. I can afford one, but I cannot carry one."

Shanar exhaled deeply. Now he understood. Now the situation was within his power. Rahab still carried the goddess within. He knew this, but she did not. "You say you cannot carry a child. Have you conceived before?" he asked sharply. He wondered if she had miscarried. The goddess within sometimes allowed that.

"No, my lord," she answered. Her next words were a soft, hoarse whisper of despair. "I fear, my lord, that I am barren. I am eighteen years old, and I have never borne a child."

186

The priest looked at her without expression. "To be barren is a curse, Rahab. You do not believe in the gods, so how can you be cursed by them?"

Some of Rahab's courage returned. "I have not said that I am cursed, but you have said my house is cursed." Her voice became a whisper. "So, too, did Balaam curse me. I want to bear a child, Shanar. Please tell me what I must do."

"If you are cursed by the great prophet Balaam, there may be little I can do." The high priest's voice now had taken on authority. To Rahab, he sounded more like the old Shanar. The priest motioned to the scrolls lying before him on the table. "But," he added, "these scrolls belonged to the great prophet, and since he is dead now—killed with the Midianites—perhaps I could have some effect on his curse."

Rahab sighed in relief. He would help her! She had been so afraid that he would laugh at her request, that he would laugh at the very idea of helping her.

"Come back in a week," the priest said. "It may be that I will have something to say to you then."

Rahab left the high priest's chambers with hope. For the first time in months, she felt that her life might, indeed, have some value. Shanar might look like a shade, but perhaps he was a sick man. He had sounded almost friendly at the end of their conversation. Perhaps Mari had lied about his action on the night of Bishna's death. Perhaps she could trust him after all.

Rahab passed quickly through the temple courtyard, but before she could step through its gates, she was stabbed by an unusually sharp pain in her stomach. She bent over, clutching herself. As she looked up, she found herself staring across the porticoes, at the dark green doors of the "goddess within." The goddess within? The phrase tormented her each time the pain in her stomach began—the goddess within! Who was she?

Staring at those green doors, Rahab remembered fleetingly the night of her dedication ceremony: the blood of the doves, the rich red wine, the terrible pain on the morning after, and that echoing phrase, "the goddess within." Perhaps the pain was causing her to be barren, or perhaps this goddess could give her a baby! She remembered the ritual of the dedication, "I shall carry the secret goddess." Was that the goddess within? *Shanar would know. I will ask him!* With instant determination, she turned to visit again the chambers of the high priest. No komer stood on guard outside Shanar's rooms—off on some errand, Rahab guessed. She was about to announce herself when she heard a strange sound from within the high priest's chambers. She listened; it was a chanting, a low, moaning, painful sound. She could see nothing but the priest's anteroom, an empty cubicle. The moaning was within the chamber itself. Rahab slipped behind the curtain and stood, hesitant again, inside the anteroom. The moaning grew more insistent; it sounded like Shanarbaal. Rahab peered into the chamber.

187

Shanar was no longer seated at the table. He sat, instead, cross-legged on the floor. His eyes were closed. He rocked and moaned. Two trickles of blood ran down each of his cheeks. Suddenly his eyes bolted open. He was staring directly at Rahab. She started to speak, but before the words were formed, the priest spoke: "Master, I will obey!" he said.

Rahab's gaze searched quickly about the room, but there was no one else there. Shanar was alone. He continued to stare blankly. "I have done all that you commanded, my lord," the priest said. "The sacrifices are doubled, the rites increased by ten!"

The priest paused. His rocking stopped. "It is enough, my lord! I have fulfilled my bargain. You must honor yours. You promised."

Rahab watched in horror as the priest scraped his face with his long, talonlike fingernails. Another stream of blood appeared. The priest seemed to tremble and cower on the floor. "No, my lord, I will not! I promise you, I will not! I would never betray you! I will tell the woman nothing. Rahab will bear no child, my lord."

Rahab gasped, but the priest did not hear her. He sat, in a listening posture, for several moments.

Then he laughed, madly. "You are right, my lord. Of course, you are right! We will never help our enemies! Never!" He laughed again, wildly, coldly, and to Rahab his laughter was like the sound of crows fighting over carrion in the wilderness.

Biting her lip, holding back her tears, she turned and fled.

Sleep refused to come, refused to ease her, night after night. She worked: thinking, searching, striving for some kind of peace, peace so that she could sleep.

Her life was filled with too much turmoil. There were too many complications. She could not forget her interview with Shanarbaal. She could not forget the threats of Habbak. He was an irritating man. She couldn't forget the words of Mari. She couldn't forget the queen and her baby. The long night hours stretched ahead—waiting.

I might as well keep working, she thought. The king would be pleased with this tapestry. She laughed to herself. *A tapestry of my life would need to be woven in black and red. Black for my anger and red for the blood that has cursed my life ever since my temple days. White—how I long for white!* It was easy as she wove the king's tapestry to forget about white. No white appeared in the royal colors, nor was there white in the goddess symbols. The white she longed for was a memory, a dim, dancing memory that always eluded her. Perhaps it was the lateness of the hour that caused her thoughts to flood with this strange, tormented longing for a dimly remembered whiteness—an innocence left behind too long ago to be recalled. Her thoughts fluttered and shivered like the shadows cast before the dancing flames of her lamp. Images, too, fluttered across her mind—images from her childhood. The idea of innocence tormented, taunted her.

The innocence of my childhood, she thought, *of my father when he was young, when he was strong, when his muscles rippled in the sun and the sweat glistened on his brown shoulders and arms as he worked in the field and in the animal pens.* She remembered the control of those arms as he handled his tools—his scythe, his knives, his hoe—as he tilled and as he fed the goat or sheared the sheep—the sheep, white against white. Of course they were dirty, but after washing they were clean, a dull white, and after shearing off one layer, they were suddenly pure shining white, as if everything were wiped away—all the dirt and mud and grime of their entire lives washed away and purged with the simple whish of her father's knives.

I wish I could shear my life of its blackness. I wish I could shear my memory of all the nights and the temple, and of what we did to Oparu—then perhaps I could sleep. The freedom she had felt when she first left the temple was gone. She was no longer bound to the goddess, but to this political wasteland—bound to this balancing of one power against another. The temple against the palace, the altar against the crown, the priest against the king. It would never end. *How I wish—a thousand wishes! If Shanarbaal were a different man. If his new gods didn't keep him bound in mad dreams, the dreams of his own mystic power within the Jericho walls. The irony of that—the Jericho walls: this ancient fortress. How I wish I could show these fools how great their ancient fortress stands.*

Fools! They are fools! I am so tired of the idiocies of men. She laughed softly, her eyes flickering over her work—the king's tapestry of idiocy! *The king makes Shanarbaal dance to his tune. Shanarbaal thinks the king dances to his. Each thinks he has the other in his control. Neither of them controls anything—not even himself. And Shanar even thinks he controls the gods, yet he bows and snivels to their imaginary voices!*

Ouch! I must be more careful. I'll hurt myself—perhaps even stain this tapestry with my blood—blood, blood, blood, blood: the feast of the gods!

"Upon whom should I call?" she said aloud, raising her eyes—"To what?" she asked herself. "The ceiling?

"To whom shall I address my prayers? Who art thou?" she asked, mocking not so much the ceiling as herself. "Who art thou?" she asked, her voice rising a little. She was amused with her own play. "Dost thou exist? Creator? God of the universe?"

Baal would be the god of the universe. Astarte would be the female power, the mother goddess owning the universe and destroying it. But no, they were not. If they existed at all, they existed as sniveling cowards in some realm demolished by its own lusts.

"Thou!" she startled herself with the intensity of her own cry. *The dark night plays tricks on me,* she thought. *It is too late, and I have been working too long and too hard. And what does it get me? A sleepless bed and walls which do not answer back. They say the Habiru are coming to destroy it all. I talk to myself in the night. And in the day I work and I work and I work, and where am I headed? I will not be queen; I will not be priestess; I cannot even become a mother! I will be only what I am: Rahab, woman of Jericho, harlot of Jericho, woman of power—ha! At least I know the irony of my own life. At least I am not caught up in my own idiocy as are the priest and the king and the cunning men who serve them, like Habbak and Onuk, fat pig of the universe!*

Certainly there are pigs of the universe, she thought. She knew many of them. *There are plenty of pigs, plenty of men, and perhaps, plenty of gods who have sunk to levels beneath human imagination. But is there no one greater? Is there any good power left in the heavens or on the earth? Dost thou exist?* she questioned her ceiling again.

Art thou the God who spoke to me? When I was young, my child's heart responded. In the days of my innocence, I thought that I knew an innocent god. Where is he now? Who is he?

"I am not becoming a mad woman," she murmured. "I am in control. I am in control of my life, for what little that's worth. Do I speak to the walls, or is there someone who listens?" *At times, indeed, I knew the Baalim were there; at times, indeed, I knew the goddess spoke. Perhaps it was caused by the wine; perhaps it was from the drugs—yet it seemed very real, and it did not seem good.*

"Art thou real? Dost thou exist?" she asked. "The shadows play strange games against the wall, and I—I call upon whom? Art thou he of whom Balaam spoke? Art thou the Lord God Almighty, God of the universe? Shall I call upon you? I am not mad; at worst, I play games with myself. In the middle of the night, what is the harm?

"If there is a just god in the heavens—answer me! Make real to me your existence, for I have not met you here in Jericho! If ever I met you at all, it was in the fields with the flowers and the flax and the sheep and the tiny, bleating baby lambs—pure and clean and loving me—almost the last love I have known.

"Hear me, O God, if God thou art! Speak to me. I am only Rahab—harlot queen of Jericho, consort of priests and kings—and thou art God. Art thou God? You can strike me if you are God indeed—you can strike me. Send your thunder down. For I believe that the thunder is God's—if God there is—in spite of Baal."

She sighed. "I am not afraid of dying anymore, for I have seen that life is an unending tapestry of death. What should I fear? That I go down to the death that we all go down to? That my bones will rot beneath the Jericho walls—beneath the rotting Jericho walls? I am not afraid.

"I have gained everything. Look at me if God thou art: I am rich; I am respected. My house is the best in the city. If you exist, there is only one thing that you can give me that I lack. Give me—I feel a fool to ask it— How can I say it? How can I be so innocent yet? You can give me one thing I do not have—give me a child!"

No voice responded. No god appeared.

She sighed in resignation. "No thunder rolls. No lightning strikes. I am a fool." She went back to her sewing.

The room seems warm—too warm. I wonder if it is the room or if I have a fever. My foolishness is probably raising a fever.

I will go to the window and cool these ravings. Yes, I am so impressive. Rahab, woman of the world, stays up through the night calling upon a god she does not know, a god who does not hear. At least you do not give me dung, God who does not exist. What will you give me?

The stars—no...those lights are too low to be stars....They must be campfires. They twinkle across the distance like the numberless stars of the heavens. Those campfires should not be there. They are there! The Habiru are there; they are coming. Oh, we shall all be killed. Oparu's death was for nothing.

She threw back her head and laughed aloud, her voice rising in a cry that sounded almost like a death wail. It was but one word: "Ha-bi-ru!"

The strangeness of her own cry jolted her. *I must not speak so loudly; I shall have the city sentries storming into my home. They will think the Habiru are already here while in truth they wait, choosing their own time, and we sit like a wounded dove awaiting the final stroke, like a bound lamb awaiting the plunge of the knife.*

I should go to bed—I should get some sleep.

Leaning into the open window, she stared out at the twinkling campfires. *How they glimmer! The Habiru come, to destroy the rotting Jericho wall, to destroy the rotting Jericho lives—and mine is one.*

She threw back her head and laughed. "The Habiru come, God of the universe, and what do they bring us? Death! If you were truly God of the universe, they would bring us life. They would bring me a child. But perhaps even you are not that powerful.

"My apologies, creator God. Perhaps in some heaven you walk sleepless tonight even as I do, contemplating the Habiru destruction of Jericho—for destroy us they will!"

39

"The people are afraid," the king told Rahab. "They tremble and their hearts turn to water."

He sighed wearily, shaking his head. "Their fear spreads like a plague. Even my personal guards are not spared! I listen to them talking when they do not know it, and what they say makes *me* afraid." He laughed, but it was not a sound of mirth. "Me! The king! Afraid!"

He leaned closer to Rahab and lowered his voice conspiratorially, speaking so softly that the roar of the wind and rain outside almost buried his words.

"The Habiru have taken Sihon and Og!" he said.

"What—the great kings of the east?" Rahab had thought them strong.

"Sihon and all his army came out to do battle at Jahaz, and the hordes took his towns and destroyed them. Then they marched from Aroer to Gilead, taking everything in their path."

"And Og?" she asked.

"Og met them in battle at Edrei, and the Habiru killed every living being—man, woman, and child—in Bashan. They took sixty fortified cities—walled, with bars and gates. They have killed two nations! And their kings!" He almost wailed, "They have met horrible deaths! Og sleeps in an iron bed, they say. Ahhh, Rahab, I fear we shall be next. Nothing seems to stop these Habiru hordes!"

Rahab shuddered at the news of Sihon and Og. "Even the children! Oh, great king, do our people know of this?"

"No!" he hissed. "And they must not know! Already the people of Jericho tremble. If they knew of Sihon and Og, their terror would overwhelm them."

Or if they knew their king shared their fear, Rahab thought, but she held her counsel.

"You are the one person to whom I can safely speak my mind in these days, Rahab," the king continued.

"You know you can trust that your words will go no further, my lord," she answered.

"If the people knew, there would be chaos. I have never seen a mob, but I have heard—and I do not wish to be torn limb from limb by my own people! Nor by the Habiru!"

"My lord—are you sure—these tales you hear—are you sure they are true? In time of war, rumors multiply," Rahab reasoned.

"Ah—if only I could hope they were rumor. No, Rahab. A captain of Og came to me. He had escaped the battle, but he died, even as he told me—so I know he spoke the truth. Dying men do not lie."

"Perhaps he spoke truth as he understood it, my lord, but perhaps his fear colored the truth."

"Not likely," he answered, "though I wish it were. He had left the city with Og and his army. They engaged the Habiru and were simply overwhelmed by their numbers! He said for every one of the Habiru struck down, twenty would rise to take his place!"

Rahab remembered the words of Balaam about "the Lord God Almighty." Did the Habiru have a mighty god, a real god, fighting for them? Rahab wished she had known a mighty god! Jericho would need a mighty god to save her if these Habiru were as strong as the king believed.

The thunder roared, shaking the earth beneath them. Even the walls of Jericho seemed to shake beneath the fury of the heavens. The rainy season was always depressing in its continuous dreariness, but this year had been particularly wet and dismal. It seemed the rain would never stop.

"The walls still stand, my lord," Rahab said reassuringly. "So long as the walls stand, Jericho is safe. We have everlasting springs within the city. We'll not run out of water or provisions even if they lay us siege."

"We would finally starve. We are lost, Rahab. They will trample us!"

"No, my lord, they will not trample us! We are safe within these walls. Shanarbaal is wise in this matter. You have repaired the walls, even whitewashed them. We are safe!" Rahab spoke with more confidence than she felt.

"Besides, my lord, the rainy season has been the wettest in memory. The Jordan has been at floodtide for months. An army cannot cross it."

"Even so, the dry season will come, Rahab. Then they will cross it."

"But, we need not go out to fight them!" Rahab tried still to encourage the king. "These walls have protected Jericho for thousands of years! They will surely continue. Shanarbaal has always said so!"

"Shanarbaal! Bah!" the king responded angrily. "Who is Shanarbaal? Where is Shanarbaal? Ever since that fool Balaam made his ridiculous wager, Shanarbaal has been nowhere to be found. He hides behind the temple door. He might as well be dead!"

Rahab was surprised. She had not realized that the changes she had seen in Shanar had extended to his political alliances.

"All my advisors are gone," the king added, almost whining. "First, Oparu ran off in the rain, taking half the royal treasury. Now, Shanarbaal has become more enamored of the gods than of the world. Habbak is a weak fool. There is no one to whom I can turn, Rahab!"

The king looked about the household. In the kitchen, Nantha scrubbed peaceably at a big pot. In a corner of the public room, Kinah's harp murmured gentle melodies.

"This is the only place in the city," he said, "that is not infected with fear. The whole city stinks of it. And I can do nothing to ease the fear of my people, Rahab. I have done everything I know to do. Last summer, we repaired the walls as Shanarbaal suggested. We improved the ramparts, built them up. We have filled the storage caves with grain. But still the people tremble."

"Why is everyone so sure that the Habiru will attack, my lord?"

"Once a people have tasted the spoils of war, Rahab, they do not easily relinquish the joys of battle. After the way they swept over the armies of Sihon and Og, they will not stop."

Rahab's thoughts escaped her lips: "Certainly, if they wish to take Canaan, Jericho is the gateway to the hill country."

The king's face blanched. "You are right," he said. "We are sure to be their target." He stood then. "I can think of only one thing left to do."

"What is it, my lord?" she asked.

"I must write to the pharaoh for help. One of his soldiers—the gods know there are enough of them in this city—can take the message to him. Pharaoh knows that I pay them tribute—and that the Habiru will not. But I will need your help, Rahab."

"Of course," she answered.

"I want Alcion to write the letter. Habbak is my scribe, but I cannot trust him. He talks too much. Anything he knows, the city will know. The people of the city must not learn of the fall of Sihon and Og, and no one must know that I have written to the pharaoh for help. If they knew, I would not live to see the Habiru attack. My own people would kill me."

"You're right, my lord. The people hate the Egyptians. No one wants more of their soldiers here."

"They won't want the Habiru here either, but we may have to choose between the two."

Quickly, Rahab summoned Alcion and explained the king's request. Without a word, the scribe prepared a clay tablet with plaster and wrote on it the king's pleas for help. The king stood, tucked the tablet within his cloak, and left.

"Rahab," Alcion asked, after the king had gone, "did I understand the king to say that the people must not know of the defeats of Sihon and Og?"

"Yes," she answered, "that is exactly what he said."

Alcion and Nantha looked at each other; they both shook their heads and sighed.

"We were in the marketplace this morning," Alcion said, but Nantha interrupted him.

"The defeat of Sihon and Og is on everyone's lips, lady. There is no one who does not know in the streets. They say that the Habiru have burned two hundred cities and that we will be the next."

40

The drunken Habbak reclined at the table with a small group of friends. Some were eunuchs; some were not. All had been drinking since before the sunset, and the hour was now somewhere between midnight and dawn. No one at the party knew or cared about the time. The king's chief eunuch had helped himself to both the king's larder and the king's wine cellar. Wine had flowed all evening. A servant brought in yet another tray covered with heavily spiced meats.

Matnar stabbed a hunk of the meat and poked it into his mouth. Almost as quickly spitting it out with a resounding "Bah!" he gulped his wine. "Habbak! This meat is spoiled!" he shouted angrily. "Is there no more fresh meat in Jericho? Not even in the larder of the king?"

"Fresh meat is difficult to get these days, Matnar, you know that." Habbak laughed drunkenly. "There is too much war in the land around us. Caravans do not get through. Farmers who are being slaughtered themselves have no chance to slaughter their animals. There is no fresher meat in Jericho than in the king's larder." He stabbed a piece of the meat and raised it to his nose. Even through the spices he could smell its stench. "But, as you say, this meat is spoiled." He waved to the servant to take the tray away.

Matnar snorted. "Jericho grows more wretched every day. There is no caravan trade, there is no fresh meat, and certainly there are no fresh faces."

Habbak snorted in return. "So it is fresh faces you miss, is it, Matnar? When the caravans avoid Jericho, there are no new slave boys to add to your harem. You do enjoy variety, don't you?"

"Hah!" the man laughed at Habbak. "It does not matter what I enjoy. I cannot enjoy what does not exist. There is no one, man or woman, in Jericho who is new to me!"

Habbak and the others laughed at this boast. Habbak's eyes gleamed narrowly. "I'll wager that there is one fresh face in Jericho, a face you may never have noticed, yet in a house that you know well."

"Bah! This cannot be!" he said, but he leered at Habbak in sudden interest. "Who is this fresh face in Jericho?"

"One who dwells in the house of Rahab," Habbak said.

The other man laughed uproariously. "Oh," he said, "Habbak, indeed you had me fooled! I thought for a moment that you were serious! The house of Rahab! Ha! Of whom do you speak? Kinah? No, that little dove has roosted in my nest. Rahab, herself? Impossible! You must mean Nantha, then! I admit she is no prize, but she is not without some charms. So you see, the house of Rahab holds no mysteries for me. You amuse me, Habbak."

"Ah, but you have left out one member of her household," the eunuch replied lazily, "and it was to him that I refer."

"Him, you say? She has a brother, but he does not live in her household." The other men frowned in thought. "Him? She has a scribe, but, ah, you are right! By the gods, Habbak, you are right! I have not, in all my nights at Rahab's house, spent an evening or even a few minutes with her scribe." He leered, leaning close to Habbak. "Should I, then? Is he worth it?"

"Ah, he is perhaps worth much!" Habbak laughed vulgarly. "Apparently he thinks himself worth a great deal. He avoids Rahab's customers. He is a creature of the day. I have seen him early in the mornings in the marketplace, but at night? He disappears into the recesses of Rahab's house, and, my friends, he disappears alone."

"Is he attractive?" one of the others asked, joining the conversation.

"Extremely so. He was the private slave of Shanarbaal for several years, and the priest is, as you know, a man who understands beauty. Perhaps you remember this boy from the temple? His name is Alcion."

"Alcion!" There were murmurs around the table.

"Hmmm. Ah, yes," several of the men nodded in agreement. They remembered the pretty slave.

Matnar smiled and waggled his head. "I would like to see this pretty boy!"

"Certainly, you may see him," Habbak teased the other man. "You may see him if you go to the marketplace tomorrow morning."

"Curse the morning!" laughed one of the others. "Let us see him tonight. The house of Rahab is not far. What's to stop us?"

The others laughed in agreement. "What's to stop us?"

"We can go right now!"

"Yes, let's see this boy who values himself above our pleasures. Let's see what he is really worth!"

"We shall see him now!"

The men lurched out of the banqueting room and into the streets of Jericho, streets that were full of merrymakers. The city of Jericho did not sleep.

The men stumbled drunkenly through the streets, laughing and cursing one another. Some of them shouted to friends they passed, and soon the group grew from a few of Habbak's friends to a larger group—all drunken and all eager to sample the favors of Rahab's eunuch.

Rahab's house was dark, the evening's guests having left hours before.

Habbak banged on her door, at the same time making lewd remarks to his friends.

"Rahab, open the door!" he shouted, banging loudly. "Raaaa-haaaab, Weee-ee've come to vis-it you!"

"Open the door, harlot!" Matnar shouted angrily. The wine was completely in control of him. "Open the door and bring us Alcion!"

"Yes, bring us Alcion!" the others in the crowd picked up the refrain. "Bring us Alcion! We want Alcion!"

"Give us Alcion!" They began to bang continuously on the door.

Inside the house, everyone was suddenly awake. Rahab lighted a small lamp and hurried to the second landing.

"Alcion, what is happening?" she asked frantically as the eunuch and Kinah joined her on the stair. "What do they want?"

The eunuch's face was pale in the light from the lamp, but his voice was hard and dry. "Apparently they want me, Rahab."

Rahab looked at him in puzzlement. "Have you made enemies, Alcion? What do they want with you?"

"Listen to them," he responded. "You can hear what they want."

Rahab concentrated on the angry, lewd shouting. Alcion was right. What they wanted was plain enough, and there were a lot of them.

"Mistress, you can't let them in!" Kinah protested.

Nantha joined them on the stair. "There are a lot of them," she said, affirming Rahab's fear. "I peeked out the kitchen window at them, and they're all drunk. Habbak and Matnar seem to be leading them."

"Habbak," Alcion whispered with understanding, for he had seen the man watching him in the marketplace.

"I won't let them in, Alcion," Rahab promised.

"You won't have to. If they bang much harder on that door, they'll *be* in," he answered.

Rahab hurried to the door. Nantha stationed herself at a crack in the kitchen window.

"Let us in! We want Alcion!" the shouts continued.

"I hear you! I hear you!" Rahab answered.

Alcion and Rahab held the door. Nantha cursed softly.

"Go home, Habbak, or I will tell the king!" Rahab threatened.

"What's the king going to do?" Matnar yelled drunkenly.

"She'll tell the king," a voice mocked. "Who cares if you tell the king?"

"Dead people don't talk," another voice shouted.

"We'll all be killed anyway when the Habiru get to us!"

"Give us Alcion! We want him now! Better for us to have him than the Habiru!"

"We, at least, will enjoy him!" The crowd laughed.

"Come out, Alcion! Come out! We want to play!"

Rahab gasped. This was unbelievable! She didn't know what to do. The voices continued.

"We'll get him anyway!"

"If you want to live, you'll open this door!"

"Come on, Rahab! We like girls, too! We won't leave you lonely!"

"Let us in, harlot!"

197

The men began to slam their bodies against the bolted door. Alcion and Rahab looked at each other wildly. "I'll go, Rahab," Alcion whispered. "These men are crazy with wine. If I don't go now, they may kill us all!"

"Aagh!" Habbak gagged.

"By the gods, out of his way!"

The banging suddenly stopped.

"Oh, no!"

Sounds of violent retching followed.

Rahab turned to Nantha. "What's happening?" she asked.

Nantha peered out the window.

"They are vomiting," Nantha said in amazement. "Several of them are vomiting in the street."

Rahab looked at Alcion. She smiled. He smiled. She giggled. He giggled. Nantha and Kinah began to giggle.

"The others are leaving," Nantha said. "I don't blame them. I'd leave too!"

Everyone in the house of Rahab began to laugh wildly.

In the street, Matnar cursed Habbak. "It was that meat you served us!" he shouted. "It was all rotten! If I don't die first, I'll kill you!"

Habbak didn't answer. He couldn't. He was sure he would die before Matnar could kill him. Alcion was forgotten. The mob dispersed.

Inside the house, Nantha stopped laughing. "Oh, what a mess!" she said. "And we'll have to clean it up in the morning. It will take a hundred trips to the springs to get enough water."

"At least we'll be alive to clean it up," Kinah answered.

"Don't worry about it," Rahab said, still laughing. "Maybe a pack of hungry dogs will come by in the night!"

41

Rahab thought at once that they were Habiru.

It wasn't their dress, for their attire was typical of desert travelers: dusty turbans, dusty beards, dusty robes, dusty feet. The sand of their travels came with them. She knew they were not camel drovers. She could smell drovers at a distance. There were two of them. One was taller than the other, and perhaps younger. They looked, she thought, a little wild-eyed, standing awkwardly in her doorway peering inside as if trying to read shapes in the darkness.

She opened wide the wooden door and gestured the two strangers inside with the customary greeting: "Welcome, strangers! May the light of the goddess grant you joy in my house."

The response was not the customary. Instead of the usual "Thanks to you, my lady," she received a searching look and strained silence. The two men exchanged glances, and finally the taller man spoke.

"Ah...lady...we, ah, do not seek a goddess, nor do we seek joy....Is this, ah, your house?"

Obviously, Rahab thought, *these men are strangers to civilized life!* She could not identify the accent. It sounded vaguely of Egypt, and yet the tones were clearer, more precise, than the speech of the men of the Nile. Very well! She would make them welcome and learn their secrets!

Her answer was smiling, gracious. "Yes, I am Rahab, woman of Jericho, and this is my house." Her eyes searched the eyes of the taller man. "How may I serve you?"

"I am Salma," he answered, avoiding her eyes, "and this is my companion, Daniel."

In the dim, soft light of the single oil lamp and the fading twilight that came in through the door, Salma's gaze took in this woman Rahab. She wore a skirt of many veils, adorned with gold. Jewels glittered in her ears, around her neck, on her arms, on her fingers, in her navel, around her ankles, and even on her toes. Never had he seen a woman so attired! He was astonished.

Salma searched for words and decided to speak the simple truth.

"We are strangers, and we were told that we might find shelter here for the night," he said.

He looked to Daniel for support. Had he phrased his request properly? They had expected an innkeeper, a man with a paunch, perhaps, and an open kettle—not this woman who dressed so shamelessly.

The woman laughed, and the sound from deep within her bosom made the necklaces quiver over her breasts. "Oh, yes," she said, "my house is widely known for its open door and its hospitality to strangers."

Rahab was well aware of the effect her appearance had on the strangers. It had been some time since she had felt so captivating, so alluring. She stepped back, motioning them to enter.

"You must be fatigued from your travels," she said after she had bolted the door. "Let me get some water. It will refresh you."

She turned toward the cooking room. "Nantha!" she called out, "bring me a basin of water and some fresh linen. We have guests!"

The men were wary. Daniel lifted the curtain over the alcove to peer quickly at the empty room. Rahab noted his furtive gesture. Surely they are spies, she thought. No simple travelers would have been so cautious. She laughed pleasantly. "Fear not, strangers. I have no other guests tonight!"

It occurred to Salma that this woman would know the city. *We can learn much from her, if we can get her to talk enough,* he thought.

"Why is that, lady Rahab?" Salma asked. "Surely such a gracious hostess has many guests!"

Schooled in the ploys of politicians, Rahab seized on this comment to confirm her suspicions. She watched the men closely as she spoke: "Not so much these days," she said derisively. "The fear of the Habiru strikes at the hearts of the men of Jericho, and it robs them of their manhood!"

Aha! Salma thought, darting a glance at Daniel. *They are afraid of us!* Daniel's glance in return assured Salma that he had read the same message. They were elated. *Why should we be surprised?* Salma thought. Joshua had told them that God had given them the country, that the people would melt in fear of them. He was exhilarated, thrilled at this confirmation of Yahweh's promise, excited and eager to see how it would be worked out.

Rahab noted their reaction. Her suspicions were confirmed. *Definitely,* she thought, *these men are spies from the Habiru!* Rahab felt alive again. She would enjoy her work tonight!

The water was brought, and Rahab began the gentle ritual of washing the dust of travel from Salma's feet. Her fingers lingered over the task as she rubbed his feet soothingly. She could feel the tension and the tiredness leave his feet and legs as she worked. *Before this night is over,* she thought, *I will know their plans, their strengths, their numbers.*

Rahab exerted her most charming demeanor. Soon they would be relaxed, well fed, and physically satisfied. In the process, they would retain no secrets.

"You have traveled far, stranger?" she asked casually as she washed and rubbed.

Salma sighed. "It seems I have traveled forever, lady!" he said. "Perhaps only now have I come home."

The shorter man gave him a hard look and snorted. "Canaan has always been our home! You are too gallant, Salma!"

"Perhaps," responded the taller man with a sigh, catching the warning to guard his words. "But I think in all my life no woman has ever treated me so—well."

Rahab laughed lightly, and again the jewels glittered. "It is my pleasure, my lord. An appreciative man gives strength to my fingers and joy to my heart. But tell me, strangers, have you been on the caravan trail?"

"We have," answered Salma, truthfully.

"If you came from the south, if you crossed the hills near Abel-shittim, did you see the campfires of the Habiru?"

His foot jumped within her hands. He was silent for a moment. Rahab said nothing, waiting.

Salma shrugged his shoulders. "Ah, lady, we have passed many campfires in out travels. We think, sometimes, we have seen the campfires of all the world." Again he shrugged his shoulders. "When you have seen one campfire, you have seen all campfires!"

She laughed again, delighted.

"I think that these campfires are different, stranger. From my window, in the night, I think that these campfires are myriad as the stars."

"Yes, that they are," he said, remembering Yahweh's promise to Abraham that the sons of Israel would be as numberless as the stars of heaven.

Completing at last the ritual footwashing, Rahab carefully dried his feet and then took his hand to lead him to the table. Nantha had prepared a variety of fruits, bread, cheese, and a pitcher of cool, watered wine. Rahab poured the wine into a cup and was surprised when the man called Daniel declined this refreshment. Her expression revealed her puzzlement, though she said nothing.

Daniel asked for water. "For all my life," he said, "I have heard of the famous springs of Jericho. Now that the Lord has brought me here, I should like to taste these famous waters."

"As you wish, stranger," she said.

Salma remembered the warnings of Joshua: "Beware the wine! When the wine is red, it lays a snare! It loosens tongues." He also requested water.

As the men ate, Rahab led the conversation back to the Habiru.

"The people here fear that those campfires across the Jordan, in the hills of Abel-shittim, portend an attack from the Habiru—siege, war. I think they're right. What do you think?"

Again, Salma shrugged his shoulders. "The Lord might say," he said, "but not I."

"And who is the Lord?" she asked.

"The Lord?" Salma repeated. *Maybe I have said too much already!* he thought. *To speak further of the one true God would give us away, yet this woman knows nothing of kings and wars. She is just an innkeeper.*

"The Lord is the creator of all things," he said, and ate.

"And what is his name?" Rahab asked.

"His name may not be spoken."

Rahab was intrigued. This was indeed a foreign god! She remembered that Balaam had said the name of the god of the Habiru. It was Yahweh. The men seemed to be more interested in eating than in talking, but she wanted to know more of this strange god.

"Then what does he look like?"

Salma was aware that he was talking too much, yet unable to avoid her seemingly simple questions. "No man has ever looked upon his face," he said.

"Surely you jest!" Rahab answered, laughing. "How can you worship a god if you cannot make his likeness!" It was an exclamation, not a question.

"He is not a god. He is *the* God. If we could make him, like a statue, how could he make us?"

"Salma, eat!" Daniel interrupted angrily. If the innkeeper knew anything of Israel and her God, Yahweh, then surely their mission was revealed. The woman seemed pleasant enough, yet he was wary. He had the uncomfortable feeling that they might be more transparent than they thought. "The food deserves your attention. It is good food." To Rahab he added, "We thank you."

"Your appetite is appreciation enough, stranger; I am pleased—" she flashed a special smile at Salma—"truly pleased that the table of my house is pleasant to your taste."

"Ah, that it is, my lady," Salma responded, relieved to turn the conversation away from the dangerous path it had been taking.

"The water, especially, is refreshing," Daniel said, indicating that he would like more.

Rahab rose, gracefully—posing? Daniel wondered—and poured more water for each man.

"Is the water always this good?" Daniel asked innocently.

"So it has always been," Rahab answered, "and so it will always be." She was amused at Daniel's clumsy attempt to pump information. The question was too elementary. Water would be a key resource in the event of siege, she knew, and she knew this would be the first and foremost question that spies from the Habiru would seek to answer.

"Water will never be a problem for Jericho," she continued conversationally, adding as an afterthought: "Jericho's tribulations will come from other weaknesses."

Both men were staring at her, open-mouthed. Pretending not to notice, Rahab rose and called to Kinah to play the harp. *The men did not drink the wine, but no matter,* she thought. *They are men, and they will respond to my dance as men respond.*

As the music began, she began the dance of love slowly. But no sooner had her body begun the undulations of the dance than both men jumped to their feet as if startled by a roaring lion.

"Stop!" Daniel shouted. This dance was too much! His senses could not withstand this onslaught of sensuality.

Kinah instantly froze, her fingers still on the harp strings. Rahab's arms dropped, and she asked, "Why? What is wrong?" Surely these men had seen the dance of love—surely.

"Ah—lady Rahab—ah, we do not wish to, to offend you—but, ah...." Daniel said, wishing he had never volunteered for this mission.

Salma spoke quickly, filling in the awkward silence. "We do not wish to offend you, lady, but we have walked many miles this day. Might we go to bed for the night? Could you show us our lodging?"

Rahab was surprised. So that was it. She could not believe that they wanted bed without the preparatory dance! They might be more interesting than she had thought, these Habiru.

She bowed, laughing in anticipation.

"As you wish, my lord. I am at your service, as is Kinah." Kinah bowed as well.

"Come," Rahab invited. "My bedchamber is upstairs, as is Kinah's."

The two men looked at one another. She had said "my" bedchamber, "Kinah's" bedchamber. Did this mean—

Rahab and the harpist each picked up an oil lamp.

"Come," Rahab commanded. She did not add the polite phrase, "The goddess calls you to her joy." She knew by now that these two men, these Habiru, would not appreciate such a reference.

Kinah led the way upward, up the narrow, dark staircase. The two travelers followed, then Rahab.

Rahab's mind flew as they climbed the stairway. She was intrigued and puzzled by these men: Salma, the taller one, his intense physical response to her touch; the other, Daniel, and his clumsy attempt at guile as he asked about the water. Their refusal of the wine, their instant, violent reaction to the dance, their candor about a god whom they obviously believed was real and powerful: yes, they were Habiru spies. They could be nothing else.

She thought of the stories she had heard of the Habiru. Shanarbaal had told her that they had attacked a generation ago and that the men of Canaan had repelled them easily. They had wandered in the desert ever since. And then she realized: *these men have been desert wanderers. They have never been to a city before. They don't know who I am or what I do. They think I am an innkeeper. No wonder they reacted so strangely!*

The realization took her breath away, and she stopped on the second landing and began to giggle and then to laugh. She caught her breath and started upward, still chuckling.

The men were already well on their way toward the third landing. Their apprehensions were mounting. Had they stumbled into a house of prostitution? How would they ever explain to Joshua that they had fallen into the hands of the very sort of woman they had been warned to avoid? They had asked, casually, in the marketplace where a stranger might spend the night, and the merchant, a seller of tapestries, had sent them here.

"Do you think—" Salma started to whisper to Daniel.

"Yes—but the Lord guides our steps. Fear not!"

Below them, in a small circle of light on the stairway, the woman Rahab was laughing. It was a soft laugh, a different timbre than her laugh as she had served them supper. It sounded as if she were delighted with some private jest.

It's a pleasant sound, Salma thought. *The prostitute has a pleasant laugh*—an odd observation, he realized, but reassuring.

They had just reached the third landing when they heard a loud pounding on the door and the shouts of angry men. "Rahab! Open in the name of the king!" The shouts reverberated up the stairs.

Rahab touched Salma's arm to be sure she had his attention, and she spoke softly and quickly: "I know that you are spies from the Habiru. That will be the king's guards—you have surely been seen. If they find you, you will not live the night. Upstairs, on the roof, I have laid out flax. Hurry—lie under the flax. Kinah, show them! Hurry!"

Handing Salma her lamp, she motioned them upward and turned back to meet the king's guard. The pounding continued. Rahab's mind moved even faster than her feet. In the darkness of these hated stairs, her sandals knew the way unerringly: no rise or indentation surprised her. She thought of the men hiding upstairs, Salma and Daniel, Habiru spies, men who believed in a god greater than Baal, stronger than Astarte, a creator god, not a destroyer.

Below her, pounding at the door, were the men of the king, the men of Jericho, the men of Baal and Astarte. The warriors of a betrayer god. Her word could betray the spies or give them life.

The Lord God Almighty, Balaam had called the Habiru God; the God of creation, the spy had said. Was he the God of the campfires she had seen in the night?

"Are you that God?" she questioned. "If you are real, give me a sign!"

As she reached the second landing, peace settled over her, a peace she had never felt before. "Yahweh?" she asked.

A blaze of light flooded the stairwell. "Yahweh!" she said with awe and assurance.

Calmly, she walked down the stairs to greet the soldiers of the king who had broken down her door. The glaring light of their torches had been her answer. She knew what she must do!

PART THREE

RAHAB: BRIDE OF THE COVENANT

*By faith the harlot Rahab
perished not with them that
believed not. When she had
received the spies with peace.*

42

INTERLUDE

And Joshua the son of Nun sent two men secretly from Shittim as spies, saying, "Go, view the land, especially Jericho." And they went, and came into the house of a harlot whose name was Rahab, and lodged there.[2] And it was told the king of Jericho, "Behold, certain men of Israel have come here tonight to search out the land."[3] Then the king of Jericho sent to Rahab, saying, "Bring forth the men that have come to you, who entered your house; for they have come to search out all the land."[4] But the woman had taken the two men and hidden them; and she said, "True, men came to me, but I did not know where they came from;[5] and when the gate was to be closed, at dark, the men went out; where the men went I do not know; pursue them quickly, for you will overtake them."[6] But she had brought them up to the roof, and hid them with the stalks of flax which she had laid in order on the roof.[7] So the men pursued after them on the way to the Jordan as far as the fords; and as soon as the pursuers had gone out, the gate was shut.

[8]Before they lay down, she came up to them on the roof,[9] and said to the men, "I know that the LORD has given you the land, and that the fear of you has fallen upon us, and that all the inhabitants of the land melt away before you.[10] For we have heard how the LORD dried up the water of the Red Sea before you when you came out of Egypt, and what you did to the two kings of the Amorites that were beyond the Jordan, to Sihon and Og, whom you utterly destroyed.[11] And as soon as we heard it, our hearts melted, and there was no courage left in any man, because of you; for the LORD your God is he who is God in heaven above and on earth beneath.[12] Now then, swear to me by the LORD that as I have dealt kindly with you, you also will deal kindly with my father's house, and give me a sure sign,[13] and save alive my father and mother, my brothers and sisters, and all who belong to them, and deliver our lives from death."[14] And the men said to her, "Our life for yours! If you do not tell this business of ours, then we will deal kindly and faithfully with you when the LORD gives us the land."

¹⁵Then she let them down by a rope through the window, for her house was built into the city wall, so that she dwelt in the wall.¹⁶ And she said to them, "Go into the hills, lest the pursuers meet you; and hide yourselves there three days, until the pursuers have returned; then afterward you may go your way."¹⁷ The men said to her, "We will be guiltless with respect to this oath of yours which you have made us swear.¹⁸ Behold, when we come into the land, you shall bind this scarlet cord in the window through which you let us down; and you shall gather into your house your father and mother, your brothers, and all your father's household.¹⁹ If any one goes out of the doors of your house into the street, his blood shall be upon his head, and we shall be guiltless; but if a hand is laid upon any one who is with you in the house, his blood shall be on our head.²⁰ But if you tell this business of ours, then we shall be guiltless with respect to your oath which you have made us swear."²¹ And she said, "According to your words, so be it." Then she sent them away, and they departed; and she bound the scarlet cord in the window.

²²They departed, and went into the hills, and remained there three days, until the pursuers returned; for the pursuers had made search all along the way and found nothing.²³ Then the two men came down again from the hills, and passed over and came to Joshua the son of Nun; and they told him all that had befallen them.²⁴ And they said to Joshua, "Truly the LORD has given all the land into our hands; and moreover all the inhabitants of the land are faint-hearted because of us."

Joshua 2 RSV

Rahab watched as the shadowy outlines of the spies blended into the dark valley below; they would be safely into the hills before the sun rose, while the king's men would be searching near the fords of the Jordan. She smiled wryly. If she knew the king's soldiers, they would return as heroes to say they had watched the spies drown in the flooded Jordan and wash toward the salt sea.

She looked across the Jordan toward the hills of Abel-shittim. The campfires still shone like innocent stars against the black sky. The sun would soon rise, and the campfires, like the stars, would disappear in the light of the day—the campfires of her new people, the people of the God she had chosen this night. A scarlet cord hung from her window as a sign of the bargain she'd made. There could be no turning back.

Guided by the pale light of the full moon, the spies raced toward the hills. Once in the shadows of the trees and bushes in the wadi, they slowed their pace but moved rapidly without waste of motion or energy. When at last they threw themselves to the ground and rested, Daniel was the first to speak: "If she betrays us, we are dead men."

Salma's first answer was a breathless grunt, but in a moment he responded. "We would be dead men already if she had not helped us."

"It's risky business to trust a harlot."

208

Salma still breathed heavily. "We have trusted one, and we left the city with our lives." He lifted himself from the ground and leaned against a large boulder. "And we have the information Joshua needs. The city will be ours."

"It will be ours," Daniel agreed. "But at a high cost. How do you think Joshua will respond to our bargain with the woman? The last thing he will want is a Canaanite in the camp."

"There was nothing else to be done; you saw that."

"I saw," Daniel responded gravely. "And I saw your eyes as you looked at her, and I saw her touch you before we left. I would be sorry to see you stoned for consorting with a harlot."

"I am a son of Judah, a servant of the Most High God. I will not forget my heritage."

"I hope not, Salma, but you are young—"

"Only three years younger than you are!"

"Nonetheless, your blood runs hotter than mine ever did. You must watch yourself when that woman enters our camp."

"I will watch myself, but it will not be necessary. The camps of Israel are large enough. I can avoid one Canaanite. She need not be anywhere near me."

"Remember that when the time comes," Daniel said, standing up. "The moon is starting its descent; I think we should find a cave to sleep in. It will be morning before we are ready."

As Salma entered the tent, Marnya, his wife smiled at him, inviting him to her arms. He had forgotten how lovely she was. Love shone in her eyes, the deep love of a child bride for the only man she had known, the innocent, trusting love of a wife who had known no betrayal and had not sinned against her vows. Gently, surely she dropped her robe. Her skin gleamed golden, rubbed gold, sun-drenched skin, the treasured midday gold of his desert wife's love.

He reached for her, but she stepped back, eluding his grasp. Her laughter sounded strangely in his ears, distant, too distant. His wife dropped onto the sleeping mat, laughing up at him. He couldn't see her face but could only hear her laughter echoing—like laughter in a strange dark stairwell—but he could see her body, pale, a blurred bareness, a softness with no edges! First she was there, lying before him, the outlines of her body soft and fluid; then she was blurring, changing, the pale skin turning into petals, petals pure and soft, soft as the lily. He was no longer looking at a woman, but staring deep into the heart of a flower whose incense drew him softly, surely—fragrant petals opening against the night, against the black night sky, long, flowing waves of black night sky. It wasn't the sky: it was her hair, long black rope that swirled around him, entwining him...slowly, surely...tightening, strangling, hanging him from the Jericho walls.

He was awake. The cave was blacker than a moonless night, and damp. He was awake and sitting up; he touched his cheek. His face, in fact, his entire body, was covered in a profuse sweat. Suddenly, he remembered his dream. He panted for breath. The woman in the dream had not been Marnya, his beloved, the first-loved wife of his youth. The woman in his dream had been Rahab, the harlot! A Canaanite guilty of—he did not know—a Canaanite might be guilty of anything. A harlot! In his dream he had confused his beloved, his precious Marnya, with the image of the Canaanite whore. He closed his eyes and breathed a prayer: "Lord God, forgive me. Forgive me for harboring the image of that woman, the lustful, provoking vision of that woman. O God of my fathers, preserve me from sin. Preserve me from these memories!"

Other images from his past, memories too strong to be denied, assailed him: his joy at Marnya's laughter, soft and childlike; her sweet, sloping, brown eyes, as trusting as any baby's.

The image of Rahab the harlot crossed his mind: the voluptuous red of her painted lips, the tinkling of the golden chains and jewels that lay sparkling across her bosom; her deep rich laughter, the incense of her perfume, the gentle caress of her hands on his feet—

"Enough!" Salma said the word aloud and forcefully. Was he no better than this, to be tempted by the charms of a prostitute? Was a judgment of death what he would claim for himself, a death that would shame both his tribe and his God? Salma was a prince of the tribe of Judah. He loved the law of his Lord; he would not disobey his God!

When sleep came finally in gentle waves, it lapped away his tensions, washing quietly upward the repeated tide of his prayer: *O God of my fathers, preserve me from sin!*

"But the spies drowned!" The king was shouting.

Shanar's yellow eyes narrowed. "Your soldiers say they drowned—but it's a lie!"

"How do you know that? My men are loyal."

"To themselves!" Shanar spat. "They failed in their mission, and now they would escape the consequences."

"By the horned god Baal, Shanar! You accuse my men, but you have no witnesses!"

"Ah, but I do," the priest responded.

The king looked at him in astonishment. "Who? What do you mean?"

"Ninunta," Shanar said, as if the name alone answered everything.

"Ninunta? The Assyrian bird god?"

"Do not mock the god," Shanar warned.

"But—" the king was incredulous.

"Ninunta came to me," Shanar began.

The king stared at him; the priest was not joking.

"He came to me to tell me that the spies are safe. He saw them in a cave."

The king turned from the priest and called to a servant. "More wine! Bring me more wine!"

"Wine will not save your kingdom! Only Ninunta can save Jericho now!" Shanar shouted.

"But Baal and Astarte are our protectors."

Shanar shook his head fiercely. "They are not strong enough," he said. "Ninunta is the true king of the universe. He has told me so!"

"But Shanar, those spies couldn't get across the river at floodtide. We are safe from the Habiru, for a while."

"They got here, didn't they?" the priest demanded.

The king looked down. "Perhaps they came around over the mountains," he mumbled lamely. He drank again from his winecup.

"And perhaps they flew!" Shanar snapped.

"They're gone now," the king said. "That's all that matters."

"They'll be back—and their armies with them."

"But the river—the river will stop them."

"Fool!" Shanar shouted, knocking the wine cup from the king's hand. "I have told you already—only Ninunta can stop them."

The king began to cry.

Shanar leaned over him threateningly and whispered, "The god demands the dedication of your son."

The king looked up at Shanar, who seemed to tower over him. "No," he said. "You will not take my boy, my only son, for your filthy Assyrian god."

"Ninunta hears you, foolish little king, and he will have your son."

"No—my son is to be king of Jericho."

"Ninunta will have your son—or there will be no Jericho."

The king stood to his feet and glared at the priest. "I am still the king," he said. "You will not make my son a priest. You will not make my son a sacrifice. My son must be king!"

The priest stepped back and bowed exaggeratedly. "King of Nothing," he said. "Tonight, King of Nothing, you will see the power of Ninunta. You will see something become nothing. Ninunta will speak to you tonight." Chuckling, the priest whirled and was gone.

Within minutes the news spread throughout the palace and then throughout the city: Shanarbaal the priest had struck the king and pronounced a curse on him, and tonight Shanar's Assyrian god would show forth his power. The people waited.

Later that night, as Shanar sat at his private ritual, he chuckled softly. He had studied the stars; he knew the secrets of the heavens. He knew the mysteries that the priests did not tell the people.

43

A full yellow moon lighted the Jordan Valley, casting eerie shadows down the wadis from the hills toward the wilderness. Sitting on his haunches, the watchman of the walls of Jericho thought of the new girl he had met in the temple that day and idly stared at the full moon. It began to disappear.

He watched, fascinated, and then touched his dozing companion, tapping the Egyptian on the shoulder. "Look!" he whispered. "What's happening?"

Abim-Akton blinked, growling like a dog in his displeasure at being disturbed.

Zabak shook him. "Look! Look at the moon!"

"What about it?" snarled the guard. He had been dreaming of a woman. He wished he were back with her, in the dream.

"Look at the moon, I said," Zabak repeated roughly. "You heard what the people were saying tonight—is this Shanarbaal's curse?"

"All right—all right! I heard. But it was just another rumor. These filthy streets are full of rumors," Abim-Akton answered, grumbling. He wished he had never left Egypt to come to this dirty outpost. It was a rotten duty. His friend Habbak was the only civilized man in town.

He turned to look at the moon, and as he did, he began to tremble. Terror gripped his spirit. Was this a nightmare? The moon was devouring itself. It was disappearing from the sky even as he watched.

Cowering on his knees, he turned toward Zabak. "What's happening?" he hissed, his wide eyes reflecting the fading yellow moonlight.

Jumping to their feet, the two men left their guard posts on the walls and ran toward the king's house, sounding the alarm. "The moon!" they shouted as they clattered through the shadowed streets. "The moon is dying!"

Alcion and Rahab had talked late into the night. Rahab had sewed as she made plans, her eyes drifting occasionally to the heavy scarlet cord draped from her window as she recalled the Habiru spy, Salma. The city had been quiet as the night edged toward morning, until she heard the cries from the streets: "The moon! The moon is dying!"

Rahab and Alcion ran up the stairs to the rooftop.

"Alcion!" Rahab gasped as she looked toward the western sky. "What is happening?"

Hanging low, near the mountains, in the clear, predawn sky, the full moon looked as though someone had taken a large bite out of it, like a half-eaten barley cake.

"Is it Shanarbaal's curse?" she asked in a whisper.

Other citizens of Jericho, awakened by the cries and clatter of the watchmen, came out of their houses, half-dressed, with swords and spears, ready to defend the city. But when they looked at the yellow, dying moon, they dropped their swords and their hearts melted within them.

Some whispered; others screamed in terror.

"What is happening?"

"The moon is dying!"

"The curse of Ninunta," wailed an old woman.

"We shall all die," another voice shrieked.

Nantha and Kinah, awakened by the shouts and noises from the streets, ran up the stairs to the roof. They watched silently for a moment.

"It's an omen!" Nantha mumbled.

Kinah clutched Rahab's cloak, her eyes wide with fear. As they watched, the moon continued to disappear, very slowly.

"I have heard of such things," Alcion said at last. "Many years ago, in Ur, the moon disappeared like this," the eunuch said softly. "I had heard the astrologers and the priests planning it." In the darkness of the rooftop, the women could not see the bitterness in his smile as he continued. "I was a slave boy, sleeping inside, and so I did not observe the great event myself, but they talked of nothing else for weeks!"

"What was it? What did it mean? What happened?" Rahab asked.

"Was it a curse?" Nantha wanted to know.

"Did you all die?" Kinah whispered.

Alcion laughed. "No, we did not all die, Kinah. A curse? Perhaps. I do not know what it was. They said it was a great sign from the gods. They said that Ninunta was angry, that he had flown to the moon and eaten her!"

"What happened, Alcion?" Rahab repeated.

The eunuch laughed softly. "The moon came back, and nothing happened! I don't understand it, Rahab....but the world did not come to an end then, and I don't think it will now."

Rahab watched as the darkness continued to eat away at the moon, edging across its surface. She shivered, thinking of the lion-bird, Ninunta, flying through the night to devour the moon.

"It does portend the death of Jericho, Alcion. I am sure of it. I feel it!" she said.

"Oh, yes," he answered quickly, "Jericho is doomed—but not because the moon plays strange tricks in the sky. Jericho is doomed because thousands of Habiru warriors stand ready to storm her ramparts and because the hearts of the men of Jericho have melted and turned to water."

As Rahab's household watched, silently now, the moon disappeared. A pale circle glowed around the space where the moon had been, and for an instant Rahab looked into a bottomless black hole of nothingness low in the western sky. It was Shanar's curse. It must be Shanar's curse.

213

As the king watched the sky, his knees began to shake, and he trembled with great foreboding. He had been awakened from a heavy, dreamless slumber by the shouting, howling watchmen, and he had hastily stumbled to the rooftop. His wife had followed him. Together, they watched as the moon seemed to fall in upon itself.

"It is Shanar's curse," Asheratti whimpered, tugging at her husband's cloak.

"Call the priest!" the king shouted. "Zabak! Bring Shanarbaal here at once! Hurry!"

The guard ran for the priest, hurrying through the streets, paying no attention to the crowds, pushing past anyone foolish enough to get in his path. Zabak grunted, flinging a moaning woman aside. He was glad the temple was close by.

Large with child, Tirnah, Rahab's sister, stirred against her husband's side, awakened by the sounds of shouting in the street. "Jaben! Jaben!" she hissed. "Something is happening outside! Wake up!"

"Be quiet, woman. I'm sleeping! It's the middle of the night," the man growled, rolling over and hiding beneath the coverlet.

Tirnah shook him again, and then she ran for the door. Outside on the street, men were darting about, screaming and crying, with swords and spears. Women leaned from windows or cowered near doors, pointing at the sky.

"She is dead!" a neighbor wailed. "The lady moon is dead!" A small child clung to her skirts with his thumb in his mouth, his eyes wide with fear, looking up.

"What is happening?" Tirnah shouted to her neighbor.

"We shall all die!" another voice nearby shrieked loudly.

Tirnah was astonished at the darkness in the streets, for the moon had been full only a few hours before. She could not see the moon from where she stood, and she was afraid to leave the safety of her doorway. "What do you mean? Where is the full moon?" she asked.

"The moon is dead!" her neighbor shouted. Lamps had been lighted in many of the houses, but the streets were dark and confused.

Tirnah hurried back to wake Jaben and shouted, "Jaben! Wake up!" She shook him hard. "Something is going on outside!"

He turned, raised on one elbow, and frowned, squinting sleepily. "What?" he demanded. "War? Is there fighting in the streets?"

"No—it's—well, Jaben," she wailed and faltered, "I don't know—it's dark!"

He reached out and pulled her roughly into bed. "Of course it's dark, foolish one! It's the middle of the night."

Tirnah began to cry quietly. It was Shanar's curse. She was sure of it. She feared the darkness outside, but she feared more to displease her husband. Jaben was already sleeping soundly again.

Leaving behind the confusion on the streets of Jericho, Zabak the watchman banged on the temple doors. "The king calls for the high priest!" he shouted.

A komer quickly admitted the soldier and led him to the chambers of the priest. The komer carried a small lamp; there was no other light. Approaching the door of the priest's apartment, Zabak could not repress a feeling of foreboding. Moaning sounds could be heard, seeming to drift on the clouds of incense that came from the room of the high priest.

"What is he doing?" Zabak whispered to the komer.

"He is with his friends, the spirits of darkness," the komer answered. "He talks to them at night, and casts his spells, but he has been expecting you."

Zabak trembled. "His magic is strong," muttered the soldier. He drew himself tall and pounded on the door. The wrath of the king was likewise strong magic.

"The king calls for the high priest of Jericho!" he shouted. "Come now!"

The moans from inside the darkness grew louder, ending on a shrill shriek: "Ninunta answers the call!"

From within the darkness, the high priest came to the door frame, his black robes flowing against the blackness of his chamber. The komer's lamp cast a pale light on Shanarbaal's gleaming eyes and yellowed teeth. The priest carried a small, carved lion with wings—Ninunta.

Zabak always felt nervous when confronted with the majesty of the priest. Close to the man now, with his heavy perfume that seemed to make the senses whirl, Zabak felt forced to act his most officious to keep from trembling.

"The king calls, my lord," the soldier said sternly.

The priest wrapped his cloak about his bony shoulders, hiding the lion-bird within its blackness. "Go, then."

The two ran through the streets to the palace of the king. Zabak said nothing of the moon, and the priest appeared not to notice. It seemed to Zabak that the priest was invisible. Everywhere, people were looking up, talking in hushed whispers, crying, shouting, but no one spoke to the priest and the guard. No one seemed to notice them; all eyes were directed toward the setting moon.

As they neared the house of the king, Shanarbaal began to chuckle, a low, raspy laugh that circled in upon itself. "Ninunta, the time has come," he said, and he followed the soldier to the rooftop and the king.

Shanarbaal squatted on his heels, wrapped in his black magician's cloak, staring without seeing into a small fire. Beside him sat the small figure of the winged lion, its glass eyes reflecting the reds and golds of the flames that lapped about a sizzling quail's heart.

Moaning softly, the priest cried to the spirits of darkness. Then he spoke in the voice of Ninunta, then as Baal, as Astarte, and as El. The voices that

215

came from the priest were angry, unintelligibly warring—the voices of the gods of Jericho.

To the west, the moon had disappeared. Only the priest did not tremble in fear. Asheratti wondered if perhaps the spirit of the priest had flown to join the dying moon.

"Ai-eeeeeee-eee-ooohh-eee!" the priest suddenly shrieked. "I am Ninunta. I am the thunderer." He leaned back on his heels and howled at the moon like a wild jackal baying for its mate. "Do you want your moon, king of Jericho?" the priest asked suddenly.

"Oh, yes!" gasped the king, falling to his knees. "Give us back the moon, Ninunta, great one."

Shanarbaal began to laugh. It seemed to Asheratti that his mocking laughter swirled into the sky.

"Has Ninunta spoken to you now, King of Nothing?" Shanarbaal asked.

"You have shown your power! Enough!" said the king.

Again the priest laughed. "Give me your son, King of Jericho. Give your son to Ninunta!" Shanarbaal was chanting now. "When the Habiru attack, give me your son, King of Jericho! Give me your son—" He laughed again, howling, "And all will be well! The god will be pleased!"

"No!" Asheratti gasped.

The king's sudden slap sent her sprawling outside the pale circle of light cast by the fire.

Hastily, the king groveled before the carving of Ninunta in obeisance to the priest and the lion-bird. "Forgive me, Ninunta, and forgive this foolish woman, great thunderer," he implored, whining. "My son is yours," he sighed.

Shanarbaal jumped to his feet, then, flinging out his cloak like wings, triumphantly. His hands passed over the flames, and the fire exploded, sending blue sparks high over the walls, spiraling up into the black sky.

"Aiii-eee, Ni-nun-ta!" he screamed. "The child is mine!"

As the king knelt before him and the queen lay whimpering in the darkness, Shanarbaal pulled his cloak close about him and looked at the king. "You may have the moon, King of Nothing," he said softly. "I will teach your son all that I know. Jericho will become the city of Ninunta. My god accepts your gift."

In the sky to the west, the setting moon began to reappear. As slowly as it had left, the moon returned to the skies above the city.

Merchants in the marketplace opened the doors as usual while the sun rose. They talked about the moon as men talk about the weather.

44

For three days, Salma and Daniel lingered near the cave, drinking water from pools in the wadi and catching quail, which they baked on a small fire inside the cave after dark. They ate barley cakes which the Jericho woman had provided.

From their hiding place, they watched the city. Many people seemed to be going and coming.

"This city was there when our father Abraham passed this way," Daniel said.

"Even then, the Lord promised us this land," Salma mused, "and now, he gives it to us. We have only to reach out and take it!"

Daniel smiled. "I think that taking the land will not be so simple. Some of us will die—"

"Death is part of life—and it is certainly a part of battle. Many died on the journey from Egypt." Salma frowned, remembering. "But if we die that our children might inherit this land, then we die well."

"You speak truly, Salma—but you have no children."

Salma laughed gently. "I think the Lord will bless me with sons."

"If you live."

"I will live, but if we stay here longer, I may starve. I'd prefer dying in battle to sitting here like a rabbit in its hollow, waiting for the wolf to catch the scent."

"The moon will rise late tonight, but it will be bright. We can get back across the river before the dawn if we hurry."

Salma looked back to the west, where low clouds were gathering. "And before the rains return," he said.

"Eight guests!" Nantha exclaimed. "Tonight? How shall we accommodate eight guests at one time? Oh, surely I can feed them; that will be no problem, but guests will expect entertainment, and there are, after all, only three of us, lady...well, not that it's impossible, but it has not been our custom in this house to—"

"Oh, be quiet, fool!" Rahab interrupted. "We will not be entertaining at all! The guests will be my family."

Nantha was immediately all smiles. "Oh, well, in that case, I am delighted, my lady. I will be happy to serve your family. We have seen too little of them since they moved to Jericho."

217

"We will see them aplenty tonight," Rahab answered. "Alcion will invite my father's entire household, and we must be prepared even to have them spend the night if the need arises. We shall have a grand feast, and then I shall make an important announcement."

"An announcement, Rahab?" Kinah was immediately curious. "May we know? Will you tell us?"

"Yes, dear one, I will tell you when I tell the others. But for now you must help Nantha with the preparations."

Neither Kinah nor Nantha was pleased with this answer, but they set to work. Kinah secretly hoped that Rahab would announce that their house had been blessed with the promise of a baby. Rahab would be happier with a baby, Kinah was sure. Nantha, however, harbored no such hopes. She felt sure that the announcement had to do with the strangers and the violent visit of the king's guard. Nantha was equally certain that no announcement connected with those events could be good news.

The time for the banquet arrived quickly. Rahab herself arranged the seating order so that her father would sit at her right and her mother at her left. In her own house, Rahab was herself the host. The women ate with the men, and they spoke freely.

At the hour for the evening meal, her family arrived. Her mother carried Tirnah's wiggling child, Mita, in her arms. Tirnah followed, complaining that her feet hurt and that the child within her womb was making her ill. Micah, Rahab's brother, came in hungry, demanding of Rahab, "Why are we having a feast?" and "What are we having to eat?" Rahab kissed them all in greeting, sympathized with Tirnah, and laughed at her brother.

Tirnah's husband, Jaben, entered the house last, scowling. Rahab greeted him kindly and looked about for her father and youngest brother Benan. They were not there.

"Mother, where are Father and Benan? Are they coming behind you?" she asked.

"They are not coming, Rahab," her mother answered. "Your father felt unwell tonight, and he asked Benan to stay with him."

"Oh, that must not be!" Rahab exclaimed, shocking them all. Her thoughts centered on the necessity of securing her entire family within her house before the Habiru attacked. If her father and Benan were outside when the attack came, they would be killed. They must come to her house immediately. "This cannot be, Mother! Father must come!" she said.

"Rahab, do not be so harsh. Your father is not well. That is why he stayed at home. He would not lightly refuse the *first*," she emphasized the word, "invitation you have offered since we arrived in Jericho."

"It doesn't matter, Mother," Rahab said. "He must come. They must both come. I will not continue this feast until they are here." With that comment, Rahab ordered Alcion and Micah to go and get her father and her younger brother. "If Father is too sick to walk—"

"He is," her mother interrupted.

"Then you must bring him on a litter," Rahab snapped. "Alcion, when you have returned with them, come to my chamber and get me. When they are here, we will proceed with the feast." Rahab turned and disappeared up the stairway.

Her mother sighed and shook her head. She could not understand this city woman, her daughter.

When Rahab returned to her public room, her father was propped up on many pillows in the place that she had prepared for him. Benan sat calmly beside his brother. Benan was a quiet twelve-year-old who took life much too seriously, in Rahab's opinion. *But,* she thought, *what should I expect? For almost as long as he can remember, the family has been plagued by my father's illness.* Benan was a child who seemed to love his father to the exclusion of all else.

Rahab joined the group and smiled. "I am honored that you could be with me tonight," she said, speaking to them all. "You are welcome here. Nantha has prepared a feast such as even the temple of Jericho seldom enjoys. I welcome you to the *shelter* of my home."

Her family smiled appreciatively at the platters of steaming food that Kinah and Nantha began to serve. Her mother ate the delicately prepared fish cakes and vegetables with great enjoyment, but she watched Rahab from the corner of her eye and wondered what her daughter was plotting.

As the meal ended, Rahab stood, staring at her family until each person, even Tirnah's child, was silent. When she had their attention, she spoke loudly and dramatically: "In a matter of days, every person in this city will be dead!"

The shocked expressions and gasps from the family seated around the public room assured Rahab that she had made her point.

"What are you talking about?" her sister said.

"How do you know that?" her father asked.

"Nonsense!" snorted her brother-in-law.

Again, Rahab waited until she had everyone's attention.

"Last night, the king's men came to this house. They were seeking two men of the Habiru who had come to spy out the city."

Jaben's eyebrows lowered, and his eyes flashed beneath the furtive lids. "So that's it!" he exclaimed softly.

"Oh, no!" her mother said.

"It is true!" Rahab responded. "The Habiru were here—in this house—but the king's men did not find them. Everyone in the city knows that the Habiru are strong. They have struck down the Moabites, the Amorites, the Amelekites—they are without number. When the prophet Balaam, the seer of the gods, came from Pethor to try to curse them—" she paused for emphasis—"he could not do it! Their god is too strong. No one can understand their god, and no army can prevail against him. Jericho will be crushed like an anthill beneath a warrior's boot. The walls of Jericho will be breached. The city will fall! Her people are doomed!"

"If what you say is true, Rahab, then our family must leave the city at once," Jaben said crisply.

"We could go to Leal at the farm," Micah interjected.

Rahab silenced them with a look. "No," she said smiling serenely. "We stay. Here."

"What?" her mother gasped.

"Have you gone mad?" Tirnah snapped.

"I do not want to be sacrificed to a Habiru god!" Jaben added.

"How do you know these things? Do you have a plan?" her father demanded from his couch.

"I not only have a plan," Rahab answered smoothly. "I have made a bargain. A bargain with the Habiru!"

"What?" Nantha asked.

"A bargain with the Habiru? Now I know you have lost your senses!" Jaben said.

"We shall all die!" Tirnah said.

Mita began to scream. Rahab looked at the child, and Tirnah hurriedly picked up the little girl, crooning to her.

"I have made a bargain with the Habiru," Rahab repeated. "And because of that bargain, you—all of us here, in this house—will live. That is, you will live if you will do as I tell you."

"This is strange business that you do, daughter," Bazarnan answered, his voice stronger than his weak frame would indicate. "To bargain with Jericho's enemies—to protect Habiru spies—for that is what you have done, is it not?"

"That is exactly what I have done, Father, and because I have done it, the people of my household will survive the Habiru attack. But—this house only will survive. All of Jericho will die, except for us. We shall be saved!"

"You have bargained for the lives of your household?" Jaben barked the question.

"For this house and the lives of all who are in it," Rahab responded impatiently. "If you are inside my walls, Jaben, you will live."

"But when do they attack?" Jaben asked. "Is there still time to flee?"

"The countryside will not stand when the city falls! To flee is to die!" Rahab answered angrily.

"You said that to stay is to die," Jaben said.

"Do you have no ears?" Rahab said sharply. "I have just said that those who stay in this house will live. Do you want to live, Jaben?"

"Of course, I want to live— But I do not trust the enemy, and I think you are a fool to do so. Don't you see? They have gotten what they needed from you, and they are gone. They will not keep their bargain. There is no reason to do so!"

"They have sworn to me by their god, and they have given me a pledge of truth that they will deal kindly with this household. They will not break their word. Their god will not let them."

"Ha!" Jaben responded. "What kind of god is that?"

"A god who is real, Jaben, a god who keeps his promises. What do you say, Father? I have made a bargain, a bargain that will be honored. Stay here in my household until the Habiru attack, and we will all live."

"If we live at all, it will be as slaves," Jaben interrupted. "What kind of life is that? I would prefer death."

"We will not be slaves. We will be alive, and we will be free," Rahab snapped, hoping that what she said was true.

Jaben snorted.

"Quiet!" his father-in-law commanded. "Why do you trust these men?" he asked Rahab.

"I know men, Father, and I have known many gods. These men were different. Their god is different. I know the promise will not be broken."

"How will they know that this is the house to be spared?"

"The house is marked with a scarlet cord which can be seen from outside the walls."

Her father nodded then. "So be it, Rahab. We will trust your wisdom in this. We will stay; we will await the attack here!"

His stunned family looked at him in surprise, but all argument ceased. Bazarnan was still the father.

Joshua was astonished.

"You have done what?" he demanded, striking his head with his hands.

Salma and Daniel were silent. They had made their report, concluding with the bargain they had made with the harlot, Rahab. Their leader had listened eagerly until that point.

"It was the right thing to do, Joshua," Salma said firmly. "She saved us when we were trapped."

Joshua frowned, shaking his head. "Did I not warn you about strange women? You never should have gone to such a house!"

"But, Joshua," Daniel attempted to speak persuasively, "we could not have stayed in the city without being seen if we had gone anywhere else."

Joshua frowned again, unconvinced. "You were seen even there—"

Salma interrupted. "Sir, had we stayed anywhere else we would surely have been captured. The Lord used this harlot's house to protect us."

Joshua looked at the two spies gravely. "Have you dishonored the Lord our God in the house of a Canaanite harlot? Tell me. If you have lain with this woman, you must confess it now and seek the mercy of the Lord."

"No, my lord," Daniel said emphatically. "She washed our feet, and she fed us, but nothing further passed between us."

Salma nodded in agreement. "We ate her food, but we did not drink her wine, nor did we touch the woman or her handmaidens."

Joshua sighed in relief. He had seen good men fall to such temptations. He feared for his people, but he remembered the words of his God: "Be strong and of good courage, for I have delivered the country unto you."

"You speak the truth," Joshua said. "You must, for if you lie, your sins will fall heavily upon all the house of Israel." He looked searchingly at them.

"We speak the truth, my lord."

Joshua shook his head in wonder. "The Lord has ways that I do not understand. He protected you I am sure...but such a bargain you have made! I pray it will not bring us to shame."

Joshua leaned back, his hands behind his head. "We shall honor your bargain. All shall be as you have promised. It is best that the people not be told that this woman Rahab was a harlot in Jericho; we will keep that knowledge to ourselves. If the people know that she was a harlot, there will be trouble in the camp. Salma, you will go immediately to Caleb. Explain to him all that has occurred and tell him it is my desire that Rahab and anyone she brings with her shall be under the protection of his household. They shall be strangers in the camp, but wards of the tribe of Judah."

Salma swallowed, but Daniel suppressed a smile. As they left Joshua's tent, Daniel did not resist the urge to repeat the words of his friend: "The camps of Israel are large enough. I can avoid one Canaanite."

Salma frowned, seeing no humor in the comment. "It will be more difficult than I imagined if she is to live beneath the banner of my uncle's household."

The two old men—Joshua, servant of the Lord, and Caleb, patriarch of the tribe of Judah—sat on a flat rock outside the camp, looking toward the walled city of Jericho.

Both the old men seemed lost in their thoughts, remembering forty years before when they had first seen the land. They had returned from their spy mission full of hope and optimism, but their ten companions had been frightened and had convinced the people not to attack.

"The time has come at last, Joshua," Caleb said. Though Caleb had seen eighty-five summers, his eyes were clear and his step was quick.

"The Lord has been good to deliver the land to us. I had thought we might not see this inheritance again," Joshua responded. "We must be ready, for tomorrow the Lord will do great things among us."

"Joshua, it is important that we harbor no evil or sin within the camp of Israel." Caleb spoke slowly and seriously.

"My friend, do you speak specifically? Are you aware of evil or disobedience among the people?" Joshua turned to Caleb, aware that the Lord's promise of blessings depended upon the obedience of the people to the laws of Moses.

"I have a particular concern, yes, Joshua." When the leader remained silent, the patriarch continued. "My nephew Salma spoke to me about the Jericho business...."

"Yes, yes," Joshua interrupted. "I told him to. He's made a bargain. I told him you'd take charge of the woman and her household."

Caleb smiled. "Ah, yes, Joshua, you understand—we must be true to what we say. It is the law of Moses."

"That is why we will give refuge to this woman of Jericho—and why you must do it, Caleb. The people will not welcome her. They will certainly harm her if they know what she is. You, Caleb, are the only man who can command the respect to protect this woman. I do not like it—it's a dirty business—but the Lord commands us to be true to our word."

His friend nodded. "That is why we must not harbor deceit, Joshua."

Joshua's craggy eyebrows jumped.

"Deceit! What do you mean, Caleb?"

"Salma says the woman is to come into the camp under my protection, but," he frowned, "that no one is to know she is—or was—a prostitute."

Joshua hung his head. "Yes...that was my order. But what would you have me do, then, Caleb? If the people know, they'll stone her!"

"If we hide it and then the people find out, they may well stone us, Joshua."

"Then what shall we do?" Joshua asked.

Caleb's eyes twinkled, and he smiled. "Let it be known to all that she was a prostitute and that she now has your protection as one who befriended the spies in Jericho, and let her household live not within the camp, but just outside the camp, beside the tents of my tribe."

"Your thoughts are wise. We will tell the truth—and if she continues to ply her trade, if she commits adultery, at least it will not be within the camp."

"May God preserve us from such sin!" Caleb responded. "Let us do what is right in the eyes of the Lord!"

Soon after the sunrise, Alcion and Micah went to the house of Bazarnan. Moving quickly through the rain, they gathered the belongings of Rahab's family and returned to the house of Rahab. Then they went to the market place for provisions.

"Remember, Micah," Alcion cautioned as they neared the vendors, "we must convince these men that your sister is ill; our lives depend upon it. Say nothing, and look sad!"

The boy giggled. "Yes, sir. I can do it."

"Then silence those giggles!" Alcion snapped harshly. "I knew I shouldn't have brought a boy for a man's task," he grumbled.

"At least I'll *be* a man," the youth snapped back.

"Just keep quiet and look sad, Micah!" the eunuch repeated.

As Alcion made his purchases, he grumbled about the high prices and scarcity of provisions.

"Don't forget; we are on the verge of war," the merchant reminded him. "You should not expect our usual selections." The man eyed the bulging bags of lentils, figs, raisins, and barley. "It looks like you're getting ready for a siege now—or does your mistress plan another party?" he added with a leer.

"Hmmpf!" Alcion snorted. "Not tonight. She's caught the pox, and her whole family has trooped in to look after her!" Alcion glanced quickly at his young helper, who looked thin-lipped and unhappy.

"I'm sorry to hear that your mistress is unwell. I was planning to visit her one evening this week."

"I would not advise it," Alcion said, "not unless you want the pox as well. We may all die from it before this is over." He shook his head sadly and looked at the ground. "She is dreadfully ill."

"What sort of pox is it, Alcion? Are we in danger?"

Alcion was prepared for this question.

"I wish I knew," he said solemnly. "Her fever rages. Half the time she does not know anyone. I have never seen anything like it."

Micah averted his face, turning as if to examine the knives in the next stall.

"Is it serious, then?" the merchant asked.

"Yes," Alcion answered, calling to Micah to help him carry the provisions. The tale, he knew, would be carried throughout the marketplace before midday. The house of Rahab would have no visitors. The men of Jericho feared the pox as intensely as they feared the Habiru.

45

The April sky hung menacingly low, and a soaking rain fell without ceasing. Moods were low and tempers were short in the house of Rahab, and throughout the city. The gray sky reflected the sodden spirits of the beleaguered town. It was harvest season, but this year the people feared that the city would reap only the harvest of death.

Seven days had passed since Rahab had lowered the spies from her window. She had continued her habit of sewing in the night. Even as she carefully embroidered, she realized the futility of completing this tapestry; still she found solace in her work. It was a design of the king on his chariot, with his spear poised to strike as his horse charged toward a lion. Beside the king was a child, the young prince of Jericho. She sighed. The child was getting bigger now, growing into a robust lad.

She had lighted her lamp and begun her labors about two hours before the sunrise. The entire house was asleep, and she enjoyed the peaceful quiet. With her family in residence, especially Tirnah's child, times of silence were more than rare. Now, in the quiet of the early morning, her mind was free to think. Food was running low: she wasn't sure how long the oil would last; the figs were almost gone; the wine was in good supply; the barley might hold out another three days; four onions were left. Alcion and Micah would be forced to go to the market today....If the Habiru did not attack soon, Rahab feared she could not convince her family to stay.

The Habiru *had* moved from the plateau of Shittim-Abel, and now their campfires could be seen just across the Jordan River. The threat had moved closer, but still it remained only a threat. To some within the city, it was a threat that could still be ignored, a threat that one could pretend did not exist.

As Rahab worked on her tapestry, the shutters of her house banged, slamming with the ferocity of a sudden wind from the west that swept down from the mountains and toward the Jordan River. The violence of the wind shocked Rahab from her reverie, and she dashed to the rooftop to save the flax and storage pots stacked there. As Rahab wrestled with the piles of flax to gather them into the room above the stairs, Alcion joined her.

Above them, the heavy, low-lying clouds fled to the east, driven by the dry, hard winds from the wilderness.

"These winds bring a change in the weather, I think," Rahab shouted.

"Look to the east, Rahab. These winds may portend other changes!"

Rahab and Alcion looked toward the sunrise. The campfires of the Habiru were gone, and the only glow in the east was from the rising sun.

The clouds obscured the scene across the river, and the howling wind drowned out all other sound. As Rahab and Alcion watched, however, the Habiru began to walk out of the trees that lined the river—hundreds of people, thousands of people, walking steadily in orderly rows, as far as the eye could see. The Habiru had crossed the Jordan River!

"Alcion!" Rahab whispered. "What is happening? How are they crossing the river? It's flooding!"

Alcion looked at her in amazement. Why was she surprised?

"But you said they would attack. Certainly they would have to cross the river."

Rahab realized her lack of reason. Of course they would cross the river. She had known they would.

"Alcion!" she exclaimed. And she began to laugh. "I never thought about how they would cross the river. I just knew that they would do it. I still do not know how they are doing it!"

"It's an interesting question, Rahab. We can see them coming, so either the river has dried up, or they have built a very wide bridge. They have been camped across the river for three days now, and that is scarcely time to build a bridge—and hundreds of people do not cross a bridge at one time. No bridge could be so wide."

"But, Alcion—the Jordan is a large river, and it *is* flooding! This cannot be!"

It was Alcion's turn to laugh. "Our eyes tell us that it is, Rahab. Perhaps their god *is* a strong god!"

As the sun rose, the people of Jericho gathered on the eastern walls, watching in awe as the people of the Habiru, by the thousands, came up from the flooded river. The men of Jericho trembled in terror as they watched, and the women whimpered. They had not believed the Habiru could cross the river at flood.

The Habiru camped at the village of Gilgal. They camped fearlessly within sight of the Jericho walls, their tents stretching in all directions, a sea of soldiers.

The inhabitants of Jericho waited. The attack should come at any moment, they thought, but the attack did not come. The city waited; the camp at Gilgal did not stir.

Inside the camp, the leaders of Israel waited, prayed, and planned. There was much to be done. It was the time of the Passover. No attack could be launched until the feast had been observed. The farmers of Gilgal had fled from their village, leaving the harvest behind. From the grain of Canaan the Israelites would make the flat, unleavened bread, symbolic of their escape from Egypt, bread made in haste. Spring lambs would be found for the sacrifice. It was the law. The Passover must be observed.

Another ritual of the law must also be observed before the attack could take place. Joshua announced that the Lord required a renewal of the circumcision covenant. Since the wilderness babies had not been circumcised, every male in the camp except for Caleb and Joshua was required to submit to the knife. They did so, but not without grumbling. Afterward, however, the camp was very quiet. Small cooking fires burned, tended by solemn, silent women. A stranger would have wondered where the mighty Habiru fighting force had disappeared, for there was no sign of the army. The men of Israel were in their tents recuperating, complaining.

"I'll never be the same again," Daniel groaned.

"No," his companion answered, grimacing at his own pain, "you will be better."

Daniel groaned again. "I feel I have become a eunuch," he said.

"The law of the Lord does not allow such a thing," his friend murmured.

"But, oh," he said, gritting his teeth, "I do know what you mean."

Other men had other reactions. Phineas, the son of the high priest, felt himself consecrated forever to the service of God. Achan, a strong warrior, felt that God demanded too much: "He has too many laws!" he growled angrily to his wife. Salma, alone in his own tent, stared fixedly at the tent's roof. He would not think of Rahab tonight, he promised himself.

Ten days had passed; still the Habiru had not attacked. Tensions rose in the city and in the house of Rahab. Tirnah complained constantly: "We could have escaped to the farm by now! I'm hungry! What if the baby comes early? My back hurts!"

For once, Rahab was not upset by her sister's constant grumbling and treated Tirnah with great gentleness and courtesy. She was kind to her brother-in-law as well, even though his complaints were a chorus to those of his wife. He seemed to take a particular delight in sarcastically teasing Rahab about trusting the enemy. "When I'm dying with a sword in my gut, Rahab," he sneered, "I'll remind you who to trust."

"When we are the only people in this city to live through the attack, Jaben, I'll remind you *whom* to trust!" Rahab responded good-naturedly, correcting his grammar. She was amazed at her own good humor, for ordinarily she considered Jaben a lout and a fool, treating him with little better than open contempt.

Kinah played with Tirnah's child endlessly, entertaining her with the harp and singing. If Kinah felt afraid, she kept her thoughts and feelings to herself. Rahab heard her crying softly in the night, however, and comforted the girl, touching her gently on the shoulder. "Kinah," she whispered, "don't cry. We have the promise of the men of the Lord that this household will be protected."

The girl clung to her mistress, and when she could catch her breath, she sobbed, "But, my lady, I am so afraid. I know what warriors do to girls. I have known warriors before! My lady, it would be better if they killed us!"

"But, my dear, they have sworn by their god that they will treat us kindly. Do not fear. We have their protection! And the protection of their god!"

"But, my lady, how can two men speak for all their warriors? I thought tonight of killing myself before they get here—"

"Oh, *no*, child!" Rahab said.

"But I knew that you wouldn't—that you would be upset—and that you need me, my help, right now."

Rahab held the girl close against her breast. She wanted to comfort her, but she did not know how—so, she became very brisk and businesslike.

"You did right, Kinah," she said, pushing the girl to an upright position.

"Now, dry your eyes. There is much work to be done tomorrow. You are the only one who can entertain Mita so she doesn't constantly cry—and I need you to help with the meal preparation as well. If one does not sleep, she will not be able to do her work! You have told me so, many times, remember?"

Kinah smiled then. "Yes, my lady," she said at last. "I will do as you say—and—" she added as Rahab turned to leave.

"Yes?"

"Whatever happens, I thank you—" her voice broke again—"for all you have done for me."

Rahab returned to her sewing, thinking of plans for the coming hours—or would it be days? She must be prepared, for it might be days, and food was running very low. When the Habiru had come across the Jordan, she had delayed in sending Alcion for provisions, thinking that attack was imminent. She remembered the spy's promise that those who were within her walls would be safe. She wanted her household within her house. But as they camped between the river and the city, the Habiru were seemingly in no hurry to attack.

What are they doing? Rahab wondered. She knew that the tension she felt was magnified a thousand times throughout the city. The Habiru had crossed the river. Why did they wait? Poor Kinah! Rahab thought of the women of the city, remembering Oparu's coarse jokes about conquered maidens. She wondered, now, how she had laughed so freely with the king's men. *If I lived in the city and if I had a little girl,* Rahab thought, *it would be a kindness to kill her now, gently.* "God of the Habiru," she whispered, "I am trusting in you and in your men. Save us, God of the Habiru."

Alcion joined her as the sun rose, and she sent him into the city for provisions. If provisions could be found, Alcion would find them. He took Micah to carry sacks and jars. They went first to the king's siege granaries, deep caverns cut into the Jericho rock. The soldiers laughed at them. "We are not yet under siege," they said. "These supplies stay where they are!"

Next, they went to the marketplace. Every door was shut. "The gates to the city are shut!" shouted one merchant. "No produce is coming in to be sold! Only death is coming to Jericho these days." The merchant laughed harshly and slammed the window shut.

"What does he mean, Alcion?" Micah asked. "We are safe, aren't we?"

"Only because we are in the house of Rahab," the eunuch answered. "The rest will surely die."

For once the boy was quiet. Alcion took him to the house of a merchant with whom he had done business since he been in Jericho—first for the temple and Shanarbaal, then for Rahab. The man was getting old, but Alcion knew that he kept provisions stored in rooms below the streets.

"Lembaal!" Alcion called loudly as he pounded on the man's door. "Are you there? I need help!"

Quickly, the old man shuffled to the door and let Alcion and Micah into his store. "Better you than Habiru!" he said shortly. "They're coming, you know. They will kill us all!"

"That may be, Lembaal," Alcion responded pleasantly. "But, in the meantime, my mistress Rahab is very ill, and I must feed her whole family! We have run out of food. I know that you have provisions stored....I have money. Could we purchase some barley and some oil? Perhaps some lentils?"

The old man frowned. He had planned to use his cache below the ground to get him through a long siege, if necessary. Still—if one survived a siege, it would be good to have money. He laughed, then, and began to bargain.

Finally, Alcion paid him twenty gold shekels for twenty kilos of barley, a pitcher of olive oil, and twenty kilos of lentils. It was enough money to buy a house, and both Alcion and the old man knew it.

As Micah toiled toward the door with the bags of grain and beans, the old man took Alcion's money, laughing. "Your gold will sweeten my death, Alcion. There, let me give you something to sweeten yours." Alcion paused, puzzled, as the merchant tottered to a chest near the wall. From it, he took a small bundle carefully wrapped in an embroidered cloth. The merchant unwrapped a small jug and handed it to Alcion.

"Here," he said. "This is summer honey from the mountains. It should be enjoyed. I will see you in the underworld!" He closed the door behind them, laughing loudly at his private joke.

Alcion and Micah hurried back to the house of Rahab. They had one more errand: water. Depositing their precious load of food in the public room for Nantha's care, they hurried to the ancient springs of Jericho. The streets had been deserted, but everyone who was not locked behind his solid doors and closed shutters was at the spring. Water would not be a problem for the city, Alcion knew, for the springs were within the city walls, and the springs did not go dry, even during the long summer droughts.

"Stay close to me, Micah," Alcion warned the youngster as they neared the crowded marketplace near the springs.

They were quickly noticed. "Alcion!" a drunken voice called out. "How is your mistress? Does she live? I have missed her entertainments sadly!"

Running to greet them was the guard Zabak. "We have busy duty to keep the peace at the springs," he said. "Tell your mistress that we couldn't catch those Habiru fellows. They drowned in the fords. Say—" he paused and rubbed his beard, "you don't suppose they brought some plague on her, do you?"

Alcion looked sad and very serious, and Micah rolled his eyes to keep from laughing. He knew if he snickered, Alcion would be seriously angry!

"I do not think so, Captain. I rather think that some of our meat was rotten. Rahab eats earlier than the rest of the household—because of the dance—and she was very ill very quickly. We threw the meat over the wall, and none of us ate it, but—I do not know, Zabak. I fear for her life."

The captain laughed drunkenly. "Don't worry, Alcion. We shall all die! It will be well for Rahab if she dies before the Habiru warriors get here." He lurched against a wall and laughed again. "It will be better if the gods of death capture her before our lady of battles arrives! Conquering warriors are not kind to women! Let her die now, Alcion."

"That may be, Captain," Alcion answered seriously. "But for now, her entire family is with us—and we need water."

"We'll need more than water to save us, my friend," the warrior answered. As Alcion started past him, Zabak reached out and took his arm, stopping his progress.

"By the way, Alcion," he said, leering, "if your mistress dies, and you want some fun, Habbak still speaks of you. You would be welcome at the king's house." He looked down at the boy with Alcion and reached out to pinch his cheek. "You too, little one," he laughed heartily. "You might as well enjoy life. It will be over soon enough."

Joshua squinted, frowning into the setting sun, looking toward the high walls of Jericho that glimmered golden in the fading light of day.

He had sought solitude away from the camp because the grumblings of the men, complaining of the pain of circumcision, had dragged down his spirit. *Children of the desert*, he thought. *They are as stubborn as their parents.*

Joshua felt his years this day and carried them heavily. His leathery, wrinkled skin, bronzed and worn by years of desert war and wandering, sat in deep furrows in his brow. There were no laugh lines, no crinkles made by smiling; his face reflected the weight and responsibility of the leadership of the nation of Israel. He had worked, always, to please the Lord. When the call came from Moses, Joshua had answered, leaving behind his Egyptian wife and his two small sons. He had, at least, spared his family the death of the firstborn—but his wife had refused to leave her family and their lands to join the nation for the exodus. So Joshua had dedicated himself to serving Moses and the Lord. There had been no time for smiles; he had fought the enemies of Israel, and he had fought the fears and rebellions that tore the nation from within.

Soon, he knew, very soon, he would be called upon to lead these sons of Israel into battle against the ancient fortress city. For thousands of years, Jericho had stood. It was old when Abraham had passed this way. It was old when the Lord God had promised that the sons of Abraham would be as numberless as the stars; it was old when the Lord God promised this land to Abraham and his heirs. And such heirs they were!

Joshua remembered when he and his friend Caleb had gone with ten others to spy out Canaan forty years before. Only he and Caleb had believed the Lord, that the land was theirs. So, Joshua and Caleb had been defeated by the fears of their people, and the sons of Israel had fled like dogs. But in the forty years that followed, those who feared had died.

And now, they had returned with a new generation of men who were not afraid, men who obeyed the Lord even to circumcision! *Yes, Lord,* thought Joshua, *they grumble—but they do obey!*

A beloved voice sounded in his memory: "Do not become discouraged; be strong and keep your faith, for the Lord our God will be with you just as he was with me!" The words of Moses had been more than a promise. They had been a prophecy!

Joshua began to pray to his God, standing with arms outreached and looking toward Jericho.

"God of my fathers! God of Moses! God of Jacob! God of this generation of grumblers! Hear my prayer.

"These people are a circumcised people. They have obeyed your commands; even in the face of suffering they obey you. They honor you, for they have given you their bodies.

"You have promised us this nation as our inheritance. We claim it, Lord God Yahweh."

The old man was silent for a moment. His body shook, as if he were sobbing, but there was no sound.

"You know that I was ready to take the land forty years ago, Yahweh! I was younger then and stronger. My bones had strength, and power flowed in my sinews. I could look to the future then and see the nation of Israel, secure in this land of milk and honey and abundant grain, even though the sons of my loins would never see it.

"And now—Lord God, the ramparts of Jericho are repaired. My spies tell me that the people of the city quake, ready to crumble before us. But my men have bargained with a prostitute—please, please, mighty God—preserve us from grief with that woman! Let not the husbands of Israel be tempted by her wiles! Preserve us from uncleanliness!

"It seems only yesterday that you brought us out of slavery in Egypt, that you brought the plagues upon the pharaoh and his people, and the ocean became dry land under our feet. You brought us across the desert, and you provided us with food and water, and our sandals did not wear out.

"Your mighty works in the past should encourage me, Lord, but the future looms before me like the walls of Jericho, and I fear. I know—even though this night I am old and discouraged—that you are a mighty God whose hand can move the earth and the oceans, for I have seen your power.

"You brought us across the Jordan River at flood tide, Lord—but, how do we win this battle before us now? O Lord, I do not know."

Joshua was on his knees, his head in the dirt and his hands stretched out toward Jericho. At the sudden and unmistakable sound of a sword being drawn from its scabbard, the old man jumped to his feet.

231

INTERLUDE

Now when Joshua was near Jericho, he looked up and saw a man standing in front of him with a drawn sword in his hand. Joshua went up to him and asked, "Are you for us or for our enemies?"

"Neither," he repied, "but as commander of the army of the Lord I have now come."

Then Joshua fell facedown to the ground in reverence, and asked him, "What message does my Lord have for his servant?"

The commander of the Lord's army replied, "Take off your sandals, for the place where you are standing is holy." And Joshua did so....

Then the Lord said to Joshua, "See, I have delieevered Jericho into your hands, along with its king and its fighting men."

Joshua 5:13-15; 6:2 NIV

46

Always Jericho had been a town well known for the revelry of its nights, but in these days as the Habiru camped outside, waiting, waiting, waiting, it seemed that the entire town was caught by a spirit of frivolous intensity. Laughter and anger erupted in the marketplace leading to fits of hysteria, passion, and sometimes murder. The air itself seemed to taunt and tease the citizens of Jericho. Every breeze carried the whispered phrase: "Habiru— Habiru—Habiru!"

Rahab's illness was talked about everywhere. The entertainments of her house were sorely missed by a populace hungry for diversion, something—anything—to keep them from thinking about the Habiru. Would the walls really hold them out? Could the king's soldiers possibly rout them? Would Jericho stand another six thousand years—or were these truly her last days?

Every day the townspeople trembled in fear; every night, the people of Jericho drank; they drank, they reveled, and they cursed. They cursed the king; they cursed the gods; they cursed the Habiru; and they cursed each other. There was no help; there was only the steady, unrelenting progress of fear. The revelries served to help them forget their terror—a terror twice as real with each new morning.

Onuk's house became the site of constant drunken banqueting. Any of the city's officials and politicians, or their favorites, might be found at any hour of the day vomiting into the fountain in Onuk's private courtyard. Fear and wine created uneasy stomachs. The servants of the household became exhausted, finding it impossible to satisfy the drunken and unreasonable demands of their host and his guests. Soon they, too, found the solace of the wine jug. Onuk and Habbak found the solace of the food and the wine, and in the manner of such men, they found solace in each other's company. The feasting had gone on for days. The men at the banquet had tired of the company of women and had sent Habbak's slave girls away. These women fell gratefully into the oblivion of deep sleep, but Onuk's guests continued their quest for diversion.

"That is seven slabs of meat you have eaten in the last hour, Onuk!" laughed a eunuch from the queen's attendants. "You will kill yourself with gluttony."

"Let me worry about my stomach, Barane, and you worry about yours," Onuk laughed in return. "If you get much fatter, you will no longer be able to wear the tight linen girdles you love so well."

Barane reddened at this comment. His love for the scarlet linen girdle had become a source of amusement for most of the men who knew him. The girdles which fitted tightly over his other garments had flattened his slender torso when he was a young lad in the royal service, but now, as the excesses of the years began to show on his middle-aged figure, the scarlet girdle about his middle drew more derision than admiration. Yet he clung to his affectation.

The other men lying about the room laughed. "Don't let them tease you, Barane. You still look beautiful to me," Habbak said with a laugh. "You men have no appreciation for beauty, but you will learn, you will learn!" Habbak turned to his host. "Onuk, with your permission, I shall invade the recesses of the brazen chest in your private chambers."

The fat man smiled and motioned his approval. Habbak put down his wine cup and touched the shoulders of the two men who lounged beside him. They were his intimate friends, these smooth-faced Egyptian soldiers. He smiled warmly at the two men. "Come with me," he said. "We shall give instructions on beauty to these untutored ones of Jericho. You, too, Barane," he addressed the other eunuch. "There is still much that we can teach these, our friends!" Habbak laughingly herded the other three men through the door leading to Onuk's sleeping chambers. "We'll be back, boys, don't miss us too much!" he teased as he shut the curtain.

"What is he up to, Onuk?" asked Elbalam, one of the city's moneylenders.

"He is being a drunken fool," Onuk responded, sipping from his own cup. "But he is an amusing drunken fool. You will see soon enough what he is about." Onuk examined a slice of aged fish and poked it into his mouth.

Elbalam dipped a dried fig into his wine cup and then chewed the fig, eating without thinking. Lying back on the floor, he placed one hand beneath his head. "What this party needs, Onuk," he said languidly, "is some music."

Onuk glanced at the young boys sleeping in the corner. "There are musicians here," he said. "You have only to wake them."

Realizing this, Elbalam picked up a small tray and sailed it across the room, where it hit one of the sleeping lads in the stomach, waking him rudely. "We want music," Elbalam bellowed. "Wake your fellows! Play something!"

The lad obliged, and soon the tinkling of his pipe and the harps of the other musicians enlivened the air of the banqueting room. Habbak looked through the opening in the curtains and smiled. "Music!" he said. "Just what was lacking. Now, men of Jericho, make yourselves ready!"

He stepped from behind the curtain. The men in the room gasped and laughed in approval. Habbak was dressed in a robe of luxurious purple gauze. It clung to his body, and its open front revealed a scarlet blouse beneath. On his head he wore three golden fillets, bands decorated with crescent moons and stars. A golden chain adorned his waist, still slim despite his years, and about his neck he wore layers of gold and silver chains. He smiled at the staring men and walked mincingly about the banqueting room so that all might view his finery.

"They are fools, indeed, who think only a woman can be beautiful," Habbak laughed. "Who can view me and think only of those wonderful creatures behind harem walls? Or for that matter, would you dispute the beauty of these, my fellows?" Bowing, he drew aside the curtain with a flourish.

The other three stepped from behind the curtain. Barane wore only the loincloth of a slave, but instead of goat's hair, his garment was a rich blue with golden borders. Everywhere else his body was covered with jewelry: pendants, anklets, nose jewels, amulets, rings, and bracelets. He tinkled as he walked, and he walked daintily, keeping time with the music.

But despite Barane's ornaments, the real attention of the crowd was drawn to the two Egyptian soldiers. They wore short tunics of glistening white. The material of their tunics was so fine and so sheer that every movement displayed the ripple of masculine muscle.

"It is Egyptian cotton," Onuk murmured to the man nearest him. "It is so finely woven you cannot see the threads."

The Egyptians had outlined their eyes and brows in black kohl. On their ears they had placed several golden rings, but it was to the simplicity and transparency of their tunics that the eyes of Onuk's guests were drawn.

Habbak laughed aloud and removed his purple robe; he wore a scarlet girdle beneath it. "Tell me that the men of Jericho do not approve!" he demanded. There were no murmurs of dissent.

In the hours before the sunrise, darkness and silence finally fell in the house of Onuk the Fat. The parade of the beauties had led to more fiercely enthusiastic festivities, but at last inebriation and exhaustion had their way with most of the inhabitants of the house.

In the private chamber of Onuk the Fat, however, one man did not sleep: Habbak stood in the center of Onuk's room, wide awake.

The fat man lay before him in a sleep from which he would never again be roused. Onuk's face wore the horrid mask of one who dies in agony, his mouth open, his eyes staring. Habbak looked about at the filth of Onuk's vomit on the couch and on the floor. *I didn't kill him*, he thought. *His own gluttony killed him.* Onuk had choked to death.

Nevertheless, Habbak reasoned, *it would not be wise to be found in his chambers. I'll return to the palace. Then no one will know I was with him when he died.* Habbak looked about the room. It was a good time to remove all trace of his presence from the room. During the last months of their friendship, Onuk had given Habbak many gifts. Some of these were still in this room.

I must take all my things now, Habbak thought, *or I will never see them again.* Quickly Habbak dressed himself in several of the beautiful robes that had been gifts from Onuk. He took all of his own gold chains, plus a few he had always admired. He covered his arms with bracelets, most of them hidden beneath the sleeves of his robes. He took only one ring for each of his fingers. Then, after wrapping a few other garments and jewels into a bundle, he flung a beautiful Babylonian cloak around his shoulders and stepped out a window into the empty courtyard. No one would see him leave, and he would be asleep in the palace before dawn.

The streets of Jericho were quiet, but they did not sleep. As Habbak slipped silently toward the palace, he was observed. Out of the shadows stepped one man. One man with a short rope was enough. In seconds, Habbak was dead, strangled. The robber quickly stripped the lavishly attired corpse of all its gold and finery.

One more naked corpse lay in the streets of Jericho. Soon the scavenger dogs claimed it.

47

In the house of Rahab, thirteen people, one of them a pregnant woman, had survived their own private siege for two weeks. The women of the two households had only endured each other's company. Nantha had long since ceased to enjoy the visitors. She made their presence the subject of constant murmuring. Perhaps the most irritable of all the family was Tirnah, who mentioned her pain and the misery of her pregnancy so often that her discomforts tortured them all. Soon even the boys began to share her complaints. They were certain *their* feet were swelling, too.

Throughout this time, Rahab continued to play the role of peacemaker. She sometimes surprised herself by her easy temper and gentle nature. She didn't know their source, but these new attributes had certainly come at the right time. Half seriously, she credited the God of the Habiru.

For Jaben, the two weeks in the house of Rahab were a time of revelation. He cursed the day he had left Bazarnan's farm, but he realized that it was too late for such cursing. He had been a fool. He had yielded to the opinion of his wife, his wife who was two years his senior, and he had come with his new family, her family, to Jericho. He watched everyone in the household carefully. Micah, almost the same age as himself, still wrestled with the younger boy. *He is still only a boy,* Jaben thought, *despite all his protest of manliness.* Bazarnan and Kora, the parents of his heart—for he had known no others—comforted each other. Bazarnan grew weaker each day, Jaben's own wife drove him nearly to madness with her simpering, and he would gladly have put the old woman, Nantha, into the street just to be free of her nagging tongue.

He watched his harlot sister-in-law most carefully of all. If he had entrusted his life to a woman—galling thought—then he must know what kind of woman she was. Jaben had never before seen Rahab for more than a few moments at a time. Now he watched her constantly. It was rumored that she was the richest woman in Jericho. Since the wives of rich men could not be considered to have wealth of their own, the rumor was probably true. Certainly her house was unlike any Jaben had ever seen before, filled with treasures and strange objects that served no purpose. But it was the woman herself who most interested Jaben.

Since the day he entered the gates of this filthy city, he had hated Rahab. On the farm he had been of service to his father-in-law. He tried not to remember how little he had known of farming before he had met Bazarnan. Here in this city, he was of no use to himself or to anyone. He lived by the kindness of a city prostitute, but he could not forgive her the robbery of his work. If he could not work, he was not a man.

Yet as he watched Rahab during these long enclosed days, he discovered an unwanted admiration for her.

She was more even-tempered than Tirnah. She had a kinder tongue than Nantha or Kora. And he suspected, but would not admit, that she was smarter than most of the men he had known. If anyone could bargain with the Habiru, he grudgingly admitted, Rahab could. He began to like her in spite of himself.

On his twenty-first day in the house of Rahab, Jaben awakened early. The house shook. The floors trembled. What was happening? He stood up. The others were awakening. The pounding persisted, loudly, regularly, like the sound of marching feet, like the sound of soldiers marching in rank. Jaben's heart jumped. Its own pounding stopped, then started again with a quiver. They were here! They had come! He hurried up the stairs toward the roof. "They're here!" he shouted. At the third landing he paused. "Rahab, they've come," he shouted. He was on the roof in an instant. He stood beside the battlements overlooking the Jordan Valley. *The nightmares of the city of Jericho are at an end,* he thought. *The worst is truly here.* Stretching before him, marching around the walls in numberless ranks, were the warriors of the Habiru.

Rahab stood beside him. "They've come," she said. He stared at her in amazement. Her eyes shone and she smiled. She looked pleased, happy, almost delighted. Rahab's exhilaration astonished him. She was not afraid at all. She was excited. She had wanted them to come, and now they were here. *She does not expect to die*, he realized.

The Habiru are going to keep their bargain, he thought. Rahab's reaction convinced him. He looked at the thousands of marching soldiers. *We are going to belong to the Habiru*, he thought.

Micah and Benan came bounding onto the roof. "What is it?" they shouted. "What is the noise?" Their shouting ceased as abruptly as it had begun. Benan's lip trembled as he stared down at the Habiru soldiers encircling the walls of Jericho.

Rahab saw and quickly placed her arms around the boy's shoulders. "It is all right, Benan," she said. "Think of them as our people—our people who have come to rescue us!"

Tirnah and the others clambered up the stairs and onto the roof. "Oh, Baal—Oh, Astarte," Tirnah cried loudly, "we are all going to die! Oh, by the power of the gods! We are lost! Oh, El! Help us!"

Her husband slapped her face. "Quiet, woman! We are not going to die! Those Habiru are going to rescue us!"

Only Rahab and Benan believed what he said.

"Shanarbaal! In the name of the gods, where is Shanarbaal?" the king demanded petulantly. He took another swallow of the strong wine he had been drinking for days, and then he spoke quietly, mumbling into his cup, as if its red reflection held an answer.

"I think he has forgotten who is king," he said. Then he stood grandly, flinging the wine across the half-dozen servants and soldiers who had attended him throughout the night.

"I am king!" he shouted. "And I am god for Jericho!"

He drank again and, seeing that his cup was empty, called for more. "Shanarbaal forgets that I am king," he whined. "I have worked all night to make plans to defeat the Habiru." He paused to giggle. "The high priest must share my plan."

He walked unsteadily around the room, carefully examining each person, expounding on his dissatisfaction with priests in general and with Shanarbaal in particular.

"Oparu was right!" he shouted suddenly. "We will take the money from the temple! What do you think of that, O great high priest Shanarbaal? That'll teach you to ignore your king!" He laughed loudly. "We'll use your money to build our siegeworks! We will climb the walls of Jericho from the inside out, and we will attack the Habiru! They have no walls to protect them! Ha! So we will win! We will win, Shanarbaal!"

He laughed again, a high-pitched laugh that ended on a hiccough, and he drank again, the red wine dribbling like blood down his chin, running through his beard and staining his tunic.

"Oparu!" he shouted. "Come back! We need your chariots to fight these Habiru dogs! Oparu, where did you go?"

The king collapsed in a heap by his wine table and began to cry. "Oparu," he mumbled, "please come back!"

And then, as the king of Jericho sat besotted with red wine, crying into his cups, and as, outside, the sun rose brightly in the east, the citizens of Jericho heard the sound, a throbbing in the floor. The servants and guards felt it first, as the floors and walls around them began to vibrate, like the drumbeats of the temple. There was no other sound, except for the simpering of the king. It was as if the building in which they stood had come to life and they felt its heartbeat. The servants and warriors looked at one another in sudden terror, and then, to a man, they fled, tumbling over one another in their haste to escape to the outside courtyards.

The commotion at the door aroused the king, and he looked up, becoming aware for the first time of the rhythmic throbbing of the floor beneath him. He grinned broadly and lurched to his feet, still clinging to his wine cup.

"Oparu! You are returning! I hear your footsteps!" He looked quizzically into his cup, realizing now that he was alone in the room. "What?" he shouted. "Have they all gone? I hear their marching. Habbak! Where are you?"

He drank again. "Curse the eunuch anyway. He never comes in early....he carouses away the night and wants to sleep all day. Bah! I spit on him!" He turned then, stumbling toward his private chambers where the queen was sleeping with the child.

"If Shanar and Oparu and Habbak want to shirk their duties, it's all right with me," he mumbled. "They can rot in the underworld for all I care! I will go in to the queen! She will have me!"

The heavy, measured throbbing awakened Shanarbaal from a deep, drugged sleep. He had been dreaming of colors—bright reds and yellows leaping like flames against the midnight sky, but suddenly he was aware that his bed was shaking in the measured cadence of the temple drums.

"Ninunta!" he whispered. "I am coming!"

As the sun brightened the eastern sky, Shanarbaal, high priest of Baal, quickly lighted a lamp and hurried to answer the call of his gods. As he traveled down the stairway toward the room of dedication, the yellow light of the lamp cast flickering shadows on the friezes of the goddess, and she danced for Shanarbaal as she always did when he entered this magic place. He ran too fast to notice on this morning, however, for he was driven by the urgency of the drumbeats that called him. He hurried past the room of dedication into the deeper chambers of the temple. His feet knew well these carved stairs, so when his lamp light dimmed and faltered—in his haste he had not refilled it with oil—he continued in the darkness. His feet knew the way; darkness was his friend. He welcomed the chilly dampness of these chambers beneath the

239

earth. The measured beat of the drums reassured him as well. He felt safe in the womb of the goddess herself, and he could feel her heartbeat all around him.

As he reached the smooth floor of the chamber of the mole, he went directly to a low altar. There, his hands felt for and quickly touched a jar of magical powders. He sprinkled them in a circle, speaking his incantations, and in the blue glow of the powder he could see his friends. Within the circle, Astarte stood with her lily and snake. Beside her, Baal sat astride a bull, holding a thunderbolt in his hands, and on the altar, the lion-bird Ninunta perched, his carnelian eyes reflecting the blue glow of the circle.

"I am here," Shanar told them.

Queen Asheratti awakened to the rhythmic throbbing of the floor beneath her bed. The little boy was sleeping, but he began to move and murmur to his mother—dreaming, perhaps. The queen lay very still, trying to discern the source of the sound. It could not be an earthquake: when the earth shook, buildings crashed and chasms opened in the earth itself. Almost deeper than the ear could hear, these sounds shook the floor and the bed, like the taut skin of the temple drum—and the rhythm pulsed, sounding like the temple drums—the call to the dance of death. Asheratti closed her eyes, and trembled.

"Wife!" shouted the king, throwing himself onto the bed and flinging aside the waking child, "I am your king!"

The child fell heavily. In pain and confusion, the little heir of Jericho began to scream. The king, his father, did not hear. Asheratti moved away from the grasping hands of the king. "Go away!" she shrieked. "You stink! What have you done to your son? You have hurt the prince!"

The king lurched toward her. She struggled against his drunken caresses, striking him in the stomach and pushing against him. "Fool!" she hissed. "You're drunk!"

Lying half on the bed, with his head on the floor, the king began to moan.

Quickly, Asheratti gathered the screaming child into her arms and fled into the courtyard. There, kneeling by a pool, shaded by the lush greenery of flowering vines and bushes, she patted the boy gently, soothing his terrors and suckling him.

Here, where the garden walls formed the walls of the city, the sounds which had awakened her were louder, identifiable. The rhythm was the rhythm of marching feet. *The Habiru! It is the dance of death beginning,* she thought, *for we shall surely die.*

The steady, pounding marching of the warriors outside the walls was syncopated by the retching of the king.

The men who marched around Jericho kept their thoughts to themselves.

They spoke no words. The Lord had commanded silence, and so they were silent.

The earth itself trembled beneath their feet, seeming to shake in rhythm with their measured tread. *Am I imagining it,* Salma wondered, *or do the steep walls and ramparts of the city tremble as well?* He smiled to himself. *The people inside the city must think we have lost our senses!*

He glanced up at the walls towering into the sky above them. They looked invincible! Yet the earth trembled, and Joshua said the Lord had delivered the city to them: He had already done it! The warriors need only have faith and be of good courage! *We shall do as you command, Lord,* Salma thought, *though your instructions seem strange indeed.*

The instructions of the Lord had seemed strange before, he remembered, thinking of how they had crossed the Jordan only three weeks before. "When the priests carrying the ark step into the water," Joshua had said, "the Lord will work wonders for us." Salma had thought, then, as he watched women with little children walk toward the raging flood—women who could not swim—that the Lord gave strange orders; he and Daniel knew the strength of those waters, for they had crossed the Jordan on the mission to spy out the land. Though they were strong and hardened, they were desert men, and they had never felt the force of the flood waters. Even for them, it had been a mighty struggle. But when the men of Israel and the women and the children had come to cross, the waters had simply dried up. Salma grinned, and his spirit soared.

As he marched around the walls, Salma would have liked to shout: *"See, Jericho! You are already dead, for the Lord God has given you to us!"* But he was silent, for Yahweh had so commanded.

As he rounded a corner of the walls, a hanging scarlet cord caught his eye. The harlot had remembered! Joshua had told them all: "The prostitute and her household are to be saved because she welcomed the spies!" *The woman has kept her covenant with the Lord,* Salma thought.

Salma's feet shook the earth, with his brothers, the men of Israel. *The Lord has given us the city! The city belongs to the Lord our God!*

48

"Where is Shanarbaal? Where is the high priest?" The king's hoarse shouts were lost in the winds sweeping across the ramparts of Jericho. The cries of the child beside him—the child he had given to Ninunta—went unheeded and unheard.

The early-morning sun shone hotly, and the brisk dry wind from the wilderness to the west whipped the king's ceremonial cloak and the ornately embroidered robes of the child. Below them, for the seventh consecutive day, the Habiru marched around the whitewashed walls of Jericho.

The people of the city had almost become accustomed to the marching, to the daily trembling of the city that matched the fearful trembling of their hearts.

Dressed in the golden horns and brilliantly embroidered robes of the goddess, the high priestess Mari-Astarte stood beside the king. The golden girdle of the goddess encircled her thin waist, and from her side dangled the gold and ruby dagger, the sacrificial instrument of the people of the gods.

Nearby, Queen Asheratti sat quietly on her knees where she had been placed. Purple marks were already visible on Asheratti's arms where the king's men had fiercely restrained her earlier struggles as Mari-Astarte had encouraged her to drink the potent libation of the goddess. No longer did the queen protest; she felt neither the slap of the winds against her face nor the sting of her hair as it blew and whipped across her dry, unfocused eyes. She heard and felt only the heavy pounding of her own heart as it shook the floor on which she knelt, and she nodded and swayed gently with its rhythms.

A komer had carried the temple drum to the ramparts above the king's palace. At a nod from the high priestess, he began the music for the dance of death, beating loudly on the drum, its rhythms joining, merging with, disappearing into the dirge from below, into the incessant, inexorable pounding echoes of the feet of the Habiru. The walls themselves picked up the refrain, the vibrations intensifying savagely as if in response to the call of the drum.

The Habiru marched on. The pounding of their feet did not fade, disappearing toward the Jordan as on the previous mornings.

Mari-Astarte began the ceremony, repeating the ancient incantations, ritual words and chants older than the Jericho walls on which they stood.

"Where is the high priest?" the king muttered. "I sent for him at dawn. He has ignored my summons for the last time!"

"Hush!" hissed the priestess. "The god has promised us the city for the

242

child, so we must give Ninunta his gift—quickly, before it is too late to save the city!" Her voice dropped, and she added in a whisper, "You are king and god—you can be priest as well!" So the ceremony continued.

A sudden blast of Habiru trumpets, so loud the city walls seemed to quake beneath them, stopped the ceremony—but only for an instant.

Deep in the bowels of the Jericho temple, in the chamber of the mole, Shanarbaal crouched on his heels within his magic circle. He rocked back and forth, his eyes darting wildly in terror. He clutched the Assyrian idol, Ninunta, tightly against his chest.

"They're coming! They're coming! They're coming!" he whispered fiercely, madly. "You promised me they wouldn't come, but they are here!" He continued to rock. He whimpered. "You promised they wouldn't come! You promised they wouldn't come, but they are here!" His words became a sob; tears rolled down his face. "You promised!" he screamed, his voice rising with his terror. "You have lied to me!"

No gods answered.

The walls of the chamber of the mole crashed down upon him.

High above, on the walls of the city, the king of Jericho ended the most ancient, most terrible ritual of the land.

As he plunged the knife deep into the heart of his only son, the floor beneath him broke, giving way, falling in. Heavy stones tumbled, crushing him in the rubble.

One final sound echoed in the heart of the dying king of Jericho: the scream of the son he had killed with his own hand.

49

Where was Nantha?

Inwardly, Rahab cursed. The foolish woman! This was no time to be separated from the family. At any second, they would be called forth and escorted away. If Nantha were not with them, she would surely die.

"Nantha!" Rahab called, pushing aside the curtain that concealed the cooking area.

Nantha stopped instantly. She had been putting her dough gods into a cloth sack.

"What are you doing, woman?" Rahab snapped.

"My lady—I was just...I was going to take my gods...." the cook stammered.

"No, you're not," Rahab said. "They are Jericho gods. Let them remain in Jericho! Put them back—now!—and come into the public room."

Rahab watched as Nantha reluctantly placed the dough figurines back into their niche in the kitchen wall. Rahab grabbed Nantha's arms and roughly pulled her into the public room with the others.

Amidst the thunderous collapse of the entire city around them, one thought held Rahab secure in the hope of rescue: Her house had not fallen!

Shock waves from the collapsing walls had shaken pottery from the shelves and broken vases and cups on tables where they stood, but the walls of Rahab's house had remained strong. A gaping hole as broad as a man cracked in the outer wall of the public room. Blocks of stone fell outward from this opening. The house shuddered and creaked, but it did not fall.

Rahab's family gasped, horrified. Tirnah's child began to scream. A warrior appeared outside, staring inward through the hole that had cracked in the wall. Tirnah fainted, but Rahab gasped in relief, recognizing the face of the Habiru spy, Salma. Alcion, too, saw the man and knew that all was well.

"Quickly!" Salma barked. "This way!" Jaben shook his wife. Micah and Alcion picked up the litter on which Bazarnan lay. "Through here, quickly!" Salma barked again.

Outside, from the city streets, they heard the shrieks and screams of the fighting and of the killing: bangings, knockings, screamings, curses and shouts and moans. The city was dying, but the household of Rahab stepped through the last opening in the Jericho wall, stepped to life and freedom.

In addition to the two spies, ten soldiers escorted them, surrounding them in a protective guard. They walked so quickly that the women had to run to keep up. The wails of the city behind them grew louder. Rahab's ears strained, hearing the cries. She bit her lip and half turned her head.

A voice sounded immediately at her shoulder. "Don't look back!" Alcion commanded. It was all he said. It was enough.

Nantha's dough gods were the first to feel the intensity of the Habiru torches, as the men of Israel consummated their victory by burning all that remained of Jericho.

The little gods huddled in their niches above a table in the kitchen; their shining rock eyes reflected the flames that lapped up from the straw mats on the floor. Their cheeks began to swell, and their edges melted and curled. They began to grimace and grin, with the dough puffing up and closing over the pebbles of their eyes. Their feet curled and blackened, and then a tiny flame burst up and licked one face and then another. The grins deepened, blackening.

Fire sprouted from lips and eyes, sending curls of smoke spiraling upward. The shrieks of the people had died away, and the roaring of the fire consumed the dough gods, as, one by one, they toppled in against one another and fell into the conflagration that had been the house of Rahab.

50

The tent of Bazarnan's family on the edge of the Judean camp drew many stares, some of them merely curious, many openly hostile.

Merab and Zerba stood at the well of Gilgal with four other Hebrew women.

"Perhaps it is nothing to the women of Ephraim that these people have come amongst us," Merab answered Zerba. "But I am of the tribe of Judah, and it is our tribe they have joined. No good will come of it, I tell you. I am amazed that Caleb and Salma allowed it."

"Caleb is old, and Salma is young—young and only a short time a widower," Zerba answered her coolly. "Salma has the eye of a lonely man. Perhaps he saw more in this family than we see."

Merab snorted. "I see too much already: strange foreign ways; shameless clothing. Joshua said this Rahab was a harlot."

"That is true," Zerba answered, shaking her head.

Abigal, another Ephraimite, agreed with her. "She is a harlot, but he has allowed her to live," she argued. "Why should this woman live when the law requires death for harlotry?"

Haggar nodded. "No one in the camps of Israel has forgotten the way the Moabite harlots seduced our men after we took Bashan. Joshua is too wise to allow a harlot in our midst. Perhaps she is no longer a harlot. Did she not bring a family?"

"Yes. They claim to be her parents and brothers and sisters—or so my man says. He has talked to the old one, the sick one, who says he is her father."

"A woman her age should have children."

"So you say, but you know what Canaanites do to their children."

The women were silenced for a moment. Canaanite practices were not to be discussed. Yet every woman at the well shuddered.

"Whether she has children or not, she is too old to remain unwed."

"She's not the only one. Several of them seem to have no man."

"Then God preserve our men from them!"

"Ah, but there's no way to help it. They'll marry into the tribe."

"It happens all the time," Hannah, a kinder woman of Judah, said. "In a few years you will forget they're strangers."

"I won't forget," Merab said coldly.

"Then, certainly, you will remember that the law bids us be kind to the stranger within our gates," Hannah answered simply.

"The law does not speak so kindly of harlots who should have died in Jericho! Remember Zimri and the Midianite whore—they died together!"

"You cannot be sure that—" Hannah started, but she stopped speaking as she realized that the old woman Nantha was approaching the well.

Nantha noticed that the chatter of feminine voices stopped instantly as she drew near. It seemed that all the women turned to look at her. *They have been talking about us,* Nantha thought. *They are surely jealous.* Automatically, she straightened her shoulders, proudly displaying her ample figure, and tilted her nose ever so slightly into the air as she walked up to the well.

She paused and looked about disdainfully. "I hope I did not interrupt your conversation, ladies of Israel," she said ironically. "I have come to draw water for my mistress, Rahab of Jericho."

Every woman looked away except for Haggar, who stood between Nantha and the well. She stared aggressively at Nantha, her fists at her waist and her elbows out.

"Indeed!" she answered sarcastically. "Haven't you heard? We have gone to war with Jericho—and we have burned her to the ground." She paused to be sure her friends could hear. "There is no Jericho."

"If it were not for my mistress you would not have taken Jericho—and you would not be here," Nantha spat back.

The women looked at one another. What did the old woman mean? Hannah wondered.

"Your mistress did not win our battle!" Zerba said sharply. "We won our battle."

Hannah stepped forward, interceding gently in Nantha's behalf.

"Come, Zerba," she said. "The Lord won our battle, and he instructs us to be kind to the strangers in our midst."

"I didn't mean that God didn't do it, Hannah! I meant that her mistress didn't." Zerba pointed rudely at Nantha. "Her mistress is a harlot and deserves to be stoned!"

Nantha was furious, but Rahab had instructed her to avoid offending the women of Israel, so she held her peace, dipping her pitcher into the waters of Gilgal. She placed the pitcher on her shoulders and walked away crisply without saying another word. But she wanted to throw the pitcher and its contents on these foolish women—these foolish desert wanderers who knew no civilization, who knew nothing and resented those who did!

Rahab sat alone on the mountain, looking across the plain to the smoldering ruins of Jericho. A pale moon lighted the landscape, casting soft shadows, and a light fog—or perhaps it was smoke—swirled within the city, softening outlines and blurring details. There was no sound in the chill night air, for the city was dead and stilled. Not even a bat swirled above the dead rocks and rubble; no mouse scurried within the ruins; no dog scavenged within the city's once-proud walls.

Then, as Rahab watched, a man began to walk toward her from the city— one man, alone, whose cloak blew and fluttered in the night winds like the black wings of an approaching spirit of death. He quickly covered the ground as she watched, until he towered over her, blacking out the moon, the city, the landscape.

It was Shanarbaal—thin, yellowed, ravaged by the depths of his obsession. Terrified, she thought, *Shanarbaal is dead; he cannot be here.*

"Rahab!" he hissed. "You are an enemy of the Baalim, whom you have offended!" He shook his long, bony finger in her face. "Traitor!" he screamed. "Traitor!" His screams were so loud that they awakened her.

Trembling, she arose and went outside. The night air was still and soft. There was no moon, but the pale light of the campfires cast a soft glow across the camp of Judah. *People were sleeping here, gently, trusting in the Lord God,* she thought, and her terror seemed to melt into the mists of the night.

"God?" she said softly. "Yahweh—Lord God—it is you who have delivered me from the Baalim!" Above her, the stars looked down, twinkling, smiling, laughing.

As Salma entered the tent, he saw that Daniel was already there, seated on the ground before Joshua. Both men looked up as Salma arrived. "The peace of our God be with you, Salma," his leader greeted him.

"And with you," Salma answered. "How may I serve you, sir?"

"The twin cities of Bethel and Ai must be scouted, Salma," his commander

247

answered with military directness. "I want you to leave in the morning, before the dawn. Both you and Daniel have proved yourselves. I must know the size and relative strength of the cities so that I can plan the best attack."

"We are your servants, sir," Salma answered in formal agreement.

"And the servants of our Lord, the most High God," Joshua responded. "He will guide you. Be strong and of good courage, men. The mighty arm of our Lord will protect you."

"We will not fail, sir," Daniel promised.

"I trust you as Moses trusted me and as he trusted Caleb. The blessing of the Lord is upon you." The old man smiled. "Get a good night's rest," he ordered gently as the two spies left the tent to make their own plans for the following morning.

Salma and Daniel traveled quickly through the countryside; they had been trained well by Joshua, who knew every military maneuver imaginable. He had been trained long ago in the armies of the pharaoh, and Salma and Daniel learned thoroughly all that Joshua taught. They were brave, yet cautious, as they traveled. An unwary soldier was soon a dead soldier, and both these men, captains of the Habiru forces, had every desire to live.

They came to the area of Bethel-Ai in the late afternoon. The two cities were within sight of each other. As the spies surveyed the spot, they realized that the cities were not alike, despite the misleading nickname *toam*, twin cities. One of the cities was considerably larger than the other. The towns were very, very old. The battered condition of their walls was evidence of their antiquity. The smaller city seemed half town, half ruin, as if a settlement had formed on the rubble of battles past.

On a ridge, midway between the two towns, Daniel and Salma watched the commerce of the people. Men gathered outside the gate of the larger town, farmers sold sheep and barley, and merchants exchanged the news and conducted the many small businesses of the day. Occasionally a woman appeared, bartering for a few moments with some merchant and then disappearing within the gates of the city. Most of the men were old, and no military forces were in evidence. The Habiru would hold a major advantage in the youth and vigor of their fighting forces.

The second town would be even less troublesome than the first, Salma and Daniel agreed, since half the city wall of this smaller settlement was fallen into ruin.

"We will take them with ease," Salma responded.

Daniel smiled. "You are right, my friend. Joshua does well to warn us against proud and haughty spirits. My arrogant soldier's heart easily forgets."

Salma understood well what Daniel was expressing. The law of Moses warned that in good times a man's heart easily turned from the God of his fathers. He laughed softly and patted Daniel on the back. "We will tell Joshua that the Lord can take the cities with the help of very few soldiers," Salma said.

Daniel laughed, too, watching the old men in the market below. What Salma said was obviously true.

They camped that night in the ruins of a house on the ridge overlooking the two cities. The house had no roof and only three of its walls remained, but these formed a shelter from the wind where the men could safely build a small campfire. They were glad to have the shelter. A cold dry wind blew across the ridge, and the creatures of the night prowled in the bushes nearby. A hyena howled, its strange wild laughter making a fierce and lonely sound.

A full, orange moon rose in the east, and in the cities below, lights began to glimmer. Salma watched the stars. "It was near this place that our father Jacob dreamed of the stairway to heaven," he mused.

"Perhaps in this very spot," Daniel agreed. "We must watch our dreams tonight."

Salma watched the rising moon. "This is an awesome place," he said.

Daniel laughed. "And tomorrow it shall be ours!"

Salma smiled. "There is still a battle to be fought," he reminded his friend.

"Yes," Daniel laughed as he replied, "and a long journey back to the camp to be made in the morning. We'll need a sound sleep and a smooth stone to put under our heads."

Salma grinned, remembering the stone that Jacob had slept on. "You'll sleep on a stone and be dreaming like Jacob—seeing angels," he teased.

Both men laughed, then looked at each other a bit sheepishly. It might not be wise to laugh about dreams in holy places.

Daniel peered across the fire. "I thought I saw a viper," he said.

"The Lord God protects us from vipers," Salma said.

"He certainly protected us from the one in Jericho," Daniel answered, "from the viper in the house of Rahab."

Salma grimaced. He did not think of Rahab as a viper. But he answered the other man lightly. "Your good sense protected us there," he said. "I'll give you the credit."

Daniel laughed at him. He was unbeguiled by his friend's casual answer. "I think my good sense was needed," he said, adding emphatically, "to protect you!"

"You must admit," Salma said thoughtfully, "that she was...well, that she is really...."

"She is, indeed," the other man interrupted him. "And she is still dangerous. You must avoid her still."

"Have I spoken to her since she has been in the camp?" Salma asked indignantly.

"Do I know?" Daniel questioned in reply. "Do I hear every word you speak?"

"Not once have I spoken to her," Salma answered. "Nor shall I!"

"Nor should you!"

Salma sighed. "Even so, that was a fine footrub."

Daniel looked at him in exasperation and handed him a large stone. "Put that under your head. We must sleep now—it will be a busy day tomorrow, and no dreams for you tonight! To dream of Canaanite harlots would not bode well for a soldier of the Lord Almighty."

Taking the stone, Salma lay back and adjusted the hard pillow beneath his head. He stared up at the moon and the stars, which seemed brighter here than he had ever seen them before, perhaps because they were closer.

Yes, he thought, *this is indeed the gateway to heaven. Jacob was right, Bethel is the house of the living God.* He thought of the stairway to heaven that Jacob had seen here, perhaps, as Daniel had said, in this very spot. He thought of the God who had spoken to Jacob from the stairway, the God who had promised Jacob that his descendants would own this land. *And now we are here to see the fulfillment of that promise,* Salma thought. He sighed and adjusted the rock. He had nothing good to say about the hard pillows of the patriarchs.

Salma closed his eyes and tried to sleep. The face of Rahab, her eyes sparkling and her lips a bright, unnatural red, intruded on his mind. *A prince of Judah must not be distracted by a Canaanite,* he told himself. *Judah, himself, the founder of the tribe, married a Canaanite,* his thoughts argued back. *Yes, and he lost his first two sons—perhaps as a punishment,* Salma reasoned. He must not think about the Canaanite woman. *The Lord God will provide me with another wife and with sons,* Salma assured himself, *but it will be in the fullness of God's time—not mine. The Lord God who provides will provide for me,* he promised himself again. He sighed, trying to get comfortable. *But whom will he provide?*

The desert sun beat down upon him. Sweat poured from his taut, tired body. And still the sun beat down. He moved one large stone slab and then another. The smooth limestone was heavy. Sometimes he stumbled beneath the weight. The stairs he built went upward. He had been building them since dawn. Where was Daniel? Daniel should have been there to help him. He would never finish this task alone. How high must this stairway be? He wasn't sure. He wished his sons were there. He needed his sons to help him. He would never finish this task alone. He moved another heavy slab. This was too much for one man to bear. He cried out to God, "Why alone, Lord God, why alone?"

He was suddenly awake and staring at the stars. This tale of Jacob had put strange visions in his head. *Go back to sleep,* he told himself.

Behind him the Egyptian slave master watched his every move as he continued to stack the rocks stone upon stone, one after another. He did not know how wide the wall must be. *Already it is as wide as a man is tall,* he thought, but it could go on forever, stone upon stone, one after another. He must finish this task. He must build this wall; this wall would keep out the stranger in the camp. Judah would be pleased. He must finish the task. *The taskmaster is too hard. I cannot finish it.* The heat of the desert prevailed against him. "O Lord God, is there no help under the sun?"

Suddenly he heard the irregular pounding of hoofs against stony ground. He turned; it was not a horse. A wild mountain ram stood staring at him. Its luminous brown eyes spoke to him of a wisdom more ancient than the earth and of the highest mysteries: the mountains and the sky. A ragged scar ran down the ram's nose, and the tip of one horn was broken, hinting of past battles fought and won. The creature reared and pawed the air. As its hoofs came down, Salma knew its intent. "No!" he screamed, but it was too late.

The ram charged, attacking the wall Salma had worked so hard to build. The wall came down, and the ram disappeared into the east. Behind the wall rose a stairway, a stairway that rose steeply, its steps disappearing into the clouds. Down this stairway came a woman wearing a long white veil. At her breast, she suckled a tiny baby boy—*my baby boy,* Salma thought. He knew immediately that the child was his. The woman looked up and smiled, her eyes soft beneath eagle brows. The mother of his baby was Rahab!

Salma awakened. The stars above him twinkled, winking, laughing at him. He had tormented himself for nothing. What the Lord God approved, man could not disapprove! What the Lord God had blessed, no man could curse. Rahab would be his wife, and she would bear sons of the tribe of Judah. The pale pink in the eastern sky promised him the morning was near.

"The Lord, the God of Abraham, Isaac, and Jacob, has spoken to me in this place tonight," Salma said aloud. He prayed silently, and then with a great sense of purpose he picked up the rock that had been his pillow and placed it on a smooth slab of limestone. From his pack, he took a small jar of oil and anointed the rock. "This shall be a memorial!" he said aloud.

On the ground beside him, Daniel turned over and looked at him sleepily. "What?" he asked.

Salma only smiled, looking at the rock. Then he turned to Daniel and laughed. "Get up, sleeping one," he said. "We have a journey before us and a battle to win for the Lord."

51

The road was familiar. The journey should have been easy: short and filled with the laughter of victorious soldiers. But the road was quiet. The only sounds were the groans of wounded men and the hum of the insects that plagued them. Dust stirred with his every footstep, clinging to the perspiration drenching his pain-laced body. Thirty-six of his men, many of them his best friends, were dead. The armies of Bethel-Ai had been old men and children, but they had defeated Salma's army the way a man brushes away a sand flea.

Salma stumbled and almost fell. Catching himself with the stick he used for support, he stopped and looked at his injured leg. A spear had pierced deep into the muscle of his upper leg. The bandage that a few moments before had been crusted with dry blood was now oozing bright red. He needed to rest.

He moved to a large stone beside the road. Several of the men who walked near him stopped to offer support. He could lean on their shoulders; they would carry him. He refused their offers, ordering them to keep going. "I'll catch up with you in a few moments. Don't wait for me." Since he was their captain, they could only obey.

Salma watched the last of the men disappear around an outcopping of rocks. He was hot and miserable, but he preferred to be alone. Each time he looked at one of his men, pain, much deeper than the wound in his leg, stabbed him. What had he done? What had Daniel done? They must have sinned terribly that God should punish all of Israel with a defeat such as this one. Salma wiped the dusty sweat from his brow. *Old men*, he thought. *Half of them were old men. And we ran before them like sheep before a lion. Perhaps that is the problem. Perhaps the lion of Judah destroys his own cubs.* He thought of his men who were dead. *I was their captain. Why could I not have stopped it?*

The face of Jophet, his lieutenant, rose before him. The spear had passed completely through Jophet's body. Salma, seeing him fall, had rushed to his defense, but it was too late. Jophet had tried to speak but had merely choked, the sound gurgling in his mouth as he died. His wife had borne him a son only two weeks ago. Jophet should not have died. No one should have died. What had happened to the Lord God of Israel? Where were his mighty promises now? Salma stabbed his stick into the ground roughly. The people of Bethel-Ai were no different from the people of Jericho. All were pagans; all were worshippers of false and vicious gods. Why had God spared these? It made no sense!

Thirty-six men of Israel are dead, he thought, *while the fat old men of Bethel-Ai laugh at our weakness! Where is the reputation of Israel now, Lord? Where are the people of a God who cannot be defeated?*

The Canaanites laugh at us, and we run like wounded dogs! The people of Canaan will not fear us. And why should they? We could not take a tiny fortress that lies half in ruins! We could not defeat old men and little boys!

Michah's smile flashed in Salma's mind. How he had loved Michah's smiling, happy face. They had played together as boys. Michah's laughter was always the loudest, the longest of all the boys of Judah. There had been no laughter on the battlefield from Michah today. His belly wound took him swiftly. "I go to be with our fathers," he had gasped. "The shepherd and the stone of Abraham protect you, Salma."

The stone of Abraham! We break upon this stone! Where is the shepherd's protection now? This is just punishment for sinners, but we are the children of the promise! Where is the promise now? We are defeated. We shall perhaps be enslaved. All is as it was in Egypt. Worshippers of false gods rule over us! Nothing has changed!

"God, why have you done this to us?" Salma said aloud, looking at the sky. No cloud of presence showed himself there now. No God responded to his pain. No ladder, no ram, nothing to signify that the God of Israel heard his bitter complaint. An empty sky stared back at him.

Salma carefully stretched his wounded leg and stood to continue his journey. *Joshua will have heard the news by the time I reach the camp,* he thought. *I have failed Joshua, and I have failed Caleb. If they had led the battle, perhaps it would have gone differently.*

It is a blessing that my father, Nashon, is no longer alive to see this day. He did not deserve to have his son bring such shame upon the tribe of Judah!

Oh, I am such an important man! How could I ever have thought that God had spoken to me? Why would the God of the Israelites, the God of all that exists, speak to such a man as I? My arrogance is being paid for by the death of my companions.

To think that I, the first captain to be defeated in Canaan, could have dared to compare myself to our father Jacob. This is perhaps the sin for which God punishes me. How could I have been so foolish? I dared to think that God would honor me with an important dream in the same spot where the ladder appeared to Jacob. Surely, this defeat is sign enough that I have not understood the mind of God! Oh, and it is worse yet! What was the subject of this dream which I took to be a sign from God? The subject was my desire for a Canaanite harlot. A harlot who sits in her camp and is even now probably laughing at the weakness of the great captain, Salma, prince of Judah. I do not deserve to live!

The pain in his leg grew more intense. He leaned heavily on the stick. *Perhaps I will not live,* he thought. *Abraham is promised his generation, Israel is promised the land, Judah is promised the sceptre. But this does not mean that sons of the promise shall come forth from my loins. Who am I to believe that God has assured me that I shall wife Rahab and get sons? I do not deserve such blessing. It may be that sin has caused the defeat; it may be that the sin is my own.*

Salma groaned and tried to clear his mind of any thinking. If his wound killed him, he thought, he would be glad.

The pile of stones was high. Men gathered the last of the largest boulders and placed them on the mound. *A memorial to sin!* Salma thought bitterly.

If only we had known of Achan's sin before the battle of Bethel-Ai! Salma lamented for what must have been the hundredth time.

The stoning of Achan weighed heavily upon Salma's heart. The execution of an entire family was a thing rarely known in the camps of Israel.

The pile of stones stood out ominously against the afternoon sky. Salma mused, *The sin of Achan caused not only these deaths, but the deaths of thirty-six of my men, my brothers, my friends!*

Unlike Moses, Joshua was a leader who rarely spoke prophetically; therefore, the camp had been shocked when Joshua spoke with the authority of one who has heard the voice of God. Joshua had announced that transgression of God's law had caused the defeat of Bethel-Ai, and in the role of prophet, Joshua had summoned all the tribes. One by one the tribes had passed before their leader. Achan's tribe and then his family had been singled out. Fearfully, Achan confessed that he had broken the law. He had willfully sinned.

Joshua had warned all the soldiers of Israel—"Do not touch the things of Jericho. Everything in this city is dedicated to God. If you disobey, you will bring disaster to the sons of Israel." Achan had brought that disaster. A beautiful Babylonian cloak, a bar of gold, and the silver shekels of Jericho had been too much temptation for Achan to resist. He had stolen all of these and hidden them in his tent. With his sin, he had brought himself and his family under the ban, the judgment of Jericho: death. The sons of Israel had stoned them all. Their bodies lay beneath a monument of stones.

As my friends lay dead in the field, Salma thought angrily, *dead because God was disobeyed, his law ignored! They were dead, because Achan had thought he knew more than the Lord himself! Dead, because Achan thought he could lie to God. Achan had deserved to die!*

The last of the men of Israel turned to leave the place of the stoning. Salma turned, too, toward the camp, toward Joshua's tent, to report to his leader that the monument was completed. The last of the stones was in place.

As Salma turned, his wounded leg buckled beneath him. He caught himself angrily. His wound was a small thing compared to the pain he felt over the loss of Jophet, Michah, and the other men who had fallen.

The force of his anger at Achan drove away his pain. There had been anger in most of the faces as they had executed the stoning, especially in the faces of the soldiers who had survived Bethel-Ai.

Suddenly, Salma remembered that the harlot's family had been there, too. They had watched, but they had not helped with the stonings. The father had looked sad, but not unduly so. Rahab's face...he had not been able to read the woman's expression.

He had looked at her closely as she left the place, and she had spoken to him: "Salma, Caleb has said that we—Nantha and Kinah and I—may treat your wounds and those of your men. We know the herbs that will draw out the pain and the fever." How strange that she would make no mention of the deaths she had just witnessed, that she should speak, instead, of healing.

He had been gruff with her. His mind had been concerned with weightier matters than personal pain. "Tomorrow, woman," he had said. And then her sister's husband, Jaben, who seldom spoke and never laughed, had approached. "Your god is a just god, Salma. I must respect him."

The interruption had surprised him. "The Lord our God is, above all, a righteous God," he had responded. *These Canaanites*, he thought, *they are observant, at least. Ah, but the woman! She is magnificent.* His mind went back, and lingered over her figure. She dressed modestly now like the other women of Israel, but he had seen her in the provocative garments of her former life. He shook himself. He would not think of Rahab.

Salma knocked loudly on the lintel post of Joshua's tent.

"Are you there? May I come in?" he asked loudly.

"You may," was the muffled response.

Joshua did not turn as Salma entered. The old man was seated on a camp stool, looking down at the sacred scrolls of Moses. The lamplight shone on a bald spot on the top of his head and made his long white hair look like clouds of gold. Joshua sighed heavily and then turned to Salma.

"I have come to report—" Salma began, but paused, confused, seeing Joshua's open expression of pain and weeping. "I did not mean to interrupt your prayers—your study—"

The old man shook his head slowly, sadly. "No, no. It is no matter. What is your report? Is the memorial completed? It is late."

"Yes, it is. The sin of Achan is covered with stones and buried forever."

Tears flowed then from Joshua's eyes, but he seemed not to notice. Salma did not know what to say. Trying to comfort his leader seemed pointless and inappropriate.

After a few moments of silence, Joshua spoke. "It seems for all my life that we bury sin and disobedience to the Lord in one place, and it grows in another. Sometimes I think it is too hard for the people. They will not obey, and they suffer sin's consequences—they suffer death."

Salma nodded, waiting for Joshua to continue. The old man would often talk to the young soldiers, instructing and sharing his thoughts, his feelings, and his faith. The young men counted themselves fortunate to be with him in such a mood. To be here on this night, with the strength of the emotions that tore at Joshua, was a special honor.

"I have wept, so many times, Salma! I wept when the people made a golden calf and began to worship in the ways of these Canaanites. I wept for I knew what would happen. Moses was angry; the Lord was angry. I thought the Lord would kill them all on the spot—but Moses prayed for them—Ah, Salma—Moses had more patience, more faith, than I could ever have." Again, Joshua paused to sigh.

"I wept when the people disobeyed the Lord and feared to enter the land forty years ago.... We were south of here, at Kadesh-Barnea, and the country could have been ours then—but they feared the men of Canaan more than they feared the Lord." Joshua slammed his hand against the small table that held the sacred scrolls. "Fools! The men of Israel are fools, Salma. Yet the Lord has chosen us, and he has given us the land!" He paused. "I cannot help wondering how we will take the land when these fools, the sons of Abraham, keep on disobeying the Lord's commands." He shook his head sadly.

Salma spoke then. He knew this answer, for it was in the law. "The Lord said that we should be careful to cleanse every uncleanness from our camp—to put away every sin."

"That is what we have done—for all my life, Salma," the old man answered sadly. "But we seem never to learn. Do you wonder that I am discouraged? I try so hard, yet we sin and we sin again—and people die because of it."

"Achan deserved to die!" Salma said angrily. "Thirty-six good men of Israel died because of Achan's sin. More men of Israel would die if we had not executed the Lord's judgment on Achan and his family."

"I weep for all of them, Salma—Achan, his children, and the thirty-six good men of Israel. Their deaths were needless," the old man said bitterly. "But Achan made his choice, and it was a choice for death—death for many. When Achan stole the trappings of Jericho, he put himself under the ban of Jericho. He chose Jericho, and he suffered its fate."

"But he had been warned! You warned us all," Salma answered. "I would not weep for Achan. As you say, he made his choice. My tears would be for the thirty-six men of Judah and Ephraim—my brothers who died at Bethel-Ai. Their choice was obedience, and they died as well: better, for they died bravely!"

"Achan was your brother also," Joshua, said gently. "He was of the tribe of Judah, your tribe."

"He brought shame and disaster upon the tribe of Judah," Salma spat angrily.

"He has brought shame and disaster upon us all. That is the nature of disobedience. But take heed, Salma. Learn from this: search your own heart; be sure that *you* are obedient to the law of the Lord."

The audience was over.

52

For three days, Caleb had sat with the old Canaanite man, Bazarnan, at his tent on the edge of the camp of Judah. The two talked until long after most of the campfires of the nation of Israel had died down to gentle smolderings.

All around him, Caleb's people questioned his friendliness toward the old man. It was improper! For the leader of the tribe of Judah to become intimate with such a stranger, it was unthinkable! He must be polite, even hospitable, to the stranger in the camp, for so the law commanded, but this daily interchange went far beyond simple courtesy. Caleb, Joshua's only contemporary, was befriending a Canaanite.

Caleb cared nothing for the sentiments of his people. He had lived with them too long not to sense their hypocrisy, and he had also lived with them too long to pay heed to their error. When his people were wrong, they were very wrong. And Caleb knew deep in his soul that his people were wrong in their opinion of Bazarnan. Caleb liked Bazarnan, who was, he sensed, a man not unlike himself. Except for Bazarnan's infirmity, the two might have been equals in every way. Caleb met few men for whom he felt such kinship. His brother Nashon had been such a man; Joshua was such a man; someday his nephew Salma would be just such a leader of Israel. But Nashon was dead. Joshua was always busy, and Salma was too young to have fulfilled the promise that was in him.

In the camps of Israel, there was but one way that Bazarnan would ever receive even a portion of the respect that Caleb knew he deserved. He and the men of his family must be circumcised; they must become Jews. Caleb had decided it the first time he saw Bazarnan on the morning after the fall of Jericho. The sick man's eyes had been wise and wary, the eyes of a man who knew life—and men. Caleb was glad that Joshua gave Rahab's family into his care. It was very much Caleb's intention that the strength of Bazarnan's line should be infused into the blood of Israel.

Caleb smiled across the campfire at the man who argued so well with him, and then he resumed his argument, an argument three days in duration: "Circumcision is a rite you owe to the God of Israel, Bazarnan. Do you think our God saved you out of Jericho for no purpose? Do not be so small in your thinking, man! Achan's entire family died because of unrighteousness. Because of his sin, his family became partakers of the ban which was upon Jericho. Yet you and your family, all of you Canaanites, were saved by the same God. Is it not right that you should become partakers of the blessings of Israel?"

Bazarnan nodded, but smiled ruefully. "Perhaps it is right. Or perhaps it is merely the whim of your god that Achan's family died and my family lived. Gods are often capricious."

"There is the fault in your reasoning, Bazarnan! The gods of Canaan are capricious, asking virtue one day and vice the next. But the God of Israel—the one true God—is always a God of righteousness. Have you noticed, Bazarnan, that there are no old people in the camps of Israel?"

"I have noticed," the other man replied. "I dared not ask why. Our gods demanded our children, so I thought perhaps your God...." he hesitated.

Caleb laughed. "No, no, Bazarnan. I see your fear, but you mistrust our God too much. He is a God of righteousness, but he is not, nor has he ever been, a God who demanded the sacrifice of our babies or—" now it was Caleb who paused, "of our old people."

"Then, why?" Bazarnan asked.

"Why are Joshua and I the only old ones in the camp?"

"Yes," Bazarnan answered simply, "why?"

"Because our long lives have been given to us as reward for righteous service and obedience, Bazarnan. Forty years ago, the children of Israel could have taken the land of Canaan. Joshua and I, with ten others, spied out the land. It was clear to the two of us that Canaan was ours for the taking—because the Lord God would give it to us. But none of the other spies nor the people of Israel were willing to take the risk. For their lack of faith, God allowed that entire generation to die before the promised land could be taken. Yet Joshua and I live, with vigor that has increased—not lessened—because the Lord rewards righteousness."

"It is an impressive story." Bazarnan smiled at the other man.

Caleb frowned. "I did not tell you this so that you would be impressed with me," he said shortly. "I want you to realize, Bazarnan, how consistently righteous are the ways of our God. He did not save you and your entire family for no reason. He has ransomed your life out from under the ban of the death of Jericho. He has called you, Bazarnan; you must not fail to acknowledge him! He has his purposes, and they are good."

Bazarnan smiled, shaking his head and staring into the fire. He had thought himself a master of argument, a magician of words, until he met Caleb. Now he bowed before the other man's reason, noting all the while that Caleb sought neither to trick him nor to manipulate him. Caleb's argument carried the strength of sincerity and a still greater strength—the strength of truth. Bazarnan sensed this with a part of himself that would not be denied. He raised his eyes to stare at his friend across the fire.

"I will be circumcised," he said.

Kora's reaction was one of total horror. "You will die!" she exclaimed. "You are not strong enough for such a thing!"

"I am strong enough," Bazarnan said with a quieter strength than usual. "Their father Abraham, the first man to be circumcised, was ninety-nine when he obeyed the Lord in this."

"That may be as it may be," Kora replied, "but he could not have been ill, as you are ill. You will die, Bazarnan; you will die and leave me alone among these strangers!"

"I will die, Kora—someday, but it will not be now. The Lord God did not bring me out of Jericho to have me die here in the camp. The Lord God will give me the strength for this, and when I die, I will leave you among your own people, a new people whose god you can trust."

Kora sniffed. "I cannot believe you would do such a thing! You will not be a man!"

Bazarnan laughed aloud at this. "I have not been a man to you for these many years, and you have not complained, my wife, my love. The Habiru God cannot take from me that which my illness has already stolen."

Kora wailed. "What of our sons, then? Would you rob them of their manhood as well?"

Bazarnan simply laughed at her again. "Caleb tells me that Abraham fathered a child in his old age within a year after his circumcision, and I do not see the tribes of Israel dwindling because of this rite. My sons will be fine, and their sons will be Israelites, servants of the most high God."

"You were, until this day, a reasonable man," his wife replied.

"I was, until this day, a man with no faith but in my own reason. Kora, this Habiru God has given me a truth greater than the mind of a man. I must obey him!"

His sons understood. The firmness of their father's conviction was enough to win their obedience. Jaben argued with Tirnah well into the night. Her resentment was shocking to him. If the Habiru God was great enough to bring down the walls of Jericho, he was a God worthy to be obeyed, Jaben argued. Tirnah acted as if she had not seen the fallen walls of Jericho. She spoke, Jaben thought, like one who was deaf and blind when they were rescued by the spies out of the rubble of the city.

"Rahab is the one who got us out of Jericho!" Tirnah argued. "Her sharp wits and not some strange god made the bargain that saved us! Father's illness has made him weak-minded, but I don't know how you will explain your madness."

"I will not explain it to you any further," Jaben said firmly, finally. "Your father has chosen to serve this Habiru God, and so have I. You are my wife and you will obey me. In my house, we will serve this God!"

Tirnah became suddenly contrite and compliant after this exchange. She knew and cared nothing for this god or any other, but in her eyes her husband

Jaben had finally become a man. If it took a strange god to bring this out in him, she thought, it was worth the cost.

Benan's fear was that his father might not survive the ritual. He ran to Alcion, seeking the older man's wisdom and comfort.

"What can I do, Alcion?" he demanded. "Not for the world would I argue with my father, yet he may be inviting his own death. He is weak. Perhaps they would let me undergo the ritual for him, Alcion! Do you think that is possible? I am healthy and strong. I could be circumcised for him."

"I do not think such a thing could be allowed, Benan. The circumcision is an individual matter. You cannot do this for him, anymore than you could die for him."

"But I would die for him, Alcion! He is my father, and I love him more than my own life!"

"As I am sure he loves you," Alcion responded, touched in his deepest heart by this young boy's tenderness. "What your father does is a covenant with a God, Benan. Perhaps the best way to be a faithful son is to discover what your own covenant with the Habiru God must be."

"Do you think this God will allow my father to live, Alcion?" Benan asked quietly.

The other man's reply was equally soft. "From what I have seen of this God, Benan, it would not surprise me in the least."

The chatter at the well hushed as Jaben walked past the crowd of women. "—should have been killed in Jericho!" Jaben caught a final indignant line of the conversation. He smiled derisively. These servants of the "most high God" seemed to know little of compassion. For himself, he required none of the gentler sentiments. Let them think of him whatever they would; he had his own opinions of some of them. Yet for the womenfolk of his family and for Bazarnan, he would have preferred some overtures of friendship, some small gestures of acceptance from the people of Israel. Only Caleb had shown them friendship.

Jaben walked through the camp, his head held high. He had told no one in his family of his purpose in visiting the camp of Judah today, but his step was sure, and his purpose certain. Everyone in his family was afraid, or so it seemed to Jaben; they were afraid that Bazarnan would die if he fulfilled his promise to be circumcised. Today Jaben sought out the tent of Caleb, patriarch of the tribe of Judah. Jaben would ask Caleb to release Bazarnan from his promise.

At Caleb's greeting, Jaben boldly entered the tent. He saw immediately that the old man was not alone. Jaben recognized the man with Caleb as Eleazar, the high priest of Yahweh. The man looked different at close range, without his ornately embroidered priestly garments. Laugh lines around his eyes crinkled as he greeted Jaben, lines that could not be seen from a distance when Eleazar performed the sacrifices. Jaben hesitated; he had not intended to discuss Bazarnan with a religious leader.

"I can come back at another time, my lord Caleb," Jaben began, taking a step backward, hoping to make a quick exit.

"No, Jaben. Come in. Your family is the subject of our discussion. It pleases me that you are here. Come in," he urged again. "Be seated."

Jaben sat down quickly, looking uncomfortable. Caleb smiled at him. "I was just explaining to the high priest that your family has chosen to become Jews. Your decision pleases all of us."

Jaben remembered the antagonistic glares from the women at the well. *"Pleased" hardly described their attitudes,* he thought, but he said nothing.

Caleb continued, "Your father Bazarnan has chosen wisely to follow the God of our people."

Jaben grimaced. There was no getting around this predicament then; he would have to discuss the matter in front of the high priest. He cleared his throat. "It is my father-in-law's decision that I have come to discuss with you, Caleb," he said. "As you know, Bazarnan is not a well man."

"Still, he may be circumcised," the priest interjected, "so long as his disease does not make him unclean."

Jaben frowned. Already the priest was making things more complicated. Jaben looked at Caleb and spread his hands. "I do not understand the meaning of unclean," he said.

"Our law specifies the conditions of uncleanliness before the Lord, Jaben, but I have talked with Bazarnan. His disease does not make him unclean."

The priest smiled. "Then there is no problem," he said in what he considered his kindest voice. The priest wanted to reassure this young stranger.

"But there is a problem," Jaben replied. "My mother-in-law and my wife—actually all of the family—fear that Bazarnan is not well enough to survive circumcision."

Caleb frowned. "Circumcision is very painful, Jaben, but men do not die from it," he said.

Jaben frowned as well. "Strong men do not die from it, Caleb—but Bazarnan is very weak, and he is old. Can he not become a Jew without this rite?"

"Without circumcision he cannot become a true son of the covenant," the priest answered. "Tell me, young man, do you truly fear for your father-in-law, or is your fear, perhaps, for yourself? Perhaps you do not want to be circumcised?"

The priest had asked the question quietly, not unkindly, but the younger man's reply was sharp. "I am not afraid of circumcision!" he insisted. "But I am afraid..." he hesitated, then continued quickly, "I am afraid to lose the only father I have known." Jaben's fierce black eyes met Eleazar's calmer brown ones. "I am very afraid of that, priest. I do not want to see Bazarnan die!"

The priest placed his hand on Jaben's shoulder. "Will you be circumcised, my son?" he asked. "Whether Bazarnan is circumcised or not, will you make covenant with the God of Israel?"

Jaben looked down at the rug beneath him. "I made a covenant with this God on the night that he saved us out of Jericho," he said quietly. "To be circumcised is a small thing for me." He looked calmly at the high priest. "But it may cost Bazarnan his life, my lord!"

"That, too, would be a small price to belong to the most high God," the priest murmured. "Then you have trusted your life to Yahweh before, young man?"

"When Rahab said we would be saved from Jericho, I believed her," Jaben answered.

"Then you saw that Yahweh is a God who can be trusted," Eleazar replied simply. "You have placed your life in Yahweh's hands before, and now you must allow Bazarnan the same privilege."

"My family does not understand," Jaben answered.

"That does not matter," Eleazar replied. "No one else can choose for Bazarnan how he will serve God. Bazarnan alone chooses. Each man's covenant with Yahweh is his own. You, Jaben, alone, choose for yourself."

"I have already chosen," Jaben answered. This was not the conversation he had planned.

"So, too, has Bazarnan. You must respect your father, Jaben, and honor his decision—whatever the outcome."

Jaben nodded, and Eleazar rose to leave. "The circumcision will be tomorrow," he said firmly. Then he looked gently at the young foreigner. "There is a good heart in you, Jaben of Bazarnan, a heart which can learn to keep the commandments of the Lord. 'Know therefore that the Lord, he is God, the faithful God, who keepeth covenant and mercy with them that love him and keep his commandments, to a thousand generations.' Trust Bazarnan into the hands of the Lord, our faithful God, Jaben," the priest said. "I will see you tomorrow," he added as he left the tent, his eyes twinkling.

Caleb and Jaben watched him go.

"Was there anything else you wanted to ask me?" Caleb said.

Jaben shook his head, smiling ruefully. "No—I think the priest has answered me completely."

The news spread through the camp like wildfire. The harlot's family would become proselytes. Her father and all the males in the household were to be circumcised by Joshua and the priest Eleazar that very morning.

Salma heard the news with something akin to relief. What he had been planning for three days now seemed not only feasible but likely. The news seemed an affirmation from the Lord. Salma hoped this was so, but he could not be certain. In the excitement of the camp over an entire family's conversion, his idea would appear not only appropriate, but even the will of God.

Only Salma himself, and God, would know that what Salma did, he did to please himself. The doubts that had assailed him ever since the defeat at Bethel-Ai held him an angry prisoner. He was not sure of his vision—his dream. He could no longer be certain that God wanted him to marry Rahab. Perhaps the dream had been nothing more than a lonely man's fantasy, but whatever it had been, he now chose to seek its fulfillment. He wanted Rahab; he hoped that the God of his fathers intended that he should have her. But whatever God intended, Salma knew that he was going to make Rahab his wife.

Bazarnan lay in front of his tent, under an awning, his eyes closed, his skin the color of death. Salma had second thoughts. Perhaps he should wait until Bazarnan was stronger. No—the old man might not get stronger. Best to ask him now.

"Sir," Salma began, hesitantly.

Bazarnan snored and jumped. "What? Who calls?" He looked around weakly and spotted Salma nearby.

"Ah," he said. "Excuse me, Salma, nephew of Caleb-my-friend. I was just lying here thinking—" he smiled, "—and I think I must have dozed off to sleep."

"Excuse me, Bazarnan. I did not wish to disturb you."

Bazarnan laughed and pulled himself to a sitting position. "What is my time these days? I am pleased to talk with you, Salma."

The younger man sat cross-legged on a rug. He was silent for a moment, trying to determine what words, what approach to use. He looked decidedly uncomfortable.

Sensing the anxiety in the younger man, Bazarnan spoke first: "Is something troubling you, my son?"

"Ah...well...sir, you may know that for the past two years I have lived alone; my wife Marnya died in childbirth in the desert." His voice faltered, and he looked down at the rug. "We lost the child as well, a son."

Bazarnan reached out and touched the younger man's hand, a gentle gesture of tenderness.

"I did not know, my friend." He sighed. "I, too, lost a wife, and two sons. I know how hard it is—" he looked down, and swallowed—"and then another son. Yes, Salma, life can be harsh."

"I want sons, Bazarnan, and I want a wife!" The words burst forth from Salma's heart, overpowering his reticence.

Bazarnan knew now why Salma had come to him. "Yes, Salma?" he said.

Salma shifted, unaccustomed to feeling ill at ease. He lowered his gaze as he attempted to explain the offer he was about to make. He could think of no gentle way to ask.

"I want to marry Rahab!" he said bluntly.

Bazarnan nodded. "I thought as much," he replied.

Salma breathed deeply and continued, "I realize that this is an unusual time to make this request, sir, but I want the arrangements to be made in case you, uh...that is, I want you to be able to tell your daughter as soon as possible, sir."

The old man's eyes twinkled. He shifted himself in order to meet the young man's eyes. The boy had almost said, "in case you die." The words had hung in the air between them. *How little faith some of these Habiru hold in their own God,* Bazarnan thought, *but this boy is Caleb's nephew, and a captain in their army—our army—*Bazarnan amended his thoughts to match his new status as a circumcised member of the tribe of Israel. *Rahab will become a woman of stature when she marries this one—if she marries this one.* Bazarnan remembered too well another marriage he had tried to arrange for Rahab. She had refused his choice—but this man was younger. She would even think him handsome, perhaps.

Both men were silent. At last, Bazarnan spoke. "You know that she was a harlot in Jericho," he said tentatively.

"Yes—but I know also that her harlotry is in the past. I know that she has been chaste since she has lived among the tribe of Judah."

"True, Salma—but you said you want sons."

"Yes, sir, for the Lord has promised me a son, and Rahab is to be his mother."

"Salma...you need to know that Rahab is past nineteen—and you know what has been her profession. Yet never in all that time did she once conceive. It may be that she is barren."

The young man shook his head. "The Lord has promised," he repeated. Salma spoke more confidently than he felt; the dream had been a long time ago; perhaps it was only the lust of his body. No matter—he had spoken for her. He would not recant.

So, his faith is not so weak after all, Bazarnan thought. "You know these things, and still you ask her hand in marriage?" Bazarnan insisted.

"Yes—I do!"

Bazarnan wrinkled his nose thoughtfully. "Then, what will you give as the bride-price, Salma? Do you think I will give you a bargain because you know that the girl is no virgin? If so, you must think again. A woman such as Rahab has already more wisdom and more skill than a hundred virgin brides. She is worth much to any household."

"The bride-price is not an issue, Bazarnan. I am a wealthy man. I am a prince of the first tribe of Israel, as was my father, Nashon, before me. I will gladly pay what is reasonable, what is fair." Salma spoke boldly now.

Bazarnan's eyes narrowed. More than once he had bargained concerning the worth of Rahab: first with Shanarbaal, then with Onuk; now he bargained for what might be the last time—if the girl would be sensible, but there was no assurance of that!

"I am in rather unfortunate circumstances at this time, Salma. As well you know, we left Jericho with little besides the clothes on our backs, so I am tempted by your proposal. Rahab will need a husband now, and if you are disposed to be that man, you could convince me to speak to her in your favor."

"To speak to her?" Salma frowned fiercely. What strange foreign custom had he stumbled upon now? "But you are her father—surely—"

"Surely I could make her marriage plans for her? If she were any other child, yes, but she is not anyone else. She is Rahab."

"A disobedient daughter should be stoned, sir! It is the law." Salma's voice was fierce.

"Indeed?" The old man's eyebrows lifted. "Perhaps that is your way, but even if that were so for us, the time for such a stoning has long passed, Salma. Does your law suggest a punishment for a father who disowns a child and then allows that child to support both his family and himself?"

Salma searched his memory. "The law does not speak of such a thing, sir. We are told to honor our father and mother that our days may be lengthened upon the earth."

Bazarnan smiled. "Again your law surprises me. I see that I have much to learn. My daughter, Rahab, has fulfilled that law, Salma, by her deeds if not by the words of her mouth. She has saved her family more than once, but she has also learned strange and independent ways. I may make the bargain, but it will be she who gives the final word concerning whether or not she will be your wife."

"I am prepared, under the circumstances, to be generous if necessary," Salma said quietly.

The old farmer laughed, and then winced from pain. "What is generous, Salma?" he asked, smiling shrewdly. "Tell me what you mean."

Rahab gasped.

"A herd of cattle, twenty sheep, ten goats—and gold as well?" she asked.

"Fifteen shekels of gold," Bazarnan answered simply. "It was as high as he would go."

"Fifteen shekels of gold! It is a fortune. You will surely become a rich man with a start such as that."

The old bargainer's ears tensed. "Will become a rich man, you say? Does that mean that you will accept Salma as a husband?"

Rahab hesitated. "It was only a manner of speaking, Father," she said. "I am surprised the man has asked. He has hardly spoken to me since we came here from Jericho." Rahab had been offended by Salma's distance, and now his proposal shocked her.

"The ways of these Habiru are not our ways, Rahab, but they will become our ways. In Jericho, a man might have made eyes and silly talk with you before a betrothal, but these people are too serious for nonsense of that sort." Bazarnan wanted Rahab to accept Salma's offer, but he knew he must choose his words carefully. He had failed miserably in the bargaining concerning Onuk. "Salma is a rich man, but I think he is also a good man. He did not make this offer lightly."

"I am not considering it lightly, Father. You need the money, and if we are to be Jews, I will certainly need a husband."

Rahab turned her back to her father on his pallet and stood facing the open doorway of the tent. "What would you do if I refused the marriage? Would you disown me again?"

Bazarnan sighed. So he had failed again; she would not have this husband either! He shook his head. "I would not disown you," he said simply. "You proved to me long ago that you love this family. You were my daughter when you supported us in Jericho, and you are my daughter here, no matter what you choose to do. I will not forsake you again, Rahab."

Rahab turned then, her eyes unusually soft and glowing. She stepped toward her father's cot and knelt beside it. "Then I am your handmaiden, Father," she said, lowering her eyes. "I accept your will in the matter of this marriage."

Bazarnan laughed heartily, too heartily, for he gasped in pain immediately. "Ah, what a strange God we have chosen to serve. He demands the very flesh of my loins, yet he returns to me the fruit of those loins! You are an obedient daughter, and you shall be a happy bride."

Rahab smiled. It had not entered her mind to consider her obedience in this marriage to be the will of the God, but now she thought perhaps her father was right.

"You have done what?" Caleb demanded.

"I have asked that Rahab become my wife, and her father has agreed."

Caleb shook his head as if in bewilderment. "All the maidens of Judah sigh for you, and you choose a Canaanite harlot?"

"Yes, I know that Rahab was a harlot—but I also know what she is now—and what she will become. I have chosen; the woman Rahab will become my wife."

Caleb laughed aloud, shocking Salma. The older man merely continued to laugh; then, at last, he said, "When I prayed that Bazarnan's strength would join the strength of Israel, I never guessed how literally the Lord God would answer my prayers!"

"What?" Salma asked. He did not understand his uncle's comment.

"Never mind, Salma, I laugh at a joke the Lord God has shared with me, but this is a good joke, and it is his will. I bow to it. She is a strong woman. I hope you will find much happiness with her. Come, let me give you my blessing."

Salma sighed in relief and knelt before his uncle.

Kinah giggled in pure delight as Rahab told her of the betrothal. "Oh, my lady," she sighed, "he is wonderful to behold, and he is a prince!"

"My life turns very strangely, Kinah," Rahab spoke softly. "I had never planned to marry, though I had hoped to bear a child. Now, I shall marry, and only this Habiru God knows whether or not I shall conceive."

"Oh, my lady, you must bear a child. A prince must have sons. It cannot be otherwise." Kinah's eyes grew large as she thought of the rejection a barren wife must suffer. "You will have sons, Rahab, I am sure of it."

Rahab hugged the younger woman. "You are more certain than I am, little one, but I will marry him. That much I know. I will marry him, and I will use all that the life in Jericho taught me in order to please him. If he must put me away because I am barren, he will give me up with much regret."

Kinah laughed. "He will not regret choosing you, Rahab. Our patrons never did."

Rahab laughed, too, but she also shook her head ruefully. "If I cannot bear him sons, he will surely divorce me—or, worse yet, he might take another wife. I could not bear to have one of these Habiru women as my competitor, my adversary. If I must have only one husband, then he must have only one wife."

Kinah laughed at Rahab again; then she apologized. "I am sorry, Rahab, but your ideas are very strange, and when you are so stern and so serious, you are also very funny."

Rahab smiled at her friend. "We will pray to this Habiru God that I may bear sons," she said. "Neither the gods of Jericho nor Shanarbaal felt pity for my barren state, but the Habiru God is a different God; perhaps he will hear our prayer."

53

Haggar, youngest sister of Salma's father, Nashon, delivered the bridal dress to the tent of Bazarnan. The lines of her mouth betrayed her displeasure at this task, but she was determined to make no scene out of respect for Caleb, who had blessed this union. With her was Hannah, a younger cousin, who smiled continually, vaguely annoying the older woman.

Faintly haughty, but excessively gracious, Rahab's mother asked them to sit and called for Nantha to serve refreshments, though she refused to partake of any herself. The visitors seemed ill at ease, but Haggar launched into her formal presentation.

"I have brought the robes for the bride of Salma," she announced, unwrapping a bulky package which she had carried under her arm. "Where is the betrothed one?" she asked suddenly, looking around.

"Rahab has gone for water; she should be back soon," Kora responded.

"Perhaps we should wait for her," the younger visitor said, but she was silenced by a fierce look from her companion.

"No!" Haggar snapped. "We have come on a mission; we will do our duty, and then we will leave—her mother can tell her." Then she turned to Kora and continued, "For many years, the women of the tribe of Judah and those who have married into the tribe of Judah have worn these ceremonial robes on the occasion of their weddings."

She held up the robe, red linen embroidered with purple and gold pomegranates. "I present you this robe for your daughter's wedding." She laid the robe down carefully, spreading it out smoothly over the rug on which Kora sat.

Kora bowed her head graciously. "The house of Bazarnan, of the tribe of Judah, thanks you for this bridal gift," she said.

"It is not a gift," the visitor snapped. "Your daughter may wear it once, and then it is to be returned to my tent to await the next wedding."

Kora bowed her head again in acquiescence, but said nothing. The visitor continued: "I bring also the veils of the bride." At Kora's feet, the woman spread scarves and veils of loosely woven white linen, edged in gold embroidery.

"These robes were made by our grandmother in Egypt. We have carried them on our travels across the desert; we have cherished them and cared for them. Salma's mother wore them at her wedding." She paused, and her eyes narrowed. "His first wife, Marnya, wore them, too!"

The younger woman gasped. "Aunt Haggar!" she said. Neither Haggar nor Kora acknowledged the girl's presence. Kora only nodded her head gently, impassively.

"If that is all you have to say, may I offer you more refreshment before you go?" the mother of Rahab asked. It seemed to Hannah that the Canaanite emphasized the word *go*, but Hannah had also brought adornment for the bride. Hannah stood and directly addressed the older women for the first time.

"I, too, have brought something for Rahab," she said softly, "but I must present it to her personally." She looked apologetically at her aunt. "I promised Salma, Aunt Haggar," she said.

The older woman stood impatiently. "I have finished my business here, Hannah," she snapped. "I have business to attend at home. You may wait if you like. I must leave."

Hannah looked distressed. She was embarrassed by her aunt's bad manners.

"If it meets with your approval, then," she said, "I will go and seek Rahab at the well."

Rahab was returning from the well when Hannah found her. In her days in Jericho, Rahab had never carried water. Here, she was the same as all other young women. She carried water, and she helped with the cleaning.

"Rahab!" Hannah called. "Stop—I need to talk to you."

Pausing to lower her water pitcher to the ground, Rahab sat on a large rock and waited for the girl to join her.

"I am Hannah! I am a cousin of Salma—and I have something for you," the girl said breathlessly.

"You are kind to bring it," Rahab responded, wondering at this gesture of friendliness from the girl. It was the first she had received from the women of Judah.

"My aunt, Haggar, sister of Nashon, has just left your wedding attire at your mother's tent—but I have a special gift for you from the bridegroom." She smiled, obviously delighted with her errand, and Rahab warmed to the girl's open smile.

"Tradition in our tribe says that the bridegroom shall give the bride, as a token of their covenant, a jewel to wear at the wedding feast."

"That is delightful," Rahab responded. "What is it?"

"Here," Hannah said, placing in Rahab's hand a long rope necklace of deep red and strands of gold that shimmered in the sunlight. A beautiful red stone hung from this cord.

"It is exquisite," Rahab exclaimed. "What does it mean?"

Hannah laughed. "Salma said to tell you the gold represents your worth, and the red cord is a reminder of the sign you hung from your window that marked the beginning of your love."

Tears glistened in Rahab's eyes, and she embraced her new cousin.

"Thank you, my cousin Hannah," she whispered.

269

Rahab waited alone, trembling. The women who had so carefully, kindly, arranged her dress had left her now. Her family was already at the tent of Salma for the wedding feast. Her father's tent had never been so quiet before. She checked her robes again, making sure that her wedding necklace was properly in place. Her veils were secure. No portion of her skin was unveiled: the beautiful scarlet gown of the Judean bride ornamented and concealed the woman beneath it. *I am a bride of the Covenanted Ones*, she thought. She heard the shouts and the singing of the bridegroom's procession as they came for her.

The curtains parted, and Salma stood before her. His white linen garment draped elegantly from the broad shoulders that Rahab had admired so often. A border of gold and purple pomegranates were the robe's only decoration. Behind the open throat of the gown, his neck and shoulders gleamed like desert gold, the well-tanned masculinity of a warrior in the sun.

Rahab was amazed at herself. How often had she stood before a man in just this way—though never before, she admitted to herself, had she worn so many veils. Why should she find herself so wordless? So without device?

The answer came quickly, and it startled her: this man alone was her husband. He alone had paid a tremendous, unnecessarily generous bride-price for her, and never again, if he lived, would she know another man's arms. She would belong to Salma, this man of Israel, for the rest of her life. She would belong to him! Finally, she had given up the control of her own life. He would be her protector. When Salma took her this day, he took all of her. The bride-price had been paid; she belonged to him. If he loved her, it would be well. If he did not? She shuddered. He must love her! She would make him love her.

He walked quickly to her. His hands surely and deftly removed the veil which covered her face. According to the wedding custom, he placed the veil across her shoulder.

"My lord," she murmured.

"My wife," he said strongly, taking her into his embrace. "I have come to take you to my tent."

Salma took his bride's hand, and together they walked out of her father's tent. They were greeted by the shouts of the wedding guests, a crowd so thick that Rahab could not see where it ended. As they stepped outside, the crowd began to divide, leaving a wide path down which Salma led his bride. The companions of the groom, Salma's kinsmen and close friends, followed immediately behind the wedding couple. As the crowd began to divide, Rahab heard one of the men behind her comment, "It looks like the parting of the Jordan River."

Another picked up the joke, "No, my friend," he said, "this I think, must look like the dividing of the Red Sea." All the men laughed, but Rahab could hear no more of their conversation, for the music had begun. Timbrels and harps and a chorus of countless voices sang that the bridegroom had come to take his bride.

Outside Salma's tent, rugs and pallets had been placed so close together that the ground seemed carpeted in a thousand colors. No one in the tribe of Judah wanted to miss the wedding of the prince. Every family came dressed in their richest clothing, and every family brought food to add to the wedding banquet. Everywhere people laughed and ate and sang.

Salma's closest relatives, all of the family of Caleb, sat on a huge blue carpet immediately in front of Salma's tent. Rahab saw everything as if in a dream. Could this really be her wedding? Could this wonderful display really accompany the wedding of one who had been a Canaanite harlot? The mysteries of Yahweh's goodness seemed too rich to be real.

Yet, it is real, Rahab told herself. *This man, this prince of Judah, has really chosen me! This is my wedding!* She smiled at Salma and said the ritual words, "This is the man that I love."

The people drank and ate and danced. The women took timbrels and danced around the camp. Circling among the many banqueting guests, they held their timbrels high above their heads, singing as they went. Then the men danced. Theirs was unlike any dancing Rahab had ever seen, a joyful, exuberant circling and kicking kind of dance, in which all the men shouted at the appropriate time. Rahab laughed delightedly when Joshua, Caleb, and Salma linked arms and joined the dance.

At sundown all the women began to sing a different song which Rahab had never heard before, but Salma told her that its words had been passed down for generations. "It is the wedding song," he whispered.

A golden wine cup had been set between them. Now Salma lifted the cup to Rahab's lips. "This is the bridegroom's cup," he said. "When you drink of it, you bind yourself to me in the presence of all the tribes of Israel. This is the wine of the promised land, my wife, and the wine of the promise that is between us."

Rahab drank deeply from his cup. Salma watched her with pleasure, then drank deeply from the cup himself, his eyes holding Rahab's.

"It is time, my love!" Salma stood. Immediately the companions stood as well. With a great flourish, one of them flung open the flap of Salma's tent.

Salma raised both his arms in the air, the wedding song softened to a gentle stirring on the air, and a new excitement traveled like wildfire across the crowd.

Salma extended his hand to Rahab. Standing, she took his hand and looked out at the wedding guests. The song rose again as, like a sea, the crowd stood, too.

Salma laughed aloud; then he swept Rahab into his arms, and marched into the tent. A shout like ten thousand waters went up around the camp.

The tent flap fell behind them, and for the first time Rahab, wife of Salma, knew the taste of her husband's love.

When Rahab awakened, morning light was streaming into the tent. Her new husband lay beside her, awake and gazing at her with a gentle, amused expression.

"You sleep like a baby," he said.

"It is not always so, my lord," she replied. "I have known many sleepless nights."

"Let us pray, then, that you shall have no such sleepless nights in my tent," her husband said seriously.

Rahab giggled, and Salma was immediately aware of her thought.

"Well, only such sleepless nights as you would choose, my love," he said.

Rahab smiled up at her new lord. "I think that I shall always rest well with you."

Salma inclined his head in gracious agreement. "I shall do my best to assure it," he said.

Then, as if in afterthought, he reached for the dagger which lay amongst his discarded clothing. "And this shall assure something more," he said sternly.

Before Rahab could grasp his intent, he sliced the knife against his right thigh. The cut was not deep, but it was long, the blood flowing fiercely onto the white linen coverlet beneath them.

Rahab gasped and looked at the man in amazement. Why had he done such a thing? What kind of husband was this man, her new lord? Was this some strange Habiru ritual?

Salma laughed, watching the blood flow onto the bed cover and hearing her gasp. "Don't be so afraid, my wife, I am not so savage as you think. There," he said, "that should be enough." He reached for one of her white linen veils and began to bandage his leg. "I think this stain should satisfy anyone of your purity. What do you think, my virgin wife?"

Rahab was amazed. "But Salma," she said, laughing, "I was a prostitute! They all know it. How can I become a virgin again?"

He grasped her shoulders and looked deeply into her eyes. There was no laughter now. "To me, you have come as a virgin. Your life begins this day, with your vows to me before the Lord our God Almighty. I will never think of you as a prostitute. You are my virgin bride—mine alone. You must never think of your life in Jericho. It is behind you—gone forever."

She could only nod her assent. He continued: "This coverlet I will give to your parents, for in our law it is written that a man may put away his wife if she is not a virgin, but if the girl's father and mother bring proof and display the cloth, then the man will be punished, and he must not divorce her as long as he lives. This cloth, marked with my blood, is my wedding covenant with you, Rahab. Do you understand?"

Rahab understood. He had paid a greater bride-price than she had imagined. He had paid a price in his own blood. Rahab knew then that Salma loved her.

In the seven nights that Rahab and Salma had been married, only during the first night had Rahab slept peacefully. In the early hours before the dawn, memories, like old enemies, surged through her sleeping mind.

Night after night, she awakened with a sigh or a gasp, and twice with screams that awakened Salma and stirred him to tenderness. But she could not, would not, tell him her dreams, only that they were frightening things she couldn't remember or didn't want to talk about. He sensed that they were dreams of her past, and he, too, was disturbed.

When his turn came to keep the night watch for the camp of Judah, Salma walked alone on the hills above the camp. Rahab's dreams stayed on his mind, causing him to wonder and to worry about the woman he had married. Would she ever sleep peacefully? Would she never stop tormenting herself with dreams and memories too dark to be shared?

The stars above Salma sparkled with the brilliant intensity of the desert night. Below him in the valley, the sheep of the tribe of Judah slept, peacefully, unafraid, untroubled by dark nightmares: These sheep he could protect. No wolf, no bear, no lion was so savage that he and his men could not ward it away from the sheep. But his wife, the wife of his heart, he could not protect. The enemies who tormented her spirit were too strong. *Like the lion that waits in hiding and attacks from the midst of the flock,* Salma thought, *Rahab's enemies attack her from within.*

What must her past have been like? he questioned. *What evils has she committed that they tear her spirit like a ravaging wolf?* She was a Canaanite, after all, and he had no idea of what her life had been before she joined the people of the Lord God. He simply did not know what she had done, and he shuddered to think of it.

"You purified her, Lord God," Salma prayed, "and I felt sure that I chose well to marry her. Why, then, if she is pure, is she tormented in the night? And why, if I did well to marry her, do I still wonder and doubt? I do not want to know about her past! But it sickens me to think that other men have known her, have held her in their arms, have touched her as I have touched her! I do not want to know!

"I promised her that I would always think of her as virgin, and so I must, yet I cannot in my secret heart forget what she was. I want to forget! Yet—yet, even if she had broken every commandment, I would still love her," Salma prayed.

In earnest supplication, he raised his arms toward the night sky. "Forgive her, God!" he prayed. "And heal her spirit! Let her rest peacefully at night!

"And," he paused, waiting, but the prayer refused to go away, "and let her love me!" He prayed desperately. "Let her love me more than any of the others! Let her love me with all of her heart! And let her bear my son! It is a selfish, selfish prayer," he murmured. "But as you are my God, you know I mean it."

The camp of Judah rested peacefully. The sheep slept. The stars glimmered in the deep night sky, their brilliance an anchor of peace, of promise, above the troubled water of Salma's soul.

"Heal her, God," the man on the hill whispered. "Heal her!"

Ignoring her troubled nights, Rahab concentrated, instead, upon pleasing her new husband. She wanted very much to be a good wife to him. She tried to discover all the secret things that would make him happy with her. He was an ardent man, and it was not long before she felt she knew him well. She discovered the sensitive spot beside his right ear lobe. She discovered the smooth, tanned skin of his neck and throat below his beard. She traced the dragonfly mysteriously created by the pattern of the hair upon his chest. He seemed to delight in her pleasure in him. She delighted that he was so easy to please.

One evening as she lightly caressed his collarbone with her fingertips, she murmured, "You are exactly as a man should be."

Salma turned on one side, surprising her when he said, seriously, "I know that I am a husband, a lover, to you, Rahab, but I want a greater love than that from you."

Rahab smiled at him, the soft provocative smile that had so often pleased the men she had known. "I love you as a woman loves a man, Salma. Do you ask for more than that?" Her eyes became quizzical, her smile questioning. There was no more than what she offered him; surely he realized that.

"In the weeks that you have been my wife, you have pleased me in ways I could not have imagined, Rahab."

She smiled again, happily. Her magic with men still worked.

"But," he continued, "something is missing."

She bit her lip and looked at him with confused eyes. Did he mean a baby? Her father had told him she was not sure she could bear a child. He had been sure that she could. He had said God had told him that she would bear his son. Was he changing his mind? Was he, perhaps, deciding to divorce her? Her face hardened.

"There," he said. "That look. That is part of it. When that hardness comes into your eyes, I see that I do not yet know you. You are now bone of my bone and flesh of my flesh, Rahab. When you bear a son, he will be heir to all that I have, but unless something changes I will not know the woman who bears him."

"I don't know what you are talking about, Salma." Rahab's voice was cold. What was this man saying? Was he trying to trick her in some way? What did he want from her?

"In all the time that I have known you," he said, "I have not come to understand the pain that comes into your eyes, Rahab. You laugh and you kiss me, but you do not tell me when you hurt, and I am sure that sometimes, you hurt."

"Have I not pleased you, my lord? Do I not bring pleasure to your tent? Am I not as a woman should be with a man?"

Salma sighed and laughed softly. "So many questions at once, yet...you are not hearing what I am saying to you."

Rahab frowned at this; these words she had not heard before. "What are you saying to me?" she asked.

"What I want to say," he began, then started again. "What I want you to hear is that I want to know more of you than merely the warmth of your body. I want to hear more than the pleasing, soothing phrases of love."

"You do not like love?" Rahab asked, aghast.

Salma laughed, this time at his own difficulty. He could not make her understand! He would try one more time. "Do not always try to please me, Rahab. Sometimes give me the pleasure of pleasing you."

"But, you do please me, my lord; you please me very much—when you do this, and this." She nibbled at his throat and caressed him. Salma sighed. She was delightful. But she had no idea what he was talking about.

He put his arms around her and gave up the battle—for a while, at least. "Promise me one thing, dove with eagle eyes,"

"Anything, my lord," she answered soothingly.

"Promise me that when you hurt, you will tell me," he answered.

Rahab hid her face against Salma's chest. He could not see how harshly she frowned. "I will try to tell you, my lord," she answered.

And then she set about making him forget about talking.

The tent of Bazarnan changed for Alcion after Rahab married. He liked her family well enough, but he did not particularly like living with them. The problem, Alcion realized, was that he no longer had a function. In the city of Jericho, there had been a thousand tasks for a man with Alcion's sophistication, but here? In a nomads' camp, there were no tasks for a Canaanite scribe. He would have to find a way to make himself useful. He could not stand to do nothing. Nor could he stand to do nothing except the menial chores of daily life.

All his life, he had lived by his wits, at first in order to survive among the intrigues and lusts of his masters and later in order to help Rahab become a rich and powerful woman in Jericho. Alcion laughed aloud. *I am bored*, he thought. *It is as simple as that.*

Caleb often visited Bazarnan, who was healing slowly from his circumcision. One morning as the two men talked, Caleb interrupted their conversation to call to Alcion, who stood nearby stirring a pot of stew that Nantha had left on the fire. "Alcion," the older man called, "I have a question for you." Alcion approached the two men. "May he sit down?" Caleb whispered to Bazarnan.

Bazarnan smiled. "Of course," he said. He often forgot that Alcion was still a servant.

"Sit with us, Alcion," Bazarnan invited the eunuch.

"Alcion, I have a question for you, and I hope that it will not offend you."

Alcion raised his eyebrow. "I am hard to offend, my lord," he answered simply. The man seated beside him looked relieved.

"Good," he said. "This is my question: Can someone who is not as you are, someone who is not a eunuch, I mean, learn to be as calm and controlled as you are?"

It was, Alcion thought, an interesting question. He smiled at the older man. "I do not know the answer to your question, my lord. I have never considered that being a eunuch might be the reason for my calmness, but I can see, now that I think of it, that it would make a difference. Perhaps quite a difference."

Caleb nodded. "But is there any way someone else could learn to be calm?"

Alcion looked quizzically at the other man. "You do not seem to have a problem with being calm, my lord," he said.

Caleb laughed aloud. "Oh, no, no, Alcion, the years have calmed the temper of my blood. No, I am not the problem, but I have two nephews, sons of my youngest sister, Haggar. They are driving the camp of Judah mad, Alcion. They are the most unruly boys I have ever encountered. I have tried everything I know—everything except having them stoned, and that is something I do not want to do. I was hoping that perhaps you might tell me the secret of your calm nature and that with that secret I might find a way to change them."

"Has their father had no effect on them?" Bazarnan asked.

"Their father is dead, has been dead since they were babies, and—I hesitate to say this about my own sister, but—she is so unpleasant no one else will marry her. Truly I can't blame them."

"The mother is the source of the problem?" Bazarnan asked.

"Undoubtedly, she is," Caleb answered. "I cannot change Haggar, but it may not be too late for her sons. Alcion, still you have not answered my question."

"But I have been thinking about it," Alcion replied. "I think that my training as a scribe has much to do with my nature. The discipline of that training calmed me, but it also gave me respect for myself that otherwise I could not have gained. It is difficult for a slave to like himself, my lord."

"Yes," Caleb answered. "I understand. All of my people were slaves in Egypt. Even our children's children will not forget. To be a scribe is an honorable thing, Alcion."

"It is, my lord, but it requires years of training."

"And these little hyenas will require a firm hand. They do not act like boys at all. They act like jackals. Bazarnan, you are my friend, and now you are my brother. I have a great request to make of you. Will you allow Alcion to train my nephews to be scribes? It is not a small task and I will understand if you refuse. I would not ask if I had any idea what else to do."

Bazarnan smiled. "To train two small boys is indeed a big job, Caleb. Alcion is servant to our family, but he is also our friend. He must decide for himself whether or not such a task is for him."

Alcion smiled. *This, at least, will be a challenge,* he thought. "I am willing to try it. But how many boys are we discussing, and how old are they?"

"The older is nine; the younger is seven. There are only two of them, Alcion, but they are as much trouble as any ten boys I have known. If they are too much for you, I will understand. They are too much for me!"

"I have dealt with boys before," Alcion responded. "If you send them to me early in the morning, I will keep them until sunset. That is the length of a scribe's work day, and they should become aware of it immediately."

"I cannot thank you enough, Alcion, but are you sure you can be spared? Bazarnan, can you allow this? You will lose a valuable worker."

Bazarnan answered graciously that Alcion was free to do whatever he wanted. Alcion thought wryly that he would hardly be missed as a soup-stirrer and carpet-shaker. Teaching little boys might be frustrating, but at least it would not be boring!

Salma and Rahab had been married only two weeks when Salma told her that Joshua had summoned him to his tent. "It will be about another battle, I'm sure," he said to her as he hurriedly left their tent.

As Rahab came to know her husband better, she realized that he loved the life of a soldier. To take the land he had been promised, to salvage Canaan from the hands of the enemy, for Salma these things were meat and drink.

He was gone for much of the afternoon, and when he returned, Rahab knew at once that he was preoccupied. His eyes glittered and his mouth was set sternly.

"Joshua offered me the honeymoon year," he told her, "but I declined it."

"What do you mean—the honeymoon year?" she asked.

"It is the law of our Lord that when a man is first married, he is not required to do battle so that he may delight himself with his bride."

"Then why did you decline?"

"We are going back to Bethel-Ai. We will win this time, and it's too important to miss!"

Rahab understood his feelings. She had known other warriors.

But then he added: "I've had a honeymoon year; this is the year for battle. Bethel-Ai will fall."

Rahab frowned. This was the first time he had mentioned his previous marriage. But she let it pass. "Just be sure that Salma does not fall," she said. "I did not wed you to become a widow."

"Have no fear. Our men died last time only because there was sin in the camp. Now we are strong, and the Lord will be with us." He hugged her close. "I will be back in a few days."

She was so alone!

Her footsteps were slow as she traced the steep trail up the wadi near her father's farm. Her sheep was lost, her baby lamb—she was searching for her lamb. It was late afternoon, and she was so tired, so tired of searching, so tired of searching alone. The lamb was her friend, and she missed him and worried about him. Her eyes searched behind every bush on the path, and then she heard a rock fall, and looking up, she saw a huge mountain goat—a ram of the desert.

His eyes spoke to her first. Her spirit was drawn into the deep brown eyes of the ram, and it seemed that the wisdom of eternity rested there, calling to her: "Peace. Peace."

Peace? she thought. *Where is there peace in the midst of this constant war? There is no peace!*

"Peace—peace—peace is!" the ram seemed to answer her without words, but with great authority.

The ram was old. Scars outlined his big nose, and the tip of one great curving horn was broken. A gentle smile played about his nose and his soft muzzle. To Rahab, the ram seemed exceedingly strong, yet he was so gentle that she dared to ask, "Who are you?"

But the ram reared, his hoofs pawing the air like the paws of the lion rampant on the standard of Judah. As he leaped upward into the hills of Judah, the words sounded within her mind: "Peace is!"

"Wait!" she cried, and she awoke. Salma was gone. She was so alone.

54

Salma's aunt looked around the tent in obvious pleasure. "Why, it is exactly as Marnya left it!" she exclaimed.

Rahab studied the older woman. *Is that why she came here—to tell me that?*

Haggar had announced that she had come to visit her new kinswoman, to welcome her. But from Rahab's observations of the older woman, such a kindness was definitely not characteristic.

Haggar continued, smiling sweetly. "What a wonderful girl she was," she sighed. "They had such a beautiful wedding—first weddings are always the sweetest. She was perfect for Salma, and she was a virgin, you know....It was a great tragedy when she died. The whole camp mourned for days. Everyone said that no one could take her place in Salma's heart. She would have been a wonderful mother. She was so gentle, so kind."

Rahab felt keenly the rebuke in the older woman's words, but she smiled as sweetly at Salma's aunt and asked, "Can I get you some refreshment?"

"Oh, no, dear. Don't put yourself to any trouble for me!" She settled into the pillows. "Visiting this tent certainly brings back memories. Marnya had such a way of making a tent into a home!"

"Oh, really?" Rahab answered, wondering when this woman would leave.

"You know, the traditions of our tribe say that the second wife should be pitied, for she walks in the footprints of the first. That is why I never remarried."

"Oh, really?" Rahab asked again, smiling.

"Oh, yes, but I have my two lovely sons. They are such a comfort to me. Good boys they are, and handsome like their father."

Rahab suppressed a giggle. "Those are the young men whom Alcion was asked to teach. I have seen them."

"Yes. They are so bright that Caleb decided they should become scribes. They have fine Judean lines—the pure bloodlines of our tribe." She paused, realizing that she had almost gone too far, and shrugged her shoulders. "But all things change—that is the way of life. Now that you are Judean, you will be learning our ways of doing things. How can I help you?"

Rahab smiled very sweetly. "It is very gracious of you to offer, but, really, I am sure that I will learn all I need to know from Salma....You've done quite enough with just the kindness of your visit."

When the woman left, Rahab looked around the tent in fury. "Just as Marnya left it," Haggar said. "Exactly as Marnya left it!" *Why did the old woman come here?* Rahab thought. *She only talked of Marnya! Bah! So his dead wife was perfect! Death makes every woman perfect—but now I must live up to her memory—and how can I? I don't even know their ways, and their law is very strict. I do not know what is right or what is wrong, in their eyes. I am sure to make mistakes. And then he will compare me to her.* She sighed. *Pity the second wife, indeed! I will not live in Marnya's shadow! I am the living one—a memory will not keep his bed warm, and he chose me! I will be very careful—I will not do anything that might be breaking his laws! Still, that woman came here to irritate me, to cause trouble between me and Salma. Well, she won't.*

Marnya's tent, is it? When I lived in the house of Shanarbaal's mother, it did not

279

seem like my own at first. Only after I made the coverlet for my bed did it become my house. Well, that's what I will do here. I will make a new coverlet, a marriage blanket, for the bed of Salma and Rahab!

By the time the army returned from Bethel-Ai, joyous in their victory, Rahab was completing the new coverlet. She had carefully woven dark linen and wool together and embroidered a design—a six-pointed star of the morning centered by the lion of Judah, like the tribal standard.

Salma will be so pleased, she thought as she sewed, eager for her husband's return but hoping to have time to finish the coverlet before he arrived. She was putting the finishing touches on the lion when she heard the commotion outside. "The men have returned!" It was a shout of victory.

Rahab dropped the coverlet and ran outside to greet her husband. The men were jubilant; there was shouting and singing. Rahab saw Salma laughing with the captains of the tribes. When he saw her, he clapped the back of the soldier nearest him, who laughed and nodded as Salma ran toward his bride. He picked her up exuberantly. "We won, Rahab! We won!"

"I know you won, Salma. The runner reached the camp yesterday," she said.

"I am so glad to be home, my wife-my home!"

"Come home, Salma! Come home and see what I have made for our home, for our bed!"

"Yes, my love, I will come with you to our bed," he answered with a grin.

Rahab laughed, and they hurried to their tent. She had dropped the coverlet where she was working, and now she quickly spread it across their pallet. She was proud of this work; it had been a labor of love.

"It is beautiful," he said. "It's lovely." He stroked the material tenderly. "But it does not feel right. It is strange."

"What do you mean?" she asked.

"The fabric," he answered. "What is it?"

"It's linen, mixed with wool," she said.

"It is what?" he asked.

"It is linen, mixed with wool," she repeated.

He threw down the coverlet as if it had burned his hand.

She had never seen him frown so fiercely. Was he angry? But he had said that the coverlet was lovely–surely he was not angry because she had changed Marnya's tent! But perhaps Haggar was right.

"What is the matter? Can I not even make a coverlet in my own tent?" she demanded.

"Not when it is sin!" he spat.

"Sin!" she exclaimed. "Is it sin to change Marnya's tent?"

"Woman, what are you talking about?"

"Oh, I know what you think. She was the perfect wife. She was the virgin! She was everything I'm not!" Rahab began to cry. She was furious.

Salma shook his head. What was wrong with his bride? She had sinned, and now she was shouting at him.

"Rahab," he said softly, "I know you did not mean to sin." He reached for her, but she pushed him away and cried harder. It was right for her to cry, he thought, for she had sinned.

Finally, she caught her breath and demanded angrily, "What is this great sin I have done?"

"You have violated the law of Moses," he said, more patiently than he felt. "You have mixed linen and wool in one cloth."

A law against mixing threads? Was there a law against everything? Every day, there was a new law. She felt she could never obey them all, and she thought this law was ridiculous!

"But Salma!" she said. "The cloth is stronger that way! That's the way we always made tapestries in Jericho."

"You're not in Jericho, now!" he snapped. "We do not do things in the pagan way."

She sighed. "I did not know," she said softly.

Himself sorry that he had sounded so angry, he drew her to him. "You could not have known, Rahab. I have not had time to tell you all the law, nor to explain it to you, but many of our laws are given to keep us separate from the worshippers of false gods. We cannot be like them, and we must always remember that. We even have a rule that a goat may not be cooked in its mother's milk, for that is the way it is done in the worship of Baal."

Rahab nodded. "That's true," she said. "It was part of the ritual."

He kissed her face. "I wasn't angry at you, Rahab. I love you too much to want you to sin, even unknowingly."

"Then you aren't angry at me because I changed Marnya's tent?"

"Marnya's tent? It is your tent now—you can do anything you like with it, but you cannot mix linen and wool."

She smiled then and said softly, "You wanted me to tell you when I hurt. When you were displeased with my work, that hurt."

"Your work is beautiful," he said again. "But we shall have to burn it."

She buried her face in his chest and sobbed.

The people of Israel left Gilgal. They packed their belongings and folded their tents and moved north, toward Shechem. Joshua had announced that they would celebrate the victory of Bethel-Ai, thereby renewing the covenant with the Lord God. It would be a great event.

The priests led the tribes, carrying the magnificent Ark of the Covenant with its golden-winged seraphim. Rahab walked with the women of the tribe of Judah, too far away to see the Ark clearly, but she wondered if the Ark itself were not a graven image. Beside her Hannah and Tirnah chattered aimlessly, and finally, Rahab could contain her question no longer.

"Hannah," she interrupted, "what is the seraphim on the Ark? Is it not a graven image?"

"It is a design of the Lord God," Hannah said. "He ordered it made in just that way—and he even designed the garments of the priests."

So the Lord God was a designer of garments, too! "What do you mean, exactly?" she asked.

"The Lord told Moses what designs—the pomegranate—and even the color—purple—that he wanted to decorate their robes," Hannah answered.

"Then what is a graven image?" Rahab insisted.

"It's anything that's made to look like a man or an animal, or any combination—like the idols of these people whom we fight."

Rahab remembered Ninunta...and the dough gods...and Astarte and Baal—and she understood, then, the reason behind the law.

The journey to Shechem took four days. At last, the people camped on the mountains that overlooked the Valley of Sechem—Mount Ebal and Mount Gerizim. The two barren, rocky peaks stood opposite each other, towering above the fertile well of the valley. Sounds carried clearly from one mountain to the other; voices were magnified, and the praise songs of the Habiru were amplified strangely by the terrain.

For two days, the captains of all the tribes labored to build an altar. On orders from the Lord himself, the rocks were carefully chosen, not quarried, not touched by any tool. Salma was honored to be one of the builders of the altar. As he helped to lay the stones, piling one smooth brown rock upon another, he remembered his dream at Bethel-Ai, the dream that God had used to tell him to marry Rahab. The sun beat down upon his sweating back, and he almost looked around for the Egyptian. But this was no slave's labor; this was a labor of love unto the Lord. He half expected to see a mountain ram knock down all his work, but none appeared.

The next morning, the ceremonies began at dawn. Joshua and the priests gathered at the altar, and, as the people sang praises to the Lord, the priests applied plaster to the altar. Then Joshua carefully drew the words of the law onto the smooth white surface.

As the sun reached its zenith, the sacrifices began. The people knelt and were silent. Rahab knelt with Salma and closed her eyes. How different from the sacrifices of Canaan. These people were quiet and solemn, sober. And the priests performed the sacrifices quickly, with great dignity. The animals were burned, completely consumed by the fire on this occasion, though Salma told her that often the meat of the sacrifices was served as food for the people.

A young sheep was led to the altar. Rahab closed her eyes, shivering in the sunshine. Tears poured from her eyes, and she trembled uncontrollably. Salma was unaware of her distress, for she made no sound and he was intent upon the rituals. As the sun began to make its descent, Joshua spoke the laws of Moses. The people on Mount Gerazim said the blessings, the promises of God for obedience; the people on Mount Ebal said the cursings, the warnings of God for disobedience.

As the people of Judah knelt to recite the laws of their Lord, Rahab knelt and looked inward. She relived the sacrifice of the lamb, the lamb that she killed for Baal. The blood of the lamb stained her hands, splashed across her bosom, covered her heart. She trembled and heard not a word that was spoken.

The next day, Salma came to Rahab with the news that they would be leaving soon. Caleb had requested, and Joshua had granted, their inheritance. Caleb had asked Salma to lead a group into the hill country to the south. They would establish Judah's claim to Hebron. They would take their inheritance from the Anakim, the giants who had frightened the Israelites forty years before.

"It is a rich country," Salma said. "Caleb remembers that the grapes were so big it took two men to carry a single branch, and we will be the first of our tribe to see it."

"If that is where we are going, we will be near my father's farm. My sister Leal still lives there with her family. Could they join us?"

"If they want to live, they must join us!" Salma responded. "Our warriors would not know them from other Canaanites."

For the first time since Rahab had seen the sacrifices of the previous day, her mood lifted. How good it would be to see Leal! She began to pack immediately.

The men of Judah sang as they marched, a joyous melodic chant. Each man sang his own song, yet the voices were woven together as if by some master design. Rahab's family—with the exception of Kora, who never sang—joined in the joyous polyphony, surprised and delighted by the ease with which their voices blended into the Habiru worship song.

Salma walked at the head of the column of marchers. Caleb, who had stayed with Joshua, had appointed Salma leader of this group: the men of the tribe of Judah, who—with their families—would go to claim the inheritance of the tribe of Judah. Joshua had given them the boundaries: from the Dead Sea in the east to the land of the sea people in the west, from Kiriath-Jearim in the north to the desert of the Negeb to the south.

Salma was elated. Sin among the tribes had been conquered; the land of Canaan was being conquered. And he had conquered loneliness, for his bride went with him to claim the land. Rahab sat astride a small donkey, which Salma led with a rope.

In the midst of the singing, Rahab began to laugh, a quiet, private chuckle that rose with the songs of the people and caught her husband's attention.

"What is so funny, my bride?" he asked.

"I was just wondering, Salma—does your donkey talk?"

Salma laughed heartily. "Certainly not! Donkeys don't talk. Donkeys bray and snort."

"Not necessarily, my love," Rahab teased. "I met a talking donkey once—at least, she was said to have talked."

Salma raised his eyebrows. "And how was that?"

"The donkey belonged to a fat prophet who came to Jericho once, and I talked to his talking donkey—but she wouldn't answer me."

"Do you mean Balaam, the seer of the gods?" Salma asked in astonishment.

"Yes, that was his name. How did you know?"

"Moses wrote about him in the Book of Law. He tried to curse us, but the Lord wouldn't let him."

"He told us about that...but I didn't believe him," Rahab said softly.

"He had a talking donkey because the Lord put words in its mouth, and the Lord put words of blessing in Balaam's mouth as well when he tried to curse us."

"Salma! Are you telling me that Balaam is truly a seer of the gods?"

"He was!" Salma answered.

"He's a vile, filthy old man! I spit on him!" Rahab said, audibly demonstrating her distaste for the prophet.

Salma laughed. "Well, he is no more, for we killed him when we took the Midianites."

The smile was gone from Rahab's face. She had preferred to think that Balaam was little more than a fat fraud; she remembered well his hateful prophecy to her, and she shivered, realizing that she had lived to see the fulfillment of most of Balaam's prophetic curse. His parting words rang in her memory: "You are an enemy of the Baalim, whom you have offended—may the unborn child die within your womb."

"Balaam was a wicked man," Rahab said. "He deserved to die."

For a time, she rode in silence.

The morning was still fresh when the marchers entered a wadi to begin the ascent into the hill country, leaving behind the well-tended barley fields of the Jericho plain. The feet of men and animals sent small stones clattering down the dry river beds as they climbed. The hill country was fragrant with green grass and wildflowers—yellows and whites, pinks and purples. Even some of the trees and bushes had blossoms.

Suddenly, a dove fluttered down before them, apparently injured, flapping her wings, and seeming to struggle to find flight.

"She is injured," Salma exclaimed.

"No, she's not," Rahab answered. "She is pretending. We have disturbed her nest."

"How do you know such things, city woman?" her husband asked.

"I wasn't always a woman of the city," she retorted. "When I was a child, my father taught me all about the animals and the birds and the flowers. I know the tricks of the doves. Look around—we are near her nest, but it is not in the direction she is trying to lead us."

The bird continued to act her distress, fluttering along the ground.

"Would you like roast dove with eggs for your dinner tonight, my husband? She would be very easy to catch, and we can find her nest as well."

"No!" Salma shouted, almost angrily. "The Lord God has given us a law for these things, Rahab, and," he added more gently, "I want our marriage to be a long and happy one!"

"What is this law about birds that the Lord has given?" she asked teasingly. "Teach me the law that Moses gave us from the Lord, Salma."

"These are the words of the law, then," he said, and his voice grew deep as he quoted: " 'If you come across a bird's nest beside the road, either in the tree or on the ground, and the mother is sitting on the young or on the eggs, do not take the mother with the young....that...that...you may have a long life.' These are the words of the law."

The woman was silent. He looked at her closely; wet tears glistened on her face. They rode on in silence. The man was puzzled. She had asked him to tell her the law, and now she was crying.

"Salma," she said at last, "the Lord is a good God, that he cares even for the birds."

"But you are crying....have I offended you?"

She laughed. "No, no, my love. There are many reasons for tears. I love this Lord of yours."

"And yours," he answered, still puzzled.

It was midday when the men of Judah reached the farm of Bazarnan. Rahab's sister, Leal, and her husband, Bazak, were crouched behind the walls of the vineyard, watching fearfully as the Habiru approached.

Rahab and Salma came to the barricaded entryway and stopped.

"Leal! Bazak!" Rahab shouted. "This is Rahab, your sister! Are you there? Open the gates."

A woman's head appeared for an instant, peeking out from behind the wall. "Rahab!" The woman shrieked as she scrambled over the barricade and came running to embrace her sister. "I cannot believe it! You are not dead! You are here!"

Rahab got off the donkey, and the women hugged, laughing and crying. Men began to tear down the barricade to allow the travelers to enter.

Arm in arm, the sisters walked toward the low stone farmhouse that Leal and Bazak had built.

Leal had a thousand questions: "Who are these soldiers with you? Did they rescue you when Jericho fell? How did you escape the Habiru? How did you not die? What about Mother and Father? Our brothers and sisters? Was it awful?"

Rahab laughed. "So many questions at once, Leal! First—yes, it was awful, but I did not die, and neither did our family. I have brought them with us."

"Oh," Leal shrieked delightedly. "The gods be blessed!"

"No, Leal—those gods had nothing to do with it. The Habiru be blessed— and the Habiru God!"

Leal was almost speechless. "I don't understand....What do you mean?"

Rahab gestured expansively at the men around her. "These are the Habiru!"
Leal's eyes widened in horror.

"These Habiru rescued us, Leal. They are our friends—and this is Salma, my
husband."

Leal took the news with astonished grace. She had never understood her sister.

Then Bazak spoke to Salma. "My home is your home, if you are the rescuer
and the husband of our beloved sister. Let us make you welcome!"

Soon the family was gathered in the house, and Leal prepared a hasty meal,
a pleasant change from the dried food brought for the journey. As they ate, Rahab and Salma told Leal and Bazak of the fall of Jericho and all that had happened since.

"Rahab! My sister! Bride of a prince of Judah! Who would have thought it—
you have joined our conquerers!"

Her husband Bazak laughed, bouncing their baby son upon his knees. "Because of her marriage we live, Leal! Our children live. I think that I like this
God of the Habiru, this mighty God who crumbles city walls and dries up the
flood—and saves our family." He laughed again and stood, holding the child at
arm's length.

"Praise the God of the Habiru, little one. He brings you life!"

Salma laughed with Bazak. He liked this jolly Canaanite farmer.

"You will come with us, then, to Bethlehem," Salma said. "Joshua, our great
leader, has given it to Judah. It shall be our inheritance. We have only to
claim it!"

Leal cast a worried look at her husband. "But, Bazak," she said, "the harvest
has just begun—all our work—the vineyard—the olive grove—can we not stay
to reap our harvest?"

Bazak's laughter was suddenly silent. All eyes turned to this man. He spoke
gently. "If we stay here, Leal, the harvest we reap will be the harvest of all the
Canaanites—the harvest of death."

Leal cast a startled look at her husband. "But Bazak!" she said. "That is the
land of the giants! No one goes there!"

"We are going there," Salma answered smoothly. "The Lord our God has
promised us this land. He promised it to our father Caleb over forty years ago.
It is our inheritance, and we will possess it."

"Have no fear, my daughter!" Bazarnan joined the conversation. "The Lord,
the God of the Habiru, has performed many miracles! Even giants will not
stop his people!"

"The offer made by your sister's husband is a generous offer. The next Habiru we see is likely to bring a sword or a spear and give us over to his God."
Bazak knelt and put his arm around her. "This God who tears down cities and
keeps his covenants is a God we will follow, my little sparrow. We will leave
our fields for those who come after us, and we will go with your family under
the banner of Judah."

He rose then, facing Salma. The two embraced as brothers. Rahab cried with joy, reaching toward her sister, Leal.

Bazarnan patted Kora's knee. "Our family is together again," he said.

As the family prepared to join the caravan, Rahab took Salma to the stable, where she showed him her horse, Shimmerance. "I have kept him here ever since my family moved to the city," she said. "I had little time for a horse then."

They walked to the enclosure where the horse was eating hay. "He doesn't even remember you!" Salma laughed.

But Rahab leaned close to the fence, making a low, soft whinnying sound, a special signal that Shimmerance did remember. The horse's ears twitched and he whirled around, rolling his eyes wildly and rearing up on his back legs.

Salma jumped away, pulling Rahab with him. Rahab laughed. "Shimmerance is only glad to see me, Salma! He is a spirited animal!"

Why did she have a horse? he wondered. Horses pulled war chariots. He had never been this close to a horse, except in the battles with Sihon and Og.

Rahab laughed again. "I will ride him!"

"So you may," he said. "The donkey suits me very well."

It was midday of the third day when they reached the hills and the villa of Shanarbaal. The singing stopped, and voices were hushed as the travelers neared the fortified structure. Rahab and Salma rode ahead, toward the villa's closed gates.

"If anyone is here, I will be recognized, my husband, and we will be welcome. I have served as hostess at this place."

"Even so, be cautious. I would not want a frightened guard to shoot an arrow through you before he recognizes you," Salma said sternly, urging his donkey to catch up to the prancing horse on which his wife sat so confidently.

"I think they were all in Jericho when it was destroyed, Salma. Probably no one is here, but there will be shelter and provisions. The place is quite large; it was built as a center of hospitality."

No guard answered Salma's call, and the couple rode slowly into the empty courtyard. The animals' hoofs clattered on the tiles, making hollow echoes that rang through the empty rooms. The villa seemed cold and tomblike. Rahab shuddered. How different the villa seemed. It was the emptiness of it, she decided.

Satisfied that the villa was not occupied, Salma called to the travelers. "We will rest here in the heat of the day," he said, "and we will stay here tonight to collect provisions for the journey."

While the people set up their camp in the courtyards and gardens, Rahab led Salma through the villa. As they walked through the long porticoes and the empty rooms, Rahab was flooded with memories: in this apartment, she had visited the king; from this banqueting hall, she had sent Oparu into the night and to his death; in this courtyard, she had been made a bride of Baal; in the corner of this room had stood Amaranthe's beautiful brass mirror; in this cubicle, Bishna had died. She wondered how many of these memories she could tell Salma, and she decided to keep her silence. She showed Salma the cooking rooms and finally, the cellar below the kitchen, where stores of oil and grain, wine and herbs, were kept.

"I am pleased at this find," he told her as they entered the lower chambers. "The grain will be useful, and the oil as well, if we have enough pack animals to carry it. Do you suppose that little horse of yours would carry two jars of grain? Surely he is good for something other than carrying you where your own two feet could take you!"

Rahab could tell that he enjoyed teasing her. Yet, her mood was tense, weighted down by the memories, memories that she could not share with this Habiru warrior.

"The priest kept his magic herbs here," she explained, leading Salma down the short, narrow stairway into the underground chamber. She had brought a lamp, knowing that no light from the sun ever reached into these inner recesses of the villa.

"I want nothing to do with such magic," Salma protested. "The Lord God has warned us to beware necromancers and witchcraft."

"All I want, my love, is to get some of the dried vegetable herbs that he kept down here. They are useful for healing, and you should well remember that Caleb permitted me to use them on you!"

"Nevertheless, I do not like the feel of this place, Rahab. There are evil spirits here!"

He held the light high. Rahab began to search, hurriedly now, as she shared Salma's unease.

Salma began to explore the room, and the light revealed a low opening that led into another, deeper, lower chamber. He leaned into the opening, holding the lamp before him, leaving Rahab, for a moment, in darkness.

"God of my fathers!" he exlaimed, his voice echoing hollowly back into the room where Rahab waited.

Salma turned to her, his face pale in the lamplight. His jaw was set, and there were harsh lines around his mouth that she had never seen before.

"Is it a snake?" she asked. "Have you found a viper's nest?"

"No—would that it were!" he snapped, grabbing her arm and pulling her roughly toward the storage room.

"Look!" he said. "Tell me what you see!"

As far as the lamp cast its light, there were earthen storage jars, the tall, wide-lipped jars that the people of Canaan used for water, oil, barley, wine, everything. Hundreds, thousands of them, as far as the lamplight went, and beyond, into the shadows of the chamber, disappearing into recesses of shadowy darkness and gloom. Some of the jars had fallen from their stacks, and had broken, spilling their contents out into the floor: bones and bodies of babies littered and crowded this underground sepulchre.

Rahab gasped, her stomach clenching and her head whirling. "Salma!" she exclaimed. "This is a tomb! It is the tomb of the children of the gods."

She fell to her knees, shaking with sobs, realizing she was surrounded by the babies who had been sacrificed to Baal and Astarte. For a moment she was aware only of the memory of Bishna's baby. Again she heard the drums and saw the drunken dancing. The cries and shrieks of the celebrants rang in her ears. She began to sob.

"Bishna! Bishna! Our baby, Bishna! They have killed our baby!"

Salma realized then, with a flood of relief, that Rahab had not been a part of the sacrifice of the children. *At least,* he thought, *she has not killed the babies.* Her sobs of grief were too intense. Breathing a quick thanks to the Lord for this confirmation, he touched her gently.

Reminded of his presence, Rahab looked at the stern warrior. "These are the cornerstone children," she said softly.

"The law of the Lord tells us what we must do, then," he answered. "Come—this place is unclean, and we must cleanse it." He took her back into the clear evening air.

In the courtyard, the people were setting up camp, talking in hushed voices and softly singing praises to the Lord.

"Men of Judah!" Salma cried, silencing all within the sound of his voice. "Men of Judah!"

"Blow the shofar," Salma commanded a soldier nearby. The youth lifted the ram's horn to his lips, and the sound that had brought down the walls of Jericho was repeated in the private gardens of the high priest of Baal, echoing and reverberating from the limestone cliffs that enclosed the sacred grove. Rahab began to tremble. Again, she heard the call to battle, the cry of the shofar!

The people were silent.

"We will meet to the west when it is over," Salma said, and Rahab realized then that she had been so lost in her own thoughts that she had not heard what he had said. She was frightened. She wished they had never come to this place of betrayal. She wanted to flee, to run with the rest of the tribe of Judah—now! But her husband held her hand. He was speaking softly now. Again, her mind wandered into her past, and she did not hear what he said.

"Come!" his voice was sharp.

Beginning with the lower chambers, pouring out the oil that Shanarbaal had hoarded, Salma and Rahab burned the villa of the high priest of Baal.

Then, running with torches lighted from the campfires, they fired the sacred grove. The mosses caught first; then the feathery leaves began to crackle and lift their fingers to the sky. A light wind sprang up from the west, fanning the flames, encouraging them to glow and to dance.

As the prince of Judah and his Canaanite bride ran down the Baalpath with their torches, the fire raced behind them, a whirlwind of red and gold; crackling, sizzling, swirling upward to the desert sky.

Though the night was clear, it seemed to Rahab that rain stung her face and the trees shrieked: "Ai-ee, Astarte." The roar of rushing water was the hiss of the flames, and the song of the goddess was the song of battles. Rahab would have sought refuge, but her husband pulled her along the Baalpath, sending her splashing into the cool wetness of the emerald pool, where she had first encountered the spirits of the sacred grove. Behind Rahab and Salma, the flames swirled into the leaves, around them, behind them, above them, leaping from tree to tree with a kiss of fire.

Struggling through the water, Salma and Rahab held their torches high, running out the other side of the pond, carrying the fire deeper into the sacred grove.

Rahab led Salma up the steep path toward the high places. Below, the fire raged, sending its searing heat upward in search of them.

"Here," she said at last, breathlessly. "This is the high place—with the pole, the ashera—and the altar, the masheba."

Salma frowned. "I didn't realize they would be so big." He sighed. "No matter—we must tear them down."

Rahab looked at him wildly. How could they do it?

"I should have brought men—but the Lord will help us. The pole will burn—no!—I can use it! Here, Rahab, get the torches over here—" He tossed his torch into small bushes nearby.

"But, Salma—it'll start a fire!"

He looked at her in amazement. "Do it, Rahab."

She complied. *Of course,* she thought, *we are starting fires.* Then, she was amazed to see Salma draw his sword and attack the ashera, hacking and slashing at the base of the ancient pole. The pole cracked, and Salma dropped his sword, pushing the pole with both hands until it fell crashing across the stone altar.

"Rahab!" he shouted. "Hurry—help me." The fire and the force of their exertion made them sweat. Salma had placed the ashera under the masheba and was using the pole as a lever to pry up the altar rock. Rahab pushed with her husband until she thought her heart would burst. At last, the ancient rock came loose and rolled. The earth released its clinging grip, and the stone rose on the lever and rolled toward the cliff, crashing finally with a great roar into the inferno below, sending up thunderings and showerings of sparks. Rahab thought that she heard screams of fury as Baal and Astarte watched their sacred grove begin to die, consumed by the yellow flames.

With a great heave, Salma threw the ashera after the masheba into the sacred grove—the flames consumed the entire valley now, in a swirling, shrieking dance of death, one final celestial dance for Baal and Astarte.

For a moment, the couple stood on the cliffs above the grove and watched.

In the light of the rising flames, Rahab could see the streaks of dirt and sweat on Salma's face. "Let's go, Salma," she said, screaming over the roar of the devouring fire storm.

"Yes," he answered, and he turned to her. "This is an evil place. It shall be hereafter barren."

He spoke the words as a prophecy. The sharp pain that Rahab knew so well pierced her. *Will his words apply to me as well?* she thought. *The evil of this place was my evil, too.*

He retrieved his sword, and together they ran toward the wadi to the west where their people waited.

Images of the fire assailed Rahab as she slept. More than once she opened her eyes to see light in the sky to the east. Was it lightning or the fire? She raised herself on one elbow. Her husband was sleeping soundly beside her. All around her, smoldering campfires cast long shadows. Were they the shadows of men? Rahab looked more closely. A dark shadow moved nearby. "Who is it?" she whispered. No voice answered her; only the night winds murmured in the grasses. *Is the camp filled with enemy soldiers?* she wondered. *Have they slipped past the watchmen? The shadows are so long—like the shadows of giants, or the ghosts of giants.* One giant had died here, she knew, in the rainy season, when the wadi was a raging flood. Did he still prowl these paths, looking for his murderers?

Perhaps his spirit could not rest. Behind her, a small snapping sound—a footfall? She turned. Was that a man standing in the edges of the light from the campfire? A man—a very large man—waited in the shadows. Oparu? She shivered and closed her eyes. The camp was silent. When she looked again, the shadow was not the same.

With the sunrise, the men of Judah continued their march toward Bethlehem. They passed many small farms, settlements, and villages. The fields were lush with flax ready for the harvest, and flowers greeted them with shouts of color, but they saw no human faces.

"The people's hearts have truly melted in fear of us," Salma said. "They have fled!"

Or hidden, Rahab thought.

"The Lord has prepared our way," her husband sang. "We serve a good God!"

Rahab could only nod in agreement. The region was empty; it was as if they were going through a land of ghosts. She half expected warriors to attack from every shadow, but none did. She felt oppressed by the vision of Oparu. Could he be alive? Did he follow them? Did his ghost defend the land? Were they going into a trap? Would the Canaanites—her former people—only flee and then set an ambush, as Israel had done at Bethel-Ai? Salma seemed so confident, so heedless. Rahab wished she could share his joy—that she could escape the lingering images of death that haunted her. Rahab forced herself to smile as they rode, but she no longer sang her husband's song.

55

The village of Bethlehem greeted them at twilight. No light, no campfires shone from these empty hills. A small flock of sheep grazed in a valley near a rock shelter, but the shepherds had left.

When Salma saw the sheep, he halted his people.

"We shall stay here!" he shouted loudly enough for all to hear. Then he spoke quietly to Rahab: "This flock shall be our inheritance. I shall be its shepherd, and this will be your home, my love."

She sighed and slid from her horse, realizing that she was very tired. Every muscle in her body ached, and she almost fell to her knees. Home? She had not imagined that she would ever have a home. She had no feeling of home. "My wife-my home," Salma called her often. *If I am your home, Salma,* she had thought, *then where is my home? What is my home?*

But Salma allowed her no time for serious thoughts now. He picked her up, sweeping her into his arms and circling around and around.

"We have come home, my wife-my home. I give you my inheritance! The inheritance of Judah is yours, Rahab! You are my bride, a bride of the covenant."

Rahab could not resist Salma's laughter. She laughed, too.

The tribe of Judah took the area surrounding the town of Bethlehem. Only the city of Jerusalem, to the northeast, held firm. Salma's men found the villages easy to take: the Canaanites left as soon as they knew the Israelites were approaching.

The tiny town of Jabez proved to be a surprising treasure. Several houses were found to contain papyrae, styluses, and many of the special instruments of the scribal profession. When Salma told Alcion about this, Alcion's response was one of pure delight. "Your God is amazing, Salma!" he said as he laughed. "He provides everything!"

Salma was happy, too, that the discovery pleased Alcion. "You have been good for my aunt's sons, Alcion. Your strict discipline has changed them from untutored ruffians into little men."

"It has not been easy," Alcion said in good-natured agreement. "And it is not over. They are constantly tempted away from their work by the enticements of the camp."

"As I have noted," Salma answered. "And so I have a plan. It is entirely up to you, Alcion, but if you would like, I will give you the city of Jabez. It will be your city, and only your scribes and those whom you choose to train as scribes shall live there."

For once, Alcion's calm demeanor faltered. A smile of unrestrained delight broke across his face. "My own city!" he responded.

"It is a small enough reward for one who has served so faithfully! It is yours, Alcion, to do with as you will."

Salma's own family he settled at the village of Bethlehem. The village was small; the tiny farm houses were set apart from each other. There were ten houses in all. Salma chose the largest of these for Rahab's family. For himself and his bride, he selected the easternmost house, "so that we can watch the sunrise together," he whispered to her as he carried their belongings into the small rock house.

Once again, Rahab made her home in a house that had belonged to another woman. The woman who had lived here had fled with only the clothes she wore, leaving behind her pots and jars, her lamps and rugs. Even her barley flour waited on a rough, low table for hands that would never knead dough in this house again.

In a corner, out of the way, Rahab found a basket with a small woolen coverlet. She knelt to examine the fabric. In the shadowy room, she could not see the design clearly. Drawing the coverlet close to her face, she noticed the unmistakable smell of soured milk. This basket had held a baby! She sighed. The woman of this house had run with her child into the hills. Where were they now?

Rahab looked more closely at the little basket. It was perfect for a baby. *Will it ever hold my baby?* Rahab wondered. Would she ever lay Salma's child down to sleep under a little blanket like this one?

Rahab looked around at the tiny room with its rough-hewn furniture. *I have come a long way from Jericho,* she thought. *I have come a long way from the night that I stared out at the Habiru campfires and challenged their God.* "You have given me more than I ever dreamed, God of the Habiru," she prayed, "but will you give me what I asked for on that night? Will you give me a baby?"

Rahab listened to the quiet. No voice answered her. *Will the God of the Habiru do what he will do—like the other gods?* she thought. *I do not know. Salma says that God has promised us a baby. He has kept other promises. Perhaps he will keep this one.*

Summer, the dry season, deepened, but the evenings were cool. Near the house was a wadi that ran up into the hills. During the dry season, its bed, smooth with pebbles, provided an ideal pathway toward the pastures where the flocks grazed. Within the wadi, small trees provided shade, and the winter rains left deep pools here and there.

One pool in particular Rahab and Salma found especially pleasant. Green trees arched over its reflecting surface, cooling the hottest afternoon with a welcome shade. This pool, beneath the curve of the canyon walls, could not be seen even from a short distance away. Often Rahab and Salma laughed and splashed like children in its pleasant waters, and on many evenings they enjoyed the pleasures of one another's embrace. Never had Rahab been so happy. She thought that she would never tire of this man, her husband. Most of all, she loved his laughter. Her heart sang within her when he laughed, and she found many ways to make him laugh.

"I do not like this Bethlehem!" Micah complained as he drove the last of the small flock of ewes into a pen.

Kinah, who had just come outside to go to the well, looked at him in surprise. "What's wrong, Micah?" she asked sympathetically.

"Better to ask what is not wrong!" he replied sharply. "That would require a much shorter answer."

Kinah smiled at him. "I'm not in a hurry," she said.

"That's part of the problem," he said. "No one is in a hurry. We take the sheep out to graze. We watch the sheep on the hills. Sometimes we bring the sheep in; sometimes we leave them out. Sometimes we sit on a rock; sometimes we sit on the ground. It is boring here!"

"You were raised in the country, Micah," Kinah responded. "I thought you liked it."

"I thought I liked it, too," he said. "But after life in Jericho—I don't know, Kinah...I just don't like it here!" Micah picked up his shepherd's staff and headed back toward the hills. A few yards away, he turned and laughed. "It's BO-OO-OOR-ING!" he shouted.

Kinah laughed, too, shaking her head and watching Micah's tall form disappear in the distance. *How tall he is,* she realized. He had certainly grown up in the last few years. *He misses Jericho street life,* she thought—*and Jericho women?* Perhaps, that was it. Kinah giggled. Pretty little Micah, Rahab's younger brother, was a grown man, a very tall and handsome grown man, and she hadn't even noticed. She laughed aloud at that. *I've been away from Jericho longer than I realized,* she thought.

Rahab had waited until she was sure to tell Salma. For three weeks, she had felt nausea with each rising sun, and it had been ten weeks since she had experienced her monthly cycle—though she had slept alone each month at the appointed time, as the law required, when she was "unclean." Her figure was full; she was beginning to feel fat, although she knew no one else had noticed yet. *Today*, she thought, *today I am sure! The Lord God is making us a baby.*

Salma had gone to check on the herds and the men who watched them. He had seemed restless lately, as if his mind were elsewhere. *He's probably worrying about Joshua and the men of Israel*, she thought. *It's as if he can no longer sit still. But when he comes home tonight, I will surprise him with my news. That will change his attitude!* She sent Nantha and Kinah to her mother's house. Tonight she would be alone with her husband!

The sun had set, and Rahab waited impatiently. She had found wildflowers to adorn her hair, and she had prepared his favorite meal. She heard the sound of the horse's hoofs as he approached. The horse was running. Why? She smiled, thinking of her husband's growing affection for the horse Shimmerance. *He is hurrying home to me*, she thought. *He will be so pleased!*

Salma's face was hard-set as he entered the room. They spoke at the same time—

"Salma, I have news—"

"Rahab, I must tell you—"

Silence followed. Rahab laughed. "Tell me, my love," she said. "What is your news?"

"I have met a rider in the hills today. The Ephraimites are struggling to the north—Daniel is in trouble—and, so," he paused, putting his hands on her shoulders and looking into her eyes, "I have summoned the men of Judah. We will march at sunrise."

"Salma!" she gasped, stepping back.

He looked at the steaming plates. "Supper smells wonderful! You have made my favorites!" He pulled her to the table. "Oh, how I thank the Lord. Oh, Rahab, I am blessed of all men!"

Rahab was silent as they began the meal. He was so excited about going off to battle that he had forgotten that she had news.

He ate heartily. "Rahab, I will need provisions for the road. I would also like to take the horse Shimmerance—would you mind?"

She smiled then, ruefully, and answered softly, "Yes, take the horse. I do not think I will be riding. I think I am pregnant."

"What!" he exclaimed. "Rahab, my wife-my home! Oh, I am blessed above all men!" His food and his battle forgotten for the moment, he came to embrace her. "My darling, my love—when? How long?"

"It has been ten weeks since my cycle. I am very sure."

He held her at arm's length, and his shouts of joy became suddenly quiet. "But, Rahab," he said, "I have already called the men of Judah. I cannot change it now."

She sighed. "I understand your warrior's heart, my love....Only...only hurry back to me."

He laughed then, heartily, and hugged her. "Have no fears, my love. The Lord has promised us a son!"

Salma had been gone a week when Rahab decided to gather herbs in the wadi. She started, alone, for the pond; she would imagine that he was here with her, playing in the water.

The pain that stabbed her was unlike any she had known before. One hundred, one thousand times more terrible than any of the sharp stomach pains of her past! She bent, clutching her stomach. She gritted her teeth, and then she screamed. The pain tore through her stomach and into her spine, and she fell onto her side and rolled. Her back crushed the grasses of the hills of Bethlehem as she rolled from side to side, trying to catch her breath, trying to think, trying not to scream. The pain came again, and once again. And then—

It was over. Blood and water seemed everywhere. She lay, wet, blinking at the sun, catching her breath, thanking the Lord God that the pain had passed. She raised herself to one elbow, looking down, and realized that her robe was ruined. At the same instant, she realized what had happened: she had lost the baby. She screamed again. She had lost Salma's baby. She knew it for a certainty. She had lost the baby that God had promised to Salma.

Her heart sank within her as she remembered Balaam's prophecy. She heard his voice as if he stood behind her now: "May the unborn child die within your womb." She shrieked. The skin across her back felt tight and parched, and she realized that she must not remain unprotected beneath the summer sun. She would have to wash herself, and quickly. The blood was beginning to dry. The bright red blood of herself, her child, was turning brown and dry.

As she shifted to rise, her leg was stabbed by a small, sharp pain, and she thought immediately of a scorpion. Quickly, she pulled her robe aside, to reveal, not a scorpion, but a small metal spiral, a golden spiral. She took it from the hem of her robe and held it in her hand. She wiped it clean and looked at it closely. "The goddess within!" The words sounded of their own accord within her mind, and she knew: this golden spiral had caused her to lose the child. It had come from her body with the child, with the blood.

As she stood slowly, shakily, trembling, she closed her eyes against the image of her baby. She could not look. She did not want to see the child who would have been. The child that would have been Salma's baby, the promised child from the Lord God. Yet, she could not leave it here, tiny and defenseless, on the hills of Bethlehem. Pulling the blue scarf from her shoulders, she forced herself to turn. She dropped the scarf over the tiny, bloody form, so small she could hardly feel it in the scarf. The blue scarf enfolded its precious burden, and holding this burden in one hand and the golden spiral in the other, Rahab hurried toward the stream. She placed her burdens—the blue scarf and the golden spiral—on a limestone ledge near the pond.

The cold water splashed on her feet as she waded into the shallow stream. She sat down. The running water washed the stains from her body and from her dress. She rubbed the white linen between her hands, watching as the blood washed away, the dark stains disappearing as the water flowed down from the hills through the wadi, into the pond, flowing past her into the valleys of the land of Judah.

She lay back in the water, closing her eyes, mingling her tears with the free-flowing water of this Bethlehem stream. She knew what she must do. She picked up the tiny burden within its blue scarf, and she picked up the golden spiral, symbol of the goddess Astarte. Nearby, the smooth flat stones waited as they had always waited; now she knew why they were here. This was the burial spot for her baby; this was her baby's sepulchre.

Slowly, moving very carefully without thinking, Rahab took a small flat stone and hollowed out a space in the dry earth. Into this small hollow, she carefully placed the golden spiral and the blue scarf. She slid a large flat stone over the hollow, burying the golden symbol of her past with the hopes for her future. Nothing was left to her now, except death. She fell to her knees, and she sobbed. Then, she closed her heart, stood slowly, and walked back to Bethlehem.

Nantha greeted her with a worried frown. "Lady—you have been gone since before the sunrise."

Rahab did not reply; she walked past Nantha, as if she had not seen her. Nantha's frown became deeper. "Rahab! Are you all right?"

Rahab lay down upon her bed and turned her face to the wall.

Much later, Nantha spread a coverlet over her mistress. The next morning, Nantha noticed that Rahab had a severe sunburn. Rahab had worn a scarf into the hills, but she had come back without it. Rahab said nothing and ate nothing. Nantha worried.

Rahab was visited by the high priest of Baal. He was swirling a golden snake, a golden spiral. "Accept the goddess within," he whispered. "Eternal virgin, eternal harlot, mother of fecundity." He laughed, then, crazily. "Eternally barren." He came at Rahab with the golden spiral, the snake of Astarte; Rahab turned her face toward the wall.

Nantha sent for Rahab's mother and her sisters. When they came, Rahab did not speak. She gave no sign of recognition. Rahab's mother shrugged her shoulders. "I don't know, Nantha," she said. "I have never understood this daughter of mine. Perhaps you should send for Salma. He is her protector now." She frowned. "The gods will take whom the gods will take—you know that, Nantha."

Nantha was reluctant to send for Salma, however. She knew that the winning of the promised land, the land of milk and honey, was important to him, and she did not want to call for him unless Rahab was seriously ill. So she hoped her mistress would soon be better.

Rahab resumed her sewing, to Nantha's great relief. But still, Rahab had nothing to say. Nantha longed for her kitchen gods; she could have talked with them. Kinah sat with Rahab for hours, playing her harp or singing softly. Rahab appeared not to notice; she sewed.

Gradually, as the weeks passed, it became obvious to Nantha and Kinah that Rahab was growing very thin. She should have been growing large with child by now, but instead she grew thinner, more hollow-cheeked, with each passing day. She sewed through the nights and slept through the daylight hours. Nantha did not know what to do. Alcion was at Jabez, teaching Caleb's nephews and other youngsters the art of writing. There was no one to ask. Rahab's father's health grew worse, and Rahab's mother visited only occasionally. Nantha became more and more worried, but she did not send for Salma. Kinah's worry grew unbearable; her mistress must be dreadfully ill.

Shortly before dawn one morning, Kinah entered Rahab's room to find her mistress still sewing, her evening meal untouched at her side.

"Mistress!" Kinah exclaimed in exasperation. "You must eat! You must rest! This cannot be good for the baby!" Her concern overtook her usual shyness, and she took the ivory awl from Rahab's hand and reached to extinguish the lamp.

Rahab turned suddenly, and her stinging slap sent Kinah sprawling across the room. "You will not put out my light!" Rahab snapped fiercely, the first words she had spoken since the day she had spent alone in the wilderness.

Kinah and Nantha were so frightened they sent for Alcion, and Alcion scolded Nantha. "You should have sent for me sooner!" he said. "She has obviously lost the baby."

Alcion sent immediately for Salma.

56

Rahab sat at her loom, holding a red thread. She gazed at it intently. Bright red thread, bright red like the entrails of the lamb, bright red like the fresh blood of the sacrifice, Bishna's blood, her own blood, the blood of her child, filling the ruby pond, filling her life. She could dive into its redness, drown in its redness, die in its redness. She could be one with the blood of the lambs; she could be one with the blood that spilled across her hands, one with the blood—

She was startled by the realization that arms held her close, encircled her, comforted her. *It is Salma,* she thought. She turned and buried her face in his shoulder. *No!* she thought, *my husband has gone to fight the wars. He is not here. I am alone. My comfort is the blood of the lambs, the blood of the lambs and death.*

"Rahab," he spoke softly. "My love." He turned her face to his but saw no recognition in her eyes. Salma patted and stroked her hair, tears spilling forth from his eyes. "Rahab! Rahab! Rahab!" he cried out. She did not respond.

"Come, my love," Salma said at last, "let us go into the wilderness. Let us be alone with the Lord our God."

He took her then by the hand, and he took the red thread from her and hung it on the loom. It reminded him of the cord she had hung from her window in Jericho, the symbol of their covenant. The Lord had rescued her from Jericho and had given her to him—for this?

The day was bright and cool. Already the sun was climbing high into the sky. They walked the familiar path through the fields, toward the gullies of the wadi, toward the pond. Rahab followed Salma wordlessly.

Salma walked with his arm around Rahab. His heart was too full to speak. It was obvious that Rahab carried no child. What had happened to her? *I should have been here,* he thought. *I should have been here.*

Salma held Rahab close as they walked, willing to her his own strength. He knew that he must seek a greater strength, the Almighty God, creator of heaven and earth. As they reached the pond, she began to tremble; her trembling grew until he feared that she would fall. He sat with her in the shade of a small willow tree, near the edge of the pond, holding Rahab in front of him, within the circle of his arms.

Alone with his wife, in the wilderness, Salma cried aloud his anguish and his despair: "God of Abraham! Ever-present strength! Be my rock and my redeemer. Lord God, you have protected me from my enemies. You have given me victory in battle, and you have brought me here. God of my fathers—what is wrong? Help me, Yahweh! Protect this woman! Give her back to me, I pray." He sobbed. "What has happened to our child? O God of the universe, you have promised us a child! Do not take away both my child and my beloved, Lord God! Strength of Israel, protect this woman whom I love! Heal this woman! Comfort her pain. Overpower her pain with your strength. Help us. Heal her!"

As Salma pleaded with his God, Rahab continued to tremble, but the sun reached through the dappled shade of the tree, warming her. Salma's arms were warm and strong. She could see a brilliant light coming into her through the tree, reaching into the depths of her spirit, filling her soul with its brightness, reaching into the depths of her spirit, healing her wounded heart, flooding her with a warmth, a vibrancy that awakened her spirit and called her forth into the day.

She looked at the man who held her close. His tears had washed the dust of travel in streaks down his face. She reached for him, then, gently touching his face, "Oh, my beloved," she sighed. "Our child is here."

Salma shook his head, sadly; she was mad.

"Come," she said softly. "I will show you." He allowed her to take his hand and lead him a short distance away to a small pile of limestone rocks. She knelt there and touched the rocks. "Salma, our child is here!" She dropped his hand, looking at the pile of stones instead of at him. Speaking so softly that he could barely hear her, she said, "After you left, I came here to gather herbs, and I lost our child here. I buried our son here, Salma, beneath this pile of rocks. This is his memorial."

Salma understood then. He gathered her into his arms.

"Children belong to the Lord," he said softly. "The Lord gives, and the Lord takes away. He is God. He gives life, Rahab. I am thankful that he gives me your life. You are my love, my delight."

For many hours, they sat at the pond, near the pile of limestone rocks. As the sun sank low, Salma drew Rahab to himself, and he comforted her with the gift of his love, tenderly, reverently.

At last the two walked back, through the fading light of dusk, to the house at Bethlehem.

Gradually, Rahab improved. When Salma was with his wife, he was the most tender of men. Gently, he lured his wife back to the real world, the world outside her own mind. With playful love, he drew forth once more her smiles and occasionally her laughter, but the enthusiasm for life that Salma had so loved in Rahab stirred slowly. She was a pleasant companion, but her laughter held no joy.

Salma blamed himself. One evening, standing alone near the sheep gate, Salma could control his anger no longer.

"How could I have been so foolish?" he demanded aloud. "The law gave me a year to bring happiness to the wife whom I had chosen. Joshua offered me the time. Why did I refuse? Rahab needed me; I should have been with her!"

But even as he berated himself, Salma knew why he had returned to the war. He had not wanted to miss a single battle! The Lord God was giving the land into the hands of his people, and Salma had wanted to see every victory. He had wanted, even needed, to lead his tribesmen into battle. Yet, he had known that Rahab needed him; he had known that the very law of Moses gave him the right to be with her. How many times had he recited it? "When a man hath taken a new wife, he shall not go out to war, neither shall he be charged with any business: but he shall be free at home one year, and shall cheer up his wife which he hath taken."

Still, he had left her, knowing that she was pregnant, and this was the result: she lost his baby. How could he blame her? Her own father had warned him that she might be barren; even so, he had not taken the warning seriously. He had been too sure of his own manhood; he had deserted her immediately after she had conceived. Now, perhaps, she would never carry a child again. How could God endure a man such as he?

"I do not give God a chance to fulfill his promises to me!" Salma accused himself aloud. "I ignore the law! I ignore my dreams, yet I expect God to bless me. I am seven kinds of a fool! The ways of God are too righteous for me! I do not deserve to be a prince of Judah!"

"Will you question what the Lord God has ordained?" The voice startled Salma. He turned to see his brother-in-law, Jaben, staring at him.

"Oh, Jaben—I do not question the Lord. I blame myself! The law of the Lord allowed me to be with her, yet I could not miss the battles. I thought only of myself—of my pleasure in victory. What does a woman care for war? But I cared—I cared more for battle than for my wife—who carried my son."

"It is a strange law that allows a soldier to stay at home simply because he has married," Jaben replied.

"It is the law of God, and it is the way of righteousness," Salma retorted, "but I considered myself—Captain of the tribe of Judah—too important to observe the law."

"You are not the first man to think himself above the law of God, Salma."

"Yes, but I have lost my son for it!"

"If you had been here, then, you could have saved the baby?" Jaben's voice held no hint of sarcasm, but his eyes were shrewd as he watched his brother-in-law.

Salma shrugged his shoulders in resignation. "I do not know what I could have done, Jaben. Perhaps if I had been here, Rahab would not have walked into the hills; perhaps she would have rested more; perhaps I could have—"

"Perhaps you think yourself too important, still, my brother," Jaben said softly.

Salma looked at him sharply. "I do not understand," he said.

"You carry too much evil on your own shoulders. Do you truly believe that everything that goes wrong is because of your disobedience? Is Rahab perfect? Has she never sinned according to your law? Or, perhaps, you mean that there was no evil in the world, no babies died, before you were born! Every sin is charged to your account, and your God blames you for all of them! What an important man you are, Salma." Jaben's voice was still soft. "I had not realized. So much misery in the world—and all of it your fault! I am awed."

Salma turned his back on the other man and breathed in sharply. Jaben was right, of course. He did blame himself for everything. Even the defeat at Bethel-Ai. Had he been, perhaps, a bit disappointed that Achan's sin was to blame? No, no, he had not been disappointed, but he had been relieved—and even surprised. Even as Achan was stoned, Salma had felt there might be some mistake; it might have been some sin of his. And Marnya, his precious first wife—she had died giving birth to his son, the son he had planted within her, and that baby had died, too. Had that not been his own fault? He sighed and spoke slowly. "I have sinned many times, Jaben."

Jaben smiled slowly and placed his hand on the older man's shoulder. "So have we all, my brother, but have you not taught me that God accepts our sin offerings? Is that not why we sacrifice?"

"Still, when we are guilty, we see the results of our sin, Jaben!"

"Sometimes, Salma, yes! But not every evil in life is the result of your personal sin—or even of mine. To what purpose are the scapegoat or the Day of Atonement if your guilt destroys your happiness on all other days? Did your God not provide the sacrifice for Abraham, Salma?" Now Jaben's voice was intense.

Salma closed his eyes and saw the ram caught in the bushes on Mount Moriah. Abraham's faith, too, had been tested, yet Isaac had not been sacrificed. The first son of Abraham had been Ishmael, yet he had not been the child of the promise. But the child of the promise had come. Again, Salma saw the ram that had brought him the dream of Rahab carrying his son. "I have lost two children, Jaben. Yet still will I trust the Lord."

Jaben sighed in relief. Salma placed his arm around the other man. "Thank you, Jaben. Your young faith has strengthened me."

"Then you will not blame yourself for everything, Salma?"

"I will try not to do it, Jaben. I will try to place my guilt on the altar of the sacrifice where it belongs."

"It is the provision of your God, Salma," Jaben answered quietly.

"So it is, my friend, and I must remember it. The ways of the Lord are righteous and straight. God is a good God; he does all things well."

Jaben smiled. "Ah, that is more like the man of faith I recognize! Salma, I have come to speak to you about something that is very important. Rahab's brother, Micah, grows restless here in Bethlehem. He is accustomed to the city and the women of the city. He is too alone, and such solitude breeds trouble."

Salma understood immediately. "Oh, I have failed in my responsibility to that boy," Salma sighed. "He should have been married years ago."

"He was old enough to have married in Jericho," Jaben responded, "but Kora is a woman who holds on to her boys. She does not say much, but her will is strong."

"Yes, I have seen that," Salma answered. "But a boy Micah's age—a man Micah's age—must have a wife. If he does not, he will fall into sin."

"We must get him a wife," Jaben said.

Salma nodded. "It can be arranged. I have many kinswomen."

"Then I will leave you to the details," Jaben answered, departing.

That night before they went to sleep, Salma told Rahab about his conversation with Jaben. "So, of course," he concluded, "I must send to the camp of Israel to find Micah a wife."

Rahab's response shocked Salma. She laughed and pushed him back against the pillows. "You are so silly, my lord," she said.

Salma sat up, looking at his wife carefully. "And why am I so silly to wish your brother married?" he asked. Was this more of her madness showing itself?

"You are not silly to wish my brother married," his wife answered. "You are silly not to know your own household! Do you not know that Kinah needs a husband as much as Micah needs a wife? They have known each other for years, so why should they not marry?"

"Kinah is older than Micah," Salma argued, because he wanted to see Rahab's response.

"Pooh," Rahab answered. "What does that matter? Jaben is younger than Tirnah, but he has taught her to respect him. Besides, the age difference is a small one. Let them marry!"

"I will talk to Bazarnan about it," Salma responded.

"Then talk to him, but this much I can tell you beforehand. Micah admires Kinah; he always has, and Kinah would not be adverse to the marriage. Oh! Let them marry, Salma!"

Salma laughed and pulled Rahab close to him. "It is good to see you alive again, Rahab, good to see that you can feel and care again. I was afraid that I had lost you forever."

"I was afraid, too, my lord," Rahab answered solemnly. Then she brightened, "Oh, it will be fun to have a wedding!"

57

Tirnah did not attend the wedding of Kinah and Micah. Both her children were sick, and she petulantly sent Jaben off to the festivities while she remained inside with two fussy babies—Mita, who was three, and the boy, who was less than a year old.

The people of the village of Bethlehem gathered at the house of Rahab's parents, bringing rugs and mats, food and wine. The celebration lasted for hours. Micah and Kinah cast shy glances at each other. Nantha laughed at them. "You'd think they were virgin babes marrying each other," she said to Rahab.

Rahab laughed, too. Nantha was pleased to hear her mistress laugh again. Rahab had been sick too long!

"Kinah is astonished with herself," Rahab said. "She told me yesterday that Micah has changed greatly in her eyes—from a little brother and a friend to a man who will be her husband, her lover. She is excited and eager for this marriage."

"It is good that she feels that way," Nantha said, glancing at the betrothed couple. "But she has always been a sensible little girl, like you, mistress!"

"Oh, Nantha!" Rahab responded. "We have not been little girls in many years!"

The older woman sniffled. "You have always been little girls to me," she said.

"Why, Nantha," Rahab laughed softly. "Where did you get this sudden gentle spirit?"

"Hmmph!" the other woman said briskly, but then she smiled. "I have always felt this way. You and Kinah are my little girls; that is all there is to it."

Rahab hugged the older woman. "It is a good life we have now, Nantha!" she exclaimed. "It is not like Jericho."

Nantha looked at Kinah, who was now playing the harp and singing for the guests at her own wedding. "No, mistress. I thank the Lord God Almighty. It is nothing like Jericho."

Winter passed. Rahab had conceived again, and as the child grew within her, she seemed to glow with health. It seemed to Salma that her beauty was a quieter beauty than before. He enjoyed looking at her, and he enjoyed telling her the law of the Lord and the traditions of his people. He had learned, word for word, the teachings of his faith, and he spent the long, rainy evenings of that winter telling Rahab the stories of his people. He especially loved the story of Abraham and Sarah and the son of their promise, the son of their old age, Isaac. God had required Isaac as a sacrifice, as a test of his father's faith.

"Abraham tied the boy on the altar; he was ready to plunge the knife," he told his wife.

"Oh, no!" Rahab gasped. "Surely he did not! What happened? The Lord would not permit it, surely!"

"The Lord did not permit it! He stayed Abraham's hand and provided a wild ram, caught in the bushes, instead."

"That is a strange story, Salma....I do not understand this God."

"No man can truly understand his ways, my precious one. But he is righteous and holy. He is a God of love, yet he is a God of terrible justice."

Rahab sighed, remembering the death of Jericho and the stoning of Achan's family and remembering, as well, the nesting dove.

"Justice and love—no, I do not understand. But I know that I have felt his love as well as his power—and perhaps that is enough."

They lingered over their evening meal, watching a golden sunset. A hint of spring was in the air, and cicadas sang in the grape arbor. The fading light of the sun spread its fingers through the bare branches of the olive grove. Rahab felt a drowsy peace with her husband and with her life.

"Your time is near, my love, and I must instruct you about the ritual cleansing of our women after birth," Salma said. "It is required by the law."

Rahab's thoughts drifted with the fading sunlight and sang with the cicadas. "Yes, my love," she said absently.

Salma's voice deepened as he quoted the Book of the Law of Moses. "A woman who conceives and bears a male child will be ceremonially unclean for seven days, just as in the time of her monthly bleeding."

"Yes, I know," Rahab said, thinking, *Have I not been a woman since I was fourteen?*

Salma continued, ignoring the interruption. "On the eighth day, the child shall have the flesh of his foreskin circumcised."

Rahab thought of her father and the pain that had been his at circumcision as an aging, ailing convert. She was thankful that her child, if the Lord blessed her with a son, would not remember the pain, even as lambs do not remember having their tails cut short at birth.

She smiled idly. "Yes, my love," she said.

Salma continued. "Then the woman must wait thirty-three days to be purified. She shall touch nothing that is holy, and shall not enter the sanctuary until her days of purification are completed."

"Yes," Rahab murmured again, concentrating on a kicking within her belly. Her hand curved around the movement, and she savored the feeling of the child within.

Salma's instruction went on: "If she gives birth to a daughter, however, the woman will be unclean for fourteen days." He paused. "Then she must wait sixty days to be purified."

Rahab nodded, wondering why so long for a girl.

"When the days of her purification for a son or daughter are over, she is to bring to the priest at the entrance to the tent of meeting, a year-old lamb for a burnt offering and a young dove for a sin offering."

"What did you say?" Rahab demanded sharply. Had he said she must sacrifice a lamb? and a dove?

"What do you mean—what did I say?" Salma spoke sharply. He thought she had been listening.

"A lamb, Salma! You said I have to sacrifice a lamb!" Her voice became a shriek, bordering upon hysteria.

"It is the law! What is wrong with you?"

"No! It cannot be!" she wailed.

He was exasperated. "Rahab! The law is the law! You may not want to do it, but you must do it!" Salma had no idea that he had repeated the exact words of Amaranthe-Astarte and of Shanarbaal.

Rahab felt again the stinging slap of the high priestess. Rahab's scream pierced the evening air and ripped into Salma's heart.

She ran; she ran until she reached the gate of the olive grove. Pushing the gate open, she ran into the grove, stopping only when she collapsed at the foot of an ancient, gnarled olive tree.

Sobs shook her body. *I do not want to kill the lamb! I do not want to shed its blood. I am sick of blood, blood, blood! No, Amaranthe, don't! Too late—the knife is covered in Asabaal's blood, spilled, like Bishna's. Oh, she is dead! The knife—No, No! Amaranthe, not the baby! Not the baby! Not the lamb! I can't! I cannot kill the lamb.* "You do not want to do it, but you will do it, won't you, Rahab?" the voice said. Again, she shrieked. She had done it! She had killed the lamb! She was guilty of his blood!

And Oparu! I helped Shanarbaal to kill Oparu. It was my fault. It was all my fault! I should have taken the baby and run to the hills. I never should have let Amaranthe take him from me. I knew what she would do. I should have protected Bishna. I should have been awake. If I had only been awake, she would not have bled to death. I have sinned! In the eyes of the Lord God Almighty, I have sinned! I have sinned all of my life, and I did not even know that I sinned!

And Oparu! I did know; I did know! I chose to sin! Oh, I have betrayed everyone. I have betrayed my people. I have betrayed my family, and my friends. Oh, Oparu! Oparu! I betrayed you unto death! I have done everything wrong! All the lies, and—oh!—all the men. Even my harlotry was a web of deception. And now—now Salma says I must kill the lamb again. How can I kill the lamb? Oh, Salma!

She felt his arms around her, holding her. "Rahab," he was saying, "Rahab, listen to me, listen! It's all right! It's all right!"

"It's not all right!" she wailed. "It's all a lie!"

He had been telling her that he loved her, but she had not heard him. "My love for you is not a lie. I love you!"

"Your love?" she asked. "I do not deserve your love. I deserve to die—as Achan died."

"What do you mean?" he asked her softly.

"I have sinned," she whispered. "I am not worthy of your love. I am not worthy of your God. I am not worthy to bear your child."

He shook his head and held her close. "What do you mean?" he asked again.

"All my life has been a sin," she answered bitterly. "You do not know, Salma. You do not know— From my first days in the temple, my life has been red with blood, and sin, and death. Oh, Salma," she sobbed. "I have brought it even unto you—with the death of our first child. My sins of the temple caused that death. It was the goddess within. I know it."

He pulled away. "What do you mean—the goddess within?" he asked.

"It was the magic, Salma. It was the magic and the curse of the temple. The gods of the temple betrayed me, and I betrayed them—and now, I have betrayed you as well." She shuddered, sighing. "If I must kill again, if I must sacrifice the lamb," her voice rose to shout, "then your God has betrayed me!"

He tried to comfort her. "The priest offers the sacrifice; you do not have to kill the lamb yourself."

She was clinging to him and crying. She did not hear what he had said.

Salma continued to explain, though he wondered if he were too blind to understand her distress or too unlearned to explain the Lord's ways. Who could explain God? But he must try. "The priests offer the sacrifice," he repeated, "and the blood of the sacrifice cleanses us of our sins. It is like the scapegoat on the day of atonement, Rahab. The sins of all the people are placed on the head of the sacrifice who must carry them away. Then we do not suffer for our sins."

Through her confusion and her tears, she did not comprehend his words. He paused and stroked her hair tenderly. She looked up at him.

"My love, my love," he sighed. "It is because he loves *us* that he provides the sacrifice—not because he loves the shedding of blood."

"Because God loves us," she repeated. It did not make sense. Blood was blood. "I am sick of blood! It is death! It is always death, and I hate it!"

"But, Rahab!" Salma said. "It is *through* the blood of the sacrifice that our lives are spared!"

"It doesn't make sense," she said.

"I have told you of Abraham and Isaac," he reminded her patiently, "and when we fled from Egypt, we sacrificed the lamb, and the angel of death passed over us. It was the blood on our doors that protected our firstborn from death."

She shuddered, remembering her firstborn. "Death and blood, Salma—it is all a betrayal. And I have betrayed even you! I lost our firstborn, and I deserve to die."

He held her closely, thinking of his own failures, the lusts and sins of his own life, and his voice was quiet. "You have not betrayed me. You are my wife, and I love you, and you will bear my son."

"And I love you, my husband, but I am so afraid."

"Do you think our Lord would have saved you out of Jericho for no reason? Don't you see, Rahab? We all deserve to die, and we will—but it is through the blood of the sacrifice that we are cleansed before our Lord."

"No," she said, "I do not see." But her sobs abated and then stopped.

He tried again. "Have you ever seen a baby sacrificed to the God of Israel?"

She looked up at him. "No," she said, "never."

"And you never will," he said.

Around them, the evening air was peaceful, silent. Salma held Rahab wordlessly for a time, hoping that the stillness of the evening would comfort the turmoil in her spirit.

"I fear this righteous God, Salma," she whispered at last. "I fear for our child, and I fear for myself."

"He is also a God of lovingkindness," Salma said. He wondered if this were an answer to her.

She shook her head. "I don't understand. I don't understand this God at all."

"His ways are beyond us, my love—but we must trust him." Now it was Salma's turn to sigh as he thought of his men who had died in Ai. Their blood had been spilled, and he had not understood—until Achan's sin had been revealed. Still he struggled with those memories. "Death is hard," he said at last, remembering the blood of his friends at Ai. "Sometimes," he added, "God's purposes become more clear after we have obeyed his laws, but sometimes they do not. In either case, we must walk in obedience!"

"It is very hard, Salma—but I do love *you*, and I do trust you. And so I will obey your law." She paused and took a deep breath. "Even though I must kill another lamb."

He was relieved that she was calm again; it did not occur to him that she thought she would have to kill the lamb herself or that she had killed a lamb before.

"Come, my love. Let's go to bed," he said. Together, they walked through the olive grove toward their home.

58

The soldier arrived at midmorning. He had traveled since the day before. His roan-colored horse had turned white and foamy from sweat.

Rahab's mother, staying with Rahab during her pregnancy, answered the loud, unpleasant knocking. Her polite eyes grew wary as she recognized an Israelite soldier at her door. It bode no good. Their God was up to something again!

Despite his desert training, the soldier gulped the cup of water she offered him. He could not wait, he said. He must see Salma at once. Kora answered him calmly, then sent Benan running to the hill. When she offered the man food, he accepted and ate as if he had never tasted hard bread and beans before.

The Salma who walked through the door at that moment was a stranger to Kora. His eyes were fierce; his bearing was stiff, military. *This is the Salma who returned victorious from Bethel-Ai*, she thought. Salma's eyes snapped at the soldier before him. "What has happened?" he demanded.

"Joshua has made treaty with the Gibeonites," the other man reported, "but Adonizedek and the other kings of Canaan have attacked them. Joshua's orders are that you assemble your men and march for Gibeon now."

Kora breathed in sharply, and Salma noted her presence for the first time. "Where is my wife?" he asked crisply.

"She is resting, my lord," his mother-in-law replied softly.

Salma went to Rahab immediately. He did not want to go to battle as Rahab approached the time of her delivery. Before, when he left, the child had died and very nearly the woman as well. He sighed. This command must be obeyed; Joshua spoke for the Lord. Yet Salma was fearful. He woke his wife with a gentle kiss. She smiled lazily, reaching for his embrace.

"You sleep late today, my love," he said.

"Ummm...yes," she answered sleepily, curling against him.

He kissed her face. "I have bad news," he said softly. She was instantly awake.

"Oh, no! Salma—not the war!"

He hung his head. "Joshua has summoned me," he said.

She sighed. "Then you cannot refuse."

"I cannot refuse," he repeated. "I would, but I cannot."

She rose then, moving awkwardly with the fullness of the child within her.

"Do you leave immediately? Does Nantha need to prepare food for your journey?"

"She has already begun, and I will leave as soon as the men are assembled...." He paused. "I do not know how long I will be gone, but I promise you this: I will return as quickly as I can."

She smiled, sadly. "I know, my love, and I pray that the Lord will keep you safe. When you return, you will have a son!"

He hugged her close. "The Lord will take care of me and keep you safe. The Lord keeps his covenants."

It was sunset when Rahab entered the stable. The master shepherd had chosen the lamb for her—a perfect lamb, without blemish. This lamb had been separated from the flock and placed in the stable where he would be safe, awaiting the appointed day.

Rahab sat carefully on the manger, where the lamb was eating contentedly.

"So you are the chosen one," she said, reaching out to touch its soft fleece. "You are an offering," she told the lamb. "You are an offering of God's mercy to me." She looked at her belly, heavy with child. "The Lord does not demand my baby. You, little lamb, are a substitute for my son."

She bit her lip, and her voice broke.

"I am not less guilty, nor is the Lord God less righteous." She sighed. "Little lamb, you are beautiful. I love you; I give you freely to my God—and, even as I do, he gives me the life of my son, his son. It is life, bought at a price—your blood. Your innocent blood cries out to God. It is the cry of my sin." She bowed her head. "It is my atonement."

Rahab began to cry, softly. "Your blood will be poured out before a God who hears and sees and knows—and who cries for you, even as I do."

Again, she sighed. "But it is right. It is even as Abraham did not withhold from God the boy Isaac, his son, his only son. Neither do I withhold you."

She looked up. "I praise the Lord who is God! He has given me a son, and the Lord who did not take Isaac from Abraham will not take my son from me! He gives me this life, and he does not require the blood of my son."

Looking down at the lamb again, she said, "Thank you, little lamb. You have no sin of your own. You will go back to God, the God who made you, the God who receives your innocence in token for my sin." Her tears flowed freely, mingling with the dirt of the stable floor.

The Jericho stairs were dark. Her feet knew unerringly the way upward through the darkness. Every indentation, every niche, was known to her; still, she wished for a light on the stair. A flash, so bright that she closed her eyes against it, flooded the stair with light. Opening her eyes, she saw herself in the blinding light—naked. *I am naked!* she realized: *Naked and ashamed.* Gazing upward into the brilliant light, she saw, at the top of the stair, an altar. An altar, for what? *Why an altar, Lord?* she thought.

In front of the altar stood Bazarnan. "Father!" she said, realizing that her father was about to perform a sacrifice. The lamb on the altar must die!

"No! Stop!" she wanted to cry out, but she could not. The lamb on the altar must die, for she must have clothes to cover her nakedness, to cover her naked body, to cover her shame. Her father was willing to kill the lamb that she might be covered.

Something was wrong. Her father was pulling at the sheep's wooly clothing—what was he doing? Bazarnan pulled back the sheep's skin; it was not a sheep at all—it was— But how could it be?

It was Benan, her father's favorite son, lying there, tied, waiting upon the altar. Her father lifted the knife....the knife fell. It was not Benan; it was Bazarnan, her loving father, willing to sacrifice all, who fell across the altar, breaking it forever. The altar fell in pieces. Benan stood beside it. The light was all around him. He was holding out a garment—the pure white covering of the lamb!

Rahab awakened suddenly, completely. *What woke me?* she wondered, listening for some sound. There was none. The stillness seemed to cover her, to enfold her. So quiet, so peaceful.

"God?" she said softly, her voice more thought than word. "Yes, God," she said, affirming her own question.

How silently, how gently this God of the Habiru had obtruded into her awareness. Here was the God as she had not suspected him before, moving so subtly upon her that she only gradually realized his presence. *There is purpose in all things.* She felt the message and whispered it inaudibly. This stillness was so close to her that it seemed a very part of her. The quiet encircled her heart: *I am the God of love, Rahab. The God of love.*

She tried for part of a moment to compare this thought to the god of death as she had known him, as she had believed in him. The comparison refused to be made. The thoughts could not form. In the presence of this gentle, stirring love, the thought of any other god was blasphemy.

If this stillness, this peace, were the only truth in the universe, it was enough. "I will have no other gods before thee," Rahab whispered. Soft tears of joy welled in her eyes. Gladly she would have died if by dying she might preserve her union with this presence of peace. She closed her eyes. Joy, like waves of light and melody, filled her. *The presence of the Lord is upon me,* she thought. "I love you," she whispered to God as the love crested within her. Her tears welled hot and fast, a celebration of love. *I am the God that hath begotten you, Rahab, the God of the universe, the God of love.* She felt the words and then whispered them to make sure they were really there. "The God of love, the God of love." The words became a melody, a song that sang within her, and she curled into a tiny circle upon her bed, babylike, melting into joy and love, the love of this God, her God.

She lay awake for a long time, unwilling to sleep, unwilling to lose the awareness of the presence. Finally she slept, a quiet dreamless sleep, a sleep of perfect trust.

59

Rahab awoke early. She felt wonderful. Usually she worked in the morning, sewing until midday, but this morning she felt no desire to work. Instead, she longed to be outdoors. She left her tapestries lying where she had put them the previous day, wandered into the sunshine, and headed up the wadi. She turned naturally toward the pond.

Green trees surrounded the pool. Their arching branches created pleasant patterns over Rahab's head as she walked along the edge of the pond. The early morning sunlight shone brightly, reflecting the feathery leaves.

A fish jumped, and Rahab laughed delightedly. How much her baby would love this pond! What a wonderful place Salma had chosen to raise his family!

Rahab's reflection laughed up at her from the pool below. *How round my face looks,* Rahab thought, and then she laughed again. *But then, I am all round.* Leaning forward, she stared at herself. Almost nine months had passed since she had become aware of her pregnancy, and her body had flowered. Her belly bulged with the promise of Salma's child.

The water rippled, and her reflection giggled up at her. "You look like a melon," she said to her belly. Her belly in the pond rippled. *Like the baby quickening within me,* Rahab thought. *What a wonderful mirror the pond makes!* A fish jumped across her face in the mirror. Rahab laughed and stepped back.

"What a beautiful world you have created, Yahweh!" she said.

No voice answered her now, no awesome stillness. A bird sang out loudly in the tree overhead. Another answered it from nearby. As the last colors of the sunrise began to fade in the east, Rahab looked into the pond again. *How dif-*

ferent from the pools of Shanarbaal's villa, Rahab thought, *and how much happier I look in this pond than I looked in the mirror of Amaranthe-Astarte.*

The mirror of Amaranthe-Astarte: she had not thought of it in years. Mari had inherited the mirror, no doubt, when she became high priestess. Rahab had never been able to find one like it. She had asked her merchant friends; she had even sent Alcion on special trips to the market when the caravans passed through. Only hand mirrors could be found. At the time, Rahab had been irritated. Now, remembering it, she laughed. *Why should I need a brass mirror,* she thought, *when God provides me with the reflection in this pond: my belly filled with child and my heart filled with love! Oh, Yahweh, you are a good God!*

The birds overhead continued their morning serenade. Rahab looked and called to them. "Do you sing to Yahweh?" she asked them. Several birds fluttered out of the tree toward the east. As she watched them fly, a well-loved melody rose in her spirit. "I will sing to him, too!" she said, laughing up at the flying birds.

As she sang, the joy of her song danced upon the hills.

> I looked toward the sunrise
> And saw my salvation
> Gleaming in a thousand campfires,
> Waiting to bring me joy,
> And solace to my soul,
> Waiting to bring me laughter
> And a child of love.
>
> Thanks be to Yahweh, Lord God Almighty!
> Praise be to Yahweh, God of the universe, God everlasting!
> That I am your handmaiden, Yahweh who lives;
> Yahweh who is; Yahweh, my God!
> Allelujah!

She recognized the pain and knew that the time had come. *I must hurry,* she thought. *Salma's baby must be born at home!*

The birthing stool was waiting for her. Nantha and her mother were waiting also. "Where have you been?" her mother scolded.

"Have you been on the hills?" Nantha demanded.

"I have been singing praises to my God," Rahab answered. "And now, I think I shall have my baby."

"What?" they said, their scolding forgotten.

She named him Boaz.

60

The horse flowed forward, like the sand before a desert wind. Salma rode with elation. His Rahab had chosen a fine animal. Salma patted Shimmerance on the neck. The little stallion had behaved as well in the battle as if he had been trained by a warrior. He had responded perfectly to every signal. But then, everything had gone perfectly.

In three weeks of warfare, the armies of Israel had suffered not one defeat. The Lord God was fulfilling his promise to his people. The Israelite camp at Gilgal had been ecstatic upon the return of the victorious soldiers. The soldiers themselves had been ecstatic. The officers of Israel had danced in the camp. The milk and honey of God's blessing in Canaan had flowed freely. The music and singing had lasted into the night, and Salma had been serenaded to sleep by the happy chanting of a victorious people.

The rhythm of the horse beneath him lulled his senses, filling his body with the languor of the long ride. He was tired, but it was the satisfied weariness of a man who has accomplished much. The armies of Israel had taken six major cities, and the confederacy of kings against Gibeon had been utterly defeated. After the battle, Salma himself had obeyed Joshua's command to stand with his foot on the neck of the Canaanite king of Jerusalem. It was a moment he would never forget. As Salma stood there with four other captains, Joshua said to them, "Fear not nor be dismayed, be strong and of good courage: for thus shall the Lord do to all your enemies!" Then the five Canaanite kings had been executed.

There has never been a god to compare to the God of Israel, Salma thought. What other god could rain huge hailstones upon his enemies and kill them? What other god could—and the memory took Salma's breath—what other god could stop the sun in the heavens until the battle was won?

For the sun had stopped! Salma was sure of it. Never before had there been a day to compare to that day of battle. The men of Joshua's army had marched all night, yet they had not weakened. Never before had Salma felt the strength that had poured into him as he fought. He had seemed to grow stronger with each passing hour.

Do you doubt me now? The words so simple, yet so strong, formed clearly within his mind.

Why did I think that? Salma wondered, surprised at himself.

Do you doubt me now, Salma?

The words came again, more insistent than before. There was no option, so Salma answered: "I do not doubt you, Lord."

What I have promised, Salma, will I not bring it to pass?

"Yes, Lord, surely you will."

Then why have you doubted my wisdom?

"Lord, I am weak."

Then be weak no longer. Shirr yourself up. Be strong and of good courage; what I have promised, Salma, I will fulfill.

"My child, Lord?"

Your child is born. Do not think that the peace of Israel is given except through the pain of woman, for it is through the woman that the blessing can come.

"Even a woman such as she whom I have chosen, Lord? Even a woman who was a Canaanite harlot?"

What I have chosen cannot be changed, Salma. What I have cleansed cannot be called unclean.

Suddenly Salma remembered the words recorded in the book of the law: "A star shall come forth from Jacob and a scepter shall rise from Israel."

Again he heard the voice, *Can I not bring all things to good, Salma?*

"Yes, Lord, even so, but can the peace of Israel come from a man of war such as I? A man so unworthy as I am?"

Out of my worth I have made you worthy, Salma, and the woman, too. I will establish the nation of Israel a holy people unto myself. I shall make of my people the head and not the tail, and you shall be above and you shall not be underneath.

"How shall these things be, Lord?"

Through the seed of the woman, Salma, "The sceptre shall not depart from Judah, nor the ruler's staff from between his feet, until Shiloh comes."

"I am your servant, Lord."

You are much more than that, Salma. You are my well-beloved child.

Tears mingled with dust on the face of the warrior-chief of Judah. The horse's feet continued to beat a path across the pagan plains of Canaan, but Salma, Prince of Judah, no longer felt himself a warrior, an alien in a foreign land.

He was a son of Israel, a son of God, living in the promised land.

A tiny girl followed her father across the hills. His shepherd's staff guided the way for both his child and his sheep. The hill was alive, bursting with the many-colored wildflowers of spring. The little girl played happily amongst the flowers. One lamb she kept near her, caressing it and arranging flowers on its back. The lamb received her attentions patiently, for this little sheep was her constant playmate, her own special lamb.

Her father guided the sheep away from the cliff, down the hillside toward the deep valley below, but the little girl dallied behind, keeping the lamb beside her. "Bring your lamb and follow me," her father called, but she ignored him, pretending not to hear. Some shining red berries on a low shrub attracted her attention, and she ran over to them, leaving her lamb alone in her eagerness for the fruit. She grabbed a handful of the bright berries, crushing their juices in her eager hands and pressing their sweetness into her mouth.

Suddenly, out of the corner of her eye, she saw her lamb running along the edge of the cliff along the ravine. Even as she looked, it was too late. The lamb was gone, over the edge. The child jumped up, running to the cliff. Looking down over the cliff's edge, she saw her lamb, broken and bleeding on the rocks below—and she saw the lion spring. Huge teeth ripped into the tiny body of her lamb. She gasped; the lion looked up, his yellow eyes flashing her a warning. She screamed.

Her father's arms pulled her roughly away from the edge of the cliff. "Don't look," he said. "Don't look, Rahab," but she had already seen the death of the lamb. She covered her face with her berry-stained hands—and seeing the red, she screamed again.

"Don't scream, Rahab, don't scream. Wake up, dear. Wake up. It's all right." Her mother's voice, her mother's hands shook her from the nightmare.

"It's all right, dear, it was just a dream!"

"Oh, Mother, it was a horrible dream! It was the worst dream I have ever had, but I am not sure why."

Her mother's arms comforted her. Kora looked anxiously at her daughter. It was not good for Rahab to be so deeply disturbed so soon after the birth of her child.

"Do you want to talk about it?" Kora asked.

"No," Rahab replied, "I want to forget it, but I can't. It's too horrible! Mother, I was a little girl playing on the hills with the lambs. Father was there guiding the sheep. He called to me, but I refused to follow him. Instead I ran to eat some berries, and while I was gone—oh, but I was only gone for a minute!—my lamb ran to the edge of the cliff and fell over, and, and—a lion killed him!"

Rahab's mother gasped in horror. Rahab did not understand why, but the other woman's face had paled as she had told her dream. Kora's lip trembled, and the older woman shuddered as if the nightmare had been her own.

"It was horrible, Mother," Rahab said again, softly.

Her mother stood and walked across the room to stand, her back to Rahab, looking out across the hills where the first glimmer of morning whispered upon the sky. "I know it was horrible, Rahab," her mother answered. "I hoped that you had forgotten it forever."

"Forgotten it?" Rahab looked at her mother in confusion. "Oh, no! Mother, do you mean it really happened? That I lost a little lamb this way? Did a lion really kill my lamb?"

"No, Rahab." Her mother hesitated so long that Rahab thought she would not continue. "It was not a lamb," Rahab's mother said finally. "It was—"

But Rahab's scream cut her mother's sentence in half. She remembered now! She remembered! She did not want to remember! Oh, why, why had she had the dream? "It was not a lamb!" Rahab screamed. "It was not a lamb! It was Josiah! It was my brother!" Rahab's sobs tore into the wall surrounding Kora's heart. For seventeen years Kora had refused to say that name aloud. Her baby—whom the gods had stolen from her—her Josiah!

"Josiah!" Kora said the word now. "Josiah!" Her voice rose as it too became a scream! "My baby! Rahab, my baby!" Kora sank down onto the bed beside Rahab. "Why do the gods steal our babies?" Kora wailed, and then her voice was lost in tortured sobs.

Rahab put her arms around her mother who clung to her fiercely, and both women began to rock back and forth and cry.

"I loved him, Mother!" Rahab sobbed. "I loved him so much."

Her mother only sobbed; the welled-up grief of all the years since his death burst forth, and she cried the first tears since her baby's death. "My baby," she finally sobbed. "Oh, my baby!"

Hours later, the two women sat quietly. Their sorrow had worn itself to quietness. Now, Kora, her eyes rimmed and deeply red, looked at Rahab in wonder at what had passed between them. She tried to speak, but her voice only cracked, hoarse and broken. She tried again, "I wanted to spare you this, Rahab," she whispered. She paused, and then, her voice growing stronger, she continued, "I so wanted to spare you what I have suffered from the gods. I thought you did not remember—all these years you had never spoken of it."

She drew her daughter to her. With her hand Kora brushed Rahab's hair from her eyes; she longed to comfort this daughter whom she had never understood. "I know what you are feeling, Rahab. Josiah was the first child of my womb, but not the first child of my heart—" She paused, searching for the words, for her truth, which she had never spoken. "I had brothers, too," she said. "Three baby boys. I raised them all." She took a deep breath and continued, "And each of them my father killed. Each of them I saw my father kill in a bloody sacrifice to Baal—to bring crops to the land—to stop a storm—to end a drought. My brothers, his own sons!" Her voice was bitter. "I vowed that I would never allow a child of my body to be given to the gods."

"Oh, Mother," Rahab gasped. "I am so sorry!"

"I was sorry, too, Rahab, but our sorrow means nothing to the gods. How they must have laughed at my silly vow! I would not give my son to the gods, but they took him anyway. Those are the ways of the loving gods of Canaan. They take and they take, and they do not give!"

Rahab remembered the first child of her heart—Bishna's baby. She understood.

"I hate the gods, Rahab," her mother said. "They kill and they kill and they laugh at us, for they know that we shall die, too. They kill our joys and our loves. They destroy all that we have, and then they demand more. When I thought they had taken everything, the goddess took even you for her temple.

"Already they have taken your first child. Who knows what evil they plan for your new baby, Boaz? I fear for him." Kora laughed bitterly. "But my fears will do him no good."

Rahab was amazed as this darkness spilled out of her mother's heart. Never before had she seen behind the wall of separateness surrounding her mother. The pit of her mother's bitterness lay before her. The hopeless black despair of her hatred for the gods. The pit was fathomless, but Rahab's compassion was deeper still.

"Mother, we have left those gods behind," she said gently. "Yahweh is the Lord our God now. He is not a killer of babies. He gives us our children, Mother, and he does not take them from us. You are right to hate the gods of Canaan, Mother. Yahweh hates them, too, and for the same reasons."

Her mother looked at her in puzzlement. Rahab searched for a way to explain what had become clear to her at the birth of Boaz. She must make her mother understand! "Do you remember when we burned the villa and the sacred grove?" she asked.

"Yes," her mother spat the word. "This Habiru God burns and kills just like the gods of Jericho. Only he is worse! There were children at Jericho, Rahab! There were children at Bethel-Ai! How many children will this Habiru God kill in the name of his holy war?"

Rahab sighed. She could understand why her mother felt this way. This war was bloody, as were all wars. But Rahab knew, had known, ever since the death of Achan, how righteously this God of Israel stood. "This war is Yahweh's war against the gods of Canaan; Baal and Astarte have caused the deaths of all the people—all the children—who have died in this war. They have caused those deaths as surely as if each child had been sacrificed in the Jericho temple!"

"I do not understand," her mother said.

"The war is no empty act of vengeance, Mother. The war is to stop Canaanite sin! In the tombs at Shanarbaal's villa, Salma and I found the skeletons of thousands of Canaanite babies buried beneath the floors. Thousands of babies, Mother, thousands of years of Canaanite sin! This generation is seeing the punishment of those sins!"

"The gods of Canaan demanded it," her mother said.

"No!" Rahab shouted. "The gods of Canaan caused it! Mother, even my first baby died because of the goddess—the goddess within. In the temple they had put a golden spiral inside my body. I only got rid of this spiral when I lost my baby. The gods of Canaan love death, Mother. They are not true gods. I do not know what they are, but their power must be stopped. The God of the Habiru will stop them. This war will stop them in Canaan. No more babies will be sacrificed on these hills, Mother. No more babies will die on their altars: that is the law of the God of the Habiru!"

Her mother looked at her in quiet amazement. "Then he is a God of justice, Rahab," her mother said at last. "And I have not known him."

"But you can know him, Mother. He called us out of Jericho, and somehow, I am not quite sure how, even the future of Canaan will be saved because of us."

"How can this be?" her mother asked.

"I do not know, but something inside me is happy, Mother. Something in my heart knows that the Habiru God loves babies!"

Her mother sighed. "You say this now, but what of Boaz? What if he should die? He is only a baby. Nothing is assured."

"I am sure, Mother," Rahab answered, realizing that she was very sure of Yahweh. "My baby Boaz will not die. I have this promise from the Lord of the Habiru, my Lord, and he keeps his promises."

"You believe this?"

"I know it. It is in the book of the law, and with every Passover lamb that dies, the Lord God renews that promise."

Kora began to weep softly. Rahab sought to comfort her, holding her close as long quaking sobs tore through her mother's body.

Inside Kora the walls of her separateness came tumbling down. The warmth of a new sunrise within her penetrated the pit of her despair, and there stood a huge rock, a rock from which a spring of hope burst forth, bright, shining waters that reflected a brilliant white light, a light of love. No hatred, no bitterness would live in that light.

Kora looked up at Rahab. The light in her eyes sparkled with tears, tears not of bitterness, but of joy. A smile broke across Kora's face. At that moment, from his pallet nearby, tiny Boaz awakened with a lusty yell. His mother and grandmother laughed and hurried to him.

61

"A lion has been seen in the hills, Rahab," Salma said as he entered the house at dusk.

"You are worried about the sheep?" she asked.

Salma nodded, frowning. "The ewes are lambing now. I fear the smell of their birthing—the smell of blood—will attract the lion."

"There is always an enemy nearby, isn't there?" she sighed. "It never ends."

Salma laughed at her allusion to the war. "It ends, my love. It ends when we kill the lion—and we will, but until then, we must watch over the sheep very carefully. Tonight, I must stay on the hillside with the flocks." He smiled and touched her shoulder tenderly. "Sleep with me on the hills tonight, Rahab. These stars in Bethlehem are brighter than anywhere else in the lands of Judah."

"But the baby, Salma. I can't leave our little Boaz."

"He won't be alone, Rahab. Your mother is still here." He smiled at her teasingly. "You aren't afraid of the lion, are you? There will be eight of my men on the hills, and we all have spears and slingshots. We will be safe."

"I am not afraid of the lion," she answered playfully.

He laughed at her. He knew she could not resist his laughter. "Sleep with me on the hills, woman!" he said, his eyes dancing.

"The baby," she said.

"Your mother can look after the baby." He smiled and drew her against his chest. "The baby will be fine, little mother."

She turned her face up to him. "As always, you are right," she murmured, receiving his kiss. "I will sleep with you on the hills tonight, my love."

As they walked on the hills, toward the pastures where the flocks grazed, Rahab's spirit drank in the beauty of the landscape. The hills of Bethlehem, infinite shades of violet and mauve, stretched before them toward the horizon and the deep reds of the setting sun. As the sky darkened, the stars began to glimmer, jewellike, twinkling against the deepening purple twilight. The night air was fragrant, heavy with the incense of the earth and the promise of the season to come. A low-lying silver mist seemed to rise from the valleys, *toward God himself*, Rahab thought as she looked with awe at the expanse of the rising stars.

"It is so wonderful here," she said to her husband.

Salma tightened his arm about her as they walked, watching the sleeping sheep in the valley below them.

"The life of a shepherd has advantages over that of a warrior," he said softly. "On the battlefield, those sheep would be the bodies of dead men."

"But they would not be the bodies of your men, Salma. Your men are victorious. The Lord God sees to that."

Salma laughed softly and hugged her.

"Yes," he said, "but the enemy prowls in the darkness. We must keep our eyes open for that lion, Rahab."

"He will not bother us, my lord. The lion would not dare to attack a prince of the tribe of Judah, who is, in the prophecies, likened to the lion's whelp!"

320

Her husband laughed. "He might not attack the whelp, but he would attack the lambs!"

"If he attacks, the Lord God will protect them," she said, "even as he has protected us."

"He has protected us, Rahab," Salma responded seriously. "He has brought us out of slavery in Egypt, and you out of slavery in Jericho. He has brought us a son, and he has brought us to this place."

"And he is here, too, Salma."

Salma stopped and held her close against him. "The Lord God *is* here," he said. "You know it, too!"

"I do know it, Salma! I can feel his peace, as I feel it when you pray for me."

"He gives us peace, Rahab. Even in the midst of the battle, I have the peace of knowing that he is with me. He *is* our peace."

Never before had Rahab felt so close to this man, the father of her child. At this moment, their spirits were one, rising like the mountain mists to soar and sing with the stars over Bethlehem.

Later, under the heavy woolen coverlet, Rahab nestled against the curve of Salma's body, warm and protected against the wind and the evening dew. She hovered between the reality of the hard earth beneath her and the soft, insistent beckonings of sleep. She snuggled closer to her husband.

Above her, the stars seemed to sing. Their glimmerings became harmonies, melodies against the night, ancient chords reverberating in timeless praise to the creator. They sang. Theirs was the joyful song of creation. Their music joined the gentle whisper of the wind through the Bethlehem grasses, carrying Rahab gently into a deep sleep.

Across the grasses of the hill, Rahab saw the wild ram. He was strong, but old. His huge curving horns revealed his antiquity. Horns such as these made the shofars that blew when the walls of Jericho came down, but this ram's strength was both gentle and kind. Looking at him, across the distance of the hill, Rahab knew that his spirit was wise and old like his horns. She stepped nearer.

Scars, old and jagged, marked the length of his nose. The tip of one huge horn was chipped—broken—at the end. She thought of Abraham and the young ram who had appeared caught in the bush at the sacrifice of Isaac.

"You have grown old," she said.

His deep brown eyes seemed to hold the wisdom of the ages, and they spoke to her: "Peace, peace in the midst of the battle."

"Peace in the midst of the war?" she asked him.

"Peace is!" came the reply, and he was gone.

"Peace is!" she repeated, and her husband stirred.

"What is it?" he asked. Had she seen something? Or was it the nightmares again?

"I had a dream," she answered. "I saw the ram—the ram of Isaac—only he

321

was very old, and he spoke to me."

"What did he say?" Never before had she told him what she dreamed.

"It was something about peace—Peace is—peace is, even in the midst of war."

"Perhaps it was a prophecy," he said. He looked at the stars. One star, near the horizon, shone more brightly than all the rest. "It is the star of the morning," he said, pointing it out to her.

"It is so bright," she said.

"It is the star of the promise, Rahab. The Lord promises that a star shall come forth from Jacob, and a sceptre shall rise from Israel."

"A sceptre—is there to be a king then? And are we a part of the promise?"

"The Lord God is our king," he answered, "and the promise is to us, and to our son, to those who follow us, and to all the generations to come. The peace of Israel comes through the pain of woman, Rahab."

She smiled at him. "Perhaps we shall have many sons," she said.

"They shall be as numerous as the stars," he answered playfully.

She sighed. "But I do not look forward to killing the lamb."

"You mean the sacrifice," he said.

"Yes," she answered. "I will do it, but it is very hard for me. I will feel like Abraham as he held the knife over Isaac."

Salma looked at her in surprise. "But you won't have to hold the knife. The priest will perform the sacrifice."

"Do you mean I don't have to kill the lamb myself?" she asked, amazed.

"No, my darling. Of course not! Our high priest will take your place."

She clung to him, her eyes filled with tears of joy. "I do not have to kill the lamb!" she said. "I do not have to kill the lamb! Oh—but," she saddened, "still the lamb must die."

Her husband held her close. "Still the lamb must die," he said. "But some-day—someday, Rahab, the sacrifices will end. Someday no more lambs will die, Rahab. I am sure of it."

A sound startled them then, and they turned. Silhouetted against the brilliant colors of the rising sun, a wild ram had bounded into view, his huge horns outlined against the golden fire of the morning light. He reared and stood, motionless for an instant—rampant—his front hoofs poised above the earth.

Rahab caught her breath, and at the sound, the ram leapt high into the air and landed, his hoofs clattering, some distance away. He paused for a moment, prancing atop the crest of the hill, and then disappeared into the mists.

Rahab stared at Salma in wonder, realizing that in her oneness with him she was more than a bride of the covenant: she was a mother of the generations of Abraham!

"The peace of Israel," she whispered.

He smiled again. "Perhaps it is a prophecy."

EPILOGUE

A table of the descent of Jesus Christ, son of David, son of Abraham.

Abraham was the father of Isaac,
Isaac of Jacob,
Jacob of Judah and his brothers,
Judah of Perez and Zarah (their mother was Tamar),
Perez of Hezron,
Hezron of Ram,
Ram of Amminadab,
Amminadab of Nahshon,
Nahshon of Salma,
Salma of Boaz (his mother was Rahab),
Boaz of Obed (his mother was Ruth),
Obed of Jesse;
and Jesse was the father of King David.

David was the father of Solomon (his mother had been the wife of Uriah),
Solomon of Rehoboam...
Matthan of Jacob, Jacob of Joseph, the husband of Mary, who gave birth of
Jesus called Messiah.

Matthew 1:1-7, 15-16 NEB